The Final Honor

A Novel

The Final Honor

A Novel

by

Stoney Livingston

This is a work of fiction

ISBN-13: 978-0692449639
ISBN-10: 0692449639

1ST printing: 2016
Chokonen Press

Praise for *The Final Honor*

The Final Honor is simply storytelling at its best. A tale of early Confederate Arizona, Cochise and his Chiricahua Apaches, a Confederate soldier, who refuses to surrender, returning home to the adobe village of Tucson at war's end with his unusual horse and dog, and of a family of settlers, trying to make a go of life in southeastern Arizona, at a time when Cochise and his people ruled the land.

"Stoney Livingston has given us a classic."
– Gordon Mustain, author of *Afterimages, Apache Tears, American Requiem* and several short stories and poems.

Chapter 1

I was leanin' over the edge of the creek, fixin' to take a fish off the end of my line when somethin' made me look up. Can't rightly say what the reason was but I looked up an' saw him sittin' a big blue roan, right across the creek from where I was. I knew the second I saw 'im I was dead.

I turned an' looked real quick for my little sister, Mel, but she musta seen this gent an', true to her teachin', she took off as fast as her little six-year-old legs would carry her without makin' a sound. She was taught this on account of all the trouble with Apaches. She sure left me in a big mess.

I forgot about the fish on the end of my line an' came up from my kneelin' position real slow on account of I didn't want to give this stranger any kind of reason to kill me too quick. He looked pretty tough to me.

The sun was at his back but I could tell he was some kinda soldier even though he was wearin' a grey duster that covered him to below his knees. I thought it a might warm for such dress but I sure weren't about to tell him that. He had a leather belt around his waist an' some kind of sword in a scabbard. It was more like a cutlass a pirate might carry, like I saw in a book before we left Ohio. One thing I noticed right off was his footwear. He was wearin' moccasins that went almost up to his knees and they had turned-up toes. He was also wearin' a cap like the soldiers I'd seen in Tucson wearin', 'ceptin' this fella's cap was grey not blue like them Tucson soldiers'.

I stood up real straight, figurin' if he was gonna kill me there weren't a whole lot I could do about it so I might as well take it like a growed man, even though I wasn't yet nine years on this earth.

Real slow-like, he picked up a sawed-off, double-barreled-ten-gauge shotgun that was hangin' by a rawhide thong from his saddle horn. I knowed it was a ten-gauge by the big holes in the barrel. He aimed it right at me an' I knew the realist feelin' of fear a body can ever experience.

"Don't move, boy. Not an inch," he said in a real calm an' kinda quiet voice, an' I knew he meant what he said, so I quit breathin' on account of that makes a body move.

I saw his finger takin' up the slack on the front trigger an' prayed I could stand like a man long enough to get killed before I fell down. When that shotgun went off I felt a sharp pain in my right arm an' heard the loudest noise I'd ever come upon. I kinda crumpled to the ground an' couldn't figure why I was still alive. He couldn't have missed me at that range with a sawed-off shotgun.

Next thing I knew, that horse was splashin' across the creek an' that stranger was jumpin' out of the saddle. I figured he was gonna scalp me before I was even dead, but my body was tremblin' so bad I couldn't do nothin' to stop him.

He jumped out of the saddle an' lit next to me like a feather. He was right fast an' smooth in his movements. He had his cutlass out an' was swingin' it down when I heard the rattle sound. He chopped at the ground right next to me a few times an' stepped back. I was so scared I couldn't look at what he was doin' but didn't reckon he was choppin' my foot off or nothin' like that on account of I didn't feel no pain. The rattle sound kept up for a few more seconds then kinda faded away.

The stranger wiped his cutlass on a nearby bush, put it back in its scabbard an' knelt next to me an' looked at my arm. "You okay, boy?"

It scared me when he spoke on account of I never expected it. Heck, I never expected to hear nothin' again.

"I think so. My arm hurts a little," I said. I could hear the tremble in my voice but I couldn't help it. I looked at my right arm an' saw a small hole in my shirt, just above my elbow. There was a little blood around the hole. I couldn't find nowhere else I was hurt.

The stranger rolled up my sleeve an' took a look at my arm. "Sorry, boy. You took one pellet. I didn't have much time to make a large selection of what to do. That big rattler was in the strike when I pulled the trigger." He nodded to his left.

I looked where he was noddin' an' saw the biggest rattlesnake I'd ever seen. What was left of its head was about the size of Ol' Blue's head. Ol' Blue was our hound, an' he didn't have no small head. I weren't afraid of the stranger as much as I was that rattlesnake by then, but it was dead enough. Even its tail had almost stopped quiverin'.

The stranger said, "It just grazed you a bit. You'll probably be a mite tender for a few days but if you keep it clean, you should be just fine."

I took a look at my arm now that my sleeve was rolled up an' almost felt embarrassed at how there weren't much more than a scratch there.

"You mind if me an' my horse drink a little of your river?" Just like that, I guessed he was through talkin' about my arm – almost like it never even happened.

At first, I just looked at him. I reckon my lower jaw musta been hangin a mite, 'cause I wasn't ready to be asked no questions, especially that one. Heck, everybody knew you could water at a creek or a river. Finally I said, "Cherry Creek ain't no river, an' it ain't mine. Anybody can drink outa it."

The stranger looked up an' down Cherry Creek then back at me an' smiled. "It sure looks like a river to me. How'd it come by the name of Cherry Creek?"

Just like that, I wasn't afraid of this gent no more. Couldn't tell you why, but I wasn't. "My pa an' Uncle George named it that on account of there's some chokecherries growin' upstream a ways."

He kinda shrugged an' said, "Oh. Well, I thought it might have been your river an' I didn't want to drink without your permission. I thank you anyway."

That big blue roan just stood an' looked at the creek then back at the stranger. He didn't make no move to take a drink. The stranger looked at my line in the water. "I think your fish just got away."

I turned real quick an' sure enough that fish was swimmin' upstream about as fast as he could go. I pert near jumped in after him but held off on account of I didn't wanna look foolish in front of this stranger iffen I didn't catch him. "Doggone it!" I said.

This fella smiled again an' said, "He was a real beauty. If you tell the story, I'll swear to it."

I liked this gent from that minute on.

He wasn't a big man – 'bout five feet eight or nine or so. I ain't much good at guessin' weight but I'd put him around a hundred seventy pounds. Couldn't really tell for sure under that duster. Solid-lookin' though, like he could handle himself proper if need be. He had rust-colored hair that was a little weedy an' it covered his ears a mite. His eyes was about the color of the top side of a cottonwood leaf in the late spring. They kinda sparkled. His face was shaved clean, 'ceptin for a bit of stubble. He was only a few years younger than my Pa. I had a feelin' about this fella, and it was a good one. Lord knows we needed *somethin'* good to happen.

The horse was a prize winner at any county fair I'd been to back in Ohio. A big stud he was too, about fifteen hands tall. An' he had four white stockings. He was built for runnin', it looked to me like, an' he didn't appear much afraid of nothin'. I could tell that by lookin' him in the eye. I could also tell by lookin' him in the eye that he was smart. I know things like that about animals. If I can just get a good look in their eyes, I can figure if they're smart or not. People too – just look 'em in the eye.

The stranger spoke English pretty good so I knew he wasn't a Federale from Mexico. The only Mexicans I had ever saw wore mustaches. I guess I figured all Mexicans wore mustaches. 'Course a lot of white men wore mustaches too, like my Uncle George.

"Your horse must not be thirsty," I said. This seemed right peculiar on account of the animal was sweatin' a little 'n' I knew he was thirsty but he just stood there, lookin' first at the water then at the man, kinda like he was waitin' for somethin'.

The stranger looked hard at his mount then at me 'n' said. "This horse has got a harder head than a bronze bust."

I didn't know what he meant at the time but I made out like I was right there in the conversation with him. "Yeah, I c'n see that."

"He knows I've got an apple left and he's gonna save his drink to wash it down."

"You got an apple?" I asked.

The stranger looked at me 'n' I could see somethin' in his face change. "You hungry, boy?"

My paw didn't raise me to beg, even though I wanted that apple somethin' fierce. "No, Sir. I just ain't seen an apple for a long spell is all."

"Well," he reached into a gunny sack tied behind his saddlebag 'n' pulled out a dark red apple. "This is what they look like."

I gotta tell you, that was the most beautiful sight I had seen in a long time, all dark red 'cept for a bunch of tiny white dots sprinkled in with the red. My mouth got to waterin' 'n' I think my breathin' stepped up a notch or two. I plumb forgot about Melanie. It ain't like we was starvin' or nothin' like that – but an apple!

The stranger pushed the right side of his duster back 'n'

unsheathed a big knife. It wasn't a whole lot smaller than that sword as far as I was concerned. It scared me for a second, but only a second. He cut the apple in two, wiped the blade on his britches, sheathed the knife, 'n' gave me one of the pieces. He gave the other piece to the horse. That horse snatched that half-an-apple right off the palm of this gent's hand so fast it looked like he was afraid the feller was gonna change his mind so he got it while the gettin' was good. It was the slickest thing I'd ever seen a horse do up to that point in my short life. Soon as he swallowed the apple the horse lowered his head 'n' drank from the river. It was just like I figured. He was wantin' a drink *after* his apple.

"Ain't you gonna eat the apple, boy? You got a name?"

"Crawford." I sort of blurted it out.

"Well, Crawford, is there somethin' wrong with the apple?"

"No, Sir. I mean, well, I'll have to share it with Melanie. That's my little sister. Are you sure it's okay to keep it?"

"Yeah. I'm sure. I got so many apples down in La Mesilla about five days ago that I'm about tired of 'em. Must've eaten a hundred. Don't worry about sharin' it. I still have some left. We'll give Melanie her own apple."

At this, I got to feelin' like I was bein' cheated. He made it sound like Melanie was gonna get a *whole* apple. Ain't folks funny sometimes? A minute ago I'd have given my favorite fishin' stick for just a *bite* of an apple 'n' here I was not satisfied with half an apple but wantin' a whole one. I felt bad about that thought for a long time. This fella must've read my mind.

"Matter-of-fact, if you and your family will take what apples I got left offa my hands I'd really appreciate it. Seems like they're makin' me sick lately. Guess I've just had too much of a good thing."

I couldn't believe my ears. I tried to act calm, though I ain't so sure my voice didn't tremble a mite when I spoke.

"Well, if it would help you some, I reckon we could do that."

"Much obliged." He stepped upstream of the horse, stooped 'n' washed his hands, then moved a little farther upstream 'n' took a real short drink. Didn't seem like that horse had drank much either. He was standin' real patient-like at the edge of the creek, kinda just lookin' around.

I said, "Ain't you afraid your horse'll run off?"

He looked at me peculiar 'n' said, "Him? That useless excuse for a horse? Nobody else would put up with 'im and he's at least smart enough to know that."

"He sure looks like a good horse to me." Not that I was a judge of horseflesh but I pretended to be.

"Oh, he'll do as a horse. It's just that he ain't all that sure he wants to be a horse. Sometimes, if he had his druthers, he'd rather be a human. That's when him and me butt heads."

I gave my best understanding nod 'n' said, "You mean like the apple?"

"Yeah, like the apple. If I hadn't given him at least half of that apple, he'd have waited till I wasn't expectin' it an' done somethin' sneaky."

"What would he do?" I wasn't really believin' everything but I wasn't so sure about that horse. I looked down at my apple. I almost took a bite but decided to wait until I was sure Mel got hers - just in case this fella forgot to give her one.

"Hard tellin'. He might wait till the middle of the afternoon to buck instead of doin' it in the mornin', or he might kick me in the pants when I ain't lookin', or he might even turn his head and take a bite out of my leg while we're ridin' down a trail on some bright and sunny day. Or maybe he'd walk a little too close to some cactus so I could get a leg full."

"Are you spoofin' me?"

"It's true. Every word. He's done all of those things." He looked at the horse 'n' raised an eyebrow. "Come to think of it,

I can't figure why I haven't killed an' eaten him yet." He smiled at me. In some ways he reminded me of Pa. Not a lot. But a little. I think it was because I was so comfortable with him right off. I reckon that was kind of peculiar on account of he'd just shot me with a shotgun.

Chapter 2

Pa had just turned thirty when he took sick last month. Ma said he had a high fever. He moaned at night 'n' slept real restless for about a week. One mornin' me 'n' Ma 'n' Melanie woke up an' Pa didn't. Ma couldn't tell us for sure what had killed Pa. It didn't matter. He was dead 'an' we missed him. He taught me how to fish 'n' hunt 'n' skin 'n' plow 'n' all kinds of things. I know it ain't exactly manly to say it, but I loved my Pa.

We buried him out behind the cabin under a cottonwood only ten days ago. Ma was awful worried. I could tell. She could tend the garden but she didn't know the first thing about the longhorns, an' Uncle George wasn't used to bein' a cowhand yet, so he worked pretty hard at keepin' the small herd together. We had forty head scattered in the hills somewhere if the Apaches hadn't found 'em. Ma wouldn't let me take Bess, our horse, 'n' go look for 'em. She said she'd lost Pa an' she wasn't about to lose me.

Pa 'n' his brother, Uncle George, 'n' me 'n' Ma 'n' Melanie, had left Ohio about two and a half years ago 'n' headed west. When we got settled real good, Uncle George was gonna send for his fiancé 'n' they were gonna get married.

We crossed a lot of desert 'n' pert near died of thirst. When we ran across this big creek 'n' found chokecherries growin' all around, Pa 'n' Uncle George agreed that this was the spot. It was the first water we'd seen since the Rio Grande. We'd run across a few washes that looked like they might carry water sometimes but they was dry when we saw 'em.

Pa 'n' Uncle George built a big cabin from all of the trees in the mountains an' we even had a shed, a tack room, a chicken coop an' a privy. We had a good start on a barn but Pa had up an' died before he finished it - that an' the well. We still had to carry water from the creek but we had the well all drilled. Uncle George was waitin' for some kinda part so's he could make the pump work. I reckon the other part musta broke or somethin'. Uncle George's house was up too, 'n' had a roof on it. It was close enough finished that he'd sent for his fiancé more than three months ago. She was supposed to be in Tucson in about a week. We were all hopin' she would get here pretty quick but with the War Between the States going on we weren't much sure when she'd get here.

We didn't know much about Indians before we left Ohio, 'ceptin there were Comanches in Texas, an' that was in the Confederate States anyway, an' the Souix was killin' folks in the Dakota Territories, so we headed for New Mexico Territory. It turns out that the part of New Mexico Territory we settled in wasn't New Mexico Territory anymore. It was called Arizona Territory an' it was Confederate. But there weren't many white folks out here 'n' Pa 'n' Uncle George agreed that if they could get the ranch started, it wouldn't matter whether we were in the United States or the Confederate States. Folks would still want beef.

I didn't understand half of what they talked about when it came to all the stuff about states an' countries but I knew I sure liked Cherry Creek, no matter what country or state it was in. The winters was cold an' the summers was a mite warm but the land was so pretty an' there was always some new adventure.

Like I said, we had forty head of longhorn cattle. We also left Ohio with three horses, two wagons, twelve oxen, some tools, six pigs , some chickens, a milk cow, a hound dog, a little furniture, an' a bunch of pots 'n' pans 'n' dishes, an' a real cook-stove and a bunch of tools.

We still had everything we set out from Ohio with except

the oxen 'n' one of the wagons. Oh yeah, an' one of the horses. Pa had sold one of the wagons an' the oxen in Tucson an' bought a lighter wagon an' two horses for carryin' supplies 'n' such. That's the only time I ever saw Tucson an' the cavalry soldiers. The horses Pa bought, an' our draft horse, well, Uncle George lost them. That's when we found out about the Apaches.

One day, Uncle George was out lookin' for them two horses Pa had bought in Tucson, on account of they'd strayed off, when he was laid upon by a small band of Indians. The way he told it, he figured he was a goner for sure but he lost sight of the Indians in a canyon for just a minute 'n' he jumped off his horse 'n' smacked it real hard on the rump 'n' hid in the bushes. Uncle George walked back to the cabin 'n' we never did find that horse an' that was too bad cause he was a draft horse 'n' we used him to pull the plow. Lost all the tack too. Never did find them other two horses either. And Uncle George lost his Sharps Rifle. After Pa died, he used Pa's Sharps.

A week later Pa ran into a traveler who told him all about Cochise 'n' his band of Chiricahua Apaches. Seems like an army lieutenant hanged some Apaches a few years back, just before the war, an' they turned out to be related to an Apache leader named Cochise. Well, ol' Cochise got so doggone mad at the white men that he went on the warpath. When the lieutenant an' the U.S. army left, the Confederates moved in 'n' Cochise fought them just like he fought the Yankees before. When the Confederates left 'n' the Yankees came back, I reckon Cochise didn't see no reason to change his tactics. He kept up his grudge. One dead white man was as good as another, I reckon, was his way of figurin'.

This fella said Pa ought to pick up his family 'n' clear out while he still had his hair. 'Course we learned later that Apaches don't normally take scalps. This traveler also told Pa that the Confederates was most likely gonna lose the war that was goin' on unless England joined up with the southern states. I asked Pa lots of questions about what all of it meant but he wasn't for sure what *any* of it meant.

I reckon I was pretty deep in my thoughts for I hadn't yet taken a bite of that apple. Right sudden that blue roan reared on hind 'n' whinnied. The stranger fell flat on his face 'n' before I knew what was goin' on, he had a pistol in each hand. I don't know where they came from. Musta been under his duster.

"Get down, boy! There's someone in the bush." He said it in a loud whisper.

I didn't wait for a repeat of that order. I wasn't keen on meetin' up with that Cochise fella I'd just been thinkin' about. I was breathin' dirt before that roan's front hoofs hit the ground.

A man's voice came rollin' over us from somewhere in the trees. "You all right, Crawford?" It was Uncle George.

I can't tell you what a feelin' came over me. It was relief like I had never felt before. "Yeah, Uncle George. I'm okay. I was just talkin' to this stranger. He shot a big rattlesnake an' gave me half an apple." I pulled my face from the dirt an' stood. The stranger still lay on his stomach, pistols in hand.

He looked at me 'n' whispered, "How itchy is your uncle's trigger finger?"

I finally realized that this situation was still a might serious to the stranger. After all he didn't know my Uncle George 'n' my Uncle George didn't know him. Grown-ups seem not to trust each other much 'n' I reckoned it was time to set everyone straight. "Don't anybody shoot," I shouted. "Everything is okay."

Uncle George, still hidin' in the trees, said, "I'm walking to the creek, mister."

"Come on out. If you're Crawford's uncle, I got no trouble with you," said the stranger. He stood 'n' tucked one of his pistols under his coat. The one in his left hand stayed there, held kinda casual 'n' half-pointin' at the ground.

Uncle George said, "You're still holdin' a pistol."

"Yessir, I am. And I'll wager you're holdin' a rifle. That gives you the advantage. Now, if you'll just step into the open, we can eyeball each other and figure out if we really wanna kill one another."

Uncle George stepped from behind a tree almost fifty yards away. He walked slow to where we waited. The stranger tucked his second pistol under his coat 'n' smiled. "I ain't gonna argue with that Sharps, mister."

Uncle George let go his two-handed grip on the Sharps 'n' carried it real loose in his right hand. "My name's George Kensington," he said when he got close enough to talk in his regular voice. He switched the Sharps to his left side 'n' offered his hand.

"Mathew Grady. Most folks just call me Matt," said the stranger as he shook hands with Uncle George.

I could tell right off that Uncle George had the same feelin' about this Matt Grady fella that I did. He smiled 'n' said, "You're welcome here, Mr. Grady." That was the way both Uncle George an' my Pa treated folks. They always let 'em know they was welcome.

Uncle George looked at the blue roan. "That's a fine lookin' horse. Bring him on up to the cabin. We have some pretty good graze north of the shed."

Matt tipped his forage cap - Uncle George told me later that's what his hat was called. "Obliged, but we probably should do something with the rattler."

"The rattler?" said Uncle George.

What, with all the excitement of this Matt fella an' Uncle George almost shootin' each other, I'd plumb forgot about that big rattlesnake. "You should have seen it, Uncle George. I didn't even know the snake was right next to me. This fella..."

"Matt 'll do, boy," said Matt.

"...Matt took out a shotgun and plugged him from the other side of the creek an' then rode across an' finished him with his sword." I guess I was gettin' pretty excited about it by then on account of I hadn't had no time to even think of it while it was goin' on. I'd been too busy sayin' my prayers an' expectin' to be killed.

"Is that so?" said Uncle George. He kinda raised an eyebrow.

"That's pretty much the way it happened, George, except he left out a couple of things," said Matt.

"What might that be?" asked Uncle George.

"First off, one of the pellets from my gun grazed his arm. It wasn't much but I had number four shot loaded an' I'm sure it hurt plenty, but he never let out a sound."

Uncle George bent over an' took a look at my arm. After a spell, he looked up at Matt. "You were on the other side of the creek?"

"Yessir, I sure was," said Matt.

"Is your shotgun a full-choke?" said Uncle George.

Matt kinda grinned an', as he walked over to the roan, said, "Hardly." He pulled the sawed-off-ten-gauge from the saddle horn an held it up for Uncle George to see.

Uncle George looked real surprised. "Mr. Grady, I must confess that I'm quite amazed Craw was struck by only one pellet."

Matt hung the shotgun on the saddlehorn an' turned around with a big smile. "I aimed about five feet left an' hoped it would still be good enough to get the snake. I didn't have time for much else. It almost worked but I had to finish him with my cutlass."

It sure looked to me like that shotgun had been pointed right at me but, when a ten gauge is pointed anywhere near your direction, I reckon it might as well be pointed right at you.

Matt went to the dead rattler an' knelt next to it. When

Uncle George saw the snake, he said, "My word! I've never seen a snake this size. That can't be a rattlesnake."

"It's a rattler all right - a timber rattler. Big an' mean, an' afraid of nothin'. Not much around it won't tackle if cornered or hungry. They carry enough poison to kill a horse."

I felt a shiver when Matt said that.

Uncle George said, "Craw, you and Mel must be very careful in the future. I had no idea there were snakes like this out here."

Matt cut the head of the snake off about six or seven inches behind where I reckon its neck woulda been iffen it had a neck. Then he slit the belly all the way to the tail an' went to tuggin' the meat an' backbone out of the skin. That snake was bigger around than Uncle George's or Matt's arms. I sure got a strange feelin' lookin' at that thing but I couldn't take my eyes off it.

"What you gonna do with that snake?" I asked.

Matt looked up from tuggin' on the meat an' said, "The meat ain't bad eatin' if you're hungry."

Uncle George said, "I don't believe we're quite that hungry, Mr. Grady."

Matt shrugged an' said, "I'll find a use for it. We can make a belt or hat bands outa the skin. And the rattles are big medicine."

"Big medicine?" said Uncle George.

Matt kept workin' at pullin' that snake's backbone outa his skin. He nodded. "Some Indian tribes use 'em to make music when they dance. This fella can make a lot of music."

He was sure right about that. I'd never seen more rattles, nor bigger ones, than this snake had.

When Matt had the skin free, he peeled the meat from the backbone an' took it to the creek. He looked back down at the creek an' then back to Uncle George. "You sure you don't want to cook him up?"

"I'm quite sure," said Uncle Geroge.

Matt walked upstream a ways an' sat the meat on top of a big rock. He looked at Uncle George when he was done layin' it out an' said, "There's a pair of red-tail hawks livin' close by. Saw 'em earlier this mornin'. Rattlesnake is one of their favorites. They prefer killin' their own food but, if they're hungry enough, they might eat it."

He put the backbone over the limb of a mesquite an' looked at Uncle George again. "Man can make needles if he has a need." Then he stretched the skin an' put little holes in the edges an' put sticks in the holes an' staked it to the ground. "I'll work it in a day or so."

All the time Matt was doin' his work, me an' Uncle George just watched him. I don't think either of us knew for sure what to make of all of it. When he was done, Matt washed his hands in the creek an' looked at Uncle George an' said, "Is that offer of graze for my horse still good?"

"Of course," said Uncle George.

Matt turned 'n' stared at the roan. "You heard the man. Let's go." He turned back to Uncle George 'n' said, "Lead the way."

That Matt never even looked back to see his horse was followin', but he sure enough was – just like a dog.

After a few steps Uncle George said, "You said there were a couple of things Crawford forgot to mention. What was the other?"

"Well, George, just before that big ol' rattler messed things up, Craw had a big fish on the end of his line and was about to land him."

Uncle George said, "I can see how he wouldn't remember to mention that in light of the fact that he had almost been fodder for the biggest snake either of us has ever seen."

Matt shook his head an' made a cluckin' sound. "Not so, George. The boy was just bein' modest."

"Modest?" said Uncle George.

Uncle George wasn't the only one who was confused. I had no notion what Matt was talkin' about.

"I'll say. That fish on the end of his line was the biggest I've ever seen. It had to be at least this big." Matt stretched his arms out full length.

Uncle George started laughin' an' I got to feelin' pretty good. I was likin' this Matt fella more every minute.

Chapter 3

Ma was waitin' behind a closed shutter at the front window of our cabin an' her shotgun was stickin' out the slot Pa had cut into 'em. She lowered the gun when she saw Uncle George leadin' us in.

Ma was a pretty woman. I used to hear her 'n' Pa talk about all her beaus before she married Pa. Seems like every young man in three or four counties was courtin' her before Pa finally won out. I'm glad it happened the way it did 'cause, like I said, I loved my Pa.

Ma had turned twenty-seven in January. She had green eyes an' red hair. An' even though she worked like a man, she somehow kept that part of her that was truly a lady. I don't know how she pulled that off. She was pretty, even in her black dress an' bonnet. She wore that on account of Pa's dyin'.

Uncle George leaned the Sharps against the wall 'n' said, "Penny, this is Matt Grady. Mr. Grady, this is my sister-in-law, Penelope Kensington."

Matt took off his forage cap 'n' said, "Pleased to meet you ma'am. I didn't mean to cause alarm. I was just waterin' my horse at the creek."

"No harm done, Mr. Grady. It's mainly the uncertainty. That's all. When Melanie came running into the house, we didn't know what had happened," Ma said.

"Yes, ma'am. I understand. I'm sorry."

Melanie peaked out from behind Ma's dress. Matt smiled at her 'n' she slid back behind Ma, but I could tell that she was playin' a game 'n' wasn't afraid no more. Even though she was hidin', her blonde hair was right easy to spot next to

Ma's black dress.

Uncle George cleared his throat. "Well, Mr. Grady. Did the southern states win the war? I see you're a Confederate officer."

I didn't know how Uncle George knew that an' I wished I'd knowed it first. But, truth be known, I didn't even know what he meant by "officer".

Matt said, "No, sir. There is no more Southern Confederacy. It's gone. All of our outfits have surrendered – well, mostly all. Me, I didn't feel like the Yankees ever whipped me so I didn't see any reason to surrender. I just rode out of Texas and headed west. This is all I've got in the way of clothes, 'cept I have a newer uniform in my bags."

Ma said, "Take off your coat, Mr. Grady. George, will you hang it for him?"

Uncle George nodded, "Of course."

Matt took off his sword scabbard belt then his duster. Was I ever surprised! He was a walkin' arsenal. I knew that word on account of I heard Uncle George an' Pa talkin' about arsenals before we left Ohio. He had two pistols, a Bowie knife, a bullet pouch 'n' a powder horn hangin' on his belt, an' a thin knife hung on a leather thong around his neck. It dangled down his back to the middle of his shoulder blades. A short-barreled Colt revolver was in some kind of holster under his right armpit. I knew it was a Colt on account of Uncle George used to sell a lot of them.

I know my mouth must have been wide open 'n' my lower jaw on the floor 'cause Matt looked at me with a sad kind of smile. "I been to a war, boy. I figured I needed all the help I could get."

Uncle George took the sword 'n' duster an' hung 'em on a peg near the door. Matt took his holster belt off and hung it with the other stuff. I noticed the two guns in the holsters wasn't Colts but Remingtons.

We didn't have much in the way of furniture but Uncle George motioned to the wooden chair at the head of the table. "Sit down and be comfortable. Where are you headed?" he asked, like maybe Matt was dressed as a banker or doctor instead of a whole detachment of cavalry.

"Now, George, that's not our concern," said Ma. I reckoned she thought Uncle George might be gettin' a touch too personal, but she did give all those guns an' knives a longer-than-usual look.

Matt sat in the chair an' smiled at Ma. "That's okay, Ma'am. It's no big secret. I'm goin' back to Tucson. I joined Sherrod Hunter's First Arizona Rangers there. That was my home."

Uncle George seemed a mite worried about somethin'. He had that look on his face. "I don't know that it would be such a good idea to go back to Tucson in *that* uniform, Mr. Grady."

"Tucson and Mesilla are the reasons there *is* an Arizona Territory. We voted to break away from New Mexico and join the Confederacy."

Uncle George clucked like he did sometimes with me when he was treatin' me like a child. "Things have changed. Ever since Colonel Carleton came through with his California Column and the Union re-took Tucson, things have been rough for any southern sympathizers. Some were burned out. Others were run out in the night; some even killed."

"Are you sure? That would have been most of the town."

Uncle George nodded.

Some of the life seemed to go out of Matt. "Well, then I reckon I'll go south to Mexico. A bunch of the men said they were goin' there after they left the outfit. I think Maximillian is trying to bring in as many non-Mexicans as he can. He's indicated that Confederates are welcome there."

There was an uncomfortable minute or so when nobody said anything, then Ma said, "Well, Mr. Grady, you certainly aren't going to leave without a meal. We have plenty. Won't you join us for supper? We'll be eating in a little before dark." My ma. She was always so thoughtful.

At the mention of supper, I realized that I was still carryin' my half-an-apple. I looked down at it at 'n' saw that it was all covered with dirt an' it was startin' to turn brown in places. I plumb forgot about it in all the excitement but I sure hadn't let go of it.

"I'd be much obliged, Ma'am. I was tellin' Crawford that I have some apples and I'd be grateful if you'd take them."

"Apples? My, we haven't had apples for more than a year. That would be wonderful. Thank you, Mr. Grady," said Ma.

I said, "I gotta go back to the creek an' wash my apple. It got dirty." I turned 'n' walked out the door.

I didn't get very far before I had a feelin' that I was bein' watched 'n' it made me real nervous. I guess I was a little edgy after thinkin' about Cochise like I had. I looked real hard at the trees to my left 'n' right 'n' in front. Suddenly somebody pushed me hard in the back 'n' I stumbled forward, loosin' my apple as I braced myself from hittin' my face in the dirt. When I gathered my wits 'n' got back to my feet, I was just in time to see that roan horse swallow my apple. I was just beginin' to see what Matt had meant about his horse.

I was madder than a treed bobcat an', at the same time, right disappointed that I hadn't held onto that apple. "What'd you go 'n' do that for?" I yelled at the horse. He nickered a soft clicking sound, almost like he was sayin' he was sorry. 'Course I knew better. That horse was only sorry it wasn't a *whole* apple. I felt tears startin' to roll down my cheeks 'n' wiped my face with the back of my hand. I'd be darned if I was gonna let that horse see me cry, even if he had taken away my apple. I thought that roan was about the finest piece of horseflesh in the world until he had pulled that trick on me. Now I was lookin' for a way to get even. I picked up a rock 'n' drew back my arm. That horse just stood there lookin' at me. It didn't even flinch at my jerky movement. That was plumb peculiar.

Well, with those big brown eyes lookin' so trustin'-like at me, I just couldn't do it. I dropped the rock 'n' stared at him as hard as I could as if to let him know he'd better never do anything like that again. I swear I saw him smile.

"He's got you now, boy. You should have hit him with the rock."

I hadn't seen Matt but, there he was, only a few feet away.

I broke into tears. "I'm sorry. I wouldn't hurt your horse but he took my apple."

Matt put his arm on my shoulder 'n' said, "I tried to warn you about his human side. Don't fret about it, boy. I'll give you another apple but you gotta promise me to keep one eye on Critter till you've eaten it."

"Critter?"

"Fits. Don't you reckon?"

I couldn't help myself. I smiled 'n' before long I was laughing an', all the time, the tears streamed down my face.

Matt pulled the gunny sack from behind his saddle, took an apple from it 'n' handed it to me. "Remember what I said. You watch him." He jerked his head in the direction of Critter. I latched onto that apple 'n' stared at Critter while I ate it, core 'n' all, without sharing so much as a seed with that horse. I figured him 'n' me was even after that because I saw him drool while I munched on that apple. I knew he wanted it more than anything in the world an' he couldn't have it. It was all mine.

Matt smiled. "Feels real good to aggravate that horse, don't it, boy?"

I swear Matt could read my mind.

"I know what you're feelin'. I go through it every day. Between Judd and me it's a contest everyday to see who can put more over on Critter."

"Who's Judd?" I asked. "Is he your partner?"

"Yeah. He's about the best partner a man can have."

"Where is he?" I asked.

Matt nodded to the small ridge behind me and said, "He's watchin' our camp, just this side of that ridge."

"Ain't you goin' to ask him down for supper?" I asked.

"You reckon it would be all right with your Ma?"

"Sure," I answered. I musta had Matt figured wrong. It looked like he was gonna leave his partner at a dry camp while he ate Ma's cookin'. I never would have figured him for that kind of man. Course, he might have figured that two men would scare us more than just one. I was startin' to get confused by my own thoughts when he gave one short, sharp whistle.

He looked at me 'n' said, "You're sure it'll be all right with your Ma and Uncle George?"

I was still tryin' to get over the sudden sharp sound of the whistle so I just nodded.

"Where's your Pa, boy?"

To save my soul, I couldn't keep the tears from startin' up. "We buried him about ten days ago."

Matt put his arm around my shoulders 'n' gave me a quick squeeze then walked to a nearby boulder 'n' sat down. "I'm sorry, boy. Real sorry."

I can't describe how good that felt - both the quick hug an' the feelin' of sorrow he expressed - but it didn't help my tears none. I went 'n' sat next to him so he wouldn't be facin' me 'n' seein' my tears.

Matt didn't look at me. I didn't know if it was deliberate or not but I was grateful for it. He said, "Boy, sometimes a man has to lose things he loves a lot. I don't know why it's so, but it is. And for each thing you lose, you become stronger, for you no longer have that thing in your life to help you stay your course. It's a lesson. Each loss is a lesson."

I just sat there for a while 'n' thought about what he said. I was about to say somethin' when a dog walked up to us real careful-like. It sure wasn't ol' Blue, our hound. I hadn't seen another dog since we got to Cherry Creek. It walked to Matt's left side - the side away from me - 'n' sat real still. I had never seen eyes like this dog had. They were blue but they had streaks of white in the blue. It looked to me like he was blind. His hair was black 'n' white an' he had a white ring of hair around his neck. For some strange reason I wasn't afraid of this dog bitin' me.

"Crawford, meet my partner. This is Judd. Judd, this is Crawford."

Like the dog understood English, it stood 'n' walked right up in front of me 'n' sat. Now, I gotta tell you, I was beginin' to feel a little peculiar. First the horse, now this dog. I reached out 'n' petted his fur. It was thick an' full of small twigs 'n' leaves, like he might 've been rollin' around in the dirt.

"Can he see?" I asked.

Matt laughed. "Better than both of us. Fella down in Louisiana told me he was born that way. I guess his eyes are supposed to be that way. I gotta tell you though, I thought the same thing you did when I first saw him. I thought he was blind and I offered to buy him to save him from bein' put down."

That made me feel some better.

"He sure looks smart," I said. And he sure enough did too.

"He's smarter than most men I've met and he's only a little over a year old."

"You had him long?"

"Almost a year but it seems like I raised him from a pup. He was only a few months old when I got him."

I had to think on this hard. His horse 'n', now this dog, seemed to have a human streak in 'em somewhere. I wondered if Matt had some kind of magical powers over animals an', if he did, maybe I could talk him into usin' 'em on our cattle. I figured I'd ask him about that after supper.

"How come you're wearin' them moccasins?" I said.

"They're about the most comfortable footwear a man can wear."

"Yeah, but what about for ridin'? I reckon your feet would get a might sore after a spell."

"Depends on how you sit the saddle an' what kind of work you're doin'. If I know I'll be doin' a lot of ropin', I might wear my boots but, other than that, the moccasins do me fine."

"How do you wear spurs?" I asked.

"I don't. Critter don't much care for 'em," he said.

"Oh," I said.

Matt stood 'n' walked to Critter, who watched Judd real suspicious. He took a rifle in a scabbard, saddlebag, bedroll, gunnysack, rope, then saddle 'n' bridal, 'n' laid 'em all on the boulder next to me. "While you're gettin' acquainted with Judd, I'll get these apples back to the house." He walked toward the house, carryin' the gunnysack of apples.

I sat there for a minute or two 'n' eyeballed the horse 'n' dog. Couldn't make up my mind about how they really got along 'n' wondered if the dog was anything like the horse. I made up my mind if I ever got another apple, I'd keep a close eye on Judd 'n' Critter both.

I petted Judd for awhile then grabbed a stick 'n' we played fetch for a time. Then we both got bored 'n' I decided to walk upstream 'n' explore. Judd went right along an', when I looked back at Critter, there he was, followin' in my footsteps. He must have felt real bad about knockin' me down or he was real mad about that whole apple I ate right there in front of him an' was waitin' for a chance to get even. I couldn't make up my mind which.

I found a red-ant hill that I hadn't discovered before 'n' squatted down to watch 'em work. I always found ants to be right interestin' - all work 'n' no play. It really ain't such a surprise they always go around bitin' everybody. If I had to work every minute of the day, I'd be pretty cranky myself. Besides, I liked to watch when one of 'em picked up something bigger than he was an' tried to carry it back to the hole. He'd get it there most of the time an', when he couldn't, another ant would come along 'n' help. They sure seemed to get along with each other.

'Course, in some ways, ants are like humans. As long as the other ant is from the same tribe they get along just fine, but let an ant from another tribe come strollin' by 'n' it's a massacre. No questions asked. No parlay. Just a massacre.

I moved a little closer to the ant hill to get a better look 'n' Judd snapped the air in front of my face. Liked to scared me into wettin' my britches. Then I could see that he didn't want me to get any closer to the ants - like maybe I didn't know they would bite me or somethin'. I laughed a little nervous 'n' told him it was okay, that I knew what I was doin'. He seemed to relax a little bit an' sat a few feet away. When I inched a little closer, I heard a real soft growl 'n' decided not to test Judd's English any more. I backed up a few inches 'n' he wagged his tail once. That's all. Just once. More like he was swattin' a fly than expressin' satisfaction but that's what it was sure enough. He approved of my move.

All this time, Critter was munchin' grass a few feet away, his heavy chewin' sound the only thing makin' any noise in the canyon. Right sudden Judd's ears went stiff an' his whole body tightened. He yapped at me once 'n' I knew it was time to leave. I wasn't sure who was teachin' who but I already knew enough about Judd to know that he was no ordinary dog. I jumped up 'n' ran for the cabin, Judd right behind me, Critter bringin' up the rear.

When I got to the cabin, I ran inside n' told Uncle George 'n' Matt that Judd had heard or smelled something in the canyon. Uncle George grabbed his Sharps 'n' Matt his pistols 'n' him 'n' Matt stepped outside. Judd was nowhere to be seen. Without a word Matt reached for the rifle layin' there with his saddle, jumped up on Critter's bare back an' rode towards the creek.

As he rode off, Matt said, "I've gotta check my camp." Then he was gone.

Uncle George 'n' I waited in the trees near the cabin. Ma 'n' Melanie was inside, Ma with the shotgun. I reckon about twenty minutes passed 'n' we heard a single shot, far off in the distance. All kinds of things passed through my mind as we waited after that shot was fired.

When Matt didn't come back after an hour, I figured Cochise had got him. I was sad 'n' real scared. Matt had seemed like the kind of man who could handle about anything that was throwed at him, an' to be killed by a single shot must for sure mean that this Cochise fella was a man to be reckoned with.

Judd came walkin' real careful-like into the clearing in front of the house. Uncle George put the Sharps to his shoulder.

"Don't shoot! That's Matt's dog," I screamed. My shoutin' so shook Uncle George that he darn near pulled the trigger but he managed to drop the Sharps from his shoulder without firin' a shot.

Judd walked up to me an' wagged his tail once. I knew everything was okay – just like that. I walked out into the clearing 'n' wasn't worried about Cochise no more.

"Crawford! Get back into the trees!" Uncle George shouted in a loud whisper.

"It's okay, Uncle George. Judd told me as much."

He looked at me like maybe I was touched in the head, hesitated, then stepped from behind a tree 'n' walked up to where Judd 'n' me was standin'. Well, Judd had assumed the sittin' position he was so fond of 'n' so he wasn't actually standin'.

Uncle George looked down at Judd 'n' said, "Good doggie. Where's your master?"

Judd laid his ears back an' barred a few teeth. Uncle George backed up two or three feet.

"I don't think he likes bein' called 'doggie', Uncle George."

Judd kinda gave me a warnin' look.

"Is that so?" Uncle George looked real puzzled. "He doesn't like being called 'doggie'?"

Judd let out a low growl.

"His name is Judd."

Uncle George looked real hard at Judd an' smiled. "Is that right? Your name is Judd?"

Judd answered with one friendly bark, stood, wagged his tail once, then took up the sittin' position.

"Well, I'll be ....." Uncle George just kind of let that sentence end itself.

"Judd says everything is okay," I said, sure that I was tellin' the truth.

"Oh he does, does he? What else does he say?" I think Uncle George was playin' with me.

I shook my head. "I don't know. I ain't learned enough of his language yet."

"*Haven't* learned enough of his language." Ma was out of the cabin 'n' right behind me. She was always correctin' my English. "So this is Judd, is it?"

Judd stood at the mention of his name, wagged his tail once 'n' sat. Ma laughed. Melanie ran up to Judd 'n' threw her arms around his neck before Ma could stop her. I wasn't so sure that was a good idea, her runnin' up to a strange dog like that 'n' squeezin' his neck, but Judd didn't seem to mind till she got to squeezin' a mite too tight. He yelped once, slipped away from Melanie, 'n' sat real quiet a few feet away, just out of reach.

"Now look what you went 'n' did, Mel. You hurt him," I said.

"She didn't mean to, I'm sure," said Ma. She turned to Mel 'n' said, "You've got to be more careful, honey. You might hurt him and he'll bite you. Then you'll both be unhappy." Ma always had a way of puttin' things in the simplest form.

"It's a wonder that dog didn't....", Uncle George started to say.

Judd stood 'n' growled.

Uncle George started over. "It's a wonder Judd didn't bite her."

Judd seemed satisfied that his message had reached Uncle George 'n' he sat back down.

About this time Matt rode up, leading a mule with packs diamond-hitched an' loaded with pans, powder, bacon, salt, flour, lead, another rifle, a pair of black boots an' other provisions. Draped over the top of the packs was a mountain lion. It was dead enough but that mule was almost walleyed thinkin' about it. I could plainly see its worry about that cat bein' on his back.

Matt tipped his forage cap at Ma. His rifle dangled at arms length from his right hand. It was a strange-lookin' thing. Had an odd-lookin' sight, and it was a lot longer than Uncle George's Sharps. "Sorry I had to leave in such a hurry but when I saw Judd was gone, I knew he'd headed for our camp. He's real attached to ol' Jack." He nodded at the mule.

Matt dismounted, in the way only he could do it, an' said, "I wouldn't have killed the cat but he was after a longhorn, not Jack. You got cattle here?"

Uncle George nodded. "We had forty head last fall. Haven't had an accurate count since then."

"This cat was after a calf. The mama was doin' all she could but I could tell she was gettin' tired. Unless she got lucky, this fella would have been eatin' beefsteak tonight. They were about half a mile away from where I was but I could see it was a longhorn for sure. That's what took me so long to get here. I had to go and get the cat after I shot him. I sent Judd back to let you know everything was all right."

Uncle George seemed real confused about something. I could tell he was tryin' to figure somethin' out. "You shot this mountain lion from a half-mile away?"

Matt nodded. "Lucky shot," he said, an' tucked that rifle into its buckskin scabbard.

"A calf?" asked Ma.

"Yes, Ma'am. They'll be here directly."

"They'll be here directly?" asked Uncle George.

"I hope they will. I paid good money for a partner that herds cattle." He looked down at Judd, who sat real patient, not movin'. "Go bring them two back to the house, Judd."

Judd stood an' left at an easy lope, disappearin' into the trees down by the creek.

"That dog... Judd herds cattle?" Judd already had Uncle George trained.

"Better'n any man I ever met," said Matt.

"A calf! Did you hear that, George? A calf! Paul was right. We *can* build a herd. We *can* make something out of this place. Someday there will be people - lots of them - and they'll want beef."

Ma was as excited as I'd ever seen her - all over one little calf.

Matt didn't say nothin' but I had a feelin' there was somethin' on his mind.

Uncle George said, "I wish Sandra were here to see our

first calf."

"She'll be here soon, George," said Ma.

Uncle George seemed to have lost his train of thought 'cause he sure changed the subject fast enough. "Mr. Grady, won't you stay with us for a few days? We could use the help to round up the cattle and, with your d... Judd, we could make short work of it. Penny is a fine cook, and we would pay for your services." Uncle George an' Ma traded quick looks. I could tell Ma approved.

"Where can I put my horse 'n' mule an' my provisions?"

Uncle George smiled. Ma smiled too. Melanie giggled some 'n' covered her mouth with her hand. Me? I felt real good inside. Like I said, it was about time something good happened an', as far as I could tell, Matt Grady was about the best thing since Pa. Didn't seem like them Confederates was all such bad folks.

"Your horse and mule can go in the coral. We haven't got the barn finished yet. If you don't mind sleepin' in an unfinished house, my cabin is just over the small hill behind this one," said Uncle George.

"Obliged," said Matt as he lead Critter to the saddle an' bridal still layin' on the boulder. I wondered how he had rode that horse without so much as a halter. There was sure somethin' peculiar about that.

He saddled Critter, draped his saddlebags, tied his bedroll, stuffed the rifle scabbard into a loop on the saddle, mounted an' led Jack to Uncle George's cabin where he unloaded the mule an' put everything in one of the unfinished rooms except for the mountain lion, which he lowered to the ground real gentle 'n' put under a tree.

"I'll tend to the cat later, " he said to Uncle George.

I know that cat was dead but it scared me to be close to it, dead or not. I sure didn't touch it. Judd eyed it with respect, keepin' his distance. Critter snorted at it a few times an' acted like maybe he wanted to stomp it but he didn't get any closer to it than Judd.

When Matt had his bedroll put away, he took Jack to the coral

Uncle George went to the house to help Ma with some chores.

I'd followed Matt to the coral 'n' was watchin' him real close. After he had Jack's tack put away I asked, kinda shy-like, "You wanna go fishin'?"

"Maybe later, boy. Right now I gotta take care of the cat."

"Can I watch?" I'd never seen a mountain lion until that day an' never would have believed they can still be scary when they're dead, an' I was plenty scared, so it took everything I had in me to ask that question.

Matt stooped down 'n' looked me right in the eye. "As long as you promise to be real quiet and not say anything, you can come along. Any notions of talkin' before I'm done, you gotta leave. Deal?" He put out his right hand.

I took his hand an' squeezed it as hard as I could but I don't think Matt even noticed. "Deal," I said.

Chapter 4

I squatted under the cottonwood, far enough away from that big cat so as to be out of reach should it come to life. Matt took his rope, threw it over a limb of that cottonwood, looped the loose end of the rope around Critter's saddle horn an' strung that cat up. He then took Critter to the coral and unsaddled him and put the tack away and walked back to where the cat was strung up.

Matt went to work and most of the time he was hummin' or talkin'. The talkin' wasn't in English. I didn't know what language it was but, whatever it was, I couldn't understand it. I think maybe Matt was castin' a spell or somethin'.

I was doin' fine with my observin' till he slit the belly open an' all the vitals dripped to the ground. It was about that time I had to step around the tree a bit. It ain't like I hadn't seen an animal gutted before but, with the mountain lion, it seemed different somehow. I can't really explain it too good 'cause I ain't sure myself why it got to me but it sure enough did. The smell was somethin' powerful awful. It didn't smell like no deer or anything else I ever skinned. I almost lost my apple but I managed to gag it back down.

I don't know how long I stood behind the trunk of that cottonwood but I don't reckon it was near as long as it seemed. I kept tryin' to think of what I was gonna say to Matt when I finally worked up enough nerve step back around the tree. Nothin' came to me. I heard diggin' 'n' I figured he was makin' a grave. I heard a ploppin' sound 'n' knew Matt had dropped the innards in the hole. Then I heard a heavier, thuddin' sound, then the sound of a shovel fillin' the hole.

After a while Matt quit hummin' and talking that funny

language and said, "I know it's a might rough, boy. Mountain cats are different than dear or elk. You don't have to feel bad. I've known many a man wouldn't come near guttin' and skinnin' one. Some of 'em were mighty brave men."

His words gave me a lot of comfort 'n' put my backbone back in place. I stepped around the trunk of the tree 'n' said, "You sure?"

Matt smiled 'n' said, "I got no reason to lie to you, boy. It's a fact. It was a hard thing for me to do. I don't like killin' things, much less guttin' 'em, but it had to be done."

I looked at the skin, stretched 'n' staked on the ground with the inside part facin' up. There was little spots of blood an' some fat left on the inside but Matt sure did a good job of skinnin'. "Are we gonna eat it?"

He looked at me in that peculiar way he did when I asked him if he was worried about his horse. "Eat a cat? Not me." He nodded. "There's your uncle's spade if you wanna dig him up but I recommend against it."

That made me feel a heap better. I'd been afraid he was gonna butcher it 'n' take it to the cabin for supper. "Then why did you skin it?"

"It's big medicine, boy. Big medicine."

I was gettin' more confused by the second. "Big medicine?"

"You'll probably get a chance to see what I mean before long. But for now, just take my word for it."

And I did. I believed everything Matt ever said to me – well, almost.

Matt poured some water from a canteen over a rag that had somethin' inside of it. He worked the water into whatever was inside the rag by kneadin' it, kinda like Ma did when she made bread. He kneaded a bit then poured some more water on the rag an' did it again. Then he took a piece of fat an' went to scrubbin' the inside of the skin real hard, almost like he was tryin' to rub the hair off from the inside. He worked at it without stoppin' for quite a spell an' then went to rubbin' the inside of the skin with that wet rag that had somethin' inside of it. When he finally stood up, he was sweatin' somethin' fierce.

He looked at me an' said, "A Comanche might have taken more time an' done a better job but this is good enough for me."

Since he spoke to me first, I figured it was okay to talk again. "What was you doin'? An' what was in the rag?"

He grinned an' said, "That was a lazy white man's version of tannin' the hide, 'ceptin' I didn't work on the outside. Squaw would've done it right an' spent two, maybe three days." He nodded down at the cat skin. "This old boy ain't gonna be made into moccasins or quivers. As for what I had in the kerchief, it was mashed up brains."

"Brains?" I said.

He nodded. "Mix it with some fat and water and scrub it good and it makes the hide more pliable."

"What's pliable?"

He scrooched up his right eye an' thought for a minute. "It makes it softer, so's it don't get stiff like an old biscuit."

"Oh," I said.

Critter whinnied 'n' I turned in the direction of the corral, real worried that he had spotted somethin'.

Matt shook his head. "That horse is gettin' too big for his own britches."

He picked up the shovel 'n' walked toward the corral. When we got there, he put the shovel in the tack room 'n' walked to the edge of the fence. Critter stood, his head drooped over the top rail, lookin' for all the world like he'd just lost his best friend. It was plumb comical. Matt stared at him a minute then said, "Don't you think you're carryin' this a bit too far?"

Critter's head drooped even lower 'n' his eyes seemed

to get real sad.

"All right, but you better stay out of the garden and away from the mare." Matt paused a second or two then said, "And stay away from the chickens." He opened the gate 'n' Critter pranced out, head held high, hoofs risin' 'n' fallin' real crisp, like he was in a military parade. Outside the corral, he trotted toward the creek.

I didn't even ask if Critter would run away. I already knew the answer. About this time Judd came runnin' into view 'n' Ol' Blue was about ten steps behind. It was the first time I'd seen Blue since lunch time 'n' I wondered where he'd been. Judd ran right by us 'n' I could tell by the expression on his face that he was havin' a grand time. He slowed a bit so Blue could close the distance an', about the time Ol' Blue was within reach, Judd bolted for the trees north of the tack shed, leavin' Ol' Blue with a confused look on his face. Blue yelped, tripped over his own forelegs, regained his feet 'n' gave chase. I laughed. It was the second time in the same day I'd laughed. An' they were the only two times I'd laughed since my Pa had died.

"You wanna see my Pa's grave?" I don't know what made me say it but it sure popped out quick enough.

Matt looked at me but I couldn't read his face. Like I said, I'm generally pretty good at readin' faces, both people 'n' animals, but I couldn't read his at that exact second.

"Sure, boy. I'd be proud to visit your Pa's grave."

We walked without sayin' anything till we got to the mound of dirt that covered my Pa. Matt took off his cap 'n' held it over his chest. He didn't say anything, just stood there, lookin' at the mound of dirt an' the little wooden cross.

I don't know how long we stood there. It was a long time though. I believe Matt would have stayed there as long as I wanted him to. He didn't seem anxious or anything like that. He held his cap over his heart 'n' stood real silent 'n' respectful.

After a while, I said, "Pa, this here is Matt Grady. I wanted you to meet him 'cause I know you'll be real good friends. You'll like him, Pa. An' he's got a horse who thinks he's a human an' a dog that's smarter than most men. Oh, an', Pa, he's a Confederate. I ain't real sure what that is, but I heard you 'n' Uncle George sayin' we should leave'em alone an' let'em go in peace before we came out west.

"Matt's gonna stay on for a while, till we get our herd rounded up. His dog can help too." I paused 'n' I could feel those darned tears startin' up. "I love ya', Pa. I miss ya' somethin' awful. An' I know Ma misses you too. I hear her cryin' sometimes at night when she thinks I'm asleep. Uncle George misses you too. His fiancé will be here pretty soon. It won't be the same without you, Pa." By now, tears were rollin' down my cheeks like a waterfall.

Matt's voice scared me, even though it was soft 'n' low. "Pleased to meet you , Mr. Kensington. I'll do what I can to get your herd rounded up. Don't worry about that. You go on about your business and I reckon you and your family will be together again one of these days."

Somehow that short speech made my tears go away. The streaks were still on my face but my eyes had dried. It was like a miracle.

"Supper's ready." The soft sound of Ma's voice scared the daylights out of me. She was only a few feet behind us an' she didn't speak very loud but it was a plumb surprise an', for that reason, I guess I jumped a little bit. I don't have any idea how long she'd been standin' there, an' she never said, but I reckoned it was for a good spell.

I thought I saw Matt flinch but he sure recovered fast if he did. He turned, put his cap on 'n' said, "Thank you, Miss Penelope. I'll need just a minute or two at the creek to wash up."

"Of course."

"Me too, Ma." I turned 'n' followed Matt, takin' note of the odd look on Ma's face. I never much cared for washin' up an' maybe that was it but I don't think so. It was a mixture of sadness, surprise, 'n' somethin' I couldn't figure, like maybe she was wishin' it was Pa instead of Matt goin' to the creek with me.

When we got to the creek, Matt splashed water on his face 'n' rubbed his hands 'n' arms. I did exactly what he did. We had some lye soap at the house but I sure didn't mention it to him. No sense in goin' to all that trouble just for supper.

Matt slammed his cap against his leg to get the dust out of it. I took my slouch hat off 'n' did it just like he did. I pert near choked in all the dust that came out of it 'n' decided that I'd have to do that more often so's the dust wouldn't have time to build up so much.

Matt looked at me out of the corner of one eye. "You wash up for supper regular, do you?"

"Naw. Not really. Just when Ma makes me," I said.

He nodded. "I know what you mean. Out here if a man washes too much, he draws a lot of bugs. Seems like they have an easier time of it gettin' to the skin if it ain't all covered with dust an' sweat."

"Yeah, I know. But most of the time, Ma don't see it that way," I said, like maybe that was why I didn't wash as much as Ma wanted me to.

Matt nodded like he understood 'n' said, "Sometimes womenfolk just don't understand us men, do they?"

That made me feel like I was a full-growed man the way he said it. "They sure don't," I said, with as deep a voice as I could muster.

Matt wiped his hands on the legs of his britches 'n' I did the same 'n' then we walked up to the house. Judd was off to our right as we walked, kinda keepin' pace 'n' I wondered if he'd gone to Pa's grave with us. I figured he had 'n' that was okay by me for I reckoned Pa would like Judd a lot. That dog sure was quiet though. You never knew for sure where he was unless he wanted you to know or unless Matt called him.

We was still a bit from the house when I said, "Matt?"

"Yeah, boy? What's on your mind?" He'd stopped walkin' 'n' turned to look at me.

"Well, it sure would be nice if you could stay a long spell," I said. That wasn't the way I meant it to come out but it did. I had planned on workin' up to it, slow-like, so's he wouldn't know that I was askin' 'im to stay longer.

Matt, he kind of smiled at me 'n' said, "Why don't we just take things a day at a time? Who knows what'll happen tomorrow? I sure don't."

"Yeah but without my pa there's only Ma 'n' Uncle George to take care of things until Uncle George's sweetheart gets here an', even then, there won't be but one man to take care of all the man's work."

"What about you? Looks to me like there's two men around here."

That Matt, he sure had me on that one. I got to wonderin' if maybe I didn't want him around so's I wouldn't have to work so much 'n' then I started to feelin' bad for those kinds of thoughts. "But what about the Apaches?" I said.

Matt kinda scrunched up his eyes a little on that one. "The way I hear it, one man, more or less, ain't gonna make much difference."

"I'll bet it would if that one man was you."

He laughed a little 'n' picked my slouch hat from my head an' mussed up my hair. "You sure got a passle of confidence in a gent you ain't known more 'n a few hours."

He was sure right about that. Don't know why I felt so safe with him around but I sure enough did. "Hey, quit that! Ma 'll get mad at me 'cause my hair's all messed up."

He knelt down 'n' smoothed my hair back with his hands then put my hat back on my head real ginger-like. "Sorry about that, boy. Don't know what I was thinkin'." He stood 'n' we walked to the house.

Chapter 5

Ma had set the table real nice. It wasn't like in Ohio when we had folks visit 'cause we didn't have all the fancy dishes but, what we did have, she had set out right proper. The house was full of cooked-food smells an' it made my stomach growl. I thought I heard Matt's stomach kick up a little too but I could've been mistaken.

Matt took off his holster belt an' hung it on a peg. I took note he didn't take off that short-barreled Colt under his right arm but he took off that knife that hung between his shoulder blades an' hung it with his Remingtons.

Uncle George motioned for Matt to sit at one end of the table but Matt kinda stood still for a second. "I'd feel a mite uncomfortable at the head of the table, George. If you don't mind, I'd just as soon sit next to Crawford and Melanie."

That caught Uncle George by surprise, I reckon, 'cause he paused for a spell till he figured out what to say. He kind of laughed a little an' said, "Well, it might unbalance the table with you and the kids sitting on the same side but the Lord knows it's big enough." He motioned to one side of the table.

Our table was made of heavy pine an' had pine benches on both sides with a chair on each end. When we wasn't eatin', the chairs was either on the other side of the room or out front where Ma an' Pa used to watch the sun set off to the right. My eyes started gettin' wet again as I thought of them sittin' outside together an' watchin' the sun go down. I had to quit doin' that.

Ma had wrung a chicken's neck an' fixed up a real nice meal. I figured it was the hen that wasn't layin' lately. I reckoned that chicken learned the hard way that she'd make food in one way or another. Besides the chicken, we had some potatoes - the last of 'em the way I figured it - 'n' gravy 'n' some corn 'n' some biscuits. It wasn't the best corn in the world but it would do. But the best part of the meal was the smell of an apple pie. I mean to tell you, I could hardly wait until everybody finished eatin' so we could have some of that pie.

Once we was all sittin' together, Uncle George, who sat across the table on my left, held my hand. Without thinkin', I grabbed Matt's left hand while Melanie grabbed his right. Ma reached over the table 'n' held Mel's right hand. I knew by the way Matt gave a little half-flinch that he'd been taken by surprise. We all bowed our heads. I could see out of the corner of my eye that Matt only bowed his head a little.

"Dear, Lord, we thank you for the bounty on our table this day and we thank you for the presence of Mr. Grady. We thank you for our health and the fine weather. We pray the states will come together again in peace and the war will be soon forgotten. We pray for these things in your name. Amen."

Instead of closing both of my eyes while Uncle George said grace, I kinda kept my right eye open a little to see what Matt was doin'. Well, he didn't close his eyes at all. He just stared at the table. I knew when we said "amen" that Ma had seen me watchin' Matt an' I figured I would hear about it later but I can't figure why she was watchin' me in the first place. I guess that's the way mothers are sometimes. They know when to catch you if they want to.

While we was eatin', Matt complimented Ma several times on her cookin'. He wondered aloud about supplies an' such. Said he hadn't had much in the way of this kind of cookin'. Said he grew up on green chiles an' beans.

I don't remember how it came out but, before the apple pie, I found out that Matt had growed up, since the age of eight, at a big Spanish mission south of Tucson. His folks had been killed by Indians on their way to California in 1846. He could speak Spanish real good an' even spoke Papago Indian.

When he got older, he helped the priests at the mission tend to horses 'n' cattle but didn't care none for farmin'. He learned to read from the priests an' read everything he could get his hands on. He even taught some of the Papagos how to read Spanish.

When South Carolina Seceded from the Union - I think that means they quit bein' a part of the United States - Matt an' a bunch of other folks in Tucson held some kind of meetin' an' voted to break away from New Mexico an' form the territory of Arizona 'n' then join South Carolina. Well, I guess some folks north of El Paso, in the town of La Mesilla, did the same thing an' the next thing you knew, Arizona was a Confederate territory. Matt said everything was official before the end of March in 1861 an' that Arizona was Confederate before Virginia or Tennessee or Arkansas. He said it kinda proud.

When he finished tellin' about the makin' of Arizona, he sat quietly an' sipped on his coffee.

Uncle George said, "Did you see much in the way of battle, Mr. Grady?"

"George!" Ma was gettin' ready to scold. I knew that tone of voice right well.

Matt said, "That's okay, Miss Penelope. I don't mind." He faced Uncle George. "When Captain Sherrod Hunter came to Tucson, I joined up with his new outfit. It was called the 1st Arizona Rangers. Before he got there all we had was a local militia we called the Arizona Guards. Anyway, after a while, we heard the Yankees were mountin' a large column out of California and headed our way. Captain Hunter sent a detail west to scout. He picked me as one of the detail because I knew the country. About two days northwest of Tucson we happened upon a small detachment of the Yankee advance party and took two prisoners. Captain Hunter figured these gents to have a lot of information so he sent a few of us all the way to Richmond, Virginia with the prisoners.

"I was only in Richmond long enough to turn over the prisoners, buy a couple of real uniforms and meet Mr. Oury, our representative from Arizona, and was given orders to return to Tucson. On the way back, I fought in skirmishes in Virginia, North Carolina, Mississippi and Arkansas. When I got to The Indian Nations, I found out that Arizona had been taken by the Yankees and my outfit was in San Antonio. I went to San Antonio and re-joined my unit. From that time on, I spent most of the war roundin' up beef to feed our army.

"In '64 the Yankees had most of Louisiana and they had a large munition store in a small town there. We were ordered to re-take the town and the munitions. The only problem with that was this town sat in the middle of a swamp. We were cavalry and Captain Hunter, who was now a Major, had to figure out how we were gonna capture it."

Matt kinda held up in his story at this point 'n' I couldn't stand it. "What did you do?" I said, half holdin' my breath.

Ma smiled at me.

Matt said, "We grabbed anything that would float and went through the swamp at night. At first light we got a look at the camp an' knew we'd bit off a bit much. We figured there musta been a thousand Yankees in that camp an' there were less than three hundred of us. Some of the boys were for leavin' them Yankees alone an' goin' back into the swamp but Major Hunter gave a quick talk an' we captured the entire garrison, complete with munitions. We took more than twelve hundred prisoners. We were all cavalry and, in this fight, not a one of us was mounted."

I know my mouth was open to my chest 'cause I was waitin'for more details. I didn't get 'em but it was still a pretty excitin' yarn. When I saw Matt wasn't gonna say no more,

"Wow," was all I could say.

"That's about it as far as the war goes, 'ceptin' when the others quit, I didn't. One of the artillerymen sold me Jack the day before my outfit surrendered or broke up – I don't rightly know which." He looked from Uncle George to Ma, then to me 'n' Mel. "The next thing I know, I wind up at your river, gettin' a drink of water."

Matt looked back to Uncle George. "Now, I don't want you to take me wrong, George, but I know you folks are from Ohio. Are you sure you want me to help you with your cattle?"

Uncle George sat back a bit in his chair. "That's a fair question, Mr. Grady, and I take no offense at all. You see, my brother and I were both opposed to a war with fellow countrymen. That's why we're here in the first place. We are not political except to say that we believe the Union was created voluntarily and could be dissolved the same way. We couldn't fight for either side, so we sold everything and came west."

Mel, who hadn't said much of anything during supper, opened up with a real surprise. "Did you own any slaves?"

"Melanie Kensington!" I thought Ma was gonna snatch her from her chair but she didn't.

Matt smiled. "No, Mel. I didn't own any slaves. Don't believe in such a thing. As a matter-of-fact, nobody in my outfit owned a slave. We were fightin' for somethin' else."

"What were you fighting for?" Mel asked.

Matt kind of went far away for a second, then he looked down at Mel an' said, "Freedom, and the rights of the states."

"Freedom?" Said Ma. She'd been pretty quiet until then.

"Yes, Ma'am. Freedom. I know that sounds a bit strange to someone from Ohio, who sees the south as the oppressors of freedom, but that's what I was fightin' for. The less confined the power of government is, the more confined are those under its control."

"What bout the Negroes?" Asked Ma.

I looked from Ma to Matt several times before Matt spoke.

"Miss Penelope, the Negroes in the north are just as bound as the ones in the south. The only difference is in the way it's done. Slavery was on its way out long before this war. In another ten or twenty years it would have been abolished in the South to my way of thinkin'. I can't speak for anyone but myself, but I fought for the freedom of all men. We just had to whip the Yankees first then we could get on with freein' the Negroes.

"All that's left now is a federal government that has too much power and will forever rule the states from Washington City."

Ma looked at Matt with a look I hadn't ever seen. "You are a strange man, Mr. Grady, but I believe you. And yes, I would like for you to help with the cattle if you are still of a mind."

"Thank you, Ma'am. I'll be more than happy to do what I can."

I didn't know what half of what I'd heard meant but I did understand the last part. Matt was stayin'. At least for a little while. That's all I needed to understand at that point. I felt a real peace inside for the first time in a long time.

"Where's that apple pie?" said Uncle George.

Chapter 6

That night, after Matt 'n' Uncle George left 'n' went to Uncle George's cabin, I could hear sawin' an' hammering 'n' figured they was workin' on the place. Sound carries a long way at night if there ain't much in the way of noise all around you. I asked Ma if I could go help but she told me it was too late 'n' that I'd had a pretty excitin' day. There would be plenty of work in the mornin'.

"But I could hold a lamp for 'em. That ain't hard work." I really wanted to be with the men.

"*Isn't* hard work, and the answer is still no. I depend on you a lot since your pa died, Crawford. You need your strength."

Well, that got me for sure. With Pa gone, I had to be the man in *our* house first. I gave up the fight 'n' went to bed. I didn't go to sleep right off though 'cause I kept thinkin' about Matt an' all them Yankees, an' that long trip to Richmond, Virginia. I knew where that was 'cause of my schoolin' in Ohio. Pa had brought some books out west an' I practiced readin' as much as I could. Uncle George told me it was real important that a man know how to read, even the big words. I paid particular attention that Matt spoke like a proper educated man an' wondered how much schoolin' he had. I'd bet he could read all them big words. 'Course I knew Uncle George could read anything. He was real book-smart.

My mind kinda wondered a bit an' I got to thinkin' about slaves an' such. I had seen slaves once when Pa 'n' me went over the river to Kentucky. He bought a bull offa a man that had some real prize livestock. This fella had a big house an' lots of Negro servants. He invited Pa 'n' me inside for a cool drink an' that's when I saw the slaves - at least I think they was slaves. The man didn't have a whip or anything, like in that book about Uncle Tom, but the servants was all Negroes. That's the only way I knew they was slaves.

A wolf howled from up the canyon behind our house an' I shivered a little. It wasn't cold or nothin' like that but them wolves always made my back shiver a little bit whenever I heard one of 'em. I thought of Cochise again 'n' conjured up all kinds of thoughts about savages that ate white people an' got to wonderin' if maybe we shouldn't have stayed in Ohio.

I missed my friends in Ohio, 'specially Billy Barnes. He was my best friend. Me 'n' Billy was always in some kind of trouble but it weren't never anything real serious. One day we went fishin' instead of goin' to school. We might have pulled it off 'ceptin' we both came home after a hard day at school with a stringer of fish. That wasn't my smartest move in life but the fish was good eatin' an' I know Pa wasn't near as mad at me as he let on. I even caught Ma hidin' a smile after supper, even though she kept scoldin' me about ditchin' school.

The worst lickin' I ever got was the time me 'n' Billy went swimmin' at the rock quarry. That was forbidden. That's one of them big words that I learned real good after we got caught by a fella who said we was trespassin' an' he snatched us up like two frogs 'n' carried us home. I got home first, so I got the first whippin', but Billy got his too. We swapped stories the next day about who got the worst whippin' but I don't recollect who won the contest.

Yeah, I missed Billy sure enough, but this New Mexico or Arizona Territory, or whatever it was called, was sure a wonderful place. They's all kinds of plants 'n' animals that I hadn't never seen before, an' lots of places to explore. An' I could fish with a stick or a pole whenever I wanted. An' the creek had pools here ‘n’ there where I could swim when the weather was warm. An’ I could ride Bess as long as I don’t go too far from the cabin. An’ everything was big out here. The mountains were bigger. The desert was bigger. The mountain lions - well, we didn’t have mountain lions in Ohio - but if we did, I bet the ones out here would be bigger. Come to think of it, we didn’t have a desert in Ohio; mountains either.

This place had lots of things we didn’t have back east. That’s what everybody calls it - “back east”. I never heard anybody say “back west”. I wonder why? Back east can be Ohio or Indiana or even Boston. It seems like a real big place if you put all them places together. I bet even Kentucky is back east. Maybe even some of them Confederate states is back east.

I heard Mel turn over in her sleep ‘n’ I listened real hard for a minute to see if Ma was cryin’. It really broke my heart to hear her cry. She was pretty tough for a woman - even if she was my ma - an’ to hear her cry made me feel kinda helpless. I didn’t hear nothin’ but silence in our cabin, an’ the sounds of saws ‘n’ hammers from Uncle George’s place. I wondered it them two was tryin’ to finish the whole job by daybreak or somethin’. I was imaginin’ a castle where Uncle George’s cabin stood when I drifted off to sleep.

Next morning I got up real early, figurin’ to join Matt ‘n’ Uncle George an’ be one of the men. It was still dark grey ‘n’ the sun hadn’t yet broke the sky, but Critter was gone. I knew Matt ‘n’ Judd was gone too. I wondered how early a man had to get up to beat Matt to the corral.

I went back into the house an’ saw Ma was up ‘n’ startin’ a fire for coffee ‘n’ breakfast.

“Matt’s already gone,” I said.

Ma looked at me, raisin’ her eyebrows. “Did he eat anything?”

“I don’t know. He was gone when I got up.”

"My. He does like to get an early start, doesn't he?"

That was all she said 'n' then she went back to workin' on the fire in the stove.

Uncle George came into the house about twenty minutes later an' Mel got up, wantin' to play with Judd, but I told her Judd was gone lookin' for cattle. Uncle George poured his first cup of coffee 'n' sat at the table.

"That Matt is a Godsend," he said after a sip of coffee. Ma didn't say anything, so Uncle George kept on talkin'. "We worked on the cabin most of the night and I figured to get an hour or two of sleep and be up before dawn - maybe take care of his horse for him while he slept. When I woke up he was gone. Couldn't have had an hour's sleep. We got a lot done last night and I figured he'd be plumb tuckered out."

Ma said, "It's good you got some help, George. I've been real worried that the place wouldn't be fit when Sandra gets here."

Uncle George laughed a short laugh. "If I had men like Matt working for me in Cincinnati, we could have made a fortune. He's no carpenter but he learns fast. I find it hard to believe the South lost the war with him on their side."

I wasn't sure what Uncle George meant an' I was about to ask him when Ma said, "I'm not so sure he believes the war is lost."

"Maybe not," said Uncle George. "Maybe not. It's a sad thing, Penny, this whole business about preserving the Union by force."

"Well, it's over now. I just hope Mr. Grady can let it lie," said Ma.

I was real confused by then so I just walked outside 'n' looked at the hills. I wondered where Matt was. I wondered if Cochise would get him. I prayed for him to be safe 'n' find all of our cattle.

I don't know how long I stood there, just watchin' them

hills, but it was pure daylight when Ma called me in for breakfast. Like always, the cabin smelled of coffee 'n' bacon 'n' fresh eggs. At least *some* of the chickens was earnin' their keep.

Blue kept his place near the door while we ate so's he'd be right there when Uncle George took out any leftovers. There was never much, but Uncle George always tried to save a little scrap of somethin' so Ol' Blue wouldn't feel left out. I had to feed an' water the horses 'n' pigs so I fairly swallowed my food whole. Ma chewed me out a couple of times 'n' said she had never seen me so anxious to get to my chores. Truth be known, I remembered what Uncle George had said about Matt an' I wanted to be just as good a worker as he reckoned Matt to be. I wanted Uncle George to be proud of me an' see that I really *was* the man of the house.

Later, after I had taken care of my chores, I mosied up to Uncle George's cabin an' eyeballed the work that had took place the night before. I couldn't believe all that got done. The windows all had frames in 'em an' was ready for screen, or maybe even glass if Uncle George could find some. I know Pa had promised Ma real glass when we had our cabin finished an' I reckoned Uncle George would do the same for his fiancé.

Uncle George's fiancé was a real pretty woman, almost as pretty as Ma. She was nice too. An' had an education far beyond most women. One time she said women was gonna vote someday. Uncle George didn't say much but I don't think he believed her. Back in Ohio, Sandra - that's her name, Sandra Miller - she was a teacher. She was pretty smart for a woman. An' she would sure stand up to a man if she was of a mind. One day when Pa 'n' me were in town gettin' supplies, we ran across her chewin' out a teamster somethin' fierce. Seems she didn't like the way he was treatin' a team of mules. The teamster told her if she was so smart, she should drive that team over to the livery herself. She climbed up into the seat of that wagon ‘n’ drove it down the street without so much as a backward look at that fella. Them mules didn’t hesitate a lick. They just up ‘n’ pulled that wagon like they’d been waitin’ for the right person to take charge.

Pa stood there for a minute, a big smile on his face, an’ said, “I think your Uncle George is gettin’ a real thoroughbred.”

I knew what a thoroughbred was ‘cause they had lots of those across the river in Kentucky. Couldn’t see how Pa figured Sandra looked anything like a horse though. Like I said, she was real pretty.

The teamster was chasin’ after his wagon, yellin’ real loud but Sandra didn’t pay him no mind. She drove that wagon clear to the livery without ever lookin’ back. I reckon that man was plumb out of breath when he finally got there.

I looked around the cabin an’ found a couple of cabinets on the floor. They was made out of some finished lumber that Uncle George ‘n’ Pa had bought in Tucson last fall. They looked almost finished an’ I figured Uncle George was gonna hang ‘em on the wall pretty quick.

In one corner of the small room in the back of the cabin, Matt’s mule pack an’ rifle was layin’. I know it ain’t right to go snoopin’ in other people’s property but I couldn’t help myself. I looked at that rifle real close. I leaned over it an’ inspected it as best I could. On the lock were the words “Whitworth Rifle Co. Manchester”. When I looked at the muzzle, I thought I was seein’ things on account of the hole in the barrel wasn’t round. It had six sides.

Uncle George’s fiancé, Sandra, had taught me some things an’ she had told me all about six an’ eight-sided things. A six-sided thing was called a hexagon. This rifle had a hexagon hole in the barrel. I wondered how it could shoot straight.

It had a strange lookin’ front sight. Oh, it had a front sight blade but a circle surrounded it. Inside the big circle was a smaller circle. The rear sight had a sight that flipped up and a sliding thing for different distances.

Finally I worked up the nerve to touch it an' one thing led to another. Next thing I knew, I had that heavy old rifle in my hands. It was all I could do to hold it up to my shoulder but I managed it. I was fightin' off Cochise an' doin' right well, I might add, when Uncle George stepped into the cabin.

I knew I was done-for the minute I spotted his face. Don't get me wrong. Uncle George is a fine man an' never done me wrong. But he had strong beliefs about mindin' your own knittin' an' stayin' out of other folks' property.

"Crawford. What are you doing with Mr. Grady's rifle?" His voice was about as stern as Uncle George's voice ever got.

"I was just lookin' at it, Uncle George. I'm bein' real careful." I was a little scared 'cause I knew I deserved a whippin' but Uncle George had never given me one. Pa was the only one ever did that an' that wasn't too often. But, maybe with Pa gone, I figured Uncle George might get out a strap an' give me a lickin'.

Uncle George was mad, sure enough, but I saw him make an effort to hold back his mad. He just stood there, framed in the doorway. Finally he said, "Put it back the way you found it, Crawford. And don't ever go through another man's things again."

"Yessir," I said. I knew by the way he said it that he wasn't gonna give me a whippin'. Like I said, I can read people pretty good mostly. I laid the rifle over the mule pack real careful an' stood away from it.

"Let's go to the field and hook Bess to the plow."

Just like that, Uncle George forgot about the rifle. But me, I wasn't quite so quick to let go. "Uncle George, what kind of rifle is that? It don't look nothin' like your Sharps an' it had a hexagon hole in the barrel. How can it shoot straight?"

Uncle George knelt next to me and said, "It's called a Whitworth and it shoots a special hexagon bullet with a twist that is equal to the lands and grooves in the barrel."

Uncle George knew about things like that on account of he sold guns in one of his businesses back in Cincinnati. I knew he was right 'cause I had read that much on the rifle. I weren't quite so sure what a land an' groove was but I didn't say so. "Is it better than your Sharps?"

Uncle George got a real sad look in his eyes. They kind of drooped a little at the corners. "Those rifles are made for killing other men at extremely long range, Crawford. The Sharps shoots a bigger caliber slug and is made more for hunting but it is also very effective at killing men. Each is very good at its intended purpose. The Whitworth shoots a .451 caliber hex-shaped bullet and is extremely accurate in the hands of a skilled marksman."

The way he said it made me feel sad - the way Uncle George looked. I knew guns was used to kill people an' protect your property an' your family, but they was used for huntin' mainly. I had never before thought of a gun that was made just for the purpose of killin' men. It was that thought made me sad.

"Do you think Matt is bad?" I asked.

"No, Crawford. I don't think Mr. Grady is a bad man. I think he is a good man who fought in a bad war. Things like that Whitworth were just the tools he used to survive."

Uncle George was sure good at explainin' things 'n' I started to feel better about my feelin's for Matt. That, an' the fact that Uncle George wasn't gonna give me a whippin', gave this day a good start.

We went to our little field where Pa 'n' Ma 'n' Uncle George 'n' me 'n' Mel was all tryin' to get something to grow. Pa an' Uncle George had done the plowin' about three or four weeks earlier. Some things was planted but we kind of forgot about finishin' our plantin' after Pa died. I had some beans planted. Mel had carrots. Ma had a bunch of things. I wouldn't know what they was till they started sproutin'. Pa had planted corn– lots of it. Uncle George was fixin' to plant potatoes 'n' rhubarb but he had to re-plow 'cause the unplanted furrows had growed hard an' needed softenin' up.

The flattest patch of land near the cabins was our field. I guess it must have been near twenty or thirty acres, but we couldn't plant all of it till we could get water to it without carryin' it from the creek. The creek was about a hundred yards away at its closest point 'n' Pa had said we could irrigate if we dug a channel from upstream far enough, an' him 'n' Uncle George had got a good start on a little trench. If Pa hadn't died, they'd probably have finished it by now. For now, we made several trips a day with buckets, waterin' two or three rows a day until we had all the rows watered, then we'd start over with the first row again. I didn't much care for that job. We used Bess for carryin' the water from the creek to the field but my arms 'n' legs were wobbly before I got my beans watered. 'Course I helped Mel. She was really too little to do her small patch of carrots by herself. Ma did her rows all by herself. I helped her sometimes but she mostly told me not to worry an' not to work too hard. I did help Uncle George though. He 'n' me did the corn. I dreaded that chore every day but I wanted Pa's corn to grow if nothin' else did, so I did my best to see to it.

The day was warm 'n' sunny an' I knew it was a bad day for plowin' 'n' carryin' water but both had to be done. Bess weren't the best plow horse in the world but she was better than the bay. The bay was Pa's horse. His name was Mud 'cause he had a little blaze with brown spots that looked like someone had splattered mud on his face. Mud was a Tennessee horse an' had lots of stamina but he didn't take much to a harness. The horse Uncle George had lost to the Apaches was our plow horse. Uncle George said we'd get another horse next time we went to Tucson an' that would be pretty soon since Sandra, his sweetheart, should be gettin' there anytime.

Uncle George 'n' Ma had a long list of supplies to get but I didn't see any way we could get all of it on our wagon. We might have to make two trips. With Pa gone, I didn't see how we could even make one trip. Uncle George couldn't go an' leave us alone with all the Apaches on the warpath an', if we all went, the crops 'n' some of the animals would die before we could get back. Ma said Uncle George could go an' we would be all right but he wouldn't have any of that. Uncle George said we would find a way.

I helped Uncle George harness Bess to the plow an' could tell she wasn't real happy about this kind of work. Can't say as I blame her. I carried water from the creak, usin' Mud as a pack horse, an' Uncle George plowed the furrows. We was still hard at it when Matt rode up in the late afternoon.

We heard the cattle before we saw Matt. They was bellowin' an' complainin' 'n' crossin' the creek. I heard 'em splashin' in the water 'n' heard Judd yip once. I don't know why but the sound of Judd made me feel good. He was right fun to be around. I liked him almost as much as I liked Billy Barnes.

Matt dismounted Critter near the creek an' draped the reins over the saddle horn then walked to the edge of the field. Critter 'n' Judd made little feints at a steer that wanted to move away from the herd an' the animal settled in next to the creek with the rest. I had never seen a horse work cattle without a rider. Not that I knew much about cattle, but I never even heard of such a thing.

Matt took off his forage cap, wiped his brow, 'n' put the cap back on his head.

Uncle George kept plowin' till he got next to Matt then he stopped an' let the harness fall from around his neck. I could tell he was gettin' tired by the way his body seemed so relieved to be rid of that leather. "How did it go, Mr. Grady?"

Matt said, "I got most of 'em but I think there's still a few left out there somewhere, if they survived the winter."

"How many did you find?"

"Forty-seven head," said Matt.

"Forty-seven?"

"Yeah. That includes twelve calves. Unless they're dead, I figure you've got twelve or thirteen more head at least, depending on how many calved."

Uncle George seemed as pleased as punch. He didn't look tired no more. "Thank you, Mr. Grady."

"I didn't really do all that much." He jerked his head in the direction of Judd 'n' Critter. "Them two did most of the work. I told you I spent a lot of time roundin' up cattle to feed our army. Those two can do the work without me if they know what needs done. They've had a lot of practice."

"That's amazing, Mr. Grady. It truly is."

Matt smiled. "What's amazing is that those two can work together so well and still manage to fight over every little thing when the work is done."

Uncle George looked confused but I knew what Matt was talkin' about an' I kinda smiled to myself.

"Are you hungry?" asked Uncle George.

"I could stand a bite," Matt said. He looked at Bess, standin' kinda knock-kneed in the harness. After a bit he said, "I apologize for not thinkin' of it before I left, but you're sure welcome to use ol' Jack for the plow work. I didn't know you had to use the mare. She ain't built for the plow."

"That's very kind of you, Mr. Grady. I'll be more than happy to buy him from you."

"You better try him out first. I don't know much about him 'ceptin' that he pulled a Napolean around. He might not care for the plow any more than I do. That would not make a smart purchase if that were the case. Besides, I'd rather loan him to you. I think Judd wants to keep him in our family."

"Very well. I'll try him out."

Matt looked at me 'n' smiled. "You helpin' your uncle, boy?"

"Best I can," I answered.

"That's good. There's a lot of work to be done, looks to me like."

Uncle George said, "You're certainly right there, Mr. Grady. And we are all very grateful for your services."

"It really ain't all that much but I don't cotton to farmin' an' I don't know how I can be of much help other than with the cattle."

"The cattle will be enough. What seems to come easy to you is something I can scarcely manage at all. You've saved our herd as far as I'm concerned. God bless you."

"I thank you for the thought but I don't need *his* blessing." Matt turned 'n' walked back towards the creek.

I knew there was somethin' powerful wrong. I had never heard anyone say anything like that about God. It was almost a blasphemy, whatever that was. I heard a preacher use that word a lot when folks didn't believe in the Lord an' I kinda had a general idea of what it meant. I couldn't let Matt walk away without takin' him to task. "Don't you believe in the Lord?" I asked.

Matt was only about thirty feet or so away. He stopped 'n' walked back to me. When he got close, he knelt next to me 'n' said, "I don't mean to disrespect you or your family in any way, boy. It's just that your God and mine are probably pretty different. I don't want you thinkin' I mean your God any ill will, 'cause I don't. But he isn't my God. Folks are different, boy. We don't all believe the same way. I respect you and your Ma and Uncle George and Melanie as people, no matter what religion you have. Can you understand that?"

I was thinkin' it over an' wasn't exactly sure of what he meant but I still liked him a lot, even though I reckoned I shouldn't if he didn't believe in God. I nodded without sayin' anything.

He stood an' walked back to the creek, mounted Critter, 'n' drove the cattle to the north side of the field. When he rode back, I noticed that Judd wasn't with him.

"Where's Judd?" I asked.

"I left him with the herd. Until we can build a fence to keep them out of this field, he'll have to tackle that chore."

"Fence this entire field?" said Uncle George.

"This ain't Ohio, George. Those are longhorns. There's deer, elk, bear, and a bunch of others out there who could make short work of your hard labor. We need to find a way to protect your crops. It's something you might want to think about."

I could tell it was something Uncle George didn't want to think about at all but he said, "Yes. I suppose you're right."

Chapter 7

That evening Matt left the cabin right after supper, sayin' he had to check the herd. Ma an' Uncle George said it wasn't necessary but Matt insisted an' excused himself. He sure had manners when he wanted to have 'em. He was real polite with Ma - shy even.

After he'd been gone a few minutes, Uncle George told Ma about Matt's feelin's on the Lord. She didn't seem very surprised - sure not as much as I'd been.

"Maybe it was the war made him that way, after all, he was raised in a mission environment. Surely he knows God," said Ma.

"Maybe," said Uncle George, "But I don't think it was the war. I don't know why, but I just don't think so."

"I don't think he would harm the children. Do you?" asked Ma.

"Surely not, Penny. There are many men - rough and tough men - who do not profess to believe, and I doubt one in a thousand would harm a child. I'm just disappointed. He has so many Christian thoughts and ways. I can't imagine him a heathen."

I knew that word too. Preacher Dawson used it from time-to-time back in Ohio. Matt didn't seem the way I thought of a heathen like Preacher Dawson described them.

"Have you given any thought to going to Tucson?" asked Ma.

"Not yet but I'll have to do something pretty soon. Sandra will be here before long."

"Perhaps if we offered to pay Mr. Grady, he would stay

with us until you returned."

"I like the man, Penelope, but I don't know him well enough to leave you and the children alone with him for a week or more."

This kind of got my dander up an', like always, I had to say somethin'. "Matt wouldn't do nothin' bad. He'd watch over us real good. I know he would."

Ma smiled. "I'm sure he would, Crawford, but your Uncle George is right. It wouldn't look proper for us to be left with a man not our kin. It just isn't done. I don't know what I was thinking. I guess I'm just concerned about Sandra getting into Tucson and trying to find us clear out here. Her brother will only be able to stay with her for a short time in Tucson before he has to return to Ohio, and I'm sure he would have a difficult time in this country. He's a banker and not very much of an outdoor person."

"Oh," I said. I could understand a banker not doin' so well in the desert an' mountains but I couldn't really understand why Matt couldn't stay with us while Uncle George went to Tucson.

After a while I went outside an' walked to the herd. Matt was sittin' by a small fire, heatin' up a plate of beans an' bacon.

"You still hungry, Matt?"

He smiled real big an' said, "No, not me, boy. But Critter and Judd haven't had a square meal in about three days. They been foragin'."

"What's foragin'?"

"Livin' off the land."

"Oh." I looked into the pan an' realized what he was sayin'. "You gonna feed a horse beans an' bacon?"

"He's not a horse this evening. He's thinkin' he's a human again. He doesn't eat the bacon but he likes the beans."

"How do you know he's feelin' human?" I asked.

"I just know." He pulled the pan from the fire an' set it on the ground. It was a big cast iron skillet. He gave it a couple of minutes to cool an', all the while, Judd was in his favorite sittin' position only two or three feet away an' Critter stood next to him, eyeballin' that pan of beans 'n' bacon with one eye an' Judd with the other. Matt spooned out a mouthfull of beans an' tested to see how hot they was then picked up the pan. Judd stood. Critter's ears picked up straight an' I could see his muscles tighten. Matt sat the pan on the ground between the two. Neither one of 'em moved. Matt stepped back a couple of paces 'n' said, "All right, you two, dig in."

Critter put his face in the pan on the side near Judd but Judd ran around to the other side of the pan an' dove in. Critter moved his rump around to Judd's side of the pan an' eased his face a little in that direction. Judd took a bunch of quick mouthfulls of beans 'n' bacon an' darted under Critter's belly an' to the other side of the pan where he snatched some more of the beans. The two continued to play this game till the pan was empty. Judd backed away while Critter mouthed the pan dry. When this was done, Critter backed up a little then reared 'n' whinnied as if to say he'd won the battle of the beans 'n' bacon. Judd barked once, wagged his tail once, an' took up his sittin' position. Critter lowered his head 'n' laid his ears flat. It looked plumb scary to me. Judd yawned an' looked over to Matt.

Matt said, "I don't know, Judd. It looked pretty close to me." Critter unflattened his ears an' looked to relax a bit. Judd laid down an' ignored him.

"Wow," I said. I'd have bet they didn't even have an act like that in a circus.

Matt picked up the skillet an' took it to the edge of the creek where he rubbed it with sand an' rinsed it proper. When he was finished, he sat near the water an' pulled a thin little cigar from his uniform pocket. I hadn't seen him smoke yet so I was a little surprised. Tobacco was hard to come by out here but now, with the war over, maybe things would get easier. Uncle George smoked from time-to-time but he ran out of cigars almost two months back.

Matt took out his Bowie knife 'n' cut a small chunk off one end of the little cigar real careful 'n' then he put that knife back in the sheath just as careful.

"How's come you cut a piece off the end of that cigar?" I asked. I'd seen Uncle George do the same thing but hadn't ever asked him why. With Matt it just seemed natural to ask, so I did.

Matt held up the cigar so's I could see the fresh cut real clear. "Take a look at the end, boy."

I did but I didn't know what I was supposed to be lookin' for in particular.

Matt pulled another cigar out of his pocket 'n' held up the uncut end. "See the difference?"

"Yeah, but I still don't see why you had to cut it."

Matt kinda smiled. "If you don't cut the end, you can't draw any air through it."

"Oh," I said. An' it made sense when I got to thinkin' about it.

He put the uncut cigar back in his pocket 'n' pulled a match safe from his britches. He took out a match, put the safe back in his pocket, 'n' struck the match on his leg.

I was wantin' to talk to Matt about Uncle George an' him goin' to Tucson an' all but I wasn't quite sure how to put it. I waited for him to get a few comfortable puffs of his cigar then I said, "Matt?"

He took another big puff of the cigar 'n' looked my way. "Yeah, boy?"

"Well, I don't know exactly how to say it, but I got a problem."

He smiled 'n' said, "Sounds right serious to me. Spit it out and we'll see if, between the two of us, we can't fix it."

"Well, Uncle George has got to go to Tucson to meet his fiancé, but he can't go 'n' leave us alone since Pa died but, if he don't go, Sandra - that's his fiancé - will never be able to get to us." I said it all in one breath an' waited for Matt to say somethin'.

It seemed he sat there for a long time before sayin' anything but I'm sure it weren't near as long as it seemed. He took a couple of puffs on his cigar an' let the smoke kinda drift up. Finally he said, "How long's it been since you been to Tucson, boy?"

"Gosh, I don't know. A long time, I reckon. I was only there once."

"It'd be a nice visit, don't you think?"

"Why sure but..."

"I'll tell you what. If I take care of the place while you all went to Tucson, you think your Uncle George might pick up some supplies for me?"

"Why sure he would. You mean we could all go an' you would stay here by yourself?"

"If it was all right with your Ma and your Uncle George."

I was pretty excited, thinkin' about goin' to Tucson 'n' all. Tucson weren't much when compared to Cincinnati but it was sure about the biggest thing in this part of the world. "Can I go ask him now?" I couldn't hardly stand it. I had to know if I was gonna get to go to a real town.

Matt could see I was excited 'cause he smiled 'n' said, "I reckon so. Tell your Uncle George I'll be back at the house in a few minutes, after I see to Jack an' Critter."

"Oh boy!" I headed, lickety-split, for the house. I ran through the door so fast I almost didn't get stopped before I hit the back wall.

"What is it, Crawford?" said Ma.

I could see she was worried about the way I came bustin' in, so I calmed down a little then said, "Matt said he'd stay 'n' watch the place an' we could all go to Tucson if Uncle George would pick up a few supplies for him." I was almost out of breath.

Ma looked at Uncle George an' him at her.

"What do you think, George? It would be nice to see people and buy a few things we could really use. It would be good for Mel and Crawford. You wouldn't have to worry about us because we'd all be together. And we could probably stay at Mrs. Lopez's again."

Uncle George kinda furrowed his brow. "I can't believe our good fortune. It's about the only way I would feel right about going to Tucson."

"Then I think we should take Mr. Grady up on his offer," said Ma.

"I don't know what he needs in the way of supplies. We won't have much room in the wagon," said Uncle George.

"I'm sure it won't be much," I said, wantin' real bad to make this trip a sure thing.

"Uncle George smiled. "No matter. We'll just make do."

That was all I needed. I bolted for the door to tell Matt the news. When I cleared the doorframe, I pert near ran into Matt but he dodged out of the way. He was pretty quick, that's for sure. Can't figure out how I missed him.

"Whoa, boy. Where you headed in such a hurry?"

"It's okay, Matt! Uncle George says it's okay! We can get your supplies if you watch the place till we get back from Tucson."

"Okay. Let's go inside and iron out the details."

Well, we did. Matt made out a list of things he needed on a piece of writin' paper that Ma had an' handed it to Uncle George. When Uncle George started readin' the list, he raised an eyebrow, then he raised both eyebrows. He looked at Matt 'n' said, "This list is pretty extensive. I'm not sure we can get it all on our wagon, what with our supplies and Sandra's luggage."

"Oh, I wouldn't expect you to get it all in your wagon. I figured on you takin' Jack. You could take my mule packs and load 'em up. There'd probably be room for more in case you needed the space. Ol' Jack can pack a proper load."

Uncle George looked at the list again. "I don't think your pay will cover everything on this list unless you're planning to stay for an extended period."

"I wasn't expectin' to cover it with what I might make in wages. I'm not sure what things cost anymore. I haven't used Yankee money for a long time but I figure this will cover everything." He handed Uncle George a leather pouch. It jingled a little bit when Uncle George took it in his hand. He opened the pouch an' poured the coins on the table. There were lots of 'em, and they was gold.

I looked from the coins to Ma long enough to see she was real surprised.

"These are all double eagles," said Uncle George.

"When we took Brashear City in Louisiana there was a lot of gold. None of us had been paid in more'n six months so Major Hunter said we could each keep a handful. I won some more playin' cards. There wasn't much to spend it on in Texas near the end of the war. I've still got most of it, 'cept what I spent on Jack an' some supplies"

"This is quite a sum, Mr. Grady." Uncle George kept three of the coins an' put the others back in the pouch. He handed the pouch to Matt 'n' said, "I think sixty dollars will be more than enough. Probably more like thirty would do it. I'll return the excess."

Matt took a coin out of the pouch and handed it to Uncle George. "Then get an extra five hundred rounds of .44 rimfire for my Henry. Use this to buy yourself and Miss Penny and the young'uns somethin' nice." The Henry was the rifle that Matt had been carryin' on the mule.

"Really, Mr. Grady. You shouldn't do that," said Ma. "It isn't like we're poor."

Matt looked at Ma for a second then said, "I ain't doin' it 'cause I think you're poor, Ma'am. I'm doin' it 'cause I want to."

"Very well, Mr. Grady. Thank you."

Matt started to say somethin' then held up. Finally he said, "When you leave here, I'd run west a day-and-a-half before droppin' down to the Butterfield Road."

"Why's that, Mr. Grady?" asked uncle George.

"That pass goin' through those big rocks is a favorite home for Cochise and his people." Matt tipped his cap. "If it's all the same to you, I think I'll turn in. That last batch of cows is gonna be a lot harder to find than the others."

"Good night, Mr. Grady," said Ma.

"Yes, Good night, Mr. Grady," said Uncle George.

When Matt had gone, Ma said, "I wonder how he knows that about Cochise?"

"He's from Tucson. He's bound to know more about him than we do."

"Maybe, but the way he said it makes me think he knows it first hand."

"Well, I'm convinced enough to take his advice. Better safe than sorry," said Uncle George.

I just stood there an' listened. Mel was already asleep, so this whole thing would be news to her in the morning. I was thinkin' about all them gold coins an' how I never had any idea that Matt had all that money. Folks can be real surprisin' sometimes.

Chapter 8

There wasn't any road from our place to Tucson, at least not directly west, which is the way Tucson was. Uncle George said due west was the shortest way in miles but the longest way in days 'cause it was over mountains 'n' such.

We loaded up in the Studebaker wagon Pa had kept when we sold our Conestoga. Uncle George had said the Conestoga was lighter and better suited to long trips an' we could get a better price for it. That's why we sold it instead of the Studebaker. I knowed it was different than the blue Conestogas Uncle George sold with his businesses. They was bigger an' heavier an' well suited for haulin' heavy loads a few hundred miles an' such but Uncle George said folks soon found out in the old days that them ol' blue Conestogas would wear out a six-ox team in less than seven or eight hundred miles an' so the folks buildin' them Conestogas had built a smaller, lighter one an' called it a prairie schooner. The Studebaker was pert near as big an' heavy as Uncle George's freight wagons an' it was a might hard on our oxen but I liked it better on account of it had more room inside.

We hitched Bess 'n' Mud to the harness, tied Jack on behind an' headed west. We really needed another team, even though the Studebaker was empty an' it was only about a hundred miles to Tucson, but we didn't have any more horses so we had to make do. Uncle George said we'd go slow an' not work Bess an' Mud too hard. We took extra harness on account of Uncle George said we'd get another team in Tucson if we could find one 'cause the load comin' back home would be right heavy.

We stayed west for the better part of two 'n' a half days. It was rough goin' an' several times we almost got stuck in sand or by hills that were too steep for our team. We had to take the packs offa Jack an' hitch him to the wagon to help pull us up a hill and it turned out he was a good leader. When we finally skirted the pass with the big rocks we headed south until we ran across the old road used by the Butterfield Stage - when there *was* a Butterfield Stage - then we headed west on the road.

It was pretty excitin' to me an' Mel, Ma too, I suppose. I didn't remember much of the country on the way to Tucson from our place on account of I was younger when I had seen it last. Uncle George was havin' a hard time gettin' Bess an' Mud to work together. They weren't much in the way of a team. Seemed like they each had their own idea of which way to go whenever there was a choice. Uncle George hooked Jack back into the team and we didn't have no more trouble with the horses tryin' to figure out which way to go.

A little bit after we were on the Butterfield road, I got to thinkin' about Cochise again an' saw him behind every bush. The feelin' didn't let up, even when we put those big rocks behind us. We'd been traveling the road about an hour when I saw the dust in front of us.

I said, "Look. Do you suppose that's Cochise?"

Uncle George reined the horses in an' let 'em blow while he studied the small cloud of dust. It didn't appear to be moving very fast an' it was too far away to tell what was stirring up the dirt. After a while, he pulled the wagon into a small dry creek bed near an outcropping of rock about a hundred yards from the road an' told us to hide on the east side of it. Ma took the shotgun 'n' led us around the rocks while Uncle George picked up his Sharps 'n' hid next to the wagon.

We laid down in the dirt 'n' rocks 'n' waited for we didn't know what. It was sure hot an' there weren't much in the way of shade. I started to crawl to a small mesquite tree about twenty yards away but Ma put a halt to that real quick.

"You stay right next to me, Crawford Kensington," she said.

Whenever she used my whole name, I knew there weren't no sense arguin'. That would be plumb stupid, so I just laid there in the hot sun. After a while I was almost wishin', if it was Cochise, he'd attack an' get it over with. I felt real bad when I looked at Mel 'n' saw how scared she was. She was barely breathin' an' her eyes was real big. I was gettin' pretty mad at this Cochise fella an' I hadn't even met him yet.

It was the better part of an hour when Uncle George said it was okay to get back in the wagon. Whatever, or whoever, it was had turned south before they got to where we was. We never did know an' I was just as glad for it.

We got back in the wagon an' continued down a big slope till we got to a river - not a wash - but a real river. Uncle George said it was called the San Pedro. A lot of things in Arizona had Mexican names. I guess that's because the Mexicans was here before white men so they got to name the places. That only seems fittin', I reckon. We only stopped long enough to take on water an' wash up a little an' let the horses drink. They sure needed it. Uncle George said we could make Tucson in about two and a half more days if we kept movin'. We was all agreed on that, so we kept movin'.

That night we camped in a canyon in a big sandy wash. We didn't build a fire, even for cookin', 'cause Uncle George said Apaches might attack at night. Ma had made some biscuits for the trip so we just had cold biscuits 'n' water.

The next day we made better time, though, I gotta say, that road wouldn't even have been called a trail in Ohio. It had ruts 'n' rocks 'n' even small bushes in the middle of it. Not much happened of interest 'cept we stopped before dark an' Uncle George built a small fire so Ma could cook us a meal.

We had corn meal bread 'n' beans 'n' some dried beef. It sure tasted good.

The weather the next day seemed hotter than anything I could remember. I felt sorry for Bess 'n' Mud. They was sweatin' pretty heavy by day's end. Jack didn't seem tired at all. We set up camp before dark an' I helped rub 'em down. They drank a lot of water an' it looked to me like we would run out. I got to worryin' about that but I didn't say anything 'cause I didn't want to scare Mel. We had more bread 'n' beans 'n' beef an' went to sleep on full stomachs.

The next day, about mid-morning, we topped a ridge 'n' Uncle George pointed to a green spot in the far distance. "That's the Santa Cruz River. Tucson sits right next to it, below that peak."

I could see the peak but not Tucson. About an hour before sunset we rode into Tucson. It was pretty excitin' to me. I could smell the river an' see the cottonwood trees on the west side of town. 'Course there was mesquite 'n' palo verde 'n' creosote too. They was everywhere. The adobe wall around the inner part of town was about half gone. I remembered that from the first time I had seen Tucson. I couldn't tell if it just wore out with the wind 'n' rain or if part of it had been torn down to build roads 'n' buildings or if maybe Cochise hadn't done it.

Uncle George stopped the wagon in front of an adobe on the east end of town. I remembered it from my only other visit to Tucson. It belonged to Mr. an' Mrs. Lopez an' they was sure nice folks. Most of the Mexicans lived on the west side of town but some, like the Lopez family, lived on the east end where most of the few white folks lived. They weren't many white folks in Tucson at the time. Mostly there was Mexicans and Papagos. Papagos was friendly Indians. They mostly lived south of town a ways.

Uncle George handed me the reins an' walked up to the

door an' knocked. Mrs. Lopez opened the door an' recognized Uncle George right off. She smiled an' gave him a quick hug then stepped around him to our wagon an' did the same to the rest of us, 'ceptin' for me. I had to stay up on the wagon an' hold the team. She did reach up an' pat my leg an' tell me *buenos tardes*. I remembered that meant good afternoon. I said it back to her an' she smiled real big. She was a real pleasant lady.

She said that Tucson was gettin' more an' more people every day on account of the war bein' over, an' she had a boarder in her only room, but her an' her husband and three children would pitch their tent out back an' that we was welcome to their rooms for as long as we liked.

Ma wasn't hearin' of no such thing but Mrs. Lopez said that would be fine with them an' they could use the money, so would we please stay in her humble home? Her English was pretty good. I reckoned it was because she lived on the east side of town where most of the white folks lived an' she musta talked with them a lot.

Finally Uncle George agreed an' gave her some money. She thanked him a lot an' asked that we come inside an' get comfortable while she rounded up her children an' pitched their tent. I reckoned Mauro, her husband, was out huntin' or somethin'. She said he'd be back in an hour or so to help her pitch the tent an' for us not to worry about it.

We unloaded our clothes an' some of our other gear an' carried it into the house. I'd tied the brake on the Studebaker so Bess an' Mudd wouldn't drag it down the street at the first loud noise. We stepped into Mr. an Mrs. Lopez's room an' Ma went right to a big porcelain basin. She put her bag down an' picked up the big pitcher sittin' next to the basin an' poured some water into it 'n' washed her face 'n' neck with a rag.

"Oh my. That feels good." She turned to me and Mel 'n' washed our faces an' necks with the wet rag. I had to agree. It did feel mighty good. It was the first time in several days I had felt any kind of cool, 'ceptin' for a quick splash in the San Pedro River.

When she was done washin' our faces, Uncle George said, "Crawford, you and I have the children's room. Put your things in there then wait for me with your mother. I'll be back in a little bit."

"Yessir," I said, already headin' for our room.

Uncle George took the wagon to the livery an' came back in about half an hour. He said he'd been able to buy a team of horses, though they weren't much for looks. I was glad for Bess an' Mudd that they was gonna have help pullin' that big ol' Studebaker home, even if the help wasn't much on looks.

Uncle George said Sandra hadn't arrived yet, so we might as well get comfortable for a few days. Mel 'n' me were ready for that. We hugged each other an' sang a verse of *Sweet Betsy*. Ma laughed for the first time in three days, an' when Mrs. Lopez came in an' said we were gonna have beef an' beans for supper, Mel 'n' me hit another verse.

'Course, with all good things come the bad, an' Ma insisted that we had to take a bath 'n' change into our clean clothes. It wasn't a real bath, but it was close enough. When it was my turn, I took the basin 'n' pitcher into my an' Uncle Geroge's room an' cleaned up the best I could. Now that I was the man of the house, Ma gave me as much privacy as she could, an' this made me feel pretty good.

Eatin' food cooked by someone besides my ma was almost like eatin' in one of them fancy eatin' places in Cincinnati. Pa an' me had eaten at an inn a few times when he was in Cincinnati on business 'n' I liked it on account of I didn't have to do no dishes an' neither did Mel or Ma. It was kinda excitin' to me that Ma wouldn't have to work so hard while we stayed with Mrs. Lopez.

The house smelled like dirt, but I guess I should have expected that, ‘cause that's what adobe is. But it still felt strange to eat with all those dirt walls around you an' only two small square windows on the side facin' the street. It was a bit hard to see at first, until your eyes got used to the dim light but, after that, it was okay. The chairs was a mixture of whatever they must'a had around, an' I ain't all that sure what the table was ‘cause it was covered with a colored blanket-like thing the Mexicans call a *serape*. The table was sturdy enough though an' I kinda liked the bright colors of the *serape*. Mel talked about it a lot. She thought it was a good idea ‘n' said we should get one for our table at home. Ma raised an eyebrow at that one, but she smiled, so I knew she was thinkin' about it.

The food Mrs. Lopez served was sure a lot different than I was used to. She did have a steak, an' Uncle George got it for Ma. I didn't know how much steak Mrs. Lopez had so I just said I'd have beans ‘n' tortillas. Truth be known, I liked tortillas. An' the way Mexicans made beans made ‘em taste almost as good as steak anyway. Beans ‘n' tortillas didn't cost nothin' extra ‘n' I figured we could eat a lot more if we didn't eat steak all the time. Mel wanted eggs ‘n' biscuits. That was a nickel on account of Mrs, Lopez usually sold her eggs, an' there weren't no biscuits, only tortillas. That didn't please Mel all that much but it did me ‘cause I knew she wouldn't eat all of her tortillas ‘n' that meant I'd get some of ‘em. I was addin' all of this up ‘n' wonderin' how long our money would last. I had no idea how much money we had. Uncle George asked for some beef mixed with green chile. That was somethin' I never saw before. He had a hard time makin' Mrs. Lopez understand what we wanted on account he wasn't sure what to call it but she finally came to an understandin' an' hustled to the rear of the house where she kept her kitchen.

I gotta say, while we was waitin' for our food, I finally got used to the smell of the adobe walls an' dirt floor ‘n' caught a whiff of the food bein' cooked somewhere out back. It was a smell I had never smelled before an' it made my mouth water plenty. Whatever they was cookin' back there was what I wanted.

Mr. Lopez came home an' he greeted us just like his wife did, with a big smile an' a hug. I liked Mr. Lopez. He was a simple kind of man an' real pleasant to be around. It didn't seem to bother him none that we had turned him out of his own house into a tent. He welcomed us just like we was family.

It turned out that what I had smelled was Uncle George's beef 'n' green chile. When Mrs. Lopez put that plate of food in front of Uncle George, I couldn't stand it anymore. I wished I had asked for the same thing.

We all held hands an' Uncle George said grace. When he was done, I asked him if I could have a bite of them green chiles an' he said 'of course', but to be careful 'cause it might be hot. Well, I blew on it a little bit to be sure it wasn't too hot, an' I got a stern look from Ma, which I always did when I blew on my food to cool it, then I put that spoonful of beef 'n' green chile in my mouth.

It was a fact, I hadn't never experienced anything quite like that. I realized too late that Uncle George hadn't been talkin' about that stuff bein' hot from the stove. What he meant was hot from the chile. My mouth got to burnin' 'n' my eyes waterin' 'n' my nose runnin', all at about the same time. A few seconds later, I started sweatin' on my forehead 'n' above my lips. I reached for the glass of water in front of me but that only made it worse. I blew air out an' sucked it back through my lips an' that helped a little. After a while I could breathe normal an' I settled back in my chair to kinda catch my breath for a minute.

"Are you all right, Crawford?" asked Ma.

"Yeah. I think so. That's the hottest thing I ever ate. It kinda took me by surprise. It has the best taste of anything I can think of. I just wish it wasn't so hot."

"Maybe if you mixed it with your beans it wouldn't be so bad," said Uncle George.

"Yeah, maybe so, but I think I'll wait until my mouth cools down before I try it again."

Mel laughed. "You sure turned red. I couldn't believe you started sweating so fast. I'm never gonna eat that stuff."

"Perspiring, Mel. Young ladies don't say 'sweat'," said Ma.

"Yes, Ma'am," said Mel. Then she said it all over, 'ceptin' she said 'perspirin' instead of 'sweatin'.

Ma could see that the emergency was over so she began eatin' her steak. I watched Uncle George, real casual-like, out of the corner of my eye an' could tell he was havin' a rough go of it with that green chile too but he put it all away. His face was about the color of a ripe tomato when he finished an' he was sweatin' all over but he did eat it all. My Uncle George was a tough an' a brave man.

When we finished eatin' we all walked around town. The sun was settin' but it sure didn't seem to cool down much. I was sure glad Uncle George was with us for there was a lot of tough-looking men, mostly Mexicans. I guess I just wasn't used to seein' Mexicans an' they scared me a little bit. When I heard 'em talkin' their language, I wondered if they was talkin' about us an' maybe were plannin' on killin' us 'n' takin' our money. Uncle George told me not to worry.

I saw a few soldiers but not as many as I'd expected. Uncle George said they was stationed just north an' east of town at a place called Camp Lowell. I was wishin' there was more of 'em 'cause they made me feel safer. Most all of 'em looked pretty long at Ma. They tried not to show it but I caught 'em lookin' out of the corners of their eyes. Like I said, Ma was awful pretty, even in her black clothes.

We took a walk down by the Santa Cruz River an' the

air was a little cooler there. Mel 'n' me skipped rocks on the water till Ma said we had to get back to the Lopez's 'cause it was gettin' too dark.

On the way back to the Lopez's the goin' was slow 'n' easy at first, even though it was a little uphill. It looked to me like the people was different than the ones we saw before the sun went down. Then Uncle George hurried us up. I think he was gettin' a little worried. I wasn't all that brave myself. I was gettin' a *lot* worried. A Mexican lady yelled at somebody but I couldn't understand what she was sayin'. Then I saw she was talkin' to a big man with a pot belly an' a bushy mustache. She weren't no bigger than a minute but she sure had that big fella dancin' to her tune. Whatever she said, he went back into their adobe with his head hung low, like a whipped puppy. Kinda reminded me of Critter hangin' his head out of the corral.

We all stopped at Ma an' Mel's room for a few minutes 'n' talked about our day an' all the things we'd seen. Ma promised we would go to the mercantile in the morning an' maybe buy some store-bought clothes. Maybe even some candy. I got a little excited about that. It had been a real long time since I'd had any candy.

Uncle George 'n' me was about to go to our room when Ma said, "I wonder how Mr. Grady is handling things?"

"I'm sure he's doing fine, Penny. He's a good hand with cattle," said Uncle George.

"It's not the cattle I'm worried about. It's the milk cow and pigs and the garden. Hauling that water is a lot of work for one person. And what about the chickens? I don't think Mr. Grady is much for tending chickens, and I'm not sure he even knows how to milk a cow."

Uncle George patted Ma on the shoulder. "Now there, Penny. Don't you worry about things. I'm sure Mr. Grady will do his best by us."

"We really don't know him, George. He could take

everything we own and be in Mexico before we got back."

"Matt wouldn't do no such thing!" It was out of my mouth before I even knew I was speakin'.

"Of course he wouldn't Crawford. Your mother is just worried. I'm sure Mr. Grady is as honest a man as I've ever met," said Uncle George.

"You're right, George. That was wrong of me to say such a thing. It's just that most of what we own is out there in the middle of Apache country, in the hands of a stranger." Ma turned to me. "I know everything will be all right, Crawford. I'm sorry I said such a thing. Mr. Grady has given me no reason to distrust him. When we get back home, I'll apologize to him in person."

That made me feel a lot better. Ma was always willin' to admit when she made a mistake. That was just another reason I had for lovin' her so much.

Chapter 9

Uncle George an' me was up before daylight, me stumblin' into things that I wasn't used to bein' there, an' bouncin' off the walls. I finally came awake enough to quit bumpin' into things 'n' washed my face in the porcelain basin. Then I ran out back to the privy 'n' took care of business. When I got back to our room, Mel was waitin' for me an' we talked, real excited-like, about goin' to the mercantile. 'Course it wouldn't be open until a little later in the day but that only made the wait that much sweeter.

We had breakfast, an' Mrs. Lopez's other boarder was there. I don't know where he was the night before but I sure wouldn't have missed him in a crowd. He had real long blonde hair an' a lot of it, an' a blonde mustache, an' he wore a wide-brimmed, tall-crowned hat that came to a peak at the top of the crown. He never took it off, even while he was sittin' at the table. Ma wouldn't have liked that in our house but she didn't say nothin'. The fella had on a cream-colored shirt with fancy cuffs an' a black leather vest with a gold chain droopin' out of a pocket. His britches was charcoal-colored with real thin white stripes runnin' the length of the leg, all the way to his waist. He also had a big Army Colt in a skinny holster with a flap on it strapped to his belt. He didn't take that off either. Not even Matt wore his guns to the table, 'ceptin' that short-barreled Colt in the shoulder holster, an' he was still a soldier. I reckoned this fella wasn't long on manners.

Turns out, this gent's name was Mr. Carter an he was in town lookin' to find a little spot to set up a stage depot on account of he figured there would be contracts let by the government any day for mail service between El Paso an' Tucson now that the war was over. I almost told him he only thought the war was over but it weren't, on account of Matt hadn't surrendered yet, but I didn't say what I was thinkin'. I didn't like Mr. Carter much. Seems like he bragged a lot an' looked at Ma too much. I think maybe Uncle George felt the same way an' we was all glad when he finished eatin' an' left.

Before he left, there was a lot of talk about the war bein' over 'n' how everyone should join together an' start life all over. After he left, Mrs. Lopez said he was really a nice man but she wished he wouldn't wear his hat to the table. I sure enjoyed her cookin'. I had beans an' eggs an' tortillas for breakfast an' I didn't even notice that the floors 'n' walls was made of dirt.

We'd just left the Lopez house an' stepped outside when the commotion started. The first thing I saw was two men fightin' in the middle of the street. One was Mexican, the other white. Both had knives an' was swingin' real wild with 'em. A crowd was quick to collect but it didn't look to me like anybody was ready to step forward an' stop the fight - not that I blame 'em none.

The white man was bigger than the Mexican but it looked to me like the Mexican was a better hand with a knife. I was about to pick him as the winner when Ma shooed me back against a wall 'n' covered me 'n' Mel with her body while the crowd kept gettin' bigger. Men was shoutin' an' cheerin' an' carryin' on like they was watchin' a cockfight.

Ma an' Uncle George was just beginnin' to push us towards Mrs. Lopez's house when somebody fired a shot. The whole crowd went quiet all at once, like somebody let the air out of 'em. I peeked around Ma 'n' saw five soldiers ridin' right into the crowd. Everyone scattered like chickens from a fox an' the two fighters stood froze. Either one could have cut the other but neither did. They just stared at the soldiers.

The leader of the soldiers - Uncle George said he was a lieutenant - raised a sword an' shouted some kind of order to the others, who spread their mounts out in a semi-circle between the two fighters an' the crowd. The lieutenant stayed mounted an' looked down at the two men who still stood real still.

He said, "Drop those knives!"

Both men opened their hands an' let their knives fall to the dirt street.

Still mounted, the lieutenant said, "You men can pick them up later at the post if you choose to do so. Now, disperse!"

An', just like that, it was over. Everybody kinda went on about their business like it never happened. I guess that's what 'disperse' musta meant.

The soldier in charge put his sword back into its scabbard 'n' dismounted 'n' picked up the knives. He stuffed 'em into his saddlebags an' led his horse to the hitchin' post where he tied down. The other soldiers stayed mounted an' watched the crowd disappear. When the man in charge saw us, he smiled an' touched the brim of his hat. "Good morning," he said. I think he was speakin' to Ma, 'cause he never even looked at the rest of us when he said it.

Uncle George nodded 'n' Ma smiled.

As the rest of the soldiers sat their horses, the man in charge stood next to Ma 'n' said, "I'm Lieutenant Barton. At your service. Are you folks new in town?"

Uncle George said, "I'm George Kensington and this is my sister-in-law, Penelope Kensington. These are her children, Melanie and Crawford. We're just in town to meet my fiancé. When she arrives, we'll be going back to our place."

The lieutenant barely looked at me an' Mel. He shook hands with Uncle George 'n' took his hat off to Ma. "Pleased to meet you." He looked real long at Ma. I didn't really like the way he looked at her but, like I said, she was real pretty.

"You have a place near here?" He didn't seem to be payin' much attention to what he was sayin'. He was more interested in Ma. I could tell.

"About a ninety or a hundred miles east of here, near Cherry Creek," said Uncle George.

Suddenly that lieutenant was payin' attention to Uncle George. "Ninety or a hundred miles east is in the middle of Cochise's territory. Surely you must be mistaken, Sir."

"Sir, if I know little of nothing, I know where we live," said Uncle George.

"Forgive me, Sir. I was just so surprised to hear it. If I became impertinent, I apologize," said the lieutenant.

"No harm, Lieutenant Barton," said Ma.

"Please. My given name is Robert," said the lieutenant.

"Very well then, Sir. No harm done," said Ma again.

I was glad she didn't call him Robert. She didn't even call Matt by his first name. I would have been surprised if she had called this lieutenant by his. It ain't like the lieutenant was a bad man or nothin' like that but it just wouldn't have seemed proper for my ma to call a man by his first name the very minute she met him. She just didn't do things like that.

"Would you folks like to join us for breakfast?" asked the lieutenant.

Uncle George said, "Thank you for the kind offer, Sir, but we have just eaten."

"Perhaps some other time then. With your permission, I will look you up. I'm interested to learn how you're doing near this Cherry Creek," said the lieutenant.

"We're staying at the Lopez house. Feel free to call," said Uncle George.

The lieutenant put his hat on an' said, "With your permission" He turned 'n' walked down the street. His men dismounted an' tied up at a couple of hitchin' posts an' followed him.

"My. He was certainly a gentleman," said Ma.

"He has good breeding," said Uncle George.

"Matt has good breedin'," I said.

Ma smiled at me 'n' said, "Yes he does, Crawford. Yes he does."

The way she said it made me think that she thought the lieutenant had more breedin' than Matt an' that kinda made me a little mad.

We walked west on Congress Street about a block or two, such as the blocks were in Tucson, an' turned right. There was dust everywhere on account of the streets was all dirt 'n' there hadn't been any rain in a spell, an' even though it was still a bit early in the day, there was enough horse 'n' mule 'n' foot traffic to stir up a respectable cloud. There was a small wash runnin' next to the street we was walkin' on 'n' I thought that was right peculiar. There weren't no water in it an' it weren't a very big wash but it stood between the street an' the businesses on that side. I reckon it didn't rain much in Tucson or somebody would'a done somethin' about that little wash.

Ma 'n' Uncle George was still talkin' about that lieutenant's manners 'n' Mel 'n' me was lookin' at everything we could see an' I was wishin' we lived in town. Like I said, Tucson weren't no match for Cincinnati but It weren't full of Apaches neither, though I was certain sure that Cochise could come in any time he wanted to 'n' kill everybody. I quit lookin' at the buildings for a while 'n' kept a sharp eye out for Apaches.

We turned left 'n' walked towards the Santa Cruz River for a spell, then we turned right again. There was a building that had a sign on it that read: "Sol Warner" 'n' underneath the "Sol Warner" was some more writin' that said, "Gen. Store". Mel 'n' me headed right for the candy. I know Mel was disappointed like I was 'cause they didn't have much in the way of sweets. They did have some licorice an' a few pieces of hard candy, 'n' they had some kind of jam made from a Saguaro cactus. The man said the Papago Indians made it. Uncle George bought me 'n' Mel some licorice 'n' hard candy 'n' he bought Ma some of the jam.

After awhile Uncle George got out the list of things Matt asked him to get 'n' he 'n' the man, who I reckoned was Mr. Warner, talked for a spell while Mel 'n' me scouted around the store. It was kinda dark inside the place 'n' Ma followed us around to be sure we didn't bang our heads on any of the stuff hangin' from the ceilin'. Seems like there was about everything up there, from pots 'n' pans to bridles 'n' shovels. I heard the man tell Uncle George he had left town in '61 on account he weren't no Reb sympathizer 'n' he was freshly back in town 'n' still tryin' to get supplies in from Fort Yuma in California. He said in a few months he expected he'd have everything back like it used to be before the war.

After a spell Uncle George left the list with the man 'n' we walked outside. It was downright hot out there. I hadn't realized how cool that dark old adobe building was until right at that minute. I was tryin' to think of a reason to go back in the store when that lieutenant rode up next to us 'n' dismounted.

I gotta admit he sure looked handsome in that uniform, an' he was real polite 'n' all but, I for some reason, I didn't care for 'im much. It was kinda like he was trespassin' into my own private little world 'n' I wasn't ready for none of that. Mel 'n' me walked a little faster 'n' got out ahead of the lieutenant 'n' Ma, so I didn't hear much of what was bein' said. Later, I got to wishin' I'd stayed closer to Ma so's I'd knowed what was said. I did hear Uncle George tell the lieutenant about his fiancé 'n' her brother, an' the lieutenant said he would keep an eye out for 'em.

Chapter 10

The next morning, that Lieutenant Barton was knockin' on our door almost before we was up. He said that a wagon was comin' in from La Mesilla with a small detachment of troops from Fort Bowie. If we had known that, we could have met Sandra just south of our place. 'Course, we still would have been in need of supplies, so I reckon we had to come to Tucson anyway.

The lieutenant said the wagon would be here in about two more days. Uncle George thanked him 'n' invited him to have breakfast with us.

At breakfast that lieutenant kept lookin' at Ma 'n' smilin' the whole time he talked or ate. I don't know how he found his mouth with the fork, he was so busy watchin' Ma. He said he was from Pennsylvania 'n' that his father had been a colonel with a Pennsylvania regiment that had fought at Gettysburg, wherever that was. He made it sound pretty important so I reckon maybe it was. He said he wanted to fight in his father's regiment but his orders had sent him west 'n' he was stuck in this God-forsaken desert tryin' to kill Cochise 'n' all his followers. I was all for that part about him killin' Cochise 'n' his followers.

After breakfast the lieutenant showed us around town a bit. He introduced Uncle George to a blacksmith 'n' said the man was real good with metals 'n' could shoe a horse real proper 'n' fix a broken wheel better than new. Then he showed us all the buildin' that was goin' on. There was lots of Mexicans makin' adobe blocks an' that was interestin' to see how they mixed the mud with grass or straw 'n' poured it into these squares of wood just sittin' on the ground. When the mud was dry enough, they picked up the square 'n' the adobe stayed on the ground 'n' finished dryin' out, an' they'd pour some fresh mud 'n' straw into the square, which they'd sat in a different spot, 'n' start all over.

There was a lot of houses 'n' stores bein' built an' I don't think the Mexicans could make the adobe fast enough 'cause some folks was chunkin' adobe blocks from the old Presidio wall. I figured there wouldn't be no wall left if they kept that up. I reckon they thought maybe they didn't need the wall with the war bein' over now 'n' there bein' so much cavalry to protect 'em from Cochise. Me, I'd keep the wall *and* the Cavalry. Couldn't be too careful with a fella like Cochise out there.

Lieutenant Barton pointed to a small mountain west of the Santa Cruz River 'n' said it was called Sentinel Peak on account of you could see all the way to the big mountains north an' east of town, an' a mighty long way to the south. They kept a guard up there a lot, watchin' for Cochise.

Ma asked if we could go to the top of Sentinel Peak 'n' look around. The lieutenant looked real pleased when she asked that 'n' offered to escort us all up to the top of the trail. That sounded like an adventure to me 'n' I was sure glad when Uncle George said it was okay. Uncle George was gonna rent some horses from the livery 'n save ours for the trip back home but the lieutenant wouldn't have none of that 'n' he said he would meet us in an hour with horses for everybody.

I don't know where that lieutenant got them horses but the mare he got for me was kinda wore out. She sure didn't seem to have a lot of spunk. I reckon the lieutenant figured that would be safer since I weren't all that experienced at ridin'. My saddle was too big but he shortened the stirrups as much as he could 'n' I made do. Mel doubled up with Uncle George.

The ride up the trail to the top was fun 'n' I was glad I was ridin' a real gentle horse when a rabbit jumped out from a bush 'n' darn near spooked the mare I was ridin', 'ceptin' I think she figured it was too much like work to get spooked, so she only jerked her head 'n' kept on ploddin' up the trail.

When we got to the top we met a private who saluted the lieutenant 'n' kept walkin' around the top of the mountain. I gotta say, it was a right spectacular sight up there. I had never seen so far before. I could pert near see our place if those mountains east of town hadn't been in the way. Off to the south, about ten or fifteen miles, there was a big building all by itself, 'ceptin' for a few small outbuildings. I asked the lieutenant about it 'n' he said it was the Mission San Xavier Del Bac an' it was on Papago land. That was where Matt had said he grew up. I wondered if he knew any of them Papagos. I wished Matt was with us. It was sad that he couldn't come home anymore just because of some old war.

It was late in the afternoon when we got back to town an' the lieutenant said his good byes. Ma told him how much she had enjoyed her day an' thanked him a lot - too much, to my way of thinkin'.

I was a little sore from ridin' all afternoon 'n' was sure glad to get offa that mare.

The next day Uncle George looked to our livestock 'n' I went with him. We had new shoes put on the horses 'n' saw to it they was given some oats. After that Uncle George 'n' me went to the "Gen. Store" where he bought a cigar for him 'n' a piece of hard candy for me. We got Mel some hard candy too 'n' we took it with us when we left the store.

By the next mornin', I was already gettin' tired of life in the big town of Tucson an' I wanted to be back at the creek, fishin' 'n' swimmin. 'Course I'd have to do my chores but there was lots of fun things to do too. 'N', besides, Matt 'n' Critter 'n' Judd was there.

It was late afternoon when the wagon 'n' its escort of soldiers came into town. It seemed like a pretty big event the way folks stood on the sides of Congress Street to watch 'em go by. Uncle George was sure glad to see Sandra 'n' she was glad to see him. I'd never seen so much kissin' 'n' huggin' in my whole life.

Sandra was a real pretty woman; almost as pretty as Ma. She had chestnut hair 'n' real pretty blue eyes. Her hair was up in a bun when she came into town but I'd seen it when it was combed out 'n' it was mighty long, longer even than Ma's.

It took a few minutes for everybody to get in all the huggin'. Even Edward, Sandra's brother, did his share. I didn't know him too good for I'd only seen him a few times while Uncle George was courtin' Sandra, but you'd a ' thought I was his closest kin the way he carried on. He was all right for a grown-up but he was sure dressed funny for bein' where he was. He had on a dark suit, just like he was goin' to the bank in Cincinnati, an' a black derby. I think his hat drew a few looks from some of the folks in town 'n' I was glad when we gathered up all of Sandra's trunks an went to our rooms. Mr. Miller - that was Edward's last name - shared the room with me 'n' Uncle George while Sandra moved in with Ma 'n' Mel. That night we all had supper together 'n' Uncle George told us that him 'n' Sandra was gettin' married the next day at noon. The arrangements was all made with Mr. Courtney, a Baptist preacher. Seems like there weren't no Presbyterian preachers in town. They was a lot of Catholics though. Uncle George musta thought Baptist was closer to Presbyterian than Catholic for I reckon he could've been married by a Catholic Priest iffen he'd been of a mind.

Everybody talked about Ohio 'n' how things was goin' back east. After a while, Sandra asked about our homestead 'n' Ma 'n' Uncle George told them about the field 'n' creek 'n' the livestock ‘n’ how Pa had died. It was real sad to listen to that last part. I started thinkin’ about Pa ‘n’ got all teary-eyed ‘n’ had to wipe my eyes a lot. Sandra patted Ma’s hands a lot ‘n’ said how sorry she was.

Edward asked if it was always so hot ‘n’ Uncle George told him the summers was plenty warm but our place was a little cooler on account of it was on higher ground. They talked for a few minutes more, then we went to our rooms. I was plumb tuckered out by then an’ had no trouble goin’ to sleep.

Next day at noon, Uncle George ‘n’ Sandra, who was now my Aunt Sandra, was married. When it was over, Ma cried ‘n’ hugged Aunt Sandra ‘n’ Uncle George real tight.

We went to the Mercantile ‘n’ collected our goods. Before we left the store, Uncle George took out that gold coin Matt had give to ‘im an gave it to Ma. She looked at it an’ said, “Why don’t I just keep it for a rainy day? There isn’t much in the way of luxury here and, who knows? Maybe next trip Mr. Warner will have more goods for the children.” She put the coin in her pocketbook an’ we went outside ‘n’ loaded up Jack ‘n’ the wagon ‘n’ set out for our homestead with our two new horses in the harness ahead of Bess an’ Mud. It was true they wasn’t much to look at, but I don’t think Bess an’ Mudd coulda pulled that wagon more’n a few miles without ‘em ‘cause it was so heavy with goods. As it was, me ‘n’ Uncle George walked next to the wagon most of the time while Ma or Aunt Sandra drove.

Mr. Miller stayed in Tucson, waitin’ for a ride back east. I guess he was my Uncle Edward by then. He was nice enough but he seemed so different than the rest of us, me included. I knew I was different than I was in Cincinnati. I think the west changed a person a lot.

On the way out of town we met the lieutenant ‘n’ some of his men. He was real pleased to escort us for the first few miles of our trip. He congratulated Uncle George on him marryin' Aunt Sandra 'n' then rode his horse on Ma's side of the wagon 'n' talked to her most of the time. I think that lieutenant was sweet on my ma.

It was late in the day when the lieutenant 'n' his men turned around 'n' headed back to Tucson. Seemed like that lieutenant wanted to keep ridin' with us but he had to go back. It would have been nice to have all them soldiers to protect us from Cochise.

Uncle George had his arm around Aunt Sandra a lot when he rode in the wagon. Back east he wouldn't have done such a thing in public but out here it seemed natural. Besides, we wasn't really in public. There weren't nobody around 'ceptin' us, an' I was hopin' it would stay that way. I sure didn't want Cochise to come ridin' up 'n' join us.

Aunt Sandra remarked on how pretty the mountains were 'n' how hot it was 'n' how the road wasn't much more than a trail. Uncle George told her the road was tolerable good compared to what was ahead. He told her how we was gonna leave the road before we got to the big rocks on the other side of the San Pedro on account of Cochise. Aunt Sandra wanted to know all about this Cochise fella 'n' Uncle George told her what he could. I even added a few things of my own to what he said. 'Course I didn't really know much of anything, 'ceptin' what I'd heard, but that was plenty.

We only made about eight miles that day, 'cause it was so late when we got started, 'n' we camped in a little draw south of the trail. It wasn't dark yet so Uncle George said we could have a fire 'n' eat hot food. I helped gather in some dead mesquite 'n' rub down the horses 'n' Jack, then me 'n' Mel went explorin'. We didn't go far on account of Cochise but there was plenty to see.

Mel found a big lizard sleepin' under a creosote bush 'n' we watched him for a long time, whisperin' to each other, wonderin' if the lizard might attack when he woke up but he didn't. After awhile he woke up 'n' looked at us for a minute then took off lickety-split. He ran smack down a hole without even waitin' to see if we was followin', which we was, as fast as we could. We watched the hole for a while but nothin' happened so we looked for more excitement farther down the wash.

I was ahead of Mel by maybe ten yards when I saw the wolf. I reckon he already knew I was there 'cause he was standin' real still. The hair on his neck stood straight out an' he had his teeth showin' like the way Judd showed his when you called him a dog, 'cept I had a feelin' that this wolf weren't as forgivin' as Judd. I was only about thirty feet from him when I saw him 'n' I stood stone-still. "Mel," I whispered kinda loud. "Turn around 'n' go back to camp. There's a wolf right in front of me. Don't run. Walk normal." I was so scared I didn't know what I was gonna do.

I heard a branch breakin' behind me 'n' saw Mel draggin' a mesquite limb towards me. "Here," she said. "You hit him with this. I'll go get Uncle George."

If that didn't beat all. She didn't show no more concern for that wolf than she would've for a duck on a pond. I never could figure how Mel was gonna act about things like this. She always surprised me.

The wolf musta had other ideas about how things was gonna happen 'cause he ducked his head low 'n' inched his way towards me, them big teeth showin' real proud. I had took the limb from Mel but wasn't so sure I would stay there long enough to use it. Mel hadn't gone five steps when I heard Uncle George's voice.

"Mel. Craw. Where are you?"

That was sure a sweet sound.

I think the wolf didn't care for Uncle George's voice as much as I did 'cause, as soon as he heard it, he turned tail 'n' ran up the wash.

When Uncle George saw me holdin' that piece of mesquite, he held his Sharps a little higher 'n' said, "What is it, Craw?"

I was shakin' so bad even my voice shook. I pointed up the wash. "A wolf." That was all I could say.

Uncle George took a few steps in the direction I'd pointed, then turned around 'n' said, "He's gone now. Back to camp with both of you. And no more wandering off. Apaches aren't the only ones out here that are unfriendly."

Back at camp, Ma 'n' Aunt Sandra had made some pan biscuits 'n' beans 'n' bacon. It sure tasted good. I kept looking at the hills around us, wonderin' if that wolf was out there, waitin' for a chance to sneak in 'n' get some grub.

I sure liked havin' Aunt Sandra with us. She fit right in like I knew she would. She didn't complain or nothin'. She almost acted like the whole trip was one big adventure. She oohed an' aahed at some of the cactus 'n' she paid peculiar attention to the Palo Verde tree. Said it had the prettiest green bark she'd ever seen.

We bedded down in an' under the wagon an', before I knew it, it was daybreak.

We stopped at the San Pedro 'n' took baths 'n' filled our water barrels 'n' then we moved on. A few miles east of the river we turned north 'n' tried to follow the same way we had come to Tucson. Mostly we did pretty good, but there was a time or two when we lost our old trail 'n' ended up havin' to help push the wagon up a hill a couple of times. It took pert near two days to skirt them big rocks but we did it without any sign of Cochise, so that made it worth the trip.

Chapter 11

Our place was sure a welcome sight. It really felt like home. It was the first time I had ever felt that way about it – home. I reckoned I had missed it without knowin' it.

Right off, I knew that something had changed. Ma an' Uncle George knew it too, but I don't think any of us knew what it was at first. As we drew closer, I saw a woman in a faded cotton dress, hangin' some clothes on a rope strung between two aspen trees that Ma used as a clothesline. She was a Negro. I didn't know what to think at first. Then I reckoned they had killed Matt, 'cause he was a Confederate, an' taken over our spread, maybe thinkin' it was his, an' not knowin' it belonged to someone from Ohio.

Uncle George reined up when the woman heard us an' turned to see who was approachin'. He looked at her a minute then picked his Sharps from under the seat an' studied the house real careful-like. I didn't see anyone around but the woman.

Aunt Sandra said, "What's wrong, George?"

Uncle George quit lookin' around long enough to answer. "There was no one here but Mr. Grady when we left. I don't see his horse or do... Judd, and I don't see him. But I do see a Negro woman hanging clothes on Penny's line."

The Negro woman smiled, kind of nervous-like, 'n' waved. "Hello. You Missah Joje?"

She sure said Uncle George's name funny.

Uncle George looked at her kinda confused as she

walked real slow at us, his hand grippin' that Sharps real tight. "I am. And who might you be? And what are you doing on our land?"

"I'm Missy, Missah Joje, an' I was jus' hangin' out some a' yo'all's clothes to dry."

"*My* clothes?"

"Yessir, Missah Joje. Missah Matt thought it be a nice surprise for y'all to have clean clothes when y'all come home."

Uncle George raised an eyebrow. "Oh he did, did he?"

"Yessir, Missah Joje, he sho 'nough did."

"Are you and Mr. Grady alone out here?"

"Sakes alive no, Missah Joje! Mah mama an' Chester wouldn't allow no such thing."

I couldn't be sure of how old she was on account of I wasn't used to guessin' ages of Negroes, but I figured her to be about twenty. She was kinda thin 'n' wispy but she had a big smile an' I kinda liked her even though I wasn't so sure it was a good idea for her to be washin' Uncle George's clothes.

"Where is your mama?" asked Uncle George.

"Why, eva'ybody be workin' a' cou'se. Dey's still plenty daylight."

"Everybody? Working? Who's everybody? And working at what?"

Ma said, "George, I'm sure there's a logical explanation. Let's get down and meet with Missy. There's no need to holler at her from up on this wagon."

Uncle George looked at Ma kinda sheepish an' put the Sharps back under the seat. "Of course. You're right. We'll unload at the corral first."

Uncle George drove the wagon to the corral an' stopped. Missy followed us on foot. We all got down 'n' Ma said, "Hello, Missy. My name is Penelope. This is Sandra. And these are my children, Crawford and Melanie."

Aunt Sandra did her "How-do-you-do's", but Mel 'n' me

didn't say anything 'cause we didn't know what to say. Seemed like Missy wasn't much used to bein' introduced either 'cause she didn't say hello to us either.

While Ma talked with Missy, I didn't hear too much of what was bein' said on account of I was lookin' so hard at Missy. I'd never really looked real hard at a Negro before an' I was gettin' an eye-full now. She was real dark-skinned an' a might thin, like maybe she didn't get enough to eat. An' her nose was bigger an' flatter than Ma's but that didn't mean much. Pa had always said Ma's nose weren't no bigger than a button. Her lips was kinda bigger than I was used to but, like I said, I never looked real hard at a Negro before. Truth be known, I was always afraid to. 'Sides, Ma said it was impolite to stare at folks.

Missy had on a faded brown cotton-sack of a dress an' she was barefoot. Didn't even have a bonnet or hat to shade her from the sun. I wondered if they got to wear hats when they was slaves. Musta been awful hot workin' in the sun without a hat.

When my mind finally drifted away from how Missy looked, I heard Uncle George say, "You say Mr. Grady allowed you to stay in *my* house?"

"Yessir, Missah Joje. Missah Matt, he say y'all a bachelor an' it be all right till you get back. He say you a fahn gentleman."

I was sure Uncle George was gonna say somethin' about Missy's family stayin' in his house, but when Missy said that part about him bein' a fine gentleman, all he did was clear his throat, look at Ma, who raised her eyebrows, then to Missy an' said, "I'm sure everything will be fine, Missy. Now where can I find Mr. Grady?"

"He maht be up in da field w' Papa 'n' Chester 'n' Billy Jo 'n' Taters."

Uncle George looked a mite surprised at the number of

folks she mentioned. "Good Lord, woman, how many of you are there?"

"Wif Mama 'n' Ebony 'n' me, they be about seven, ah think."

Uncle George appeared to have lost his tongue for a minute or two there. He didn't say a word. I reckon he was tryin' to think of what to say. After a while, he said, "I see." I guess he couldn't think of anything else. Ma kinda glanced at him 'n' smiled. Aunt Sandra didn't know what to think, I suppose, but she knew Uncle George pretty good an' she was smilin' too.

Ma said, "Come, Sandra. Let's get the wagon unloaded." Just like nothin' unusual was goin' on. That was my Ma. Missy pitched in an' they started unloadin'.

About this time, Judd came runnin' up to the corral. He stopped about ten feet from the wagon, wagged his tail once, an' took up his favorite sittin' position. Mel ran up 'n' hugged him. She didn't squeeze as hard as she had the first time an' Judd took it like a man. When Mel was all done huggin' Judd, he got up an' approached Aunt Sandra real careful-like.

She smiled 'n' said, "Who is this handsome fellow?" She knelt next to him.

Uncle George said, "His name is Judd, and I suggest you use it and never call him a d-o-g." Uncle George spelled it out. I gotta say, he was sure well trained by now - Uncle George that is.

"Really?" said Sandra. She rubbed Judd's neck. I could see Judd took to her right away. He wagged his tail once an' sat.

Uncle George cleared his throat, "Hu-um. Well, I'll walk up to the field and see what's going on around here. I'll be back at the house to help with the wagon in a little bit."

Ma smiled real big 'n' said, "You take your time, George. I've got a feeling you may need to take a while to digest some of the changes Mr. Grady has made during our absence."

As Uncle George walked up the gentle slope to the field, I heard him mumblin' about how President Lincoln should have let the Southern States go in peace an' how Mr. Grady had an odd sense of humor an' how we wouldn't be goin' through this if there hadn't been a war to preserve the Union.

I wanted to go with him but I had to stay 'n' help unload the supplies. I didn't pay much attention to what I was doing for thinkin' about what Matt was up to 'n' how Critter was doin' an' what was goin' to happen now with all these Negroes at our place.

I led Jack up to Uncle George's house an' unloaded the packs. Jack was a big mule an' it weren't the easiest job I ever had, but I finally got it done an' was just about to lead Jack back to the corral when I saw the strange-lookin' house about a hundred yards west of Uncle George's place. It weren't a house really, more like a bunch of trees 'n' bushes piled up, but I could tell it was for livin' in. I led Jack up to the thing 'n' looked inside. All of Matt's soogans - that's what he called his bedroll an' other personal stuff - was there. I reckoned he'd been livin' there for quite a spell the way things looked. I didn't go inside on account of what Uncle George had told me about gettin' into other folks' things. I just led Jack back to the corral 'n' put him inside.

As I was closin' the gate, here come Matt, ridin' Critter an' leadin' a pinto mare. I don't know where Uncle George was. I had thought he was talkin' with Matt. I reckoned they must have missed each other.

Matt smiled down at me 'n' said, "Howdy, boy. How was your trip to Tucson?"

I tried to act like it wasn't all that much. After all, a fella my age shouldn't get all that excited about a trip to town. "It was fun. They had candy, 'n' an a little mountain that we went to the top of an' we could see for a hunderd miles, 'n' they was a river they called the Santa Cruz, an' soldiers..."

"Soldiers?" Matt's eyes kinda narrowed.

"Yeah, but they was friendly."

Matt's smile was back. "Oh. Okay. I reckon that's all right then."

I wondered about the pinto. "Where'd you get that horse?"

"Traded for her."

"For real? You mean she's your horse? What about Critter?" Critter's ears picked up at the sound of his name. I never thought to ask who he had traded with at the time.

"Well, I didn't think it through at the time I traded for the pinto. That was an oversight. Seems like Critter is actin' all human about the situation and he's jealous as all get out."

"Serious?" I said.

Matt made the sign of an x over his heart. "Cross my heart an' hope to die."

"Now what are you gonna do?" I asked. She sure was a pretty horse.

Matt rubbed his chin, like maybe he was thinkin' real hard. "Say, maybe you can help me out. I sure could use it."

"How can I help?" I had no notion of anything I could do.

"Well, if you would make me a trade for the pinto, I think Critter could live with it."

I got so excited, I could feel my heart beatin in my chest. My knees got to feelin shaky an' I felt weak all over. Then I realized I had nothin' to trade. "I sure would like to help but I got nothin' worth as much as that mare."

"I ain't so sure about that. I took a real shine to that fishin' pole of yours." He waited for a second then said, "Now, I know the pole is worth a lot to you, but this here is a fine mare. She's got stamina an' she's fast an' young. And it took me a while to break her."

I started to say somethin' but Matt beat me to it.

"Okay, I can see you're a first rate horse trader. Bein' as that pole of yours is one-of-a-kind, I'll throw in a saddle blanket next time I get to town. I guess I better throw in a bridle too. Wouldn't want you to put a Spanish bit in her mouth."

I was struck plumb dumb. For as smart as I figured Matt to be, he sure was beatin' himself to death on this deal. I whittled that ol' fishin' pole out of a piece of aspen in less than an hour. I sorta felt like I was takin' advantage of him if I accepted the offer the way he put it so I sweetened it up a little. I tried to talk like Matt when I said, "I reckon you made a deal but you gotta take some licorice that we got in Tucson for it to be fair."

Matt raised one eyebrow. "Real licorice?"

"I promise." I crossed my heart, just like he'd done.

He'd been sittin' the saddle, his hands restin' on the horn, loosely holdin' the lead rope on the pinto. He leaned a little forward an' held out the rope. "Then it's a deal. Take your horse so Critter will quit givin' me grief."

My legs felt like they was made of water as I walked up an' took that rope. I wasn't sure I was gonna make the trip but I somehow managed. The pinto just looked at me with her big brown eyes an' I looked at her. I could tell right off that I had just made the trade of a lifetime. I patted her on the neck an' withers.

"What's her name?" I asked.

"She ain't got one. Didn't have her long enough to give her one. She's your horse now so I reckon namin' her is your duty."

"What should I call her?" I was so excited I couldn't think straight.

"First thing that comes to mind is always the best bet," said Matt.

I looked at her an' the splotches of brown 'n' white all

over. "How about Patches?"

Matt rubbed his chin again. "I believe you hit the old nail right on the head. Fits her just right. Patches it is."

"You want the licorice now?" I said. I wanted to make sure the deal was sealed an' I could keep Patches.

"That and my fishin' pole," said Matt.

I handed Matt the reins an' couldn't get to the house fast enough. I ran in, grabbed my pole, an' ran back to where Matt still sat Critter. I couldn't give him the pole quick enough to suit me. Then I dug every piece of licorice I had from my little leather pouch 'n' handed it to him. "There. I guess we have a deal, huh?"

Matt smiled 'n' said, "Too much licorice. I'll just take a piece now and another piece when you get your saddle blanket. That may be awhile. Never know when I'll get to a town." He took a piece of licorice, put it in his mouth, an' handed me back the rest.

I couldn't believe it. Patches was mine!

About this time Uncle George walked up to us. I couldn't hold it in. "Uncle George. Look at my horse! I just traded Matt for her."

"Traded?" He looked at Matt, who just sat real quiet-like in the saddle, grinnin'.

"I had an extra horse an' no fishin' pole," said Matt.

Uncle George looked at Patches then at Matt. "Mr. Grady, may I have a word with you?" When Uncle George didn't say nothin' about Patches, I knew he was real anxious to find out about them Negroes.

"Sure, George. How was your trip? Did you find your fiancé?"

"Fine and yes. Now, if you don't mind, I'd like to talk to you for a moment."

I could tell without bein' told that it was time for me to become scarce. "Thanks, for the trade, Matt. I'm gonna take

Patches to the corral."

"My pleasure," was all he said. He turned to Uncle George 'n' said, "I would'a' met you but I wanted to get that pinto down here. I might have to explain a few things."

"That would be nice," said Uncle George. "Let's start with Missy washing my ..."

I took my new horse to the corral an' rubbed her down real good an' fed her fresh grass from my hand. I wished I had an apple but, then again, I didn't want her to be ornery like Critter so I decided it was a good thing I didn't have one.

Chapter 12

We all sat outside, eatin' supper, 'ceptin' for Matt. I didn't know where he was. Probably out lookin' for lost cattle I reckoned. I thought it peculiar that he'd miss supper though, an' got to wonderin' if Cochise might have got him this time.

Missy's mama, whose given name was Olissa, was pushin' another biscuit at me an' fussin' over how skinny I was, an' Missy was pourin' Uncle George 'n' her husband, Chester, a cup of coffee. We'd drug our table outside an' the benches an' chairs too, an' set 'em near an old tree stump that made do as another table. Us kids had found rocks an' branches we used for chairs an' we was all sittin' together at the stump.

After lookin' Missy over so careful when I first saw her, it seemed real natural to be with her brothers and sister. They weren't nothin' scary about 'em at all. They was people just like me. Onliest thing was, they had darker skin - an' they did talk a mite different.

Billy Jo - he was about fourteen - looked like a scrapper to me but he was real friendly an' I was glad enough for that.

Tater was about my age an' no bigger than me. He was funny. I liked him a lot. It seemed like forever since I had a friend my age, an' I knew right off that me 'n' Tater was gonna be good friends. Don't ask me how I knew. I just did.

Ebony was the youngest. She was six. Her skin was almost pure black. Mama - I was already callin' Missy's ma that 'cause everybody else did - well anyway, Mama said they named her Ebony on account of that was a real dark wood -

sorta' the way I named Patches - on account of it fit. Ebony an' Mel was kinda watchin' each other close-like. Didn't seem to me either one of them was sure about the other.

Mama's husband said he took the name of Abraham Lincoln after President Lincoln, but everyone just called him Papa, even me. Now, I didn't do it 'cause he was replacin' my Pa but more 'cause it was his name - like Mama. That was her name as far as I was concerned.

We learned about how they had all been slaves on a plantation in Georgia. That's one of them Confederate States, I think. Anyway, Papa said he'd been owned by the master of that plantation since he could remember, an' all his family too. Once, durin' the war, it looked like the master was gonna have to sell Chester 'cause times was hard but the master's wife wouldn't hear of it. Papa said they had a good master an' was better off than a lot of Negroes. But good master or no, bein' free was better, even if it meant bein' hungry, he said.

I'd seen their wagon just before supper an' it was a good sturdy one - big too. Papa said his master had give it to 'em after Atlanta fell to the Yankees. The master had told 'em about the homestead act in the United States 'n' said it would be better out west than in the South now. He'd give 'em a few provisions 'n' sent 'em packin'. The master said he would rather Papa and his family have the wagon than the Yankees. It didn't seem to me that Papa liked Yankees much better than Matt the way he said the word. Might have been the way he talked though. I'd never heard that kind of talk before. It was like Kentucky talk, only more. I don't know how to explain it.

When Uncle George asked Papa how he came to be at our place, Papa said that Matt had stopped them south of the ranch about ten miles. Said he'd seen their dust an' came to investigate. The children was afraid of that dog, he'd said. Uncle George corrected him an' said the animal's name was Judd.

Papa laughed real loud 'n' said, "Ah see y'all had da same 'sperience with Mistah Judd Ah had."

About then me 'n' Ma 'n' Uncle George got to laughin' so hard I pert near choked on a piece of biscuit. Aunt Sandra looked real confused, her not yet crossin' the bad side of Judd's path. She couldn't figure out what was so funny.

When he could draw a breath, Papa said, "Y'all know dat horse be scarier dan Judd fur sure. Dat big stallion, he come prancin' up to da wagon an' go ta sniffin' around da place like he lookin' fo sumpthin' ta eat. And sho' 'nuff, he was. Found it too. Got Mama's last apple. Ah know'd she'd a' swatted 'im good wid a switch but dere sat Mistah Matt, wi' his Confedrit Uniform.

"We 'bout thought da end o' da world had come. We ain't seen no Confedrit soldiers in a coon's age an' we figures Mistah Matt be one a dem guerillas, like Quantrill. Turns out, nuttin' could be farder from da troof. Mistah Matt, he say he sorry for da way his horse act an' he offer to feed us all. Next thing ah knows, we all diggin' a trench from da little rivah to da field. One thing, it lead to anudder, an' da next t'ing, we be settin' up house in y'all's cabin an' workin' da field, plowin' an' plantin an' irrigatin'. We sure 'nough are grateful to Mistah Matt an' y'all fo' helpin' us out of a tight. We was gettin' a mite hungry."

Nobody said anything for a few seconds, then Uncle George cleared his throat. "Papa, you and your family have worked a miracle here. I've never seen a straighter furrow in any field, and the crops are lush beyond any expectations we ever had. You've more than earned your keep."

"It be da irrigation dat make dem crops so lush, Mistah George an' it be Mistah Matt dat boss dat job. An' he work as hard as any of us." Papa stopped speakin' for a second an' looked around. He looked back at Uncle George. "Y'all sure Mistah Matt ain't here?"

"I'm sure. He said he was goin' to La Mesilla. He won't be back for ten or twelve days," said Uncle George.

That was the first I heard about that an' it kinda took me by surprise. He didn't even say goodbye.

Papa said, "Ah sho am glad. Ah forgot. He tol' me not to let you or Miss Penny know dat he'd been diggin' in da groun' lahk a dirt fahma."

Ma 'n' Uncle George looked at each other 'n' grinned real big. Ma said, "Don't you worry, Papa. Your secret is safe with us." Even Ma was callin' him Papa.

Papa relaxed a bunch 'n' I could tell he was relieved. "Thank y'all, Miss Penny. Ah surely am grateful. Ah didn't meant t' tell on Mistah Matt like dat, but it don' seem proper an' fittin' for y'all t' be thinkin' we did ever'thin' around heah. Mistah Matt, he be like a whirlwin'. He evawhere at once. Ah never see'd no man could work as long or as hahd. He was real 'xact about dem cabinets in y'all's house, Mistah George. An' when he tol' us to move inta y'all's cabin, he built dat funny-lookin do-dad of a shelta ova yondah. When ah axed him why he di'nt move inta da udder cabin, he said he could nevva do such a thing. It belonged ta Miss Penny an' her chillins."

"I see," said Uncle George. He kinda gave Ma a quick look. I couldn't read what it meant.

Aunt Sandra said, "I would like to have met this Mr. Grady before he left. Why was he in such a hurry?"

Uncle George said, "Well, he said he could make better time in the cool of the night with as much moon as we have, and it would be safer."

"Why was he goin' to La Mesilla?" I said.

"He said he had some business to take care of. That's all I know. And it's none of our business what Mr. Grady does. He did say he might pick up some stray longhorn cattle on the way back. According to Mr. Grady, they're all over west Texas, just for the taking."

"Oh." That was all I could think of to say. At least he was comin' back. I was hopin' Cochise wouldn't get him. It was almost two hundred miles to La Mesilla. Anyway that's what Pa had said.

I gotta say, that was probably the happiest supper I ever ate without my Pa. I never even talked to a Negro in my life an' here I was eatin' supper at the same table with a whole family of 'em, even if the table *was* the stump of a tree. They was good folks an' I think they musta had a pretty rough go of it. I couldn't even imagine bein' owned by someone. I was real glad they was at our place. I knew Uncle George wouldn't never let anyone own 'em again. Knowin' that made me feel real good.

Chapter 13

It was like life changed overnight. I had a new pinto horse an' a new friend. I didn't have to carry water to the field. I had a new aunt. The crops was growin' good, an' supper was special every evenin'. We all ate together.

I don't know for sure when or how they made up their minds, but Papa an' his family found some land next to our place an', in the corner of it nearest our house, they started a cabin. It was only about a quarter mile from our place. They worked part of the day at our place an' part of it on their cabin. Uncle George helped 'em everyday with their cabin 'cause he knew a lot about buildings an' he showed 'em a lot of things to do to make their place sturdy 'n' comfortable.

Me 'n' Tater 'n' Billy Jo dug out a privy behind where their cabin was goin' up. That took the better part of four days. The sun was tolerable hot an' we had to break for water a lot. Ma wouldn't let us work too long without sendin' us to the creek. While they was buildin' their cabin, Papa's family slept under a big tarp tied to their wagon which was next to our house. 'Course me 'n' Tater got to sleep together since we was such good friends an' both of us could fit on my bed. At night, Tater would tell me stories about Georgia 'n' the plantation, an' I'd tell him about our life on a farm in Ohio. We got to know each other pretty good. In a little more than a week, I knew more about Tater 'n' his family than I did about my ol' pal, Billy Barnes.

I couldn't understand why so many white folks, even the ones in Ohio, treated Negroes so mean. Tater was my best friend. It ain't like he spoke a foreign language, like the

Mexicans. He was just like me 'ceptin' his his skin was darker. The more I got to know him, the more his skin seemed about the same color as mine. Pretty soon, I couldn't see no difference at all.

One of the sudden changes I could have done without was schoolin'. Now, don't misunderstand me, I loved my Aunt Sandra, but she was never gonna quit bein' a school teacher. I could see that right off. The second day after we got back from Tucson she got all the kids, 'n' Missy 'n' Chester too, out under a big mesquite tree an' started in teachin' us proper English. An' I mean *proper* English. I don't mind speakin' English proper now 'n' again but sometimes it's better understood if you speak it the way people can understand it best, an' that ain't always *proper*.

I gotta admit that I was surprised how different Missy 'n' Chester sounded in only a few days, an' they sure was proud of how well they was gettin' on in *proper* English, so I reckon some good came of that schoolin' after all.

I didn't have much time with Patches, what with all the work 'n' schoolin', but that was okay 'cause I was waitin' for Matt to come back before I rode her. I weren't the best rider in the world 'n' I didn't want to get throwed in front of Tater an' look like a plumb greenhorn. That would never do. Me 'n' Tater 'n' Billy Jo would feed her the best grass we could find 'n' pet her 'n' give her water 'n' a lot of attention when we could but nobody rode her, not even Uncle George. 'Course Uncle George wouldn't ride my horse without askin' but he was too busy to ask, I reckon. Besides, he had Mud, 'n' Mud was his horse now. I wished Billy Jo 'n' Tater had their own horses. I almost felt bad that I had Patches 'n' they had nothin', but I would never give up Patches.

Tater would ride ol' Jack once in a while if we hadn't worked him too hard on that day. I gotta say, Jack was one fine mule. Didn't seem like there was much he wouldn't tackle.

One day, down at Tater's place, Papa had his oxen hitched to a big rope that was wrapped around a tree stump. Papa 'n' Chester had been diggin' under that stump for the best part of the day an' it still weren't movin'. Papa added Jack to the team 'n' Jack leaned into that rope 'n' harness an' took two powerful steps an' that stump ripped right outa the ground like a gopher leaving a floodin' hole. Tater 'n' his whole family patted Jack 'n' carried water to him in a bucket. Papa wouldn't let Tater ride Jack on that day.

My Pa's corn was tall 'n' sweet, an' we shucked some one evening. We all shared, an' even Mama said it was some of the best-tastin' corn she ever ate. That was all I needed to hear to know that my Pa was the best farmer in the world 'cause I knew Mama was a good judge of corn. I thought I saw Ma cry a little when she saw how beautiful that corn was. I know she was thinkin' of Pa. So was I.

I wasn't real surprised at how easy Aunt Sandra took to life out here in Arizona. It was a lot harder than the way she lived in Ohio but I kept recallin' how she had showed that teamster how to drive a wagon. I always knew she had the makin's. She seemed happier than I had ever seen her back east. I could tell she loved Uncle George by the way she always smiled at him an' held hands 'n' such - like Ma 'n' Pa used to do.

Missy was puttin' a little meat on her bones an' she looked a lot healthier than that first day I had seen her. I reckoned it must be awful to be hungry for a long time. It was all I could do to miss supper once.

Chester could sure handle an axe 'n' a plow. He'd work all day, plowin a rocky piece of ground on their land, then chop trees for their cabin till late at night. He had real strong arms. I was glad he was my friend.

Mel 'n' Ebony was always together. Seems like they got over whatever was ailin' 'em when they first met. I reckoned they was almost as close as me 'n' Tater, an' me 'n' Tater was as close as the pupils on a cross-eyed flea.

Billy Jo didn't have no one his own age around but he went fishin' with me 'n' Tater whenever we got a chance. Mostly he helped Chester 'n' Papa build their cabin.

Uncle George spent his time tryin' to keep the cattle out of the field. He tried to teach Ol' Blue to herd cattle like Judd but that didn't work out too good. Blue tore up the crops worse'n the cattle, an' all he really got done was to run the meat offa them cows. Uncle George gave up on Blue after a while an' spent more time helpin' Papa with his cabin.

Ma spent a lot of time with Aunt Sandra an' I reckon they was good company to each other.

I was sure Cochise had got Matt by now. It was late June an' we'd seen neither hide nor hair of him.

Papa's family was livin' in their cabin, even though it still needed some things attended to, but it was mostly done an' now all of us had real cabins to live in. The weather had been awful hot 'n' dry 'n' we had to irrigate a lot more than before. Papa got to worryin' about the creek 'n' wonderin' if it might not run dry if we didn't get rain soon.

Chapter 14

One day Tater caught a big green beetle called a June Bug an' tied a string around it. He held the string up while the June Bug flew an' followed it so's not to pull back on the string an' make the June Bug tired. Anyways, that's what he said. He was runnin' along behind his June Bug about as fast as he could go, an' me right behind him, when we both ran plumb into Cherry Creek. Hadn't neither one of us been payin' attention to anything but that June Bug.

When we hit the water, Tater lost his hold on the string an' the June Bug got away. We jumped out of the water real quick an' went to lookin' for that bug before he could get too far and found it flyin' around a Cat Claw bush on account of the string had snagged on the thorns an' the critter was tethered to the bush. The June Bug crashed into the ground. Tater said it was tuckered out from all that flyin' an' carryin' the string behind it, so he bent down an' untied the string an' let it go. It didn't fly too far before it crashed into a Palo Verde tree. I reckoned that bug was gettin' real tired iffen it couldn't see a Palo Verde tree.

We got to lookin' for more June Bugs an' found a place upstream where there was a bunch of 'em. We each caught one an' Tater showed me how to tie the string to 'em so's they could still fly. I got to lookin' at that beetle real close an' found it to be right pretty. They was the prettiest, brightest shade of green I ever saw on top, an' a real shiny blue-green on the belly. There was a gold line all around the top of the shell that covered the wings. My but they was pretty.

Besides bein' pretty, they stunk somethin' awful. It was a real peculiar smell, kinda like a skunk, but not quite as strong. It sure made my hands smell terrible. I figured I might even have to use some of Ma's lye soap to get rid of it, an' I wasn't real sure that lye soap would do the job.

We had a grand time, followin' our June Bugs around, hangin' on to the string so's they couldn't fly away. After a spell the bugs would get tired an' we'd untie 'em an' find some more. I guess we musta flew them June Bugs for the better part of two hours. Finally, I couldn't stand the smell on my hands no more an' told Tater I was gonna go get some of Ma's lye soap. He asked me if he could have some too so I reckon he was feelin' the same way about the smell I was.

We'd just let our bugs loose an' was gettin' ready to go back to the house when Mel an' Ebony came walkin' up to us an' wanted to know what we'd been doin' for so long an' I told her about the June Bugs. Of course, Mel an' Ebony just had to tie onto a June Bug an' try it out for themselves. Well, that only lasted until we caught a couple of bugs an' handed 'em to the girls.

Mel said, "You tie the string. Its legs scare me. Does it bite?"

Tater laughed. "Dey don' bite. Ah don' tink dey got no teef."

Mel put her nose a little closer to her hand. "Peuw! These bugs smell somethin' awful!" She threw the June bug into the air an' it headed south as fast as it could fly. Ebony flung hers about twice as far an' it pert near passed Mel's bug on its way south. Mel ran to the creek an' put her hands in the water. Ebony was with her all the way. They rubbed an' rinsed an' rubbed some more, smellin' their hands between each rinsin'. Finally, I reckon it reached a place where it was tolerable enough to live with, for they finally quit washin' an' looked up at me 'n' Tater.

Mel said, "That was pretty sneaky, you not tellin' us about the smell."

I looked at Tater 'n' smiled. "Seemed tolerable enough to me. You find the smell tolerable, Tater?"

"Ah t'ink maybe it tola'ble fo' men but no' fo' womenfolk."

Ebony said, "Tater Lincoln! You rascal! Ah'm gonna tell Mama on you."

Tater, he didn't look like he cottoned to that idea so much. I looked at Ebony an' tried to help my friend out of a tight. "Now, Ebony, we was just funnin'. We didn't mean no harm by it. We'll catch you some bugs an' tie 'em right proper an' you can watch 'em fly without gettin' the smell on your hands."

Ebony knew she had me an' she smiled. "You promise?"

"We promise." I looked at Tater. "Don't we, Tater?"

He kicked a little dirt up an' said, "We sho 'nuff do."

So, we did. Them girls had us catchin' June Bugs the rest of the day. An' they never had to touch a one.

Chapter 15

It was on one of them hot, dry days that Billy Jo came runnin' up to our place, yellin' real loud that Indians was comin'.

Real quick, Uncle George took charge an' decided that we'd hold up in our cabin since it was the biggest an' had a better view of things than the other two cabins. We all sat inside, waitin' for the Indians, 'cept Uncle George. He was out by the tack shed where he could see the approachin' dust. We reckoned there must have been more than a hundred, judgin' from the size of the dust cloud.

All of us had our duties. Pa had trained us for that. Mine was to keep the shotgun 'n' sharps loaded for Uncle George 'n' Ma. Papa had an old musket, an' I took particular notice that Billy Jo was holdin' a powder horn. Chester had a big thing that looked a little like Matt's cutlass. He called it a machete.

I admit, I was scared plumb stiff. My muscles got so tight I started to shakin' all over. I just knew Cochise had found out about all those thoughts I had about him. He got Matt 'n' now he was comin' for me. Maybe if I gave myself up he'd leave everyone else alone. I was thinkin' real hard on that idea when Uncle George came into the cabin.

"They're headed right our way," he said.

Ma said, "How many of them are there, George?" I could hear the worry in her voice. That made me even more scared.

"I can't tell. There's so much dust, I can't make out anything."

Nobody in the room said a word. It was like we was already dead.

"Everybody take your positions," said Uncle George.

I knowed we was doomed. Ma's shotgun was only good at short range, an' that old musket Papa had didn't look to me like it was good for one shot. Uncle George's Sharps was our only hope an', against a hundred Apaches, it wasn't much hope.

Seems like we waited the better part of an hour. It was hot 'n' stuffy in that cabin with all them doors an' windows shut but nobody complained. I reckoned that was the least of our worries.

I peaked through one of the slots Pa had cut in the shutters an' stared until my eyes watered. Just when I thought I couldn't stand it no more, I saw the first rider. Well, not the rider, but the horse. It was Critter! The only trouble is, the rider wasn't wearin' no Confederate uniform 'n' forage cap. He had on a brown, low-crowned hat, a brown shirt an' a yellow bandana over his face. His britches was grey, like Matt's, but that was all. Even his leather was different. He didn't have no flaps on his holsters an' the holsters was different. They was both left-handed, one of 'em bein' worn backwards on the right hip.

"They got Matt!" I screamed real loud. "That's Critter!"

Uncle George said, "Not so loud, Craw." He took a real close look at the lead rider. "That *is* Mr. Grady," he said after a while.

It was then that I saw them funny-lookin' moccasins that Matt always wore.

Still nobody moved. We all waited to see who the other riders were. After a while I heard Judd yip, like he did when he had an ornery steer try to drift. In a little bit, I could see that there weren't nobody else but Matt in all that dust. He turned his back to us for a minute an' rode left to right 'n' I could see

Judd bunchin' 'em up. Longhorn cattle! I figured there musta been more'n a hundred of 'em. When the cattle was all bunched, Judd sat in front of 'em in his favorite position 'n' Matt rode up to the cabin.

He pulled the bandana from his face 'n' smiled real big. His teeth looked real white 'cause his face was covered with dirt, 'ceptin the part of his face the bandana had covered. It was a little whiter than his neck 'n' his forehead. "Hello the house."

Uncle George stepped out first an' I knew he was as glad to see Matt as I was. Maybe his reasons was different, but he was sure 'nough glad.

Matt looked at the Sharps in Uncle George's hand 'n' said, "Expectin' trouble?"

I could feel my legs shakin' 'n' couldn't figure out why they'd start such a thing now the danger was past, but they sure was wobbly. They barely held me up.

Uncle George said, "We saw your dust and thought it was Apaches."

Matt looked real confused. "Apaches? Me?"

"Well, with all that dust..."

"With all that dust, I reckoned you'd know it *wasn't* Apaches. They ain't fool enough to raise such a ruckus if they're raidin'. I'm real sorry, George, if I put a scare into you folks."

We was all driftin' out of the cabin by now. When the women came out, Matt took off his hat. "Howdy, Miss Penny, Missy, Mama, Ebony, Mel." He looked at me 'n' smiled. "Howdy, boy. You ridin' Patches good yet?"

"Not yet. I been waitin' for you to get back so's we could ride together," I said.

Matt looked at Chester, Billy Jo, Papa 'n' Tater. "Sure am sorry I didn't ride ahead, folks. I had no notion you'd take me for Apaches." I could tell he meant it too.

Ma said, "It's good to see you, Mr. Grady. I trust you had a pleasant trip?"

"Thank you, Ma'am. I did. I spent a bit on improvements."

"Improvements?" asked Ma.

"Yes, Ma'am. Improvements."

"I see you have a new hat and shirt,"said Ma.

"I'm not so sure that qualifies as an improvement. I've still got my uniforms."

"I see you've traded pistols," said Uncle George.

"No. They're the same pistols. I had a gunsmith convert 'em to cartridge. Had the barrel shortened to five-and-a-half inches on one of the Remingtons. Left the other alone for longer-range shootin'."

"That's quite a gunbelt. Mighty fancy leather work, and two left-handed holsters," said Uncle George.

"Mexican fella I met durin' the war. He does mighty good work. Made a lot of harness for Colonel Sibley's outfit. He lost them an' all of his mules at Glorietta Pass," said Matt.

I noticed the Colt was still in the same shoulder holster under his right arm. Seemed to me he'd get awful tired of carryin' around all that weight. He didn't wear the shoulder holster around our place but I reckoned he took it special for the trip on account of Cochise 'n' all.

I had hardly paid attention but Matt was leadin' a pack horse, loaded down right proper. He dismounted 'n' started pullin' things from the packs. He handed Papa a rifle. "No offense, Papa, but you gotta admit, this here Spencer is an improvement over that musket. I got ammunition for it somewhere."

Papa said, "But, Mistah Matt, Ah can't ....."

"Later, Papa. Later." Next, he pulled another rifle from atop the packs 'n' said, "Chester, if a man is gonna protect his wife out here, he needs a little help. This here Sharps oughta do just fine." He tossed the Sharps to Chester 'n', without lookin' to see if he caught it, he was pullin' out some more stuff. He gave Billy Jo 'n' Tater each a fine skinnin' knife. Mel 'n' Ebony each got a real doll. Missy got a new bonnet. Mama got a heavy coat. He gave Ma a real pretty green shawl. When it came to Aunt Sandra, he said, "I never met you, Ma'am, but George told me a lot about you an' I reckon you could make use of this." He handed her a leather-bound book.

"But, Sir, I don't know you"

"Oh, I'm sorry. My name is Matt Grady. Now you know me." He looked at Uncle George. "Tell her it's all right, George."

Without waitin' for an answer, he grabbed a wooden box of cigars 'n' handed it to Uncle George. "Hope you like 'em, George. They're the best they had in town. And I know you prefer the big cigars to them little cigarillos I smoke." Then he turned back to the pack horse 'n' took a bridal 'n' saddle blanket from the pack 'n' set it on the ground. "This completes our deal, 'cept for that piece of licorice." He turned to Ma. "Miss Penny, I got somethin' else for Craw but, you bein' from back east an' all, I reckon it's proper I ask your permission to give it to him since he's a might young." He reached up an' pulled another rifle from the horse.

It was a beauty! I couldn't believe it was for me. I looked at Ma real hard. I was beggin' her with my eyes to let me have that rifle. It was shorter than the others but it was a real rifle. I could help protect Ma 'n' Mel if I had it.

Ma looked at me for a while, then at Matt.

Matt said, "It's a First Model Maynard Carbine, Miss Penny. Some of our cavalry outfits used 'em. It's a .56 caliber but it's easy to load and clean. It should help give piece of mind to you and your family."

I could tell Ma was weakenin'.

Uncle George said, "Let the boy have the gun, Penny.

Between Mr. Grady and me, we'll see to it he learns to use it properly."

Thank you, Uncle George. That was what I needed. Ma nodded. "Very well, Mr Grady you may give him the gun."

"Carbine, Miss Penny."

"You may give him the carbine, Mr. Grady."

"Thank you, Miss Penny." He turned to me 'n' handed me the carbine. "Don't you ever make your Ma sorry she let you have this carbine, boy."

"I won't, Matt. I promise. Gee. Thanks."

"I'll give you the ammo when we go out to shoot. Don't be snappin' the trigger with the hammer cocked on account you'll most likely ruin the pin."

I just nodded and stared at the carbine.

He turned and pulled a big bolt of red cloth from the pack horse 'n' handed it to Mama. "I reckoned you might be able to make use of this."

It looked to me like Mama was gonna cry. Instead, she tucked that whole bolt of cloth under her arm 'n' hugged Matt real tight.

Everybody started thankin' him a hundred times but Matt had enough of it. "I'm glad to see everybody is alive an' well. Now, if you folks don't mind, I gotta wash this trail dust offa me." he mounted Critter 'n' rode downstream while Judd sat, watchin' the cattle.

"He must have spent a fortune in La Messilla," said Uncle George.

Aunt Sandra looked at her book then at Ma. "This is a fine edition of *Hamlet*. Mr. Grady is a very unique individual."

Ma smiled 'n' said, "That he is, Sandra." Even though it was a mite hot, Ma had that new shawl around her shoulders. She was lookin' at it when she spoke to Aunt Sandra.

I watched Matt 'n' Critter disappear around a bend in the creek then looked at my carbine. I couldn't believe it. Matt was back 'n' I had my own gun, 'n' I could learn to ride Patches like Matt rode Critter, 'n' maybe he would even teach me how to rope cattle.

Chapter 16

It was late dusk when I strolled down to the creek lookin' for Matt. He'd been gone quite a spell. I found him 'n' Critter both layin' down near the edge of the water. Critter was plumb stretched out an' Matt was layin' on his back with his hat pulled over his eyes. His head was restin' on Critter's neck. Judd was stretched out on top of Critter's side, his paws folded over his nose. I stood there for a minute, eyeballin' those three, thinkin' I'd never knowed anybody like anyone of the three of 'em.

Without a move, Matt said from under his hat, "Howdy, boy."

It surprised me a bit 'n', after jumpin' back about a foot, I said, "Howdy, Matt. You tired?"

He pulled his hat up on his head enough so's his eyes could see me 'n' said, "A mite. But not so tired I can't visit a spell. What's on your mind?"

I sat on the ground nearby an' held out my hand. In it was my last piece of licorice.

Matt took it 'n' put it in his mouth. "I was wonderin' when you'd get to it," he said.

"Will you teach me how to shoot 'n' ride 'n' rope 'n' work cattle?" I just kind of blurted it out.

I saw his hat move a bit as he raised his eyebrows. "Sounds like a lot a' teachin' to me," he said around the licorice.

"Yessir, it surely is, but I need it bad."

"You reckon?" he asked.

Now, mind you, Critter 'n' Judd, neither one had moved. They was both still sleepin' real comfortable. "Yessir, I do. Why, if I could do all those things, I'd be a big help to Ma 'n' Uncle George 'n' Aunt Sandra."

"That's true," he said. "When do you reckon we'd have the time for all of this teachin'?"

"I'd get up real early an' go to bed real late." I was kinda gettin' desperate. It was lookin' like Matt wasn't gonna have much to do with all this teachin' I needed.

He sat up. Critter didn't move a muscle but Judd's ears picked up a bit. "I'll tell you what we can do. If your Ma can spare you tomorrow, we'll go work those longhorns I brought back. You gotta promise me you'll be real careful, boy. Them longhorns can be a little rough at times."

"I promise. I'll do everything real careful."

"Okay, boy. Now go ask your ma. If everything is all right with her, meet me at the corral about half-an-hour before sunup."

Just like that, he was done talkin'. He pulled his hat back down over his eyes an' laid his head back on Critter's neck. Judd's ears went limp an' everything was quiet.

I walked back to the house real slow, thinkin' about how our lives had changed for the better since Matt 'n' Critter 'n' Judd had come to our place. It was like a miracle.

When I got to the front of our cabin everybody was outside 'n' ready to eat. Tater was sittin' at the stump, a fork in one hand, even though he didn't have any food on his plate yet. That boy sure liked to eat. Even more than me.

"Where is Mr. Grady, Craw?" asked Ma.

"Sleepin'. I don't think he's gonna eat with us tonight. Seemed like he was right tired."

"Oh. I see," said Ma.

Uncle George said, "It's no wonder, what with him bringing in all those longhorns by himself and right through the middle of Apache country too. He deserves a rest."

"Now can we eat?" said Tater.

Ma smiled real pretty. "We certainly can, Mr. Tater." Ma had taken to callin' him "Mr. Tater" once in a while. I could tell he liked it whenever she did it.

It was full dark by the time everyone finished eatin' 'n' Papa drug out his banjo like he did a lot, an' Billy Jo took out his mouth organ. Him an' his family sang lots of songs, most of which I'd never heard, but they was all pretty. Papa had a real deep voice an' it was pretty too. As a matter-of-fact, all of 'em had pretty voices an' could sing like angels. I wished I could sing like that. Aunt Sandra sang some with 'em an' so did Ma 'n' Uncle George. Aunt Sandra had a beautiful voice. I never knowed she could sing like that. The glow from the small fire sure lit up a lot of happy faces that night. I was wishin' that Matt was with us. I wondered if he could sing pretty like Papa.

I met Matt at the corral before sunup. He showed me the proper way to saddle a horse accordin' to his rules. He showed me how some horses draw a deep breath an' hold it while you're cinchin' 'em up. They do this, he said, so's they could let the breath out later 'n' the cinch strap would be real loose an' the saddle would slip 'n' fall, usually takin the rider down too. He told me Critter tried it almost every day. That didn't come as no real surprise though.

Patches was a little jumpy when I put the saddle blanket on her 'n' Matt told me to pet her a bit 'n' tell her that everything was all right. I did this 'n' she calmed down real good. I had a little trouble gettin' the bit in her mouth but Matt told me it would come easier with practice. He had to help me throw the saddle up but I knew I could do it by myself if I stood on a stump or somethin' high. I watched real close when I went to cinch the saddle but Patches didn't try to pull that trick Matt told me about.

Matt checked to see how tight the cinch was 'n' he

nodded ‘n’ said, “Good job, boy. Now, take note of which hole it’s in an’ how much you got folded through the ring, an’ do it the same way each time you saddle this horse with this saddle.”

I gotta say, I was pretty excited when I had Patches all saddled ‘n’ ready to go. I started to climb into the saddle ‘n’ Matt put his hand on my arm.

“Why don’t you walk her around the corral a time or two and talk to her a little bit?” he said.

“But she’s so tame. You done a good job of breakin’ ‘er.”

“Suit yourself, boy,” said Matt, ‘n’ he turned to finish saddlin’ Critter.

I managed to get a foot in the stirrup an’ was tryin’ to throw my right leg over the saddle when Patches came apart. I mean, she went in about five directions at once an’ I went in a sixth. She was still kickin’ ‘n’ snortin’ when I hit the ground. I wasn’t hurt, unless you count pride, but that was hurt real bad. I looked up at Matt, who was cinchin’ down his saddle on Critter. He didn’t even look to see if I was hurt. That got me even madder than bein’ throwed.

I stood ‘n’ dusted myself off ‘n’ was about to grab Patches’ reins, since she’d finally quit buckin’, when Matt said. “She’ll be all right, boy. Step out of the corral for a minute. Critter’s feelin’ human this mornin’.”

I wasn’t sure exactly what he meant but I did have an idea. That’s all it was too: an idea. I stepped out of the corral ‘n’ watched the show. Critter started buckin’ before Matt had his leg over the saddle. Matt hung on ‘n’ somehow managed to get his right leg over the saddle an’ find the stirrup. As soon as he had his foot in the stirrup, Critter started spinnin’ around in circles, then he went up on hind ‘n’ pawed the air. Next thing he did was put his nose on the ground an’ throw his hind legs about as far in the air as any horse ever did. It’s a good thing the moon wasn't out or he'd a kicked it right out of the sky. He made so many moves, I could scarce keep track of 'em. When nothin' seemed to be workin', he slammed his side against the corral fence so hard it knocked the top rail out. Matt musta' been expectin' it though 'cause he had his foot alongside Critter's neck. When that didn't work, Critter just stopped real quick 'n' stood stock-still.

Looked to me like it was all over so I ducked under the middle rail. Matt said, "Not yet, boy."

About then Critter went to sunfishin' like he was fresh 'n' ready for the kill. He squealed 'n' snorted 'n' stomped his feet 'n' tossed his head back like he was tryin' to knock Matt out of the saddle with his head. Right sudden, he stopped 'n' stood. He was quiverin' all over. To tell the truth, I was plumb scared.

"Wow." I couldn't think of anything else to say.

Matt dismounted 'n' let go of the reins. He walked right in front of Critter 'n' looked him in the eye. It was grey light now so I could see pretty good.

"You done now?" Matt asked Critter.

Critter backed up a few feet an' reared. He whinnied so loud, I was sure he could've woke the dead. When his forelegs hit the ground, he stomped 'em a few times 'n' then stopped. He laid his ears back 'n' made as if to bite Matt's hand. Matt pulled his hand back 'n' said, "You're sure a sore loser."

Critter's ears stood up real straight an' he pranced around the corral, ignorin' Patches 'n' Matt. I stepped back from the fence a few feet, figurin' that Critter could bust that corral into splinters if he wanted to, 'n' I wanted a runnin' start if that happened. After three trips around the corral, Critter stopped in front of Matt 'n' drooped his head. I almost laughed but didn't for fear that Critter might not like it an', that bein' the case, take out his mad on my puny body.

Matt put his hand out 'n' rubbed Critter behind the ears. Critter held his head high 'n' stood real still.

"Is he gonna do some more?" I said from my safe spot outside the corral.

"No. He's had enough for today, I think," said Matt.

"Does he do that real often?" I asked, still afraid to go into the corral.

"Not quite like that. He was showin' off for Patches," said Matt.

"Oh," I said. "Is it okay to come in now.?"

"Yeah. Just talk to Patches 'n' give her some attention. Walk her a bit before you take to the saddle."

"You bet I will," I said.

I musta' walked her five minutes before I worked up the nerve to mount up again. This time she gave one little kick an' settled down. I patted her real good on the neck 'n' told her what a good girl she was, all the time shakin' 'cause I figured she might change her mind at any second an' start to buckin' again. When I looked at Matt for his approval, I saw Ma standin' in front of the house, watchin' us. I don't know how long she'd been there but I knew she was a mite worried. I could ride Bess all right but Bess was as gentle as a snowflake. I figured Critter's ruckus musta' woke her up an' she probably thought I was bein' killed or somethin'.

Matt leaned over 'n' opened the corral gate. When he rode past Ma, he tipped his new hat 'n' smiled. "'Mornin', Miss Penny. Nice morinin, ain't it?"

Ma smiled back 'n' said, "It surely is, Mr. Grady." She looked at me as I rode by an' smiled real proud-like. "You be careful, Crawford."

"Yes, Ma'am," I said.

We weren't fifty yards from the corral when here come Judd. He kept pace on our right, dodgin' trees 'n' bushes 'n' a cactus now an' then. After we'd rode about a half-mile, Matt stopped 'n' took his rope from his saddle. He pulled another rope from his saddlebag 'n' handed it to me. "This is your own rope, boy. Take care of it. It can be the most important thing in your life sometimes."

"Gee, Matt. My own rope?" Every day got better with Matt around.

"Yep. Your very own rope, or catch twine, or whatever you want to call it. It's thirty-five feet long - a grown man's rope. I expect you to learn to use it like a man."

All of a sudden I got to feelin' real grownup an' important. That rope made me feel as big a man as the carbine had, an' that's sayin' a lot.

We spent a couple of hours ropin' branches 'n' stumps. Matt showed me how he doubled the loop back about a foot to keep it open 'n' how to dally 'round the saddle horn without losin' a finger. He really made a point to mention keepin' my fingers out of the way when I dallied - an' when Matt made a point, I listened real good.

After breakfast we went out again an' he had Judd cut out a calf for me. Once the calf was away from her mama, Judd kept the mama away while Matt hazed the calf my way. I caught that little rascal on my first throw 'n' I was so proud I forgot to dally. It was about the time I remembered what I forgot when that calf hit the end of my rope an' I was snatched out of the saddle like I weren't nothin'. Not only did I forget to dally, I forgot to let go of the rope. After I was drug about twenty feet, I finally let go 'n' Matt hocked the calf 'n' jerked the rope tight 'n' dallied quicker 'n' I could ever tell it. That calf fell like it'd been struck by lightning 'n' Critter dug in 'n' backed up just enough to keep the rope tight while Matt walked it down to the calf 'n' took my rope off it.

I was sure embarrassed when he handed me my rope 'n' Matt knew it too. He said, "Don't worry about it, boy. That was one of those lesson's you can afford to learn by experience." He smiled 'n' walked back to the calf. Critter eased up enough for Matt to loosen his rope without so much as a word from him. The calf stood up bawlin' 'n' ran, lickety-split, for its ma. Matt mounted Critter without even payin' any attention to my face, which was bleedin' a bit from bein' drug through the dirt.

I got better as the day wore on. Trouble was, Patches didn't know what to do once I roped the calf. Matt showed me how to low-rein her 'n' make her back up a little every time I hit with the loop. Before we was done for the day Patches was already knowin' what to do. I think she even liked workin' them cows. She sure was a smart horse.

We looked for strays 'n', a little later in the day, found one, but Matt said I wasn't quite ready to tackle this one. He dismounted 'n' told Critter 'n' Judd to get that steer up with the others. Next thing I knowed, Critter was herdin' that steer on one side 'n' Judd on the other. That steer was outnumbered 'n' he knew it early on. He marched right up to the little herd without so much as an argument. I couldn't figure why Matt needed a rope with Critter 'n' Judd around. I reckoned he must have fed the whole Confederate Army with the help of those two.

Chapter 17

The day after my first ropin' lesson, me 'n' Matt went to the big mesa about a mile or two east of our cabin 'n' he showed me how to load 'n' shoot the Maynard Carbine. It was right heavy and I had a hard time holdin' it steady so Matt took me to a mesquite and put the barrel in a low fork. He taught me how to get a good sight picture and to align my front and rear sights. The Maynard liked to knocked me backwards the first time I pulled the trigger, 'n' the noise weren't nothin' to be ignored either, but I got the hang of it the second time I tried it, 'n' by the third shot I was feelin' like maybe I was as good as a cavalry man. Then Matt shot that Henry of his 'n' I knew I had a ways to go. He was about the best rifle shot I ever saw. When he had finished shootin' a rock three times while it was still movin', he reloaded 'n' put the Henry back into that buckskin scabbard of his 'n' said. "Time to go to work, boy. I've got to work on that fence."

I could tell he didn't like that idea but he was gonna do it anyway. The field was almost all fenced off now 'n' I knew he wanted done with it. The fence wouldn't keep out rabbits 'n' such but it would keep out the cattle.

I'd been wantin' to ask him a question ever since I'd seen them pistols but I had never got around to it. "Say, Matt, I ain't never seen you shoot your pistols. How come?"

He kinda smiled at me 'n' said, "Boy, a man should use the best weapon he's got for the job at hand. A rifle is almost always better than a pistol. Pistols are for close in work, or maybe when you haven't got time to bring a rifle to bear. They're kinda like a last resort."

"Oh." Was all I said. We rode back to the house real quiet, just enjoyin' the beauty of the mountains 'n' the desert; me feelin' like I had maybe growed up some this day. My shoulder was achin' a little from shootin' the carbine but that only made me feel more growed-up. I reckoned that's what a cavalryman must feel like at the end of a hard day of shootin' Apaches.

Next mornin' I was woke up by a strange sound. It was kinda like a pig squealin' but not quite. I'd never heard nothin' like it. I jumped out of bed an' put my britches on an' grabbed my carbine.

Ma musta been fixin' biscuits on account of she had flour on her hands. "Craw, you stay put." She walked over to the wall an' picked up her shotgun. "You stay right behind me." An' I followed her out the door.

Turns out it was Critter makin' the noise. He was layin' on his side an' groanin' somethin' fierce. I leaned my carbine against the front of the house an' ran next to him an' squatted down. Critter looked at me an' his eyes was real big, almost wall-eyed. It scared me plumb to death on account of I figured he was gonna die any second. I patted him on the neck an' petted him some. I didn't know what else to do.

I said, "It's gonna be okay, Critter." Course, I had no sure knowledge of that bein' a fact, but it made me feel better to say it. I don't know if it helped Critter any though.

Next thing I knowed, Matt was on his knees next to me. He never said a word to me. He just opened Critter's mouth an' got to lookin' inside. He took one of his fingers an' scraped Critter's teeth until he had somethin' under his nails. He sniffed his fingers an' looked at whatever it was he had scraped out of Critter's mouth, then he looked up at me, then Ma, then towards the creek.

"Where are those chokecherry bushes?" he said.

"About a half a mile upstream," I said.

He held out his hand an' showed me the end of his finger. "I don't know much about chokecherries but I heard the Mountain Apache say the leaves would kill a horse. They never let their livestock near the stuff." He looked down at Critter an' didn't move for maybe a full minute, then he looked up at the mornin' sky, like maybe he could find an answer for Critter's ailment.

Right sudden he looked at Ma an' said, "Have you any whiskey, Miss Penny?"

"No, Mr. Grady. We have no whiskey. We don't use it."

"Right about now, I'm wishin' you did. No offense, Ma'am."

He looked back down at Critter an' rubbed him behind the ears. "You big dummy."

I could tell Matt was right worried an', to tell the truth, it scared me a bit. I figured Matt could fix anything but it was lookin' like maybe he couldn't help Critter an' Critter was gonna die.

I hadn't noticed before but Judd was sittin' off to the side, watchin' all of us. When Matt rubbed Critter behind the ears, he came walkin' up next to Critter an' laid down right in front of him. He licked Critter's nose an' whimpered. I got to feelin' awful. I was for sure Critter was gonna die.

"You got any kind of brush I could get into his mouth, boy?"

I tried to think real fast but I was so worried about Critter, I couldn't think of nothin'."

I don't know where she'd been but Mel was standin' right next to me. "I have a brush, Matt."

Matt looked at her an' kinda smiled. "That's real kind of you, Mel, but I'm afraid it will ruin your brush."

"I can get a new one someday, can't I?"

"You sure can. Get it for me, Mel."

She was off for the house, lickety-split. Next thing I

knowed she was back an' holdin' out her little hair brush. Pa had got it for her special. I knowed that brush meant a lot to Mel but she couldn't let Critter die an', if her brush could help, Matt was welcome to it. That's the way Mel was.

"Salt, boy. Get me some salt."

I didn't even have time to move before Ma was in the house an' back outside with a bag of salt. Matt took it an' said, "Thanks, Miss Penny." Then he sat it next to the brush an' started fast-walkin' to his wickiup. He looked back over his shoulder an' said, "Get a bucket of water."

I ran an' grabbed a bucket an' filled it with water from the creek. By the time I got back, Matt was kneelin' next to Critter. He dipped the brush in the bucket then poured some salt over it an' went to brushin' Critter's teeth. Critter didn't care much for it an' he started puttin' up a fight. Matt put his knee on Critter's neck an' said, "I don't care for it much either, old boy, but it's all I can think of. You ain't seen nothin' yet."

I had no notion of what Matt was talkin' about but Critter seemed to calm down a mite.

"Help me hold his mouth open, boy."

An' I did. I Pert near lost a finger when Critter took a notion to bite but I jumped back a second then dove back in an' got a better grip on his jaws. I was gettin' real serious by that time an' I weren't gonna fail Matt - no way.

After a few minutes, Matt threw a bunch of water in Critter's mouth until he pert near drowned. He got to coughin' an' heavin'. After a minute, he settled down an' breathed real heavy. Matt dipped the brush in the water again, salted it, then took out some reddish powder from a leather pouch. He sprinkled the powder over the brush and shoved it in Critter's mouth an' went to brushin'.

"You might as well get out of the way, boy. I ain't sure how he's gonna take to this."

I was sure glad Matt said somethin' for, just about the

time I let go of Critter's jaw an' went to stand up, that horse came plumb unglued. I mean, he started paddlin' his feet an' snortin' an rollin' his eyes. Matt jumped back to keep from gettin' killed, an' kinda back-peddled a few paces. Critter made his feet an got to jumpin' an' buckin' an' carryin' on somethin' fierce. I had no notion of what he was plannin' on doin' so I headed for the corral an' jumped inside.

Critter went for Matt an' stopped short an' went on hind. He looked ten feet tall, his front hooves danglin' over Matt's head. Matt raised a hand an' Critter came down on all fours, his forelegs hittin' the ground only an inch or two from Matt. An' then he turned an' headed for the creek at a wobbly run. I never saw a horse run sideways before. Matt just stood there an' watched him go. Judd watched for a few seconds, then up an' took off after Critter.

I ducked under the corral fence an' came runnin' up to Matt. "Ain't you gonna stop him?" I asked.

Matt looked at me an' smiled. "Boy, if that horse ever taught me anything, it was to get out of his way when he had his mind set on somethin'."

Mel peeked around the corner of the house. "Is he gonna be all right, Matt? He sure was runnin' funny."

Matt pert near laughed when he saw Mel's head peekin' around the corner. I could see him holdin' it in. "Can't say for sure, but he's a pretty tough nut."

"Mr. Grady," said Ma.

I hadn't even thought about Ma durin' this whole thing but there she was, standin' in front of the door of the house.

"Yes, Ma'am?"

"Are you going after Critter or would you like some breakfast?"

Now, if that didn't beat all. Critter was out there somewhere dyin' an' Ma wanted to know if Matt wanted breakfast. I was even more surprised by Matt's answer.

"That would be nice, Miss Penny. I believe I would like a bite."

I was right confused. Seemed like everybody forgot about Critter. Well, not me. I went to runnin' to the creek.

When I got to the creek, Critter was rollin' around in a shallow spot. He was splashin' an' carryin' on like nothin' I'd ever seen. His squealin' could'a woke up the dead. Judd stood next to the creek with his head cocked to one side like maybe he couldn't quite figure what Critter was tryin' to do. That made two of us.

Every once in a while Critter would stop rollin' an' squealin' an' take a big drink of water. After doin' that, he'd vomit a bit, then start to rollin' an' squealin' some more. I was for certain he was gonna die on account of I'd never seen a horse act like that before.

Seems like he musta vomited three or four times an', about the time I was sure he would die any second, he seemed to rest a little bit an' his breathin' got a mite easier. I knew things was gettin' better when Judd yipped once an' Critter kinda wobbled out of the water an' stood next to him.

I don't know for sure how long all this took but it musta been quite a spell, 'cause Matt came walkin' up to the creek an he had a big plate of bacon an' beans. He stopped about ten feet from Critter an' said, "You feelin' any better?"

Critter looked at him an' snorted whilst he was shakin' his head.

Matt grinned an' said, "It's about time. I reckon you better stay away from them chokecherry leaves. They don't seem to agree with you."

Critter didn't do nothin' but Judd yipped once. I couldn't be for sure if he was agreein' with Matt or if he wanted some of them beans.

"What was that powder you put on Mel's brush?" I asked.

"I ain't for sure what all it had in it but it was a mixture of things given to me as part of the trade I made for Patches. I was told it could fix almost any serious problem. It seemed to me that Critter had a serious problem, so I gave it a try."

"Wow. It sure looks like it worked. Critter's not lookin' so peaked now," I said.

Matt set that plate of beans on the ground. "This will be the real test." He looked at Critter an' Judd. "All right, you two. Dig in."

Judd went for them beans right off but Critter just stood there for a few seconds, watchin' Judd. I don't reckon he really felt much like eatin' yet but the idea that Judd might get alla them beans was more than he could stand. Judd stopped eatin' the beans an' looked at Critter like he was tellin' him the beans was all his. He barked once an' wagged his tail once. Critter laid his ears flat against his head an' dove at that plate like there was nothin' else in the world. I could tell Judd was expectin' it by the way he managed to keep from bein' stomped into the ground. The battle of the beans was on again an' both of 'em put up a good showin'. When the plate was clean, I could tell Critter was feelin' a lot better. He reared an whinnied real proud.

"Not bad," said Matt.

Critter shook his head from side to side an' Judd barked once as if he might be protestin' Matt's judgement.

Chapter 18

Things was goin' real good on our place. I even got to likin' the schoolin' Aunt Sandra was givin' me on account of it helped shorten the work part of the day. She sure was smart. An' a good teacher too. Chester came 'n' sat under the mesquite whenever he could put off his chores a spell so he could get in some book-learnin' an' Aunt Sandra weren't worried about him at all. She said he was doin' fine. So was Billy Jo. He sure wanted to learn to read real bad. I guess maybe that's because he wasn't allowed to read when he was a slave. I ain't sure what happened to Tater. He was more like me an' didn't care much one way or another about readin' proper English, but Mama saw to it he went to Aunt Sandra's schoolin' every day.

Abraham "Papa" Lincoln an' his family finished their house, an' it was a beauty too. Mama said it was the nicest house in the world 'n' she cried a lot. Ma cried with her. I couldn't figure that one out. If everybody was so happy, an' if was the nicest house in the world, why was everyone cryin'?

Uncle George let Billy Jo an' Tater use the horses that we bought in Tucson to go with me an' Matt so's they could learn to rope an' work cattle too. Papa said he would pay Uncle George for the use of them horses when he got some money but Uncle George said he considered it a good investment on account of Billy Jo an' Tater would be learnin' to work cattle from the best there was - that bein' Matt - an' they could put their learnin' to good use later on.

It weren't no time at all when we all saw that Billy Jo had found his callin'. He learned about ridin' an' ropin' faster than I ever thought of. Even though he weren't mounted as good as me an' Matt, he got to where he could tell which way a longhorn was gonna go before the longhorn knew, an' he was there an' ready with his rope. He didn't have a rope as long as mine, an' it weren't near the quality neither, but Billy Jo was always in the right spot at the right time. Matt said it was called "anticipatin'." Matt said only a chosen few could do it as good as Billy Jo.

I was a little jealous of Billy Jo at first but I got over it pretty quick when he pulled me out of a jam or two when I got in over my head. Seemed like he was born to the saddle but he swore he never rode anything but a mule in his whole life, an' that hadn't been very often.

Whenever Matt was explainin' somethin' about them longhorns, he'd be real sure that Billy Jo understood what he was talkin' about. It ain't like he ignored me an' Tater, but it was right clear that he reckoned Billy Jo was special when it came to horses an' cattle.

Billy Jo got to where he knew each move that Judd was gonna make when he was after a bunch-quitter an' he was right there to help Judd if Matt an' Critter wasn't nearby. I ain't so sure Judd liked him buttin' in at first but, after a spell, Judd got to likin' it on account of he could start a steer in Billy Jo's direction an' Billy Jo would take over an' Judd would move on to the next bunch-quitter. Them two worked together almost as good as Critter an' Judd did.

I knew Billy Jo wanted a good cow horse real bad. An' I knew Matt wanted him to have one on account of Billy Jo could do twice as much with half the work if he had a real good horse.

Billy Jo was as happy as I ever saw him. He weren't lonely no more an' he could do work that he really loved, an' I know for sure that nobody ever loved his work more than Billy Jo when he was workin' cattle. I got to be a fair hand with the rope but I couldn't hold a candle to Billy Jo.

Everybody was so busy on account of there was so much to do that Billy Jo was about killin' himself, what with him doin' all his chores an' then learnin' how to work cattle but, no matter how tired he was, when Matt went out with the cattle, Billy Jo was right there with him. An' he almost never missed learnin' *prope*r English from Aunt Sandra either. I don't know how he did it but I do know why. Matt said his book-learnin' had to come first an' Billy Jo respected Matt a lot. An', besides, Matt wouldn't let him near the longhorns if he missed one of Aunt Sandra's classes, so I reckon Billy Jo was gettin' to be one smart cowhand.

One day, Matt 'n' me 'n' Billy Jo an' Tater was lookin' for strays about two miles south of our place when Matt reined up next to a big mesquite an' dismounted. We didn't have no idea why he'd do such a thing on account of we'd only been out about an hour an' hadn't yet come upon any cattle. He motioned us to dismount an' rest a spell then he reached into his saddlebag. I thought he was gonna pull out the biscuits Ma had made for our lunch an' we was gonna eat real early. I wasn't hungry yet but it didn't matter for he pulled a pistol from the saddlebag.

I thought maybe he was gonna teach us how to shoot a pistol but he turned to Billy Jo. "Billy Jo, I talked to your papa an' he said you were old enough to have this." He held out the pistol.

For a minute, Billy Jo just stood there an' looked at the pistol. I reckoned he was just as dumbstruck as we was.

Matt said, "It's a Navy Colt. Thirty-six caliber. It's a good gun. I'd rather you had a rifle but I don't have one to spare. I figure you might need it someday."

Billy Jo still stood there, his mouth open, starin' at that Colt.

Finally, Matt said, "Billy Jo, will you please take the

pistol? My arm is gettin' tired."

Billy Jo reached out real gentle an' took the pistol. He looked at it a long time an' then he looked at Matt an' there was tears streamin' down his face. Billy Jo was almost a growed man at fourteen an' I was plumb surprised to see them tears.

Matt grinned an' said, "I know it's not the newest pistol in the world but it ain't that bad."

Billy Jo threw his arms around Matt an' went to huggin' him an' bawlin' like a wounded heifer. I ain't never seen the like. Matt hugged him back an' patted him on the shoulder blades. After a spell Billy Jo stepped back an' looked at Matt, them tears still flowin' down his cheeks like maybe a dam had busted behind his eyes.

He said, "Missah Matt, no white man evah give me nothin', an' here y'all is a Confederit an' y'all give me a gun. Ah don' unnerstan' this worl' sometimes, Missah Matt. Y'all saved us all from stahvin' an' then seed to it we was treated lahk whaht folks. Ah love you, Missah Matt." An' he threw his arms around Matt an' went to cryin' some more.

Matt didn't say nothin'. He just left his arms around Billy Jo till he got the cryin' out of hisself an' backed up a step or two.

"Thank you, Missah Matt," said Billy Jo.

"You're welcome, Billy Jo. Don't ever use it wrong and I'll never regret you got it."

Matt's eyes looked a little wet but I couldn't be for sure.

"Ah'll never use it wrong, Missah Matt. Never."

"That's good enough for me." Matt turned his back to us for a second an' wiped his eyes, then he turned around an' said, "You can have my powder horn. I don't need it now that my pistols are converted. I've got a mold an' some lead, caps and powder for it too."

He reached into his saddlebag an' pulled out some ball

an' powder an' percussion caps an' proceeded to give us all a lesson on how load the Navy Colt. He showed us about how much powder to put in each chamber in the cylinder an' how to put the ball on top of the powder an' pack it with the lever underneath the barrel an', finally, how to put the percussion cap on the nipple of each chamber. He told us that, most often, he left the cap off of the chamber under the hammer on account of it might fire iffen the hammer was bumped hard enough. He said it was easy enough to push a cap onto the nipple once you had a need.

We spent almost an hour shootin' an' re-loadin' the pistol. Matt showed us how to hold it an' aim it but he never pulled the trigger on account of he wanted us to shoot the ammo. Matt shot a pistol left-handed an' told us that it was the same for right-handers except that if we closed an eye, we was supposed to close the left one. Billy Jo let me an' Tater shoot his pistol an' he didn't take no more shots than we did. I ain't so sure I would a' been so generous iffen it had been my pistol.

Seemed like none of us was a real good pistol shooter but it weren't for lack of tryin'. Matt told us there was two basic ways to use a pistol an', as far as he was concerned, neither was real good on account of a rifle would be better. He said the first way was to shoot at a target twenty-five or thirty yards away by takin' aim, just like a rifle, an' squeazin' the trigger real gentle. The other way was to snap off quick shots at real close range by pointin' the pistol, almost like pointin' your finger. He said that kind of shootin' took a lot of practice an' gettin' used to your gun on account of each gun had its own special feel.

When we were down to the last six balls, Matt called a halt to the shootin' an' said it didn't make much sense to carry an empty pistol around, so Billy Jo loaded it an' gave it back to Matt to carry in his saddle bags on account of Matt didn't have no holster to give him. Matt didn't say much about a holster but Chester had made him one an', when we got home, he gave it to Billy Jo with a big hug. The holster was a little big but it held the gun real good. It even had a flap on it so's the gun wouldn't fall out while Billy Jo was workin' cattle.

When I saw the flap, I got to lookin' at Matt's holsters 'cause his guns never fell out an' he didn't have no flaps. Matt's holsters had a rawhide thong that looped around the hammer an' kept the gun from bouncin' out. The other end of the thong went through a hole near the top of the holster an' was knotted to keep it in place. It didn't look as safe as the flap on Billy Jo's holster but I reckoned that Matt knew what was best for him. The holster on his left side was tied to his leg with a rawhide thong. I didn't know why he did that.

Billy Jo put his holster on his belt an' I don't reckon he ever took it off. If he did, I never saw it.

Chapter 19

It was late July before the first good rain came, an' it was a gully-washer. There was a lot of lightning an' thunder 'n' Matt was out in it with Critter 'n' Judd. They had the cattle all bunched up in a small canyon 'n' was guardin' the mouth so's they couldn't scatter 'n' run.

I was in the house with Ma 'n' Mel 'n' Uncle George 'n' Aunt Sandra 'n' all of Papa's family. We was all listenin' to Aunt Sandra readin' from the book Matt had give her. We had a lantern goin' an' it weren't the best light but it was good enough. I was havin' trouble payin' attention to the story though. It was a good story mind you, but I was worried about Matt out there in that wind 'n' rain 'n' lightning. An' the way that fella talked that wrote that *Hamlet* book, a body had to have all his attentions on what was bein' said or he'd get plumb lost. That was the most proper English I had ever heard.

"It ain't right that Matt has to be out there all by himself," I said right sudden-like.

Aunt Sandra stopped readin' 'n' looked at me. "You're right, Crawford, but Mr Grady said he didn't need any help and there was no sense in everybody getting soaked to the skin."

It's true. He had said that. But it still didn't seem right an' I said so. "It still ain't right."

"I'm sure he'll be all right, Craw," said Ma.

"Maybe ah' go see if he be okay," said Chester. "Dat wind blowin' mahty hahd, an' dey's 'nuff lightnin' to make it dangerous out dere at tahms."

"I'll go with you, Chester," said Uncle George.

About this time there was a knock on the door. "Hello

the house." It was Matt.

Ma opened the door 'n' Matt came in. He was soaked plumb through. Rain dripped offa his hat like a waterfall. He took a quick look at everybody 'n' said, "We've gotta get up to the creek 'n' build up the dike on our irrigation trench or the crops are gonna be flooded into Mexico."

"What about the cattle?" asked Uncle George.

"I borrowed the boy's rope and, with mine, I made a single-strand fence across the mouth of the draw. It might not be enough but the crops are more important right now."

Seemed like there was a lot of confusion while everybody went for tools but we all met in less than five minutes, ready to go. Matt led the way on foot 'n' we all followed. It was still rainin' real hard an' it was as dark as pitch 'cept when the lightning struck. The wind was howlin' an' drivin' the rain right into our faces so bad, I couldn't keep my eyes open very long 'n' kept blinkin' so's I could see.

I don't know how Matt found the creek, much less the irrigation ditch, but he sure enough did. Led us right to the spot where the ditch left the creek, like maybe he had a light in his head and could see through his eyelids.

The creek was awful high 'n' runnin' real strong. It weren't really a creek anymore. It was truly a river. Not near as big as the Ohio but, I mean to tell you, it was a lot faster, an' I could see where the water had already taken a big chunk out of the little dam we had built to hold it out of the ditch. Water was pourin' into the ditch almost as much as if it was the creek.

Chester 'n' Uncle George 'n' Papa went to work throwin' mud into the broken piece of the dam with their shovels while me 'n' Tater 'n' Billy Jo gathered all the loose branches we could find 'n' threw 'em into the hole caused by the water. Seemed like that water washed everything away faster'n we could fill. We kept at it for a good fifteen minutes, maybe more, an' we had only lost ground against the water.

I was out of breath 'n' about give out when Matt said, "We ain't gonna win it this way." He kinda had to holler a little on account of all the wind 'n' rain.

Ma said, "But Mr. Grady, we'll lose everything. We have to keep trying."

Matt kinda turned his head down a little, so's his hat would afford a bit of protection from the rain, an' said, "That doesn't work, Ma'am. We kept tryin' in the South, but heart and spirit need help when the odds are this steep against us."

"What can we do?" asked Ma.

Uncle George 'n' Chester 'n' Papa was still shovellin'. They wasn't ready to give up just yet.

Matt just stood there for a minute, lookin' like he was thinkin' real hard. "I don't know for sure. I might have an idea. You folks just do what you can. I'll be right back." He disappeared in the dark, runnin' like an Indian.

We kept it up all right. We kept losin' more dirt to that creek that was now a river. In a little while Matt came back, ridin' Critter 'n' leadin' a big steer with his rope. Judd was nippin' at the steer's hind legs to keep 'im goin' the right way, I reckon.

Matt hollered real loud, "Everybody back away from the ditch. Move to the side toward Miss Penny's place."

The way he said it didn't leave no room for questions. We just done what he said without thinkin' about it. As soon as he figured we was far enough away, he led the steer right into the middle of the ditch an' shot 'im square between the eyes. That was the first time I ever saw Matt use a pistol. He used the long-barreled one in the backward holster on his right hip, but he held it in his left hand. The steer dropped right at the mouth of the ditch, without so much as a twitch, an' stopped a lot of the water. They was still some washin' over 'n' around it but it was considerable slowed.

The sound of the shot kinda scared us all for a second but Matt didn't leave no time for thinkin' about bein' scared. He said, "Fill in behind an' left 'n' right of 'im. Build as high as you can. I'm goin' after another if I can find one. I had to drop the rope fence 'n' they've likely scattered. I'll be back as soon as I can."

Nobody said a word. We all went back to shovellin' 'n' carryin' tree branches, 'n' what rocks we could find. I reckon nobody had the energy to talk. We was all tired 'n' soaked to the bone.

It seemed like a long time before Matt came back. 'Course it might've been only a few minutes. I couldn't be for sure. He didn't have another steer.

"Couldn't find 'em in this weather," he said as he dismounted 'n' dropped Critter's reins.

We'd done a right proper job of stoppin' the water but if the creek got much higher it would still take all our work right into our field. We all worked maybe half an hour more, pilin' things as high as we could before we all fainted dead away. Finally Matt said, "That's about the best we can do. If we take any more mud from this area, the creek could break through somewhere else. And I don't think we have the strength to carry it down here from higher ground."

Uncle George said, "The creek will continue to rise."

Matt said, "That it will, George. Me 'n' Critter will stay out here a spell."

Papa said, "Whatchoo 'n' dat crazy horse gonna do out chere by yo'sef?"

Matt kinda grinned at him an' said, "Not a whole lot. We'll probably take a nap."

"Take a nap? Whatchoo talkin' 'bout?" said Papa.

"Don't you worry about me 'n' Critter, Papa. Just get on up to the house 'n' out of this rain. All of you. Go on," said Matt. An' the way he said it didn't leave a lot of room for a parlay on the subject.

Matt called Critter 'n' unsaddled him, an' the next thing I knowed, Critter was layin' on his side, right on top of the dam. Matt laid down on his back in the mud next to him with his head on Critter's neck, like I'd seen him that other time, 'n' pulled his hat down over his eyes. "I'll call you if I need anymore help," he said.

"But, Mr. Grady," said Ma.

"Goodnight, Miss Penny. Get you an' the others back to the house before you catch your death."

And that was that.

When we all got back to our cabin Uncle George started a fire on account of we was all wet 'n' cold, even though it was the middle of summer.

Ma said, "Mr. Grady has never used such a stern tone of voice before."

I saw Uncle George smile. "He's used to giving orders, Penny. And I don't imagine he's used to being questioned while he's giving them."

Chester said, "Dat sho' was a good idea he done had about shootin' dat beef cow."

"I never would have thought of that," I said. It felt real good to talk with the grown ups, like I was one of 'em.

"I must say, when he fired that shot, it startled me," said Aunt Sandra. "I wasn't expecting it."

"Neither was the steer, I dare say," said Ma.

As sad as it was to have to kill the steer to save our field, the way Ma said it kinda made everybody grin a mite. Chester even laughed out loud. Then so did me 'n' Tater. Then we all laughed together. I think we all felt like one big family. I know I did.

Chapter 20

I reckon everybody was plumb give out, ‘cause I was the first one to wake up an’ I knew for sure *I* was give out the night before. The sun was just peekin’ over the mesa east of the cabin an’ there wasn’t a cloud in the sky when I jumped up ‘n’ ran outside to see if Matt was still at the ditch. We’d all slept in our cabin that night ‘n’ it was a mite crowded, so I woke Tater when I got up. He followed me to the ditch, hitchin’ up his britches as he ran to keep up.

When we got to the ditch, Matt ‘n’ Critter was gone. I could see the big hollow where Critter had laid down but that was all. I was feelin’ a touch of disappointment when I, right sudden-like caught the whiff of beans ‘n’ bacon. An’ they sure smelled good! Matt was upstream about fifty yards, cookin’ over a small fire. Must been rough gettin’ that fire started with all the water.

Matt looked up at me ‘n’ Tater ‘n’ said, “Mornin’, boy. Tater. You gents hungry?”

Was I ever! That food smelled so good, I couldn’t hardly wait to dig in. “Yes, Sir. We sure are. You got enough?” I said.

Matt looked at Judd, who was in his favorite sittin’ position only a few feet away. “What do you think, Judd? We got enough to share?”

Judd looked at me ‘n’ Tater real quick an’ barked once. It was a friendly bark, but I took notice he didn’t stand ‘n’ wag his tail once, like he did if he was real happy about a situation.

“What about it, Critter? You feel like bein’ neighborly this mornin’?” asked Matt.

Critter laid his ears back an’ shook his head.

"That ain't no way to be, Critter. These gents put in a hard night's work."

Critter pawed the ground 'n' whinnied real soft.

Tater's eyes got real big. "Dat horse, he be speekin' English. 'Least he be unnerstannin' it."

"Yeah, he does," I said. "He surely does."

Matt said, "Looks to me like he was sorry he didn't wanna share his grub once he remembered how hard you worked. You boys want some coffee?"

I sure liked the smell of coffee but it never tasted up to its smell as far as I was concerned, 'sides, Ma didn't like me drinkin' it. "No coffee for me," I said.

"Ah'd sure like some a' dat dere coffee," said Tater.

Matt dug out about everything he had that would hold food an' dished us each out a big helpin' of beans 'n' bacon. He even had some pan biscuits. Critter had his ears laid back the whole time Matt was dishin' out the grub. I know it made him mad to think me 'n' Tater was gettin' so much of them beans 'n' bacon.

When we had our chow, Tater started to dig in but Matt stopped him. "Ain't you forgettin' somethin', Tater?"

Tater said, "Oh, yessah, Missa Matt." An' he commenced to sayin' grace.

When he finished, Matt said, "That's fine, Tater, but I was thinkin' of somethin' else."

Tater, who was about to put a big spoonful of beans in his mouth, held that spoon in midair, right in front of his face 'n' looked at Matt. I could tell he had no notion of what Matt was talkin' about an' neither did I. After a few seconds, Matt said, "Always take care of your animals first."

Tater looked at Critter 'n' Judd, then at Matt. He put his spoonful of beans back in his bowl 'n' stood up. He walked to a bunch of tall grass 'n' pulled a handful out by the roots 'n' walked up to Critter. Critter looked at him like he must be plumb crazy. He weren't about to eat grass with all them beans there. 'Course Tater didn't know this an' was a might confused when Critter didn't take the fresh grass.

Matt grinned 'n' held out the pan he'd been cookin' in. There was still lots of beans 'n' bacon left. "Would you mind settin' this pan over there by that little rock?" he said.

Tater was proper confused but he did as Matt asked, then walked back 'n' sat next to me. He picked up his spoon an' looked at Matt. "Now?" he asked.

Matt looked at Critter 'n' Judd. "Grub, you two."

An' the show was on again. Even though I'd seen it before, it was somethin' to watch. Critter tried his ol' trick of movin' to Judd's side of the pan 'n' Judd darted under his belly 'n' came out on the other side. Critter musta' thought Judd was gettin' more than his fair share 'cause he kicked some dirt at Judd with a foreleg. Judd didn't take that too good. He clamped his teeth around the handle on the pan 'n' started draggin' it away. Critter kept his nose in the pan 'n' tried to follow but he couldn't keep eatin' 'n' keep up with Judd. Finally, he laid his ears back 'n' squealed real loud. Judd let go of the handle 'n' barred his teeth. I gotta say, he looked right scary. The two stared at each other for a bit, Critter with his ears laid flat 'n' Judd with his teeth showin' clear to the back of his mouth.

Matt said, "That'll be enough, gentlemen. Eat. We got work to do."

Just like that, they both dove right back into them beans.

When I looked back at Tater, his spoon was in the air in front of his mouth. I don't reckon he'd yet taken a bite of his food. Me 'n' Matt was about half finished.

Tater looked over to Matt 'n' said, "Da's one crazy horse 'n' dog." Tater realized his mistake as soon's he said "dog" but it was too late. Judd stopped eatin' long enough to look at

Tater 'n' show his teeth.

Tater put his spoon back in his bowl 'n' held up his hands. "I'm sorry, Missah. Judd. Ah didn't mean nuttin' by it."

Judd went back to his breakfast. Matt grinned 'n' said, "That's his one fault, Tater. He's real serious about bein' called one of them, you-know-whats. It's okay. He accepted your apology."

Tater looked real suspicious at Judd. "Y'all sure 'bout dat?"

Matt laughed a short laugh. "Yeah, I'm sure about that. Now eat your grub."

Tater picked up his spoon 'n' dug in.

Matt wasn't jokin' none about a lot of work. We checked our crops an' found 'em to be mostly okay. There was a row or two washed out pretty bad but that was nothin' compared to what it would'a been iffen we hadn't plugged up the irrigation ditch. We started in right after mornin' chow, workin' on improvin' that ditch. Pretty soon, everyone else joined us 'n' pitched in. We uncovered the steer Matt had shot 'n' Matt threw a rope around it an' him 'n' Critter 'n' Jack drug it up the hill a ways. Matt skinned it 'n' stretched the hide. He said we couldn't eat the meat but it might feed a coyote or wolf or some such other critter.

Mama 'n' Ma 'n' Aunt Sandra 'n' Missy left a little before noon to fix us some lunch an', by the time we got back to our cabin to eat, we was all covered with mud. Ma wouldn't hear of us eatin' whilst we was so dirty 'n' she made us all go back to the creek 'n' wash up. I weren't none too happy about that but I went along without gripin', mainly 'cause Matt didn't say nothin'. He just hung his head like me 'n' Tater 'n' led us back to the creek.

We had fun dunkin' each other in the water 'n' splashin' around like a wounded buffalo. Tater held his nose 'n' put his head under the water for a long time. I got a mite worried 'cause he was under there so long, but he came bobbin' back up to the top with a big grin on his face. I splashed him 'n' musta caught him unawares 'cause he started coughin'. I felt bad for a bit but he stopped coughin' after a while 'n' splashed me back. We was still soakin' wet when we got back to the cabin.

We had biscuits with chicken gravy an' it sure tasted good.

We was about done eatin' when Critter whinnied real loud. I heard his hoofs hit the ground.

Matt sat his plate down real quick 'n' said, "Get your guns." He ran in the direction of Critter's whinny.

We all went lickety-split for our cabin 'n' everybody got their guns, even me. Ma looked at me real good 'n' said, "Crawford, you be real careful and don't shoot unless Uncle George tells you to."

"Yes, Ma'am," I said. It was plain Ma weren't all that comfortable with me havin' that carbine in my hands but she knew Matt had taught me proper, so she let it be.

Uncle George stepped outside with his Sharps 'n' stood in front of the door. We all waited. Seemed like forever before we saw anything. I was wonderin' where Matt was. Everything was awful quiet. I could hear my own breathin'. Tater was next to me, 'n' I could hear his breathin' too. Billy Jo had his Navy Colt up to one of the slots an' he wasn't movin' a lick. He looked like a statue.

Then we saw 'em. About eight or nine Indians came ridin', real careful, up to within forty feet of our cabin door. Uncle George just stood there an' didn't move. His Sharps was ready though. I saw the Indian in front look at all the guns stickin' through the slots in the shutters of our cabin windows. I couldn't tell if he was afraid or not. I don't think he was.

Then I noticed one of the Indians was leadin' Critter with a short rope. I knew this was not gonna be good for him when

Matt found out. About the time I noticed Critter, Matt stepped from behind a cottonwood about thirty feet from the lead Indian. He said something to the Indian 'n' the Indian said something back. We was too far away for me to make out what was bein' said, an I think they was talkin' Indian anyway, so it wouldn't have made no difference if I heard every word.

The Indian pointed to Critter 'n' said somethin'. Matt shook his head. The Indian looked at our cabin 'n' said somethin' else. Matt looked at our cabin 'n' said somethin' back to the Indian. The Indian laughed a short laugh 'n' got off his horse. He walked up to Critter 'n' fashioned a halter from the rope 'n' jumped up on Critter's back. Critter just stood there 'n' didn't move. The Indian jerked the rope reins to the right 'n' gave Critter a proper kick to get him started. Well, I reckon that was about all Critter wanted to take. He turned his head 'n' took a bite outa that Indian's leg 'n' then threw him about ten feet in the air.

When the Indian hit the ground he rolled over a couple of times then got to his feet 'n' limped to his own horse 'n' took his rifle from its scabbard.

Matt said somethin' kinda hurried-like to the Indian but the Indian didn't pay him no mind. He cocked the hammer back 'n' raised that rifle to his shoulder. My heart stopped beatin' 'n' I started to pull my carbine outa the slot 'n' run outside but, before I ever got the carbine from the slot, Matt had drawn that short-barreled Remington 'n' shot that Indian plumb though the ear. I never saw a pistol come out of a holster so fast. Next thing I knowed, Matt had his other Remington out in his right hand 'n' was blazin' away at all the rest of them Indians with both guns. They started shootin' back but he just stood there 'n' kept shootin', takin' aim each time, first one hand, then the other. Bullets was flyin' all around him but Matt paid 'em no mind. Them Indians was tryin' to hold their horses, which was all jumpin' 'n' buckin' 'n' tryin' to run from the gunshots an', at the same time, tryin' to shoot Matt. They wasn't havin' much luck at either. Judd came out of nowhere an' spooked the horses even worse. He was right in the middle of things, barkin' 'n' bitin' 'n' jumpin' all over the place. Critter rammed into one horse after the other, kinda like he was tryin' to run 'em over. This didn't help their aims none either.

Missy 'n' Mel was screamin' 'n' so was me 'n' Tater. I think Uncle George got off a shot but none of the rest of us did. When both of Matt's guns was out of ammunition, he took that short-barreled Colt from under his arm 'n' shot the last Indian that was still mounted. Just like that it was over. Maybe six or seven seconds.

It was so quiet, I didn't think death was even that quiet. The first thing that moved was Critter. He walked up to Matt 'n' stood next to him. His hoofbeats sounded like slow drumbeats. Matt patted him once, all the while lookin' at all them Indians layin' all over the place.

Uncle George said, "Are you all right, Mr. Grady?"

Ma went for the door. Chester was right behind her, then me 'n' the rest.

Matt didn't answer Uncle George. He just stood there lookin' at them Indians. He started re-loadin' his pistols. One of them Indians musta moved 'cause Judd growled. Matt holstered the pistol he was loadin' 'n' pulled his Bowie knife 'n' started to kneel down. Judd was only a foot or so away an' was lookin' ready to move in for the kill.

This time it was Ma who screamed. "Mr. Grady! No!"

Judd jumped back like somebody had just hit him smack-smooth in the face with a blacksmith hammer.

Matt looked down at the Indian, then stepped back a pace 'n' looked at Ma. "He's dyin' for sure, Miss Penny." His voice was so calm it was scary.

Missy was runnin' out of air by now 'n' Tater was holdin'

his breath ‘n’ turnin’ red in the face, even over his dark skin. Mel was breathin’ real fast. I ain’t sure what I was doin’.

“We’ll tend to his needs, Mr. Grady,” said Ma, an’ her voice was kinda tight.

Matt looked back down at the Indian, then up at Ma. “He won’t need any tendin’ now, Ma’am.”

Ma said, “Mr. Grady. Are you all right?” She was pretty close to him by now ‘n’ I could tell she was lookin’ for blood on Matt’s clothes.

Matt looked at Ma ‘n’ said, “I’m sorry, Miss Penny but I couldn’t let ‘im shoot Critter. Once I shot the one, I knew I’d have to shoot ‘em all. There wasn’t much future in hesitatin’. It had to happen fast. Sorry you ‘n’ the young’uns had to see it.”

“That was murder, Mr. Grady,” said Aunt Sandra.

If I thought it was quiet before, I was wrong. I don’t think anything on the earth made a sound for a minute or two. Matt looked at Aunt Sandra a long time ‘n’ said, “Murder?” He acted like maybe he wanted to say something more but he didn’t. He took Critter’s rope ‘n’ led him away towards the creek without sayin’ another word, like maybe he was disgusted.

I wanted to follow him but I didn’t. Somethin’ told me to let him go alone. When he disappeared, I turned to see Chester with his mouth hangin’ wide open. Nobody had said a word since Matt. I don’t think anybody knew what to say. Tater was takin’ in big gulps of air, ‘n’ Missy was kinda moanin’.

After a while Chester said, “Dat Missah Matt, he be the fightin’st man I ever seed. He kilt all nine a’ dese Indians ‘n’ never flinched a muscle.”

Uncle George said, “I think I got the one on the big bay but it doesn’t really matter. I have every confidence Mr. Grady would have gotten him if I hadn’t.”

Aunt Sandra held on to Uncle George’s arm ‘n’ said, “Oh, George, I can’t believe what just happened. This doesn’t even seem real.” She looked at the bodies layin’ all around.

Uncle George said, “It happened all right, my dear. And I have a feeling that, but for Mr. Grady, we would all be dead now. He did what he had to do. I think you were hard on him. Things are different out here.”

Papa said, “It warn’t jus’ the horse, Miss Sandra. Dem Indians was gonna take evathin’ afore they was done. Mistah Grady done us all a service. It was dem o’ us.”

Aunt Sandra said, “Perhaps you’re right, Papa.” She looked at Uncle George ‘n’ said, “Are you all right, George?”

“I’m fine, Dear, except I’ve never shot another man before and I don’t feel very good about that.”

Aunt Sandra put her arms around Uncle George ‘n’ hugged him real tight.

Ma said, “Mr. Grady - was he okay? He never did answer me.”

“I don’t know for sure,” said Uncle George. "He seemed all right when he walked off. If he’d been hurt, I’m sure he would have said something.”

Mama said, “Wid all dat shootin’, he bound to be hit by sumpthin’. Ah never heard da like, even when dat Yankee Sherman, came trew Joja.”

Chester said, “How can a man jus’ stan’ dere, all calm-like, ‘n’ keep shootin’ like he done? Ah was scared ta det, ‘n’ I was in da house behind a wall.”

Uncle George said, “I think Mr. Grady is not afraid to die. I think he’s just looking for a way to do it.”

Ma said, “George! How can you say such a thing? Mr. Grady is kind and thoughtful, and very good to all of us. He has friends here. That’s a silly notion.”

Uncle George looked at Ma a long time. “Then you tell me how a man can face down nine other men and calmly stand and shoot like he was in a gallery, while they’re shooting back at him?”

Ma said, “I don’t know, George. I don’t know.” She

turned to Aunt Sandra. “Sandra, I don't know why Mr. Grady shot all of them but I am sure he's no murderer.” Then she walked real fast into the cabin.

Aunt Sandra looked at Ma's back, real surprised-like.

Uncle George said, “We better bury the dead. Everybody grab a shovel.”

We buried all nine of ‘em a little ways from Pa's grave. We didn't know their names. We didn't even know if they was Apaches. Each grave got a little wooden board at the head that said “Unknown Indian, Killed July, 1865".

Chapter 21

It was way past dark when we finished buryin' them Indians 'n', I gotta say, I was awful sad about the whole situation. It was peculiar to touch a dead person. I know 'cause I had to help get 'em into the wagon an' to the graves. I didn't ever want to have to do it again.

We saw nothin' of Matt that night, nor the next day until about dusk, when he came in herdin' a bunch of our cattle. Judd was yippin' at the bunch-quitters 'n' Critter was keepin' a watchful eye.

Me 'n' Uncle George was up by the field when he brought 'em in. He had Judd take 'em south of the house where there was good water an' still some good graze. He rode up 'n' dismounted. "Howdy, George. Boy," he said.

"Hi, Matt," I said. I sure was glad to see him. I think he knew that.

"How are you, Mr. Grady?" said Uncle George.

"Fair to middlin', George. Sorry about not stayin' around to help you bury them Indians. I had to round up as many head as I could an' find a way to pen 'em in before we get hit with another storm."

"Do you know what kind of Indians they were, Mr. Grady?" asked Uncle George.

"That I do, George. They were Apaches."

Now I was for sure Cochise was gonna kill us all.

"Are you certain?" said Uncle George.

"Yep. They were Mimbrenos. They're a bit far west for Mimbrenos, but that's who they were."

With that news, I figured maybe Cochise might not be as mad at us as I thought he would at first.

"If they don't normally range this far west, what do you suppose they were doing here?" asked Uncle George.

Matt loosened the cinch strap on Critter 'n' patted him on the belly. "That I don't know. Maybe they figure it's safer here than it is near the Rio Grande. After all, Cochise and his people control all of this land around here and the Mimbrenos are close to the Chokonen - that's Cochise's band of Chiricahuas. The Mimbrenos are another band of the Chiricahuas. I think there are two or three more bands that are all part of what they call the Chiricahua Apache. The white man doesn't really understand how they're related and, more often than not, they call the same band by a bunch of different names. Anyway, they've banded together before to fight the white man. Last time I know of was a few years ago under Mangas Coloradas. Maybe they're gonna do it again, under Cochise this time."

"Do you really think so?" I asked. Now I wasn't so sure how Cochise might feel about this situation.

Matt smiled at me 'n' said, "Probably not. They might've figured since the Chokonen was raisin' such a ruckus over here, they could get in a little raidin' 'n' blame it on Cochise and his people."

"I bet that would make Cochise mad," I said.

Matt grinned real big 'n' said, "I think Cochise is already mad enough."

Uncle George said, "Mr. Grady, Sandra feels very badly about using the word 'murder' in connection with the shootings. She feels so badly about it she's afraid to face you."

"That's okay, George. You tell her I understand."

"That's decent of you, Mr. Grady. I will tell her."

Matt looked at Uncle George a minute, then said,"George, if I could have done it any other way, I would have."

"I'm sure of that, Mr. Grady."

"Just so you'll understand why I did what I did, I'll tell you what happened."

"You don't have to explain yourself, Mr. Grady."

"Maybe not, but I want to."

Uncle George kinda nodded.

Matt said, "I speak their language pretty well. Their leader, the one who tried to ride Critter, told me he was gonna take your horses and women. I told him there would be a fight and at least some of his people would surely be hurt, even if they killed all of us. He said he would take my horse instead if we would not put up a fight. I agreed. Trouble is, Critter didn't. At that point, I knew he was gonna shoot my horse an' try to take Miss Sandra an' Miss Penny. Them Indians didn't really leave me much of a selection when it came right down to it, George."

For a long time Uncle George didn't say anything. Finally, he said, "You were going to give up that fine horse for only two women?"

Matt smiled. "It was kind of a silly notion, wasn't it?"

Both him 'n' Uncle George laughed.

"Are you hungry, Mr. Grady?" asked Uncle George.

"For the kind of cookin' that goes on around here? What kind of question is that? I'm starvin'."

Uncle George patted Matt on the back 'n' said, "Let's go eat."

Uncle George sure musta liked Matt a lot 'cause I never saw him pat another man on the back. I was glad for that.

We ate outside of Tater's cabin that evening. Sometimes we'd do that, you know, change supper from one house to the other. It was fun for all of us 'cause the cookin' was different at each house, though I gotta say, Aunt Sandra wasn't as good a cook as Ma or Mama but she was improvin'. On this night we had some smoked ham that Papa had been savin' for a special occasion 'n' I guess he figured this was a special occasion for some reason. When he saw Matt, I swear I saw his eyes tear up a little. That old man sure liked Matt. Come to think of it, you had to like Matt. He never did nothin' but good for folks, 'cept for killin' them Indians what was gonna kill us. It weren't much good for the Indians but it was good for the rest of us.

After supper Papa took out his banjo 'n' Billy Jo his mouth organ an' they played some more of them songs that I liked so much. Ma 'n' Aunt Sandra had taught 'em some of the songs that they knew 'n' Papa 'n' Billy Jo played those too. Everybody sang together 'n' we all had a lot of fun. I felt real close to all of 'em. Matt even sang a little. He sang soft, so's hardly nobody could hear him, but I heard him 'n' he had a pretty good singin' voice too.

After a while Matt drifted off to his little wickiup, sayin' he had a bunch more strays to bring in tomorrow. We sang songs for almost another hour then we was all tired 'n' went to bed.

The next mornin' I went out with Matt to look for strays. We were south of our place about a mile or two when Matt reined up 'n' dismounted. He took out his knife 'n' cut a red bulb off the top of one of them prickly pear cactus things 'n' slit it down the middle. It was a deep reddish-purple color inside 'n' had lots of little black seeds in it. He scooped out a bunch of the fruit inside 'n' put it in his mouth. I could see he was workin' them seeds outa the fruit 'n' pretty soon he spit out a bunch of 'em 'n' swallowed the fruit. Then he took out another chunk of fruit with his knife 'n' handed it to me.

"It's like eatin' a little watermelon, only I like the prickly pear better. Spit out the seeds an' tell me what you think."

I took that stuff in my mouth off the end of that knife real ginger-like 'n' got to workin' them seeds real good. I could tell the flavor was delicious. I spit out the seeds 'n' swallowed the fruit. "That was good," I said 'n' dismounted, figurin' to cut me one of them things for myself.

"Easy, boy. They got tiny little stickers in 'em that you can hardly see. You gotta be real careful how you handle 'em. It's okay to eat 'em the way we just did but it's better to have a small fire so you can burn the stickers off. Then you can eat 'em like an apple."

He picked up a few dead mesquite branches 'n' built a small fire. While the fire was startin' up, he said, "We'll pick a bunch an burn the stickers off, then I can tie 'em in a gunny sack behind my saddle. You reckon your Ma might make a jam of 'em?"

"You bet she will," I said.

After we had the first few prickly pear fruit ready for the gunny sack, Matt gave one to Critter for every ten we put in the sack. Matt said it was what Critter charged for carryin' prickly pear fruit. Judd got a couple too. He wasn't as greedy as Critter.

When we had the gunny sack full, we searched the desert 'n' hills, findin' sixteen head of cattle which we drove back to the ranch. Funny how I was startin' to think of it as a ranch. In Ohio, nobody owned a ranch. They all owned farms, even if they just owned livestock. Folks talked different out west 'n' I guess I was becomin' a westerner.

Everybody thought them prickly pear fruits was wonderful delicious. When Ma found out they was only ripe once a year- in August or September - she organized all the women 'n' girls to go pick 'em in the mornin' so's she could make jams 'n' preserves.

It turned out that Chester had learned somethin' of blacksmithin' on the plantation where he grew up 'n' when Matt found this out, he wanted to make a trip into La Messilla to get some more "improvements" but he couldn't get away just yet on account of the cattle 'n' the summer storms.

I wasn't for sure what kind of arrangements Matt had made with everybody about them cattle, but he didn't pick out any land 'n' he didn't separate his cattle from ours. They was all just bunched up together. One day, I overheard Matt talkin' to Uncle George.

Matt said, "That's the way I feel about it, George. You're gonna have to register a brand 'n' get them hides scorched. Folks will be comin' this way before long now that the war is over. You'll need a way of keepin' your cattle separate from others."

"I agree with you, Mr. Grady, but you have kept no cattle for yourself."

Matt grinned 'n' said, "I reckon that's your responsibility. I just want twenty percent of the profit from the first sale, from both you and Papa's family. He gets thirty head and you get seventy-five. I can't register a brand. They'll want to see my parole papers."

Uncle George said, "Surely, Mr. Grady, it's just a formality by now. If you sign the surrender papers, you will have all the rights accorded any United States Citizen."

Matt lost his grin 'n' said, "George, I have no desire to be a United States Citizen. You think about a trip to Tucson to register a brand an' let me know." He turned 'n' walked towards the creek.

Uncle George shook his head 'n' said, "I wish Mr. Grady could forgive and forget."

I said, "Forgive 'n' forget what, Uncle George?"

"Forgive our government and forget the war." Uncle George walked up the little grade to his cabin 'n' I sat there on a stump, thinkin' about what Uncle George had said.

He was right about that, I think. The only time Matt

wasn't the Matt I liked was when somebody talked about Yankees or surrender. Whenever that happened, Matt seemed like he was a different person. It scared me a little. Not for me, 'cause I knew Matt would never hurt me or any of us. But I was afraid for Matt. Don't ask me why 'cause I can't explain it.

I didn't see where he came from, but Judd was sittin' next to me. I reached out an' petted him. He wagged his tail once. I squeezed him around the neck 'n' patted him some more. Judd 'n' me was becomin' good friends.

Chapter 22

Me 'n' Matt was out south of our place quite a distance, lookin' for the last few missin' head of cattle. It was awful hot 'n' I was wantin' to head back to the creek 'n' cool off a mite. We was pushin' three head in front of us - well, Judd was doin' all the pushin'. Me 'n' Matt just kind of rode along. Anyway, I noticed Matt rein in 'n' study the lowland south of us. I watched his face for a few seconds then looked in the direction he was lookin'. I barely saw a wagon 'n' a few horses with riders. They was raisin' a bunch of dust, 'n' they was headed our way. Behind 'em, maybe a half a mile, was a bunch more riders, maybe twenty or so. Looked like they was tryin' to catch the wagon 'n' the riders that was with it.

I heard Matt mutter somethin'. Couldn't rightly tell what it was 'n' it's probably a good thing too. Then he pulled that Whitworth rifle from its rawhide scabbard 'n' dismounted. He knelt behind a low fork in a tree 'n' pointed the rifle at the lowlands whilst he rested the barrel in the fork. Mostly, he carried his Henry, but he brought the Whitworth on this day 'cause he was gonna teach me about long-range shootin'. He pulled a little cigar from his shirt pocket 'n' unsheathed his Bowie knife 'n' cut a little piece off one end, then lit the cigar with a match he pulled out of his match safe from the same pocket. He puffed on it a few times, till it was lit proper, then he stuffed it into the ground next to him with the lit end up. He watched the smoke drift from the cigar for a few seconds then put his shoulder into the stock of his rifle. I could barely see the horses 'n' people. They weren't no bigger than little dots 'n' I figured Matt was gonna wait until they got a lot closer before he fired. It sure surprised me when that big ol' rifle went off. I liked to wet my britches.

I looked down at all those horses 'n' people 'n' still couldn't tell much. They was an awful long ways off yet. Nothin' happened right away 'n' I figured Matt had missed whatever he was shootin' at. Then the horse leadin' the second bunch of riders fell 'n' its rider went rollin' across the desert for a spell. The fella got up 'n' stood real still. All the rest of the riders in that second bunch stopped chasin' the wagon 'n' rode up to that fella whose horse had fallen. The wagon 'n' the three riders with it kept comin' our way. I don't think they even knew we was there yet. They was just headin' for the hills to escape them other fellas.

Matt pulled his lookin' glass out of his saddlebag 'n' stretched it out. He was lookin' real quiet 'n' still at all them fellas down in the desert. I looked too but without the lookin' glass, I couldn't tell much of nothin'.

When I looked back at Matt, he was packin' a ball down the barrel of the Whitworth. At least I thought it was a ball, but I took a quick look just before he shoved the paper cartridge down the barrel. It wasn't a round ball at all. It was long an' had six sides to it that looked like somebody had put it in a vise an' twisted it a mite. So that was how come the rifle had a hexagon bore. It shot hexagon bullets, just like Uncle George had said! I'd never seen a bore like that before the Whitworth an' wondered if maybe somebody hadn't made some kind of serious mistake. It didn't seem to bother Matt none. He rammed the bullet home then took aim. I was ready for it this time when the rifle fired. I looked back down to the bunch of men gathered around the fella who was standin' on the ground . Nothin' happened for a few seconds, then, all of a sudden, one of the horses fell. Its rider jumped off before the horse hit the ground. Then everybody scattered like rabbits runnin' from a fox.

Matt sat behind the tree 'n' took off his hat 'n' wiped his

brow a bit. He smiled at me 'n' said, "Well, boy. I think you better go back to the house 'n' fetch me four of those horses we took from them dead Indians. Bring the best of the bunch, 'ceptin' for that bay mare that Billy Jo picked."

"What are you gonna do?" I asked.

"I hope I'm gonna make peace with Cochise. Take Judd with you an' leave the cattle. I'll be needin' them too."

My legs plumb gave out. "Cochise?" I said as the seat of my britches hit the ground.

"Yeah. I do believe that's Cochise and a few of his band."

I knew it. I knew someday Cochise was gonna get me 'n' it looked like this was the day. I couldn't leave Matt alone, even though I was scared to death. I don't know where I found the strength in my legs but I sure enough did, 'n' I got up 'n' ran over to Patches 'n' took my carbine out of the scabbard Matt had made me outa that steer he had skinned. My hands was shakin' so bad I almost dropped it.

"What are you doin', boy?" asked Matt.

"I ain't leavin' you here by yourself with all them Apaches down there. I ain't gonna do it!"

I don't know for sure what I expected Matt to do when I said that but it was probably somethin' like maybe him sayin', "Thanks, boy. Together we can whip 'em all." 'Course that ain't what happened.

"Boy, we got only one chance to come out of this. And I'm countin' on you. You gotta get four of them horses back to me as fast as you can. That's Cochise down there. And he knows we're here. This won't be a surprise like with them other Indians. Take a good look, boy. You might not be able to tell from this distance, but those Apaches down there are some of the best soldiers in the world. Now get to work." He turned his head. "Judd. Go with Crawford."

My hands wasn't shakin' quite as bad when I put the

carbine back in the scabbard. I mounted Patches 'n' looked at Matt real long, not for sure I would ever see 'im again. "Don't get killed, Matt," I said. I was pert near cryin'.

Matt grinned real big 'n' said, "I'll do my best, boy. Now get out of here."

I rode like the wind. Judd was doin' his best to keep up, 'n' he'd pass me from time-to-time when we hit a wash or draw, then we'd hit a flat 'n' me 'n' Patches would pass him back. I got hit in the face a few times by mesquite branches, 'n' one of 'em pert near unseated me, but I hung on 'n' kept urgin' Patches to run faster. I felt blood runnin' down my cheek where the branches had hit me but my face was so numb I didn't feel any pain.

I was hollerin' so loud when I got near the house that everybody came a runnin' 'n' they was all carryin' weapons of one sort or another. I jumped offa Patches before she ground to a halt an' somersaulted about three times before comin' to a stop.

Ma was the first to reach me 'n' she put her arms around me 'n' asked what was wrong 'n' was I hurt an' she went to wipin' my face with a kerchief.

"It's Cochise!" I blurted. "They was this wagon 'n' three riders 'n' twenty or more Apaches. Matt shot two of their horses 'n' the Apaches stopped but the wagon kept goin'. Matt told me to get four of the best horses we have 'n' get 'em back to him as fast as I could." I said it all in one breath.

"Good Lord!" said Uncle George. "Chester, get four of those horses. The chestnut, the dun and two of the sorrels."

"Yes Sir, Missah George," said Chester.

Everybody was runnin' around, roundin' up horses 'n' ammunition. I was still catchin' my breath when I realized that Patches was plumb give out. I got to my feet 'n' loosened the cinch.

"Crawford. What are you doing?" said Ma.

"I gotta get another horse, Ma. Matt's out there all by hisself. I gotta go help him." I know there was a note of beggin' in my voice but I couldn't help it. Matt was the biggest part of my life besides Ma 'n' Mel.

Ma looked at me for a second then said, "Come on, I'll help you saddle another horse." I sure loved my ma. She was the greatest ma in the world.

We was all ready in five minutes or less. I led the way 'cause I knowed it, but I couldn't go as fast as I'd come ridin' in on account of we was leadin' horses 'n' Ma 'n' Aunt Sandra was with us. The only ones we left behind was Missy, 'n' Mama, 'n' Mel, 'n' Tater 'n' Ebony. Tater was real mad about that.

I don't know how long it took us to get back to the spot where I'd last seen Matt but it musta been close to half an hour. When we got close, I slowed a bit 'n' told everybody we was gettin' close. Next thing I knowed, Matt was standin' in a little clearin'.

"Howdy," he said, grinnin', like he almost always did.

We all stopped in our tracks 'n' just sat there.

"You might wanna dismount an' let them horses blow. Looks like they could use a rest," said Matt.

"Are you all right, Mr. Grady?" said Uncle George.

"That I am, George. And I'll be even better if you brought some good horses."

"We brought the best we have," said Uncle George.

"I reckon that'll have to do. Now, if you'll just give me a minute or two, I'm hopin' to resolve this situation," said Matt.

"Mr. Grady, Crawford said you were fighting Apaches," said Ma.

"Not yet, Miss Penny. I'm tryin' to avoid that. If you will all just sit and rest your horses, I'll take the four extras." He walked up to Chester 'n' took the lead ropes. Next thing, he was disappearin' into the trees.

We all dismounted 'n' Uncle George made us form a fightin' line behind a bunch of trees 'n' then we just sat 'n' waited. We was all a mite nervous, not knowin' what was goin' on outa sight behind them trees.

I couldn't hardly stand the not knowin', so I slipped away from our fightin' line an' skirted the right side of our position. After a spell, I came to the crest of a hill an' hid behind a big rock. Below me, maybe sixty or seventy yards, was Matt an' them Apaches. I couldn't hear much of anything that was bein' said 'cause I was too far away but, every once in a while, the breeze musta been just right or somethin' 'cause I could catch a few words. It didn't do me no good though, 'cause Matt an' the tall Apache was talkin' a foreign language. I reckoned it was Apache.

I got to worryin' that Ma or Uncle George might find out I wasn't where I was supposed to be an' get to frettin', an' it didn't look like them Apaches was gonna kill Matt, so I went back to our fightin' line. Nobody had even knowed I'd been gone.

It musta been close to half-an-hour before Matt walked back into the clearing. We was still hidin' behind the trees when he said, "There won't be any need for shootin'. As a matter-of-fact, with your permission, I've asked Cochise to meet with all of you. He said he would if you are in agreement."

I wasn't so sure I liked this idea.

"Meet with Cochise? *The* Cochise?" said Uncle George.

"The one and only," said Matt.

"Do you think it safe, Mr. Grady?" asked Ma.

"Cochise gave his word no harm would come to any of us," said Matt.

"Can he be trusted?" asked Aunt Sandra. She was tough for a woman, but I could see she was a little worried.

Matt grinned 'n' said, "More than any man I ever met."

"That's good enough for me," said Uncle George. "Tell him we would be honored."

Matt said, "It might be good if you all stepped into the clearing an' pointed your weapons down a mite." Then he turned 'n' disappeared into the trees again. In a few minutes he was back, an' right behind him came twenty of the toughest-lookin' Indians I ever saw. 'Course I hadn't seen many Indians but they was tough enough, I promise. And they was all mounted. I noticed one of 'em was ridin' the dun we had brought from the house.

The Apache ridin' the dun slid from the horse's back 'n' stood next to Matt. Matt made a motion with his left hand. "Folks, this is Cochise." Matt turned to Cochise 'n' said somethin' in a language I didn't understand. I recognized all of our names mixed in with the other words but that was about all I got out of it.

We all kind of stood there, struck plain dumb. Cochise was taller than the other Apaches 'n' kind of handsome in a rough sort of way. He was dressed in cotton britches 'n' shirt, 'n' he had a cloth in front 'n' back of his waist. He carried a breechloadin' carbine of some kind.

Uncle George was the first to speak. He stepped forward 'n' offered his hand. "I'm pleased to meet you, Sir," he said.

Cochise looked down at Uncle George's hand 'n' sort of smiled. He took it 'n' shook it up 'n' down real hard a few times.

I know Uncle George was pleased to meet Cochise certain 'cause not many white men met him 'n' ever lived to brag about it. Not that Uncle George would brag about it 'cause he wouldn't, but that don't make no never mind. If he was shakin' Cochise's hand that meant he was still alive, just like the rest of us. An' that really confused me 'cause I'd never heard any man, Indian or white, ever cursed as evil like Cochise was. I kept watchin' Cochise 'n' the rest of them

Apaches real close, lookin' for any sign of a trick. I was about as nervous as a cricket in a hen house an' twice as jumpy. Seems like every move one of them Apaches made had me jumpin' to see what he was doin'.

Cochise shook hands with Chester 'n' Billy Jo 'n' Papa. He looked at 'em real hard 'n', then, the next thing I knew, that tall Indian was standin' smack smooth in front of me 'n' lookin' down at me like he was on a mountain top. I was in his shadow 'n' it seemed to cool off a mite with him shadin' the sun.

"You are Crawford?" His voice liked to scared me to death. He didn't say it mean or nothin' like that but he had a strange kind of accent an' it seemed like his words was shorter than when I said the same words.

"Yessir," I said. I tried to sound brave but I don't think it came out that way.

I'm right certain I saw him smile. He must 'ave 'cause he didn't kill me or stab me or nothin' like that. I looked over at Matt, who was just a bit left of Cochise 'n' I realized that Matt was grinnin' from ear to ear. About that time, I also realized Cochise had his hand out, waitin' for me to shake it. I put my hand out 'n' Cochise pert near tore it off my arm, he shook it so hard. When I stopped bouncin' up 'n' down after he let go of my hand, I said, "Pleased to meet you, Sir." Just like Uncle George had said.

"You are brave boy," said Cochise.

"Yessir," I said. I didn't want to brag but I sure wasn't gonna tell him he was wrong. I didn't know what else to say.

"He sure is," said Matt with a big smile. Then his face got real serious. "But sometimes he doesn't obey orders and gets to hidin' behind boulders with his carbine where he makes a real good target for lookouts."

I thought sure I was gonna faint dead away. So, them Apaches had lookouts an' they knew I was there all the time, an' coulda killed me anytime they wanted. I didn't have long to think about my close shave with dyin' though.

Cochise looked right into my eyes 'n' said. "Did you help Matt Grady shoot my horse?"

That about did it for me. My legs got that real puny feelin' in 'em 'n' I knew I was a goner for sure. I didn't actually help Matt but I sure didn't try to stop him.

Matt cleared his throat. "He didn't know at the time it was you, Cochise, or I'm sure he would have told me not to shoot."

Colchise grunted 'n' said somethin' in Apache.

Matt answered him in Apache. At least I reckoned it to be Apache.

Cochise turned to Matt 'n' smiled an' I felt a little strength comin' back into my legs.

Matt kinda faced us all 'n' said, "I reckon you folks are a might confused about the goin's on here, so I'll try to explain."

We all kinda took up comfortable positions so we could hold our breaths 'n' listen real close.

Matt said, "When I first saw the Apaches chasin' that wagon an' them riders, I didn't know it was Cochise. 'Course I don't know that would have made much of a difference." He glanced at Cochise real quick. "I figured if I could shoot the horse out from under the lead Apache at that range, they wouldn't even hear the shot 'n' maybe they'd give up the chase, not knowin' how many of me there was or where I was hidin'. I had to take the second horse to let 'em know I was serious.

"I had taken out my eyeglass between shots an' recognized Cochise."

Ma said, "You *recognized* Cochise? Have you met him before, Mr. Grady?"

Matt kinda looked a little shy 'n' said, "Well, truth be known, Miss Penny, I'm a brother to one of Cochise's sons."

"Brother to *one* of his sons?" Sounded to me like Ma was askin' too many questions.

"Yes, Ma'am. You see, when I was a youngster, I rode up on an Apache boy that had broken his leg pretty bad in a scrape with a mountain lion. He wasn't dead yet an' neither was the lion. All I had was an old single-shot musket. I shot the lion instead of the Apache. Turns out the Apache was Taza, one of Cochise's sons. I got him back to Cochise and his people all in one piece an' I been Taza's brother ever since." Matt only paused a second then said, "Now, you gotta understand, this was in the days before that Yankee lieutenant hung Cochise's people, and Cochise and his people were friendly to the whites at that time. Matter-of-fact, Cochise had a wood-cutting contract at the stage station in Apache Pass once."

For a long time nobody said a word. Finally, Uncle George said, "Patches. Where did you get her?"

Matt grinned 'n' looked at me. "Remember the mountain lion, boy?"

I nodded. I wasn't yet able to speak.

"I traded ol' Taza outa his best mare with that hide. Told you it was big medicine."

Then it hit me. I owned a horse that once belonged to the mighty Apache. The son of Cochise even. I looked up at Cochise. "Does Taza want his horse back?"

"She not Taza horse. She Crawford horse." A shorter, stouter Apache walked up next to Cochise.

Matt said, "Boy, meet Taza."

Chapter 23

Taza was real strong-lookin', like maybe he could kill anybody he wanted to just by lookin' at 'em. I was right glad he didn't look at me like he wanted to kill me 'cause I would'a' been an easy target right about then. He shook my hand an' when he let go, I weren't real sure it was still on the end of my arm until I looked down an' saw it was still there.

We had a real nice visit with Cochise 'n' his warriors for a spell, then Matt said he 'n' Critter 'n' Judd was gonna go look for the wagon an' them three riders. Cochise musta offered to help in Apache but Matt said he didn't think that was such a good idea. I had plumb forgot about the wagon in all the excitement of seein' Cochise.

Matt rode off 'n' I got nervous again. Without him bein' there, I wasn't so sure Cochise wouldn't change his mind 'n' scalp us all. I wasn't the only one thinkin' that way either. Chester was all bug-eyed 'n' he was breathin' kinda funny. Uncle George 'n' Papa seemed to be the only two that wasn't real nervous.

After a while I got to feelin' more comfortable 'n' tried to talk to Taza. He spoke English, but he was hard to understand, but I got most of what he said, or at least I think I did. He told me all about the mountain lion Matt had shot in "the olden days" 'n' how Matt was a friend to the Chiricahua. He said he had give Matt the Mexican name of El Gato. Cochise told me that was Mexican an' it meant "the Cat". That's when I first really started to thinkin' of Cochise 'n' his people as Chiricahua Apaches instead of just plain old Apaches. Matt later told me that Cochise and his people were Chokonon Chiricahuas.

Seems like them Chiricahuas was a big family of about five different tribes or something like that.

Taza showed me his rifle ‘n’ I showed him my carbine. He was a growed man like Matt but, in some ways, he seemed more like my age. I started to likin’ him a little bit, even though I was scared of him. Him an’ some of the others showed me some ridin’ tricks, like pickin’ up another man at a gallop ‘n’ leanin’ under the horse’s neck to shoot. They even speared cactus at a full gallop with the long lances they carried. That was scary. I took note that when some of the Apaches talked to Cochise they called him Cheis. Later, Matt told me that’s what his people called him. He said the name meant “strong, like an oak.”

Cochise tried to talk to Papa ‘n’ Chester a lot. He knew English pretty good but I think the Georgia accent was hard for him to understand an’ the goin’ was slow. He stared at ‘em too. I guess his ma hadn’t ever told him it was impolite or something. Cochise wanted to know how Chester’s skin got to be so dark. Papa told him they was all born that way but I don’t think Cochise believed him.

It was only about an hour before sunset when Matt came ridin’ in, leadin’ the wagon ‘n’ three riders. They was Mexicans. Uncle George had told me how Apaches hated Mexicans ‘n’ Mexicans hated Apaches ‘n’ I figured the fight was gonna start all over again but it didn’t. Them Mexicans was scared sure enough though. I could see it plain on all their faces, but Cochise ‘n’ his warriors didn’t do nothin’ more than keep a sharp eye on ‘em.

When the driver of the wagon, a man about fifteen years or so older ‘n’ my pa, pulled the wagon to a stop, I could see a bunch of people under the canvas. They all popped their heads out at about the same time ‘n’ I was surprised to see a lady about the same age as the driver, ‘n’ two kids ‘n’ a woman about Ma’s age.. The kids looked like maybe the oldest, a boy, was maybe eight or nine, 'n' the youngest, a girl, was six or seven. The three riders was two men an' a women dressed like a man. They was all about Ma's age, maybe a few years younger.

Them horses was still lathered up good 'n' I reckoned they'd been worked pretty hard that day.

Matt said, "Folks, this is the Peralta outfit. We'll get around to formal introductions later, seein' as they don't speak much English."

He turned to Cochise 'n' started speakin' that funny language again. After a while Cochise turned to his Apaches 'n' spoke some to 'em. Whatever he said seemed agreeable to 'em 'cause they was all noddin' 'n' smilin'. Cochise said somethin' to one of the Indians 'n' he walked to his horse 'n' rode off without so much as a backward glance. Cochise said somethin' to Matt 'n' Matt turned to the Mexicans 'n' started speakin' Mexican. Sounded to me like he spoke it real good. 'Course I didn't really know for sure.

Seems like the Mexicans weren't as scared after Matt finished talkin'. They was even smilin'.

Then Matt turned to Uncle George. "George, I hope I haven't overstepped my authority."

"What have you said, Man?" I could tell Uncle George wasn't too sure about what was goin' on at this point.

Matt looked at Ma 'n' then Aunt Sandra. "I hope I haven't put too much of a burden on you, Miss Penny, Miss Sandra."

Ma said, "What is it, Mr. Grady?"

"I asked everyone to stay up near our place tonight 'n' tomorrow. I told them we'd butcher a beef 'n' the two horses I shot an' have a big meal. I told 'em the final decision was yours. I'll pay for the steer, Miss Penny. "

Ma stepped right up to him. I wasn't quite sure myself what she was gonna do. "You'll do no such thing, Mr. Grady.

Those cattle are as much yours as they are ours. And if it weren't for you, we wouldn't have any of them." She looked first at Cochise, then to the Mexicans. "You are all welcome."

Cochise 'n' some of his people knew what she said right off but the Mexicans was havin' a hard time understandin'. Matt looked at 'em 'n' smiled 'n' said somethin' in Mexican 'n' I could hear the thanks rollin' off 'em in the forms of smiles 'n' sighin' 'n' what not. It made me feel real good. I felt real sorry for them Mexicans. They'd been scared as much as me 'n' maybe more, since they didn't know Matt 'n' Critter 'n' Judd. An' they looked pretty hungry to me. I wished I had somethin' right then 'n' there to give 'em to eat but I didn't.

Uncle George looked at Matt. "You told them the final decision was Penny's?"

Matt almost laughed. "I didn't reckon they'd skin someone like Miss Penny as fast as they might you if they didn't like the answer."

Uncle George thought about it a minute, real serious-like, 'n' finally he got to grinnin' 'n' pretty soon it turned into a laugh. Cochise was watchin' the whole thing 'n' I don't reckon much got by him. He started laughin' too, 'n' then a few of his Indians took it up, 'n' pretty soon the Mexicans was laughin' too. I ain't sure how many of 'em knowed why they was laughin' but I guess it didn't really matter. At least they wasn't tryin' to kill each other.

We all went to the big cottonwoods by the creek near our house. After Missy 'n' Tater 'n' Mama 'n' Mel 'n' Ebony got over the shock of all them Apaches, we all built little fires 'n' cooked beans 'n' bacon 'n' pan biscuits. At first, everybody kinda stuck with their own kind. It was us 'n' the Apaches 'n' the Mexicans. Then Matt moved from fire to fire, draggin' a couple from each group to the other until we was all mixed up. I heard him tell Cochise in English that it was an old Scottish custom. I don't know if Cochise knowed what that meant or not. I sure didn't.

That was one of the strangest nights I ever knowed. I was scared an' yet I wasn't. I met new friends 'n' tried to learn Mexican 'n' Apache 'n' teach English. I learned the names of the Mexicans but it would take a while to remember 'em all. I know that don't make a lot of sense but that's the way it was.

When the evenin' was pretty late, the Apaches moved away from the creek 'n' rolled out what little they had with 'em for sleepin', an' it weren't much. Ma 'n' Aunt Sandra 'n' Mama gave what extra blankets we had 'n' the Mexicans gave some too. The Mexicans drew their wagon closer to our house 'n' bedded down in or under it.

The next mornin' I was up at first light. I stepped outside to use the privy, but when I took a look at the Indians surroundin' our place, I plumb forgot about the call of nature. There musta been three hundred or more, an' most was mounted.

Chapter 24

I was mid-step, right in front of our door. My right foot seemed like it didn't wanna touch the ground. I didn't know if I wanted to run or hide or what. It didn't seem like there was much use in tryin' anything. There was just too many Indians. I thought for a minute that I might make it into the house 'n' get my carbine 'n' maybe get off a shot before they killed me but I weren't none too sure of that. It didn't seem all that likely, the more I thought about it.

None of them Indians made a move. They just sat there in the grey light of dawn 'n' watched me. I figured right then to die like a man. I wouldn't give 'em no satisfaction at seein' me beg for my life, even though I sure wanted to. I wasn't gonna be no coward within sight of my Pa's grave. I finally managed to put my right foot down.

"Crawford." I knew it was Cochise without ever seein' him. He had a way of speakin' that only he had.

I looked off to my left, 'n' there he stood, his rifle in his hand. 'Course, I didn't know at the time that a Chiricahua Apache never went anywhere without his rifle, so I figured Cochise was gonna kill me hisself. I turned to face him like I know my Pa woulda done. I just stood there, waitin' for the end. There weren't no use in tryin' to rouse Ma or the others. It would probably be better if they didn't have the time to worry about dyin'.

Cochise waved his free hand. "These are my people. I bring them here so they know this place. Your people are safe from all Chiricahua who know this place."

I think it was about that time that I completed nature's call. At least I thought I might have. I almost fainted dead away at the very least. I managed to say, "Thank you, Sir."

"You are a brave little warrior." He seemed to be tryin' to find more English words. He couldn't 'n' so he finished in his own tongue.

"Much respect." Matt's voice came to me from the end of the house. "He said he has much respect for the brave little man."

"Can I go to the privy now?" I said.

"I think you better," said Matt.

I took off lickety-split.

By the time I got back to the house, everyone was up. The Apaches was mainly near the creek but Cochise an' Taza an' a young Apache, maybe ten or thereabouts, was talkin' to Matt near the corral. Matt spotted me an' waved me to him.

When I stopped next to him, he said, "Boy, this young fella here is Na'itche, Cochise's youngest son. He brought him along because he wanted you to know him. He thinks you can be friends."

Na'itche was tall an' slender, nothin' like Taza, an' he was sure a lot younger. He looked a lot more like Cochise than Taza too. I held out my hand. Na'itche looked at it for a spell, then he looked at Cochise. Cochise gave a little nod an' Na'itche took my hand an' shook it. He sure shook hands different than Taza an' Cochise an' I'm just as glad for it 'cause I didn't have to look at the end of my arm when we was done shakin' to see if my hand was still attached.

About this time, Tater came strollin' up an' I made him an Na'itche shake hands. Next thing I knowed, the three of us walked down to the creek an' skipped rocks. Na'itche was pretty good at it, an' he did better than me an' Tater. I didn't see no difference in him an' me an' Tater an' I think Na'itche knew that, for we became friends right off.

Na'itche spoke pretty good English an' didn't have such an accent as Taza, an' he was a lot easier to understand. He sure seemed different than Cochise an' Taza in a lot of other ways too. Cochise an' Taza was both tough an' scary but Na'itche weren't scary even a little bit. He was just like me 'n' Tater, 'ceptin' his pa was right fierce an' famous.

Ma made as many eggs as she had 'n' rationed 'em out as far as they would go. The Apaches had brought some venison, 'n' prickly pear fruit. Mama made a bunch of biscuits an' Ma got out some of her prickly pear jam. It took a long time to get everybody fed but the Apaches was special impressed by Ma's jam. They couldn't figure how she made it.

Matt snatched a couple of biscuits when he thought nobody was lookin' 'n' took 'em to Judd 'n' Critter. I never saw him eat anything that mornin'. I guess he figured he gave his share to Critter 'n' Judd. Preparations was already underway for the afternoon meal before we was done eatin' breakfast. Chester slaughtered a beef 'n' the Lincolns 'n' Mexicans started makin' stuff up right away. Ma 'n' Aunt Sandra helped.

The Apaches had brought one of the two dead horses up from the lowland 'n' dressed it up real proper. I think they took the other one to their camp. The carcass was hangin' from cottonwood limbs over by the creek. I'd never seen a horse hangin' up all dressed out like a deer before 'n' it was a strange sight. I wasn't too keen on eatin' horse but I knew for sure I'd eat a whole one if Cochise asked me to. Matt said they had took the other horse to the women.

It was about this time I realized there weren't no women with the Apaches. I asked Matt about this 'n' he said that Cochise had only brought the men 'cause he wanted them all to know this place so we would be left in peace. The women 'n' children 'n' a few warriors were at a rancheria someplace. Later, I learned that a rancheria was a place where they set up a camp 'n' lived there for as long as they could before runnin' out of food or bein' found by the cavalry. That didn't seem right to me.

Me 'n' Tater 'n' Billy Jo showed Na'itche an' the Mexican kids - the boy's name was Pancho and the girl's was Christina, but everyone called her Tina - our favorite play places near the creek. There was an old dead tree that had fallen across the creek 'n' sat about five feet above the water. Beneath it there was a deep enough pool for jumpin' without hittin' bottom most of the time, 'n' so we did - all of us. It was real cold at first but once you got used to it, you didn't pay it no mind. We had great fun 'n' I wasn't feelin' so different from Na'itche an' the Mexicans anymore, even though I couldn't understand the Mexicans when they talked. We was all workin' on that though.

Judd came to the creek 'n' jumped offa that dead tree more than all of us put together. He musta thought it was a bunch of fun too, 'cause he pushed me 'n' Tater off the tree a few times by slammin' into our legs with his rump then jumpin' in after us. Critter stood at the edge of the creek 'n' kinda gave us all the evil eye. After a while, he waded in 'n' stood there, withers-deep, in our pool. No amount of coaxin' would get him to move. He just stood there, blockin' us all from jumpin'. After a bit, Pancho decided he would jump anyway. I tried to warn him but he didn't speak no English 'n' he jumped in, landin' right close to Critter. I was for certain that Critter would stomp him to the bottom but he didn't. He just stood there like he was enjoyin' life in general 'n' the creek in particular. Pretty soon we was all jumpin' in next to Critter an', the next thing you know, we was climbin' all over his back, for it was easy enough to do in such deep water. Critter hardly moved a muscle. He seemed to enjoy it as much as we did. That Critter was one strange horse.

Judd stood on the tree 'n' yapped at Critter once or twice but Critter didn't pay him no mind. This musta made

Judd mad ‘cause he jumped on Critter's back ‘n’ stood there. Even then Critter didn't do no more than turn his head a bit ‘n’ lower his ears a tad. Judd finally jumped into the water, paddled to the bank, an’ made another run at the tree. He'd jump from the tree to Critter's back, then into the water ‘n’ swim to the bank ‘n’ do it all over again. That was one fine time we all had that day.

When it came time to eat, us kids was near starvin’ from all the swimmin’ ‘n’ playin’. And such food I ain't never seen before. There was beef stew, made with vegetables from our field, ‘n’ steaks, ‘n’ roast, ‘n’ liver, ‘n’ ribs, ‘n’ stuff I'd never heard of. Mama had made somethin’ called tripe, ‘n’ the Mexicans had made some kind of shredded beef thing with chiles in it. The Mexicans also made tortillas. I figured that was good enough reason to let ‘em stay on our place, for I surely liked them tortillas.

We all had corn - Pa's corn - the best there ever was, ‘n’ I bet he woulda been proud to know he was feedin’ Cochise with that corn. We had tomatoes too. There was even a few scrub potatoes. The Apaches had cooked up the horse just like a cow. They had horse steaks ‘n’ ribs ‘n’ roast ‘n’ everything. They used a lot of black pepper ‘n’ cooked it over an open fire. I tried a little of it ‘n’ I gotta say, it wasn't too bad. I liked the beef the best though. It was about the best meal I had ever ate. I wasn't afraid of the Apaches anymore. They was people too. Life was very good for me on this day.

Chapter 25

It was pretty late when everybody finished eatin', 'n' I don't think any of us ever had a better supper. I noticed the Apaches was even talkin' to the Mexicans by the time it was dark, though I ain't real sure the Mexicans trusted 'em. I think maybe they was still a little afraid. Can't say as I blame 'em, after all, they was pert near massacred by them same Apaches. Seems most of the Apaches spoke Mexican on account of they traded a lot down in Chihuahua. Matt said they also raided a lot - anywhere in Mexico.

Matt didn't seem worried about how the Mexicans was gettin' along with the Apaches, so I didn't worry much either. After a while I saw Matt 'n' Cochise 'n' Taza walk away into the cottonwoods. I couldn't stand just standin' there, so I ran up to Matt 'n' asked him if I could walk with 'em. Matt looked at Cochise.

Cochise smiled an' looked from me to Matt. He said something in that funny Apache language 'n' patted me on the shoulder.

I looked up at Matt to see if it was all right but I knew if Cochise told me to come along, I was sure enough comin' along. Matt said, "I think you have your answer, boy."

The four of us walked through the cottonwoods to the creek an' went upstream a ways before Cochise sat on a large rock. He pulled out a tobacco pouch an' started to dig into it. Matt said something in Apache 'n' Cochise put his pouch away. Matt handed him a small cigar then gave another one to Taza. Matt took out his Bowie knife 'n' cut one end of his cigar 'n' then handed the knife to Cochise. I ain't all that sure I'd of given that knife to him but it worked out 'cause all Cochise did was cut one end of the cigar like Matt had done, then he handed the knife to Taza, who did the same thing, then handed the knife back to Matt. Matt lit his cigar, then Cochise's 'n' Taza's.

After a puff or two, Cochise said, "You will come with us, Matt? With your rifle we can kill many soldiers." I was kinda surprised he spoke in English.

Matt took a puff of his cigar 'n' let the smoke out real slow, like maybe he was concentratin' on enjoyin' that smoke. He looked at me 'n' then at Cochise. "No, my friend. You honor me with your thoughts but I would only bring you more trouble."

"More trouble is no bother. Your rifle will be good for us. Bad for the soldiers. You have no love for the bluecoats."

I could tell Cochise was workin' real hard to say the right words in English, 'cause his speech was kinda broken.

Matt said, "You're right about me not havin' much love for Yankees but If I joined you, they would double their efforts to find you."

"What will you do, brother?" said Taza. He spoke English too.

Matt took another puff on his cigar. "I don't know for sure. I think I'll try to live out here as long as I can before the Yankees find me out."

"When they find you, they will try to kill you?" asked Taza.

"Most likely," said Matt.

"If they not kill you, where you go?" said Taza.

Matt waited a long time before he answered. "I don't know. I ain't all that sure I'll go anywhere. I'll just have to wait 'n' see."

Cochise said, "They will find you, El Gato. There are too many of them. They will kill you like they will kill all of us. You should come with us and die with your brothers."

Cochise said it like he was talkin' about the weather. He was so calm, it scared me pretty bad. I knew as sure as I was sittin' there that the cavalry was gonna kill Matt 'n' all of the Apaches. I couldn't understand it. They was all people.

Matt said, "Your council warms my heart, Cochise but I cannot bring more trouble to you and your people."

"They your people too," said Taza.

"Even more of a reason not to bring trouble to them," said Matt.

Cochise waved his hand toward our cabin. "You have great love in your heart for these people?"

"Yes," said Matt.

"The Mexicans?" asked Taza.

Matt smiled. "Even the Mexicans."

Taza looked a little disappointed. He shrugged.

Cochise said, "No harm will come to them from the Chiricahua."

"I thank you for that."

"They are not bad - for Mexicans," said Cochise with a big smile.

Matt laughed a little 'n' Taza joined in. I reckon even Apaches had a sense of humor 'n' that made me feel a little better.

Cochise looked at me 'n' said, "Crawford, you have friend in Chiricahua. I am glad we did not kill the Mexicans and I am glad we met." He turned to Matt 'n' talked Apache for a bit.

Matt looked at me 'n' said, "Cochise doesn't have the English words, so he asked me to tell you that you would make a good Apache and that your ma is beautiful and kind and very smart and that you and your family can count on him to stand by his word that you will all be safe from attack by his people. He would like to know if it would be possible for him to visit with some of the women and children someday and maybe learn some of your ma's cookin'."

I looked right at Cochise like I know my pa woulda done 'n' said, "Thank you, Sir. I bet my ma 'n' Aunt Sandra would be proud to teach you their cookin'."

Cochise smiled.

After a while, everybody put out their cigars 'n' we walked back to the cabin.

The next morning, Cochise and his people left. Most of the food that was left over went with them. I guess most of us figured they needed it more than we did.

Chapter 26

Cochise and his people had been gone for a few days 'n' I was gettin' to know the Peraltas pretty good. Ignacio - he was the oldest - he was kinda like the father of their clan. He was fifty with grey hair. His mustache an' little beard was even grey. He was about as tall as Matt but he was skinnier, maybe twenty pounds. He had a funny-lookin' guitar that he played real good, but I couldn't understand none of the words to his songs. I liked the music though. Consuela, his wife, was about forty-seven but you wouldn't know it to look at her. She didn't look all that much older than Ma to me, 'ceptin' she had streaks of grey in her long hair. She wasn't real tall but I'll bet she could whip her weight in mountain lions. She just seemed like someone I wouldn't want to cross.

Chuy, Pedro 'n' Socorro were Ignacio an' Consuela's kids. They weren't kids no more but that's the way they were called.

Chuy was about twenty-two 'n' he had black hair an' a black mustache 'n' he was a pretty fair hand with a horse 'n' pistol. I saw him shootin at cactus in a draw north of the house 'n' he hit pert near everything he shot at. Pancho told me Chuy loved a girl in Mexico an' weren't none too happy about leavin' their hacienda there but he killed a man over that girl he was in love with 'n' they all had to leave. It took the better part of an hour for him to tell me the story on account of he didn't speak any Emglish.

Pedro, he was the oldest son. He was about thirty. Him 'n' Chuy was about the same size - about an inch or so taller than Matt - 'n' he had black hair 'n' a black mustache. He was a real horseman an' a riata man; carried that rawhide rope everywhere he went. He sure knew cattle good. I heard him 'n' Matt talkin' about cattle 'n' even though I didn't understand it much 'cause they was talkin' Mexican, I could tell Pedro knew what he was talkin' about. Pedro, he had a real strong sense of duty 'n' he sure loved his wife, Marguarita.

Maguarita was about a year younger than Pedro 'n' she had long black hair 'n' the biggest eyes I ever saw. She was Christina 'n' Pancho's mother. Everybody called Christina "Tina" 'n' she was about Mel's age. She was a regular ball of fire. Couldn't hardly any of us kids keep up with her when she got her mind fixed on somethin'.

Pancho was my age but he seemed older, I guess 'cause he was so proud. If you ask me, he had too much pride. It gets in the way sometimes. Pancho was about the most curious kid I ever met 'n' he was real smart too. He started learnin' English at our little school the very first day. He could speak a little after only two hours of learnin'. Pancho was a good rider for his age but I could handle a rope better.

Socorra was Consuela's daughter an' the sister of Chuy 'n' Pedro. She was about twenty-one an' the prettiest woman I ever saw, 'ceptin' for my ma of course. She dressed like a man most of the time an' rode better'n most of 'em 'n' she was sort of a tomboy but she sure was pretty. Her hair went all the way to her waist 'n' it was as black as coal. She would bring Matt fresh tortillas whenever she made some. I think she was kinda sweet on him.

Pancho 'n' me 'n' Tater 'n' Billy Jo fished 'n' explored a lot. We found a cave one day about a mile or two northeast of our cabin, partway up the side of that big mesa, an' the day after we discovered it, we went back with some candles so we could see how far it went. Billy Jo said they had a secret cave in Georgia that they used to explore once in a while. Since he had cavin' experience, we all elected him the leader of our party.

Billy Jo said it was best if we only burned one candle at a time so's our candles would last longer. That sounded like a good idea to me 'ceptin' that whoever was in the back couldn't see unless we all bunched up real tight. After only a little while, we agreed to burn two candles at a time so nobody would fall 'n' get hurt. That made it more fun 'n' interestin' 'cause we could see better.

The cave got smaller 'n' smaller until we finally reached a little hole, no bigger'n a good-sized pig. Tater thought we oughta go back but Billy Jo said it was all right, so we crawled through the hole 'n' that cave opened up into a huge cavern. There was them long rocks that grow from the ceilin' an' the floor, an' it was a sight to see.

From that big room, there was three openings, an' we picked one 'n' went on with our explorin'. After a while Tater got to complainin' that he was hungry so we all stopped 'n' ate the biscuits 'n' bacon we had brought. While we was eatin', Pancho discovered a white bug. We all got to lookin' at it real close in the candle light an' decided it was an albino cricket. Pa had an albino horse once. It had pink eyes. Pancho played with the cricket a while then turned it loose 'n' it disappeared in the dark.

When we finished eatin' we couldn't agree whether to turn back or keep on explorin'. After a while Pancho said we should turn back on account of we hadn't but two candles left. That ended the discussion real quick. We turned 'n' started back the way we had come but, after a while, parts of the cave seemed like I'd seen 'em more than twice. Pancho said the same thing I was thinkin'.

"I theenk we are lost, Billy Jo," said Pancho.

I was still doin' good until I heard Pancho put voice to what I'd been thinkin', then I got a twinge of bein' scared.

Billy Jo said, "Y'all might be raht. Ah ain't for sure

wheah we is."

Pancho didn't say anything, probably because he didn't know enough English yet, but I sure did. "What do you mean, you ain't sure where we is?" I said. There was more scared in my voice than there was mad 'n' I knew it. It made me kinda mad at myself.

Billy Jo said, "Ah thought we was goin' raht, but we done passed dis here place about t'ree tahmes."

Pancho blew out the candle he was carryin' 'n' after a bunch of English 'n' Mexican 'n' hand-signal conversation, we all understood that he thought we should save our candles as much as we could since we didn't know how long it would take us to find our way out. That made sense to me.

As it turned out, it didn't matter much. We was so lost, we kept going by the same places over 'n' over. Pretty soon our last candle burned plumb out. Let me tell you, it was serious dark in that cave without so much as a single candle lit. We all got proper. scared 'n' I thought I heard Tater whimperin' a might but I'm not for sure. I wouldn't blame him none if he did though 'cause I sure felt like cryin' myself. We didn't know what to do. If we couldn't find our way out with a candle, we sure weren't gonna do it in the pitch dark.

We sat for a spell 'n' just talked quiet-like, so each one would know where the other was. That helped some until we all agreed that it wasn't gettin' us outa the cave. Worst thing was, nobody knew we had come to this place. It might be weeks or months, or years, or maybe never, when they found us. I started feelin' sad 'n' sorry at the same time. I was sad that I would never see my ma 'n' Mel 'n' Matt 'n' Uncle George 'n' Aunt Sandra 'n' Critter 'n' Judd 'n' Blue 'n' Patches. I was sorry 'cause I reckoned I had a lot more livin' to do 'n' I swore an oath to myself that if I got the chance, I'd be nicer to everybody.

After a bit, I started to shiverin', not that it was so cold but because it was dark ‘n’ a mite damp. I asked the others if they was cold ‘n’ everyone but Pancho said they was. We huddled closer together to keep warm, but I think we also did it to know that we was all still alive ‘n’ together. It helped some on both counts.

I don’t know how long we huddled there without speakin’ but it was a right long time. We didn’t have any food but there was water somewhere in the cave. We could all smell it. I wondered out loud how long we could survive with just water. Tater said we could make it a month. Billy Jo thought maybe two weeks. Pancho didn’t understand enough English yet so he didn’t have no opinion. He got mad ‘cause he couldn’t understand what we was talkin’ about so we had us an English lesson, a real long one too, though I couldn’t rightly say exactly how long. It helped to pass the time ‘n’ take our minds offa almost certain death.

Durin’ a slow spot in the English lessons, Billy Jo said, “Donchoo think we needs ta do sumpthin?”

“What can we do?” I asked. I had no ideas runnin’ around in my head at all.

Tater said, “We could all split up an den maybe one a us would find a way out ‘n’ he could get some hep to find the rest of us.”

I had to admit, that didn’t sound like such a bad idea.

“But what if one of us gets hurt ‘n’ dey ain’t nobody dere ta hep him?” asked Billy Jo.

I hadn’t thought of that. It was darker than the inside of a cow, an’ you couldn’t see your hand only one inch from your face. A fella could get hurt real easy. Heck, he might even fall over a ledge or somethin’ ‘n’ disappear forever.

“Splittin’ up is no good,” I said. “If one of us gets hurt, he’d have to lay down ‘n’ suffer till he died.”

“Da’s right,” said Billy Jo. “‘Sides, we don’t know what lives down heah. They could be dragons ‘n’ such.”

"What's a dragon?" said Tater.

"I don't know for sure but I's heard of 'em. Dey breed fire 'n' eat peoples."

Tater said, "You prob'ly right, Craw. We just stay togedder."

I can't say for sure how long we just stayed there 'n' nobody said nothin'. There wasn't nothin' to judge time by - nor nothin' else for that matter. After a while I wasn't even sure I was alive. I wasn't sure what alive was. I wondered if this was what it was like to be dead. I wondered if my pa was in a place like this 'n' I got to cryin'. Not out loud or nothin' like that but I could feel them tears again. I was glad it was so dark so nobody could see 'em.

Tater was the first one to hear the growlin' noise. He said, "Wha's dat?"

We all listened real hard 'n' then we all heard it. It was more like a mix of a growl 'n' a whine. We all agreed it must be one of them dragon things 'cause none of us had ever heard such a sound. It wasn't very loud but we couldn't tell if it was 'cause it was far away or 'cause whatever was makin' the noise was tryin' to be quiet.

I figured I wasn't goin' out without a fight, so I started feelin' around for a rock or anything I could use to hit it a lick. I didn't have any luck. There just wasn't anything to be had. "If it finds us, I reckon we should all attack it at once," I said. "Billy Jo can't use his pistol. He might hit one of us in the dark. And, besides, the bullets might bounce off the walls and kill us."

"Why don't we jus' run lickety-split?" said Tater.

"How y'all gwan' run when y'all can't see nothin'?," said Billy Jo.

Ahm scared," said Tater.

"I think we're all scared," I said.

"I know I sho 'nuff is," said Billy Jo.

Pancho didn't say much of nothin'. Even if he spoke

good English, I don't think he would admit to bein' scared.

I saw a light 'n' then I was certain sure it was one of them dragons spittin' out fire. The light came from about fifty or sixty feet away from where we was all huddled together 'n' it was wigglin' on the wall of the cave like maybe a fire-breathin' dragon's breath might do. I figured it was the end for sure 'n' I was about to yell when I heard Matt's voice.

"You down here, boy?"

About then, I saw Judd come around the corner. He yipped once 'n' all of us started jumpin' up 'n' down 'n' callin' his name. Matt wasn't too far behind 'n' he was carryin' a lantern. That lantern looked almost as good as Judd 'n' Matt. I hadn't been so sure I'd ever see light again.

Judd wagged his tail once 'n' sat down about three feet from all of us. Matt stopped 'n' held up the lantern to get a good look at all of us 'n' then he smiled. "I ain't real sure, but I'm thinkin' you boys had better have a good story ready when you speak to your folks. When I last saw 'em, they was all a bit worried 'n' real concerned about your welfare but I reckon that'll change pronto when they see you. They'll be wantin' to know what you thought you were doin' 'n' such."

Billy Jo 'n' Tater didn't say a word. I knowed they was sure that Matt was about the toughest man in the world 'n' they didn't wanna make him mad. None of us would ever forget them dead Indians. Pancho didn't say anything 'cause he didn't understand what Matt had said.

"It was my fault, Matt," I said. Then I wondered why in the world I had said it.

Matt was grinnin' real big now. "Then I reckon you better be the first one out of the cave. Might look better for the rest of 'em if you was still leadin'." Without sayin' anything else, he turned 'n' started walkin'.

"Yessir," I said, kinda quiet-like, 'n' I fell in behind him like a whipped pup. Tater followed me, then Billy Jo 'n'

Pancho. I didn't see Judd but I think he was last in line.

When we got outside it was after dark. I reckoned it to be about eight or nine o'clock. Turns out it was closer to midnight 'n', when we got home, everybody was waitin' at my house. Ma ran to meet me out front of the house 'n' she gave me a big hug 'n' wiped a bunch of tears from her face 'n' then she stood up real straight 'n' looked me right in the eye, leastwise I think she did. It was a mite dark to be for sure.

"Crawford Kensington, where have you been?"

It had been a mighty long time since Ma had used that tone of voice on me 'n' I knew I was gonna get a whippin'. Ma had never given me one but Pa wasn't here anymore, so I figured it was up to Ma, for if anyone ever deserved a whippin', I surely did.

"We was lost in a cave, Ma," I said.

Then I heard Matt talkin'. It was almost like a dream. I wasn't sure he was talkin' 'n' yet I was. I heard the other boys gettin' proper scoldin's too, even Pancho. 'Course I couldn't understand what his mother was sayin' but I could tell by the tone of her voice it weren't much in the way of praise.

"Miss Penny, could I have a word with you?" said Matt.

"I'll talk to you in a moment, Mr. Grady, after I've dealt with Crawford." I had never seen my ma so upset.

Matt said, "That's what I'd like to talk to you about, Miss Penny."

Ma turned to face Matt 'n' I could tell she was gettin' madder by the minute. "Mr. Grady, this is a family matter. I'll not tolerate interference from an outsider."

There was just enough moonlight for me to see the look on Matt's face. I ain't sure what kind of look it was but I hadn't never seen him look like that before. He stared at Ma a second or two then said, "He's a boy, Ma'am. Let him be a boy while he can. It ain't long out here." Then he turned 'n' walked in the direction of the corral.

Ma stood there a long time 'n' it was then I noticed that everybody had quit talkin'. I reckon they all heard Ma 'n' Matt 'n' they wasn't sure what was goin' on or somethin'.

Uncle George was the first to speak. "Penny, I know you're upset but Mr. Grady was just trying to help."

Aunt Sandra put her arm around Ma's shoulders 'n' Ma started cryin'. I wasn't for sure what was goin' on. Uncle George put his hand on my shoulder 'n' said, "Craw, I think you'd better get to bed. We'll finish this in the morning after we've all had a good night's rest."

"Yessir," I said, an' I walked to the house real quick before Ma got back on the warpath. I pulled my shoes off 'n' got into bed with my britches still on 'n' pulled the blanket over my head. Next thing I knew, it was mornin'.

Chapter 27

Uncle George 'n' Aunt Sandra was sittin' at our table, sippin' on coffee. Ma sat at one end of the table 'n' she had a cup in front of her but she wasn't doin' nothin' but lookin' at the cup. I stayed in bed, lookin' through the open door at the three of 'em. I had to hold my breath to hear what they was sayin', but hold it I did.

Ma said, "I've never been so upset. I didn't mean to hurt Mr. Grady's feelings."

Uncle George said, "Well, you *were* a little harsh with him, Penny. You gave him a pretty good tongue-lashing."

"George!" said Aunt Sandra. "You're not helping things with talk like that. She feels badly enough."

Uncle George said, "I'm sorry, Penny."

Ma reached out 'n' patted Uncle George's hand. "I know, George. But you're right of course. I was wrong." She looked at Aunt Sandra. "Whatever will we do without him Sandra?"

"I don't know but we'll manage," said Aunt Sandra.

"I didn't realize it before but, without Mr. Grady, we would have been done for a long time ago. He held us all together. He showed us the way," said Ma.

"That he did," said Uncle George.

"George!" said Aunt Sandra.

Then it hit me - right in the chest. Matt was gone. I was outa that bed 'n' standin' next to Ma at the table.

"What are you talkin' about?" I blurted, my own problems plumb forgot.

Uncle George stood 'n' patted me on the shoulder. "I'm

afraid Mr. Grady has left, Craw."

"No!" I screamed, 'n ran outside, barefoot, not even feelin' the ground under my feet. I didn't slow down till I reached Matt's wickiup. It was empty. Nothin' was left. "No!" I screamed again.

I heard Ma 'n' Uncle George 'n' Aunt Sandra come runnin' up behind me but I didn't care. I didn't care about anything. I turned to 'em 'n' said, "Where is he? Why did he leave?"

Uncle George said, "We don't know, Craw. Maybe he'll be back in a little while."

"I'm sorry, Craw," said Ma. "It was my fault. Maybe he'll forgive me and come back."

"Penny. Don't be so hard on yourself. You were upset. Surely Mr. Grady knows that," said Aunt Sandra. "He'll be back in a day or so."

I don't know what came over me but I started shoutin', "You ran off Matt! He never done nothin' but good. He was brave 'n' smart 'n' tough, 'n' he knows Cochise. He taught me lots of things 'n' he wouldn't never hurt nobody what didn't deserve it."

"Now. Now, Craw. Your mother didn't mean to run anybody off, least of all Mr. Grady. It's all just a big misunderstanding. Mr. Grady will come back."

Uncle George's words helped considerable 'n' I calmed down a bit. "You think so?"

"Sure he will, Craw," said Aunt Sandra. "He'll probably be back before dark."

But he wasn't.

That night, I sat out in front of the house 'n' just looked into the shadows, seein' Matt everywhere. I missed him somethin' fierce. I missed him as much as I missed my Pa. I knew that night that Matt was sent to us by God to take up where Pa had left off. Pa had probably even had somethin' to do with it. After a while I was sure Pa had picked Matt out of all the men in the world to come an' take care of us.

I heard Ma comin' up behind me but I didn't move. She put her hand on my shoulder 'n' said, "I know you miss him, Craw. I'm sorry."

I could tell by Ma's voice that she really was sorry an' then I got to thinkin' how I had started it all by goin' to the cave 'n' gettin' her so worried 'n' all. I couldn't stand it no more. I started cryin' 'n' turned 'n' put my arms around Ma's waist 'n' said, "I'm sorry too, Ma. I won't never do nothin' like that again."

Ma knelt down in front of me 'n' wiped away my tears. "I miss him too, Craw."

I started cryin' all over again. "I love Matt, Ma." I squeezed her as hard as I could 'n' she squeezed me back.

The next mornin' I was up earlier than usual 'n' I went to Matt's wickiup 'n' sat in it for a long time. I was late gettin' to my chores but Ma didn't say nothin'. I don't even remember what I did that day 'ceptin' pine away for Matt. It didn't help much though.

The Peraltas started talkin' about leavin' since Matt wasn't there to protect 'em from Cochise but Uncle George told 'em that Cochise had given his word 'n' that it didn't have anything to do with whether Matt was there or not. Socorra said she was stayin' even if her family left. She said El Gato would come back. Ma kinda looked at her peculiar when she said it. Finally they decided to stay 'n' continue to build a place about a half-mile from ours. Everybody agreed that it might be a good idea to build another building between our place 'n' the Lincolns. Uncle George said it could be used as a school in the winter during the day 'n' the Peraltas could sleep in it at night 'n' be near the rest of us if somethin' happened.

We all worked as hard as we could to put up a building before winter. Chuy an' Pedro an' Uncle George an' Chester cut most of the trees for the walls. Ignacio an' Socorra took care of the cattle. That Socorra was a natural. She was as good as any man at workin' them cows, I bet - 'ceptin' Matt. Billy Jo an' Poncho an' me an' Tater tended to the milkin' an' pigs an' chickens an' we all got along real good.

Ignacio's wife, Consuela, did a lot of cookin' an' carryin' water, an' for no bigger than she was, she did a right fine job. Pedro's wife, Marguerita helped her a lot when she wasn't tendin' the fields with Ma an' Aunt Sandra an' Missy. Mama did more than her share of cookin' an' mendin' clothes 'n' such an, before long, every one of the Lincolns was wearin' a red shirt. Missy had a pretty red dress an' so did Ebony an' Mama. She was sure makin' the most outa that bolt of cloth.

Tina an' Mel an' Ebony did a little bit of everything. They helped with all the chores, includin' cookin' an' mendin' an' milkin'. I was sure glad to get a break from milkin' That was one chore I could do without. Next thing I knowed, Mel an' Tina had red dresses too. I gotta say, we sure was a peculiar-lookin' bunch of folks with all them red clothes.

'Course, Uncle George an' Chuy an' Pedro an' Ignacio an' Chester an' Papa had to work on their own places some too, so it took quite a spell to finish our buildin', but we got it done in early October. It was pretty good-sized 'n' had a big room 'n' three smaller ones. We even gave it its own privy out back.

Not a day went by that I didn't check the horizon for Matt. Shucks, I expected to see Critter 'n' Judd at any minute. Jack was still with us an' that was a little comfort to me 'cause, not only was he a good mule, he was a part of Matt to me.

All of the Peraltas was speakin' pretty good English 'n' Poncho spoke it even better'n me. I let Tater 'n' Billy Jo 'n' Poncho shoot my carbine once in a while 'n' they was all surprised that I could shoot it so good. I told 'em Matt had taught me how to shoot.

Right after we finished the schoolhouse - for that's what we all called it - that lieutenant Barton from Tucson, an' twenty troopers, happened on our place. It was late afternoon when they rode in. I was kinda glad to see him 'cause it was like bein' reminded that there was still other people in the world. I'd almost forgot what it was like to see anybody but the Lincolns 'n' Peraltas.

I saw Ma brushin' her hair real quick-like 'n' pushin' it back before she went to the door to greet 'em.

Lieutenant Barton touched the brim of his hat 'n' bid us good day. 'Course the Lincolns 'n' Peraltas came runnin' up to our place to meet the soldiers. The lieutenant had his men set up camp near the creek about three hundred yards south of the house 'n' then he 'n' a soldier with stripes on his sleeve came back to call on Ma.

The lieutenant introduced the fellow with stripes on his sleeve as Sergeant Dwight Culpepper. I liked him right off. He was a might older than the lieutenant an' he spoke with a funny accent - Uncle George told me it was Irish - 'n' he was always smilin'. I reckoned he was a pretty capable gent. A bit rougher than the lieutenant but he struck me as the kind of fella who could be real gentle or real tough, whichever was needed.

The lieutenant said him and his men was on a patrol 'n' would camp for the night if that was all right. Ma invited him 'n' the sergeant to have dinner with us 'n' Lieutenant Barton said they would. He left 'n' went back to his men 'n' came back just before supper with Sergeant Culpepper.

It just so happened that this was the night to have supper at our house 'n' the Peraltas 'n' Lincolns were there. All the women had pitched in to do the cookin', so it wasn't much trouble to set two extra places. Ma 'n' Uncle George 'n' Aunt Sandra 'n' Lieutenant Barton 'n' Sergeant Culpepper sat at our table, which had been drug outside. The air was a might cool but we had a big fire goin' 'n' that kind of made things warm 'n' cheery. Everybody was dressed in their red clothes that Mama had made 'em an' the lieutenant looked at all that red real peculiar but he never said nothin'.

Durin' supper, Lieutenant Barton remarked on how nice our place looked 'n' how surprised he was to see so many people here. He said we had almost started a town. Uncle George laughed at that 'n' said if a man had to live in a town, he might as well know everybody who moved in, right as they moved in, 'n' we knew everybody.

Towards the end of the meal Lieutenant Barton said they was lookin' for Cochise. No one said a word. We was all sittin' pretty close together, the Peraltas 'n' the Lincolns 'n' us. Everything got real quiet. I don't think the lieutenant even noticed. He went right on talkin'.

"Two weeks ago, a patrol raided one of their rancherias and was surprised by a party hidden in the rocks nearby. We lost four men. The survivors said the Apaches were led by a white man wearing a Confederate uniform and riding a blue roan. My men say that horse ran right over two of our own"

I swallowed that bite of food I had in my mouth without so much as one chew. Ma dropped her fork an' put her hands to her face.

"Now, Mrs. Kensington, I didn't mean to upset you. Cochise doesn't work with whites. They were probably a bunch of renegades led by a die-hard seccesh. We'll get them. Don't you worry."

Ma didn't say anything. She just sat there, starin' at the table, tremblin' a might.

Uncle George stood up 'n' said, "I have some cigars, Lieutenant. Would you and Sergeant Culpepper care for a smoke?"

Lieutenant Barton excused himself 'n' him 'n' Sergeant Culpepper followed Uncle George closer to the fire to have their smokes.

I looked at Ma, then at Aunt Sandra. Ma was gettin' white as a sheet. Aunt Sandra seemed real worried. She patted Ma on the shoulder 'n' said, "Let's get these dishes done."

I helped with the dishes 'cause I didn't know what else to do. I didn't dare speak a word. I was real scared for Matt 'n' I was afraid if I said anything it might help that lieutenant find him. After the dishes was done, Papa broke out his banjo 'n' everybody sang songs, 'cept me. I went to Pa's grave 'n' sat next to it. I asked him what I could do to help Matt 'n' I told him that I loved him 'n' that I loved Matt too. I even liked Lieutenant Barton, but I didn't want him to find Matt.

After a while I got cold 'n' went back to the fire. By the time I got there it was late 'n' most everyone had gone to bed. I could see the faint glow of low campfires where the soldiers was sleepin'. Lieutenant Barton 'n' Sergeant Culpepper was gone. I stood by our fire quite a spell, almost until it had burned itself to embers. Finally Ma came out of the house 'n' stood next to me. She didn't say anything for a long time. When she did speak, it was real low 'n' quiet.

"I don't know what to do, Craw."

"About what, Ma?"

"About Mr. Grady. There are too many soldiers. They will find him eventually."

I could feel my body gettin' colder even though I was standin' right next to them glowin' embers. "What will they do when they find him, Ma?" I already knew the answer.

Ma said, "I can't think about that right now. Come on, Craw. Let's go to sleep." She took my hand 'n' we went into the house.

Chapter 28

The soldiers was gone when I got up the next mornin' 'n' I wondered where they was 'n' if they would find Matt that day. I didn't eat my breakfast 'n' Ma didn't eat much either. Mel just played with her food. She might have taken a bite or two but that was about all. Aunt Sandra 'n' Uncle George came in about the time we was feedin' Ol' Blue the best breakfast he ever had.

"Good morning, Penny," said Uncle George.

"Good morning, you two. It's a pretty day, isn't it?" said Ma. Her voice didn't match her words. She didn't look like she was enjoyin' a pretty day, more like she was sufferin' a lot of pain.

"That it is," said Uncle George.

"Would you like some coffee?" asked Ma. I knew we was gettin' low on coffee but that didn't matter. Ma would give away her last cup if someone wanted it.

"No, thank you," said Aunt Sandra.

"Maybe, if you've got any grounds left in the bottom of the pot," said Uncle George. He loved his coffee, no matter what was goin' on around him.

Ma poured him a cup 'n' sat at the table with Aunt Sandra. Uncle George kept standin' while he sipped real ginger-like at the edge of that hot cup of coffee. After a spell, he said, "Sandra and I are gettin' a little low on some staples and we thought it might be a good idea to take the small wagon into Tucson and pick up supplies. Pedro and Chester will go with me. Why don't you make a list of what you need?"

Ma nodded.

Uncle George sipped at his coffee again and said, "Mr. Grady knows this country pretty well, Penny. He'll be all right."

Ma looked up at him. "Will he, George?"

Uncle George finished the coffee 'n' set the empty cup on the table. "I'll be back in about half an hour to pick up your list." He walked out without answerin' Ma's question.

I wanted to go to Tucson real bad but I didn't want to leave our place, even for a minute, in case Matt came back. I didn't ask Uncle George if I could go. Ma knew what I was thinkin'. I know she did.

By the time the teams was harnessed 'n' Chester 'n' Pedro got to our place, it was near eight o'clock. They left without much talk an' was soon out of sight.

Pancho 'n' Billy Jo 'n' Tater came by about an hour later 'n' we put our coats on 'n' went to the creek for some fishin'. We had all come to callin' ourselves the Apache Gang. After all, we was almost part of Cochise's tribe. Anyway, our gang went to the creek an' dropped hook 'n' lines in the water. We didn't pay much attention to fishin'. We all tried to figure out a way we could help Matt hide from the soldiers.

"I don't think Missah Matt needs no help hidin' from dem Yankees," said Billy Jo.

"You are right, Billy Jo," said Poncho. "He is like a puma. They will never catch him"

Tater said, "But dey's so many a dem Yankees, jus' like in da war."

"Well, dey didn't get him in da war nieder," said Billy Jo.

Tater thought about that for a minute 'n' said, "By golly, y'all could be raht. Maybe dey won' fine him."

I thought about the soldiers from Tucson with their fat horses 'n' new uniforms 'n' all their guns. From where I sat, things didn't look all that good for Matt. The more we talked about it, the sicker I got. Maybe Matt could surrender 'n' they would give him one of those parole things they gave the rest of them Confederates. I didn't hold much hope of Matt surrenderin' though.

Sudden-like, a thought came to me. "Hey, why couldn't we find Matt 'n' tell him he could hide in the cave 'n' we could bring him food 'n' water?"

"Senor Matt would not hide in a hole like a dog," said Pancho.

The way he said it made me realize it was true. I was runnin' out of ideas. "There must be somethin' we can do," I said.

"We could take your carbine and join him," said Pancho.

"I don't think my Ma would like that too much," I said.

"Mahn nieder," said Tater. "Mama would give me a raht proper whuppin' iffen she even caught a whiff a' me thinkin' such notions."

"I think Senor Matt will die with Cochise someday," said Pancho.

"You liar!" I screamed. I jumped up from the edge of the creek 'n' popped Pancho right in the nose. He fell backwards 'n' covered his face with his hands.

I wasn't done yet. I moved in, fixin' to give him another lick when a voice said, "Whoa, boy. We don't treat our friends that way."

I plumb forgot about Pancho 'n' turned to look at who had said that, knowin' that it could only have been Matt. He was leanin' against a cottonwood, right behind us.

"Matt!" I yelled, 'n' ran to him. Without even thinkin' about it, I hugged him 'n' held on real tight. He rubbed my hair and un-hooked my arms.

"Ain't you forgettin' your friend?"

And I sure enough had. I turned 'n' looked at Pancho, who was sittin up 'n' lookin' at Matt, a trickle of blood runnin' over his upper lip. He wasn't even coverin' his face. He just looked at Matt without movin', a big grin on his face.

"I'm sorry, Pancho."

"Do not worry about it, Craw. I shouldn't have spoken like I did." He wiped at the blood on his face.

I helped him up 'n' we all gathered around Matt. Then I remembered. "Matt, you can't stay here. The soldiers from Tucson were here. They left early this mornin'."

"I know, boy. They left just after daybreak."

We all sat next to the water 'n' started askin' a bunch of questions, all at the same time. Matt just smiled 'n' waited for us to settle down 'n' then he said, "I been to the mountains south of here. It was gettin' a mite cold, so I came back here. Ain't much warmer here. Guess I'll join Cochise down in the desert."

"No!" I threw my arms around him 'n' hung on for dear life.

Matt didn't move for a long time. Finally, he said, "I missed you too, boy. And Mel too."

"What about Ma?" I said.

"Yeah. I missed her too."

"She sure felt bad, Matt. I never saw her fret like that. She misses you somethin' fierce. We all do."

"Yessah, Missah Matt, we sho' 'nuff do," said Billy Jo.

"And I miss all of you," said Matt.

When he said that, all of us hugged him real tight. They was tears in everybody's eyes. I think maybe even Matt's.

He stood 'n' said, "You reckon your ma would speak to me, boy?"

"Would she ever!" I said.

"Well, then I reckon we should walk to the house 'n' get it done," he said.

I had never been happier in my life than I was at that minute. I figured everything was gonna be all right from now on. Matt whistled 'n' Judd appeared out of nowhere. He ran up to us, wagged his tail once 'n' sat down. We all hugged 'n' petted him 'n' he tolerated it real good.

When we got done sayin' hello to Judd, I said, "Where's Critter?"

Matt nodded to the hill behind us. "Couldn't risk bringin' him any closer with all them Yankees movin' about. He's kinda recognizable, an' I do believe they might be lookin' for such a horse."

He turned to Judd. "Go get Critter." Judd stood, wagged his tail once an' lit out for the hill. Matt started walkin' for the house 'n' we all fell in behind.

When we got to the house, Matt stopped outside 'n' just looked around. I don't know exactly how long he stood there but, before he went for the door, it opened 'n' Ma 'n' Aunt Sandra walked out. When Ma saw Matt, she put her hands to her mouth an' stood real still, right in front of the door.

"Howdy, Miss Penny, Miss Sandra." He touched the brim of his hat. He was wearin' that forage cap again, like on the first day I saw him.

Ma just stood there. Aunt Sandra was surprised too but she kept her senses better'n Ma 'n' she said, "Good morning, Mr. Grady. How have you been?"

"Tolerable well, Ma'am. Thanks for askin'. How have you 'n' George been?"

"Well. Thank you."

There was a little stretch where nobody said anything, then Ma said, "Mr. Grady, it's very good to see you." My Ma was back. I don't know where she went for a while there but it weren't near here.

"It's good to see you too, Ma'am."

"Mr. Grady, I want to apologize for..."

"Ma'am, you got nothin' to apologize for, so please don't speak on that subject anymore. I'm the one who owes all of you the apology for leavin' like I did. There was a lot of work to do and I reckon you could have used the help." He looked west, at our schoolhouse with its own privy, 'n' smiled. "I see you folks have been workin' real hard to make this place like a regular town."

Ma said, "Mr. Grady, the soldiers are looking for you. They say you were with some Apaches who attacked one of their patrols."

Matt was still standin' in front of the house, about fifteen feet from Ma. "I was livin' with those Apaches, Miss Penny. Those soldiers attacked our rancheria. All we did was protect our homes, just like I'd do if they attacked you here. It isn't like I was searchin' 'em out. I just want you to know that."

"Thank you, Mr. Grady."

About this time, Judd came into view, followed real close by Critter. Ma saw them 'n' smiled for the first time in a long time. "I see your companions are still with you."

"Judd an' me are pardners 'n' Critter is like the plague. I can't get rid of 'im."

Ma almost laughed. She held it in but she did smile a big ol' smile.

Chapter 29

I didn't know where Lieutenant Barton an' his men had went but, if they was lookin' for Matt , they went the wrong way. Things settled down to what they was before Matt left 'n' he seemed busier than ever. He helped everybody. I went with him a lot 'n' Ma let me do it. She knew I was afraid he'd change his mind 'n' leave again. Besides, goin' with Matt meant workin' harder than not goin' with him 'n' Ma knew that too.

We cut firewood for three days without stoppin'. I got blisters on both hands 'n' was sore all over. Matt kept tellin' me the hurtin' would quit after a few days 'n', sure enough, it did. On the fourth day I started feelin' better 'n' by the fifth day I was as good as new.

One day we was out ridin' an' Matt spotted a deer. It was quite a ways off but I could tell it was one of them big mule dear they got out in this part of the country. I wanted to take a shot but Matt said it was too far away for my carbine an' he'd have to work a bit east an' around it an' maybe he could push it my way. I took up a position behind a big mesquite an' waited while Matt rode off. In about half-an-hour, I saw the deer start to move in my direction. After a bit it went out of sight behind a little ridge an' I figured it would stay in that draw an' I'd never see it again. Next thing I knowed, it pert near ran me over as it flew by my mesquite about as fast as I ever saw a deer run. I fired a panic shot at its backside but it kept on goin'.

A few seconds later, Matt came gallopin' up to my tree an' dismounted. "You get him, boy?"

I kinda looked at the ground an' said, "I ain't sure. He kept runnin'."

"Well, that don't mean you didn't get 'im. It might mean you just wounded him. We can't have a wounded deer runnin' around. If you fired a shot at 'im, you gotta track him an' make sure he isn't hurt. If he is, you gotta finish the job."

I was wonderin' how I was gonna do all of this when Matt said, "Boy, you reload your piece. Judd an me will give it one more go. Stay right here an' be ready." He mounted an' rode off, Judd runnin' at his right flank.

When my hands stopped shakin', I reloaded an' waited. An' I waited some more. It was almost two hours later when I heard that deer crashin' through the mesquite an' Palo Verde. I was nervous but Matt was sure givin' me a lot of notice on this one an' I didn't wanna miss again. I was ready when that muley broke into the little clearing, runnin' almost directly at me. He was sure panicked an' I knew why, 'cause I could hear Matt an' Critter hot on his heels.

This time I looked right through the sight an' squeezed the trigger, just like Matt had taught me, an' that deer fell like he'd been pole-axed, rollin' to a heap about thirty yards from where I stood. Matt 'n' Critter 'n' Judd came along directly, an' I could tell by the sweat coverin' Critter that Matt had worked him pretty hard. I felt bad about that but Critter didn't seem to mind it at all. When Matt dismounted, Judd went to sniffin' at the deer for a few seconds, then he backed up a bit an' stood real still. He wagged his tail once an' sat next to the carcass.

Matt grinned from ear-to-ear. "I'll help you get him back to the house an' hang him up, but the rest is up to you."

I was sure proud of that deer. I skinned it all by myself. We had plenty an' we shared with everybody on account of the meat wouldn't last all that long anyway. Everybody had venison steak an' roast, an' Matt showed me how to make jerky an' we jerked everything we couldn't eat in two days. It was a chore cuttin' them thin strips of venison so they'd dry real fast but it was sure worth it when it came time to eatin' it.

Matt was sure peculiar about some things. The day before Thanksgiving he told Ma an' Uncle George an' Aunt Sandra to tell all the folks we was gonna have turkey an', if they had the fixin's to get 'em ready. Him 'n' Critter 'n' Judd left that morning an' he said he'd be back as early as possible on Thanksgiving. Aunt Sandra remarked that she was real surprised that Matt would even concern himself with such a thing as turkey on Thanksgivin'.

Uncle George said he had no notion of where Matt could find a turkey in a little over a day.

Next mornin' just after daybreak I was feedin' the chickens when Matt rode in. He had two of the biggest wild turkeys I had ever saw. He was grinnin' from ear-to-ear when he dismounted. He took the turkeys from his saddle horn an' set 'em on the ground, then unsaddled Critter an' turned him loose. Judd came up to me an' said hello by waggin' his tail once then sittin' down.

Ma an' Aunt Sandra an' Uncle George was in our place havin' coffee an' they come out the door grinnin' even bigger than Matt.

Ma said, "I see you are a man of your word, Mr. Grady."

He looked at her, then down at the turkeys, then back at her. "It wasn't all as easy as I figured it would be but the worth of it will be in the eatin'."

Uncle George said, "Where in the world did you find wild turkeys out here in this desert?"

"I didn't," Matt said. He nodded to the big mountains pert near half a day's ride southeast. "I knew there were turkeys in those mountains but I wasn't so sure I could get there an' back in time."

"Your timing is perfect, Mr. Grady," said Aunt Sandra

while she eye-balled those two big turkeys.

Ma looked at me an' said, "Craw, run over to the Peraltas and the Lincolns. Ask Mama and Mrs. Peralta to come to our place so we can get started on dinner."

"Yes, Ma'am!" I said. An' I took off, lickety-split. I didn't even bother to ride Patches. I ran all the way an' never even got tired.

When I got back to our house, Ma an' Aunt Sandra already had water gettin' hot so's they could pluck the feathers easier. Matt was gone. Uncle George said he went to the creek to wash up. He even took some of Ma's lye soap. I figured he musta been powerful dirty to do that.

Late that afternoon, we was all set up outside. The air was a mite brisk but we had a big fire goin' an', with our tables next to it, we was all plenty warm. Papa said the blessin' for all of us, an' it was right touchin'. Everybody kinda teared up a bit, even Matt, I think. While Papa was sayin' the blessin', the fire was cracklin' an' the smell of autumn was real plain. It was crisp an' pure. That was the best Thanksgivin' I ever had. There's been others that was good, but nothin' like that one.

After Thanksgivin', Matt started takin' a lot of his meals with the Peraltas. I figured he liked Mexican food best of all but I couldn't help but notice that Socorra sure gave him a lot of attention, an' she quit wearin' man's clothes too, an' she was sure pretty. I felt kinda peculiar about that on account of I wanted Matt to pay more attention to Ma. It ain't like I wanted her to forget Pa - never - but Matt was real special to me. 'Ceptin' for my pa, I never came as close to another man.

Matt took the whole Apache Gang out to look for stray cattle one day 'n' gave us all a workout. Critter 'n' Judd did most of the work but, every once-in-a-while, us kids would find one in the open 'n' Matt let us give chase. Patches was gettin' a mite better at cuttin' but she weren't no match for Critter. Tater was gettin' to be pretty good at ropin' an' ridin'. He was probably better than any of us 'ceptin' Matt 'n' Billy Jo.

We'd put in a good day's work 'n' was pushin' six head home when Matt spotted a small herd of horses. We rode up next to him 'n' took a good long look at the small ridge north of us. There was about a dozen wild horses led by a big buckskin stallion. He was sure a proud one. He stood real tall 'n' arched his neck 'n' was showin' off to the rest of them horses.

"Can you boys get them mavericks home?" asked Matt.

"Sure," I said. "You mean it?"

"If you feel confident about it."

"We can do it, Missah Matt," said Tater.

"There is no doubt," said Poncho.

"Dey's right, Missah Matt," said Billy Jo.

"Take Judd with you. I'll be back later tonight." He called Judd who came runnin', lickety-split, 'n' sat next to Critter. "Stay with the cattle, Judd." 'N' without so much as a goodbye, he rode off in the direction of the ridge.

We got the cattle home all right but, truth be known, we couldn't have done it without Judd. He kept 'em all headed in the right direction when they wanted to drift to the creek.

Ma met us at the big corral 'n' opened the gate. It was big enough to hold about a hundred head if you packed 'em in real tight. That was another of Matt's ideas. She smiled 'n' asked us where Matt was, 'ceptin' she said Mr. Grady, like she always did. I told her I thought he might 've gone after some wild horses.

"Alone?" she said.

"I don't reckon he figured we'd be much help. He ain't never taught me how to catch wild horses," I said.

"Oh," was all she said but she was smilin'.

After supper I walked to my fishin' spot 'n' sat for quite a spell, waitin' for Matt, but he didn't come back that night.

It was mid-afternoon the next day when he came draggin' in. He looked a sight. His face was all bloody on one side 'n' his right hand was cut up a mite. His britches was torn at both knees 'n' one of the sleeves on his shirt was hangin' by a thread or two at the shoulder. He was ridin' Critter but it looked to me like it was painful for him. Behind Critter, on a short lead rope, was that buckskin. He wasn't standin' quite as tall as he was the last time I saw him. He looked plumb tuckered out but he still had plenty of fight left in him. I could tell by the look in his eyes. His ears was laid back a little, like maybe he was gettin' ready to attack something, most likely Matt.

Aunt Sandra 'n' me was carryin' wood into the house for the cookstove 'n' we was right close to the door when we both spotted him.

"Mr. Grady!" Aunt Sandra's voice told me she must'a' figured Matt was about near dead.

Matt put his bloody hand to the brim of his forage cap 'n' said, "Mornin', Miss Sandra. It's a fine mornin', don't you think?"

"Are you all right, Mr. Grady?" she said.

"I could use a cup of coffee, if you have some to spare." He pulled Critter to a stop 'n' took a quick look at that buckskin, then turned back to Aunt Sandra. "I brought a new horse for the string I'm startin'"

"Looks to me like rough start, Mr. Grady." I hadn't heard Ma come through the door, but there she was, holdin' a hot cup of coffee."

Matt slid out of the saddle 'n' hit the ground like a cat. He smiled real big 'n' said, "That it was, Miss Penny."

Ma held out the cup of coffee. "After you've had your coffee come inside and I'll tend to your injuries."

Matt took the cup 'n' said, "I thank you, Ma'am." He took a sip 'n' looked down at me. "You get them cows home, boy?"

"Yessir," I said. He looked awful

He took another sip of the coffee. "I knew you could, boy."

"You look a mite rough, Matt. Did that horse do that?"

Matt kinda looked disgusted. "*Those* horses did it." He nodded at Critter 'n' the buckskin."

"Critter too?" I didn't understand.

He took another sip of the coffee. "Yep. Had my catch twine around that dun an' was walkin' the line when Critter decided the world wasn't big enough for him an' that other horse. I was in between 'em when he came to that conclusion."

Ma put her hand in front of her mouth 'n' I couldn't tell if she was hidin' a laugh or if she was in some kinda shock. I kinda think she was hidin' a laugh. Matt seemed like he was takin' it pretty good, so I guess she musta figured he wasn't hurt too bad, 'n' she was beginnin' to think it comical.

Aunt Sandra said, "We know from the looks of you who lost. What I want to know is, who won?"

Matt smiled real big 'n' I saw him wince a bit. Musta hurt him a little to smile too big. "I ain't real sure of anything but who the loser was."

Ma laughed for sure this time. "Mr. Grady, will you put the horses away so I can get you on the road to healing?"

Matt tipped his cap, took a long sip at the coffee, handed the cup back to Ma 'n' said, "Yes, Ma'am. Thank you for the coffee."

He turned to me 'n' said, "She sure made that sound easy when she said to put the horses away, didn't she?"

"It sounded easy to me," I said.

"Where's Judd?" he asked.

"Last I saw, he was aggravatin' Ol' Blue," I said.

Matt whistled but it wasn't much of a whistle. I think his lower lip was split a little and it didn't have the clear, sharp sound it usually did. It was loud enough for Judd though. He came around the corner of the house at a dead run 'n' stopped right in front of Matt. He took up his favorite sittin' position 'n' waited real patient.

Matt knelt down 'n' spoke real soft. "Judd, Critter's actin' stupid again. I'm gonna put that dun in the corral if I can. You keep Critter away from him." He stood 'n' undallied his rope from around the saddle horn 'n' started walkin' toward the corral.

"Aren't you gonna lead him in with Critter?" I asked. I was gettin' real nervous about Matt walkin' that buckskin to the corral, even though it wasn't that far.

"Can't, boy. Critter won't have anything to do with it. I got my dallies figured if that dun breaks."

I looked around for places Matt might hang his end of the rope if that buckskin broke but it looked to me like he was pushin' his luck for a little ways. Sure enough, that wild horse reared on hind 'n' started pawin' the air. Matt pulled down hard on the rope 'n' that horse's head came down like maybe Matt had shot him. Matt went hand-over-hand down the rope until he reached the horse's nose. He kept the rope pulled down tight 'n' put his face right in front of that horse's eyes.

"Listen, Dunny. We can do this the hard way or my way. My way is easier. Which do you want?"

My jaw musta dropped all the way to the dirt. That horse stopped fightin' 'n' just stood real still. Matt had barely spoke louder than a whisper. It was then I noticed that Matt had made a halter out of his rope 'n' that was why he had so much control over that horse. 'Course that didn't explain why that horse quit fightin' when Matt spoke so soft.

All of a sudden I heard a big commotion behind me 'n' I turned to see Judd nippin' at Critter's face. It was plain Critter had plans to come after the buckskin 'n' Judd was doin' his best to keep him from it. Just as I was certain sure that Critter had got by Judd, that dog jumped up 'n' bit him real quick on the end of his nose. That was more than Critter could stand, I reckon, 'cause he plumb forgot about that buckskin 'n' turned on Judd. He went to stompin' 'n' snortin' 'n' pawin' the ground. His ears was layed back so flat, it looked like he didn't have no ears at all. I was afraid Judd was gonna get hurt, maybe even killed. Matt ignored 'em both 'n' headed for the corral at a slow walk. That buckskin kept lookin' behind him at Critter 'n' Judd but he followed Matt like a puppy. I didn't reckon I was ever gonna get used to bein' around Matt 'n' the way he did things.

After the buckskin was let loose in the corral, Matt closed the gate 'n' said, "You reckon I oughta let your ma doctor on me? She got any experience?"

"Ma can do anything. She's doctored me 'n' Mel 'n' Pa a lot," I said real quick. There was no doubt in my young mind that Matt needed doctorin', 'n' I was just as sure that Ma was the one to do it.

Matt kinda smiled 'n' said, "Well, I reckon I'd best get this over with."

He headed for the house 'n' I was right next to him, just like his shadow.

Aunt Sandra 'n' Ma was both ready. Ma had some clean cloths 'n' liniment, 'n' Aunt Sandra had a pot of hot water. They both worked Matt over for quite a spell 'n' he was right brave about it. He didn't cry nor complain even once. Had it been me, I'd a' been screamin' my head off. He had some right deep cuts 'n' scrapes 'n' I know they hurt real bad when Ma cleaned 'em with lamp oil 'n' hot water. His right hand was cut pretty deep in the palm 'n' Ma said she should sew it up. Matt raised an eyebrow at this one but he nodded 'n' said, "Well, Miss Penny, if you think you're up to the job, go right on ahead."

I watched as long as I could but after a while I had to leave the room for a spell. When I was sure that the sewin' was done, I came back in. Matt didn't look none too happy but he didn't complain so's I could hear it. His shirt was off 'n' his back was rubbed raw. I reckoned he musta been drug a spell by that buckskin, or maybe even Critter.

Ma tied a bandage to his right hand real careful 'n' said, "You'll be needing rest and quiet for a few days, Mr. Grady. You'll be welcome to stay with us."

Aunt Sandra gave Ma a quick look 'n' I know Matt caught it. I could tell by the way he looked at her. He looked at Ma 'n' said, "I thank you, Miss Penny, but my little wickiup will do just fine. Besides, I'll be as good as new by tomorrow."

"Mr. Grady, if you use that hand before it has a chance to heal, you may cause serious damage to it," said Aunt Sandra.

"I'll be careful of the hand, Miss Sandra."

"Have you another shirt, Mr. Grady?" asked Ma.

"I've got my uniforms, Ma'am."

"That won't do, Mr. Grady. The war is over." Ma turned 'n' walked into her bedroom 'n' came out in a bit with one of Pa's shirts. I wasn't sure how I felt about that. At first I was kinda mad that Ma would even think about given one of Pa's shirts to anybody. Then I got to thinkin' about how Pa had probably sent Matt to us 'n' he for sure would have given him a shirt if he needed it. I reckoned it was a good idea after all.

Matt looked at the shirt that Ma was holdin' out to him 'n' said, "Miss Penny, I appreciate the offer but I can't take that shirt."

Aunt Sandra sure surprised me when she said, "Mr. Grady, the shirt is of no use to Penelope and you are in need of one."

Matt gave her a quick look 'n' said, "You reckon?"

Ma said, "Mr. Grady, you have given us all more than we can ever repay. You have helped everyone here. Why won't you accept even a small token from one of us?"

Matt looked at Ma, then Aunt Sandra, then me. "Is it all right with you, boy?"

"It sure is, Matt. Pa would be real proud to have you wear that shirt."

He smiled at me 'n' turned to Ma. "I thank you for the shirt, Miss Penny."

Chapter 30

It took Matt more than one day to heal, on account of he was up early the next mornin' 'n' down in the corral, workin' with that buckskin. He just called the horse Dunny. He musta called him that a hundred times that mornin'. I had most of my chores caught up 'n' I watched him work ol' Dunny for a couple of hours. He had a strange way of breakin' a horse, I'll say. Now, I knew this was gonna be Matt's second horse 'n' not just some ol' bronc that he was gonna sell, but he sure gave that horse a lot of attention.

First thing he did was walk up to him real slow 'n' talkin' real soft. That horse laid his ears back 'n' showed a fine set of teeth. Matt stopped about two feet from him 'n' said, real soft, "Ain't no sense me an' you fightin'. We already been down that road. I know it looks to everybody like you won but we know better, don't we?"

Dunny kinda eased up on his barred teeth.

"That's a little better but not quite good enough. You know, you're gonna get mighty hungry 'n' thirsty if I don't bring you food an' water an', so far, you ain't given me much reason to do that."

I hadn't noticed before but the water bucket in the corral was empty. Matt picked it up 'n' said, "I'll be back in a little bit, Dunny. You just be patient."

Critter came prancin' up to the corral about this time. He whinnied real loud 'n' reared up on hind. Matt looked at him 'n' said, "That'll do, Critter. That'll do."

Critter came down on his forelegs 'n' looked at Matt. He laid his ears back real tight 'n' shook his head. Matt laughed.

"You askin' for another go at me?"

Critter stopped shakin' his head 'n' looked at Matt a long time. Finally he turned around 'n' trotted off. Matt smiled 'n' looked at me. "I think he's gonna take his time warmin' up to this idea."

I hadn't noticed Judd before, but he was in his favorite sittin' position at the corner of the corral. He fell in behind me 'n' Matt as we walked to the creek.

"You gonna teach Dunny how to cut like Critter?" I asked as we walked under a cottonwood.

"What I can. Judd will teach him the rest."

"Judd's about the smartest dog I ever saw," I said. Then I realized too late I had said that word. Judd reminded me. I heard him growl once 'n' I turned to my right just in time to see he had a fine set of teeth. He was showin' 'em real plain. "Sorry, Judd. I forgot."

He let his lips fall back over his teeth 'n' wagged his tail once.

"Matt, how come Judd hates that word so much?"

"I ain't for sure, boy. I think maybe whoever owned him when he was a pup must have used it a lot 'n' I don't think ol' Judd had a lot of likin' for the man. That's the only thing I can figure. He's always gotten a mite carried away anytime he hears the word. He can pick it out of the middle of any sentence, in any tone of voice. You might even be talkin' about the weather, an' you could slip that word in an' he'd let you know he heard it. You wanna try it?"

I looked at Judd again, then back at Matt. "No thanks."

By now we was at the creek 'n' Matt stooped down 'n' rinsed out the bucket 'n' filled it almost to the top. He didn't say anything until we got back to the corral 'n' then, when he did say somethin', it was to the horse.

"This is your water, Dunny." He held up the bucket. Dunny stood stock still. He didn't even move his ears. Matt let the bucket drop to his side.

"This thing gets heavy, Dunny. If you want a drink, you're gonna have to come and get it." Matt kept holdin' the bucket at his side. Dunny didn't move. Neither did Matt.

After a long time, Matt said, "If you got chores to do, boy, you might as well get to 'em. I don't reckon much is gonna happen around here for quite a spell. This horse is almost as stubborn as Critter."

I stayed for a few more minutes 'n' nothin' happened so I left 'n' went back to the house. Ma 'n' Mel was makin' butter 'n' I knew it was hard work so I took my turn at the churn 'n' worked at it real hard. I liked butter a lot 'n', with the prickly pear jam, it was special good.

"How is Mister Grady feeling this morning?" asked Ma after I'd been workin' that churn for about five minutes.

I stopped churnin' 'n' said, "He seems tolerable better but I think he's still a mite sore. That bandage is gettin' dirty already."

"Is he using a rope in that hand?" asked Ma.

"Not that I saw. He was mainly just talkin' to that new horse. He calls it Dunny."

"Talking to it?"

"Yes, Ma'am. Talkin' to it. I reckon he's gonna talk that horse into doin' what he wants it to do."

"Mr. Grady has some strange ways to our way of thinking but they seem to work for him."

The way Ma said it gave me a strange kinda feelin'. I said, "Do you like Matt, Ma?"

"What kind of question is that? He's given me no reason to dislike him."

"We all like Matt," said Mel, who'd been watchin' me churn while she rested some. "He's wonderful."

I reckon Mel had learned a new big word 'n' was tryin' it out. I'd never heard her say 'wonderful' before.

I ignored Mel 'n' her new big word 'n' looked at Ma. "But do you like him?"

"I think Mr. Grady is a fine gentleman," said Ma.

"But do you like him?"

"Yes, Craw. I like Mr. Grady."

I smiled real big 'n' got to pumpin' that churn so fast I figured the butter should be ready in no time.

After lunch, I went out to the corral to see how Matt was doin' with Dunny. Matt was layin' on the ground in the middle of the corral. That buckskin had his head next to Matt's 'n' I figured he was chewin' Matt's ear off. I started runnin' as hard as I could for the corral. I felt my heart thumpin' so hard, I thought it was gonna bust right out of my chest. I was about to scream at that horse when I saw that he wasn't hurtin' Matt none at all. Matt was layin' on his back, smokin' one of his cigars, 'n' ol' Dunny was drinkin' outa that water bucket right next to Matt's head.

I musta' quit breathin' there for a second or two 'cause I felt myself drawin' in a big breath of air. I stopped at the gate 'n' just stood there.

Matt took the cigar from his mouth 'n' said, "I wouldn't come in just yet, boy. Ol Dunny here ain't all that sure what he's gonna do yet."

I didn't say anything. I just stood real quiet. Dunny finished drinkin' 'n' looked Matt over real good. He musta liked what he saw 'cause he didn't go to snortin' 'n' stompin' 'n' such. After a while he nudged Matt's face real gentle-like with his nose. I found that right peculiar, what with the way he'd been carryin' on earlier.

Matt talked to him in a real soft voice the whole time Dunny was nosin' around. Dunny took another drink 'n' slobbered all over Matt when he was done. Matt pulled a little carrot out of his shirt - Pa's shirt - 'n' gave it to him. Without lookin' away from the horse, Matt said, "Tell your ma I owe her one carrot. I took a real scrubby one."

I didn't say anything. I was too busy watchin' Dunny gobble up that carrot. He sure seemed to like it. I don't reckon wild horses get much in the way of carrots 'n' he sure enough wanted another one. He started pawing the ground with his right foreleg.

"That's it, Dunny, ol' boy. I don't have anymore," said Matt.

Real slow, Matt sat up. Dunny backed off a pace or two 'n' just stood there. Matt stood, talkin' real soft to Dunny the whole time. He walked to the fence, where his saddle 'n' blanket sat on the top rail, 'n' picked up the blanket. Dunny was startin' to get a mite suspicious 'n' I figured Matt was pushin' his luck. Dunny was pawin' the ground in earnest now 'n' I was sure he was gonna give Matt a swift kick any second. Matt ignored the warnin' signs 'n' walked up real slow 'n' placed the blanket on his back 'n' rubbed him with it real gentle. Looked to me like Dunny wanted to buck but he weren't quite sure about how he felt. Matt patted him gentle on the withers 'n' rubbed him there. Dunny settled down for a second. Matt went to the fence again 'n' got his saddle. Dunny looked at him like maybe he must be crazy if he thought he was gonna put that thing on his back. Matt set the saddle on the ground 'n' started rubbin' Dunny with the blanket again. Dunny really liked that. His ears was up 'n' he looked like the horse we had seen that first day on the ridge.

I had all kinds of questions but I was afraid to say a word. It was like watchin' magic.

Matt quit rubbin' Dunny 'n' walked over to where I was standin'. "I'm gonna give him a minute or two to look the saddle over. It has my scent on it 'n' he'll see it won't hurt him."

I kinda looked at at Matt sideways.

He said, "I just sat on it for a minute or two while it was on the fence, in case he can't smell so well."

I almost laughed but didn't for fear I'd scare ol' Dunny. I just nodded 'n' watched Dunny. He sniffed the saddle 'n' shook his head. It was plain he wasn't none too sure what that saddle was all about. He sniffed some more 'n' finally reckoned it wasn't gonna hurt him, leastways not while it was layin' still at his feet. He looked up at Matt 'n' started walkin' our way real slow. Matt started talkin' to him real soft 'n' he seemed to like it pretty good. He nuzzled up to Matt 'n' Matt patted him 'n' stroked his neck 'n' rubbed him behind the ears.

After a bit Matt picked up the saddle 'n' put it on Dunny's back real gentle. Dunny just stood there like a brood mare. Seems like he 'bout trusted Matt for any action he might take. After the saddle was cinched down proper, Matt walked away 'n' took a bridle from the tack shed. He came back through the corral fence real slow 'n' smooth 'n' held the bridle up 'n' out in front of him 'n' just stood there for a minute or so.

Dunny didn't take to the bridle all that easy but, after a bit, Matt finally got it on proper 'n' didn't break none of Dunny's teeth. After he had the bridle on he talked to Dunny some more 'n' stroked him real good. Then he told Dunny it was time. If Dunny didn't understand what he meant at first, he sure learned it quick. Next thing I knew, Matt was in the saddle. I didn't know what to expect but, whatever it was, it sure wasn't what happened. What, with the way that Dunny had taken to Matt, I think I expected everything to be like as if Dunny was plumb broke. But he weren't.

For a second or two nothin' happened. Dunny just stood there 'n' Matt sat the saddle like he had no care in the world. Then ol' Dunny broke in two. He went to buckin' 'n' squealin' 'n' havin' wal-eyed fits. I couldn't rightly tell who was a worse bucker, Critter or Dunny. Matt sat the saddle like he was homesteadin' it 'n' it looked to me like maybe old Dunny would get wise 'n' quit carryin' on, but he slammed into the corral fence so hard he knocked off the top rail. Next thing I knowed, he cleared it in one mighty jump. He slammed into the tack shed so hard he knocked it sideways a mite.

All this time Matt was hangin' on for dear life. He lost a stirrup but found it again before Dunny spun the other way. By now Dunny had bounced 'n' spun his way halfway to the house. Next thing I knowed, he slammed into the front door. Matt pert near lost his head on the edge of the roof. I could see he was bleedin' pretty bad from his forehead.

Dunny headed for the chicken coop, a squealin' 'n' snortin' 'n' buckin' 'n' spinnin'. By now Billy Jo 'n' Tater was runnin' up to see what all the commotion was about. I seen others out of the corner of my eye but I kept concentratin' on watchin' Matt 'n' Dunny, so I couldn't be sure who they was.

Dunny hit that chicken coop like a tornado. Feathers 'n' chickens went everywhere. The coop came down. I heard ol' Blue howlin' from somewhere 'n' then I saw Judd on the other side of what was left of the chicken coop, in his favorite sittin' position. Seemed like he was enjoyin' the show. I heard hootin' 'n' shoutin' behind me 'n' turned just long enough to see Pancho 'n' the rest of the Peraltas cheerin' Matt on. At least I think they was cheerin' Matt. They might have been on Dunny's side.

After Dunny was done with the chicken coop, he spun 'n' bucked his way to the creek. He pert near took Matt's head off with a cottonwood branch 'n' then gave a few weak bucks 'n' stopped. He stood real still, breathin' hard. I had never seen nothin' like what I had just witnessed in my whole life. Matt had to be the greatest bronc rider in the world.

For about a minute there weren't no sound 'cept for ol' Blue howlin back at the house. Then, all-of-a-sudden, the Peraltas 'n' the Lincolns let out such a cheer as I never heard before. Matt looked up from Dunny's ears to all of us standin' nearby. He smiled real big 'n' said, "I believe Ol' Dunny'll do just fine."

He slid from the saddle 'n' handed me the reins. "Would you mind hitchin' him to the corral?"

I reckon I showed my bein' a little scared 'cause Matt said, "He'll be okay, boy. Don't you worry none."

That was good enough for me. I reckon I trusted Matt more than anyone in the world, 'ceptin' my ma. When I took the reins I noticed that Matt's hurt hand was bleedin' pretty bad 'n' his shirt was torn a bit. His hair was soaked with blood 'n' his britches was tore again at the right knee - Aunt Sandra had sewed them up yesterday. He was limpin' a mite too.

"Dat wa' da fanciest ridin' I evah saw," said Chester.

"Si, Senor. That was the best ride I have seen," said Ignacio, the father of the Peralta clan. An' he was old enough, I'll bet he'd seen a lot of buckin' horses.

Matt kinda bowed but he didn't have no hat to take off 'cause it was somewhere between the creek 'n' the corral.

"Senor Grady, we need a doctor here all the time to take care of you," said Chuy.

"You do look a sight, Mr. Grady," said Aunt Sandra. You better come up to Penny's and we'll get you doctored up."

Matt sighed, "Yes, Ma'am."

I kept walkin' towards the corral. I didn't see Ma or Mel. Couldn't imagine how they could have missed all the excitement. Seemed like everyone else in this part of Arizona Territory had seen it.

Dunny followed me with no trouble. His knees was shakin' pretty bad but I could tell by lookin' into his eyes that he was still mad. I was hopin' he wouldn't take out that mad on me before we got to the corral 'n' he didn't. I put him inside 'n' tied him to a post. I knew I'd have to get help 'n' get that top rail fixed pretty quick or Ol' Dunny would be gone first chance he got.

I unsaddled Dunny 'n' rubbed him down pretty good with a curry comb an' some hay. He seemed to like that a lot 'n' I talked to him like I was Matt. I think he liked that too. When I was about done, Critter came prancin' up to the corral. He took a notion to take a bite out of Dunny's rump but Dunny wasn't havin' none of that 'n' he kicked at Critter through the corral fence. Critter barely got out of the way 'n' then he came runnin' at the fence like he was gonna come right through it.

From out of nowhere, here comes Judd. He planted himself between Critter 'n' the corral 'n' showed a set of teeth like you wouldn't believe. I believe he curled his lip up till it pert near went over the top of his head. Critter pulled up short 'n' thought things over. I could tell he wasn't none too happy about a little dog standin' up to him but he didn't want Judd jumpin' up 'n' bitin' his nose. He laid back his ears 'n' shook his head 'n' squealed but Judd held his ground. They stared at each other for a spell, then Critter turned around as if he wasn't interested anymore 'n' trotted off towards the creek.

Chapter 31

When I got back to the house Matt was sittin' on a bench at the table. Ma 'n' Aunt Sandra was washin' his face 'n' head. He musta been dealin' 'em fits 'cause not a whole lot had been done. He still had his shirt on 'n' he was holdin' his right hand under the table.

Ma said, "Mr. Grady, please let us dress your injuries."

"I'm fine, Miss Penny. There ain't no reason to make such a fuss."

Aunt Sandra said, "Your hand is bleeding, Mr. Grady, and you have a serious head wound."

I gotta admit, he did look a mite rough.

Matt said, "I appreciate your concern, Miss Sandra, but I can wash the blood off in the creek. There's no sense in bleedin' all over Miss Penny's house."

Ma said, "Mr. Grady, let me look at your hand, please."

Matt, kinda sheepish, pulled his hand out from under the table. "I'm real sorry about tearin' up that fine stitch-job you did on me. I really am."

Ma looked at his hand 'n' I saw her face kinda screw up a bit. "Mr. Grady, you should see a doctor. The stitches are all gone and I think the hand is broken. Your bones are exposed."

"There ain't much can be done about the broken bones in a hand, Miss Penny. If you could see your way clear to sew it up again, I promise I'll be more careful about it."

Ma looked at Aunt Sandra, who was starin' at Matt's hand. "Sandra, will you try to talk some sense into Mr. Grady's head?"

I could tell Ma was gettin' upset.

Ignacio came into the house about this time. He looked at Matt's hand and made a face. "Senor Matt, I think we should take you to Tucson. They have a doctor there."

Matt said, "That ain't necessary, Ignacio. I learned a bit about doctorin' durin' the war. All I gotta do is clean it out real good an' sew it up."

I took a peek at his hand 'n' pert near lost my stomach. It looked mighty bad 'n' I got real scared for Matt.

"What would your Confederate doctors have done with a soldier in your condition, Mr. Grady?" asked Ma.

Matt kinda gave a weak smile 'n' said, "If it was in Richmond in March of this year, he'd a given the soldier a scarf to stop the bleedin' and a carbine instead of a rifle so loadin' would be easier."

"That hand needs immediate attention," said Aunt Sandra. "Not to mention that ugly gash you got on your head."

Matt grinned real big. "That's what I was tellin' Miss Penny, Miss Sandra. If we clean it an' sew it up an' maybe try to set that one bone, it'll be just fine."

Ignacio 'n' Aunt Sandra 'n' Ma all looked at each other. Finally, Ma said, "Very well, Mr. Grady, I'll clean the wound and sew it up. I don't know that I'll be much good at setting the bone. I'm not sure I have the stomach for it."

"Papa can set bones," I said. "I seen him set a tiny bone in a bird's wing." And it was true. Papa had found a dove with a broken wing and had doctored it proper. When the bird was well it flew off but it came back a lot. It wasn't afraid of Papa and his family much.

"Fetch him, Craw. Please," said Ma.

I was out the door 'n' runnin' for the Lincoln's house lickety-split.

It turns out, I didn't have to go very far. Papa was just outside the door with some of the Peraltas. They was all talkin' about Matt's ride.

"Papa!" I said. "Ma needs your help to fix a broken bone."

He beat me through the door 'n' was kneelin' next to Matt in a few seconds. He took Matt's hurt hand, real gentle, 'n' looked at it careful-like. After a bit, he looked up at Matt 'n' said, "Missah Matt, you hurt real bad. Y'all need to see a docta'."

When Papa said it, it was a for-sure thing. Matt needed a doctor. None of us had any questions about it.

Ma was daubin' the cut on Matt's head when Papa said it 'n' she kinda stopped for a second or two 'n' looked at Matt. He looked at her, then at Papa. "You know, Papa, you could be wrong." He didn't sound like he meant it. He knew things weren't right, 'n' he knew it before Papa said anything, I could tell by the way he acted.

Ma said, "Mr. Grady, I'm going to clean your hand as best I can, then we are taking you to Tucson as fast as we can get there."

Matt said, "I appreciate it, Miss Penny, but I think I'll see the doctor in La Mesilla. There are too many Yankees in Tucson now."

"La Mesilla is four days ride, Senor Matt. Tucson is only two on your horse," said Ignacio.

"Can't help that, Ignacio." He looked at Papa. "If you'll just set them bones the best you can, Papa, I'd appreciated it."

"Yessah, Missah. Matt." He took hold of Matt's hand 'n' went to work. I couldn't watch what he was doin' 'cause it made me feel kinda sick, so I looked at Ma 'n' Aunt Sandra 'n' Ignacio. Matt grunted once but that was the only sound he made the whole time Papa was workin' on that hand. It seemed to take forever but I'm sure it weren't more'n four or five minutes. When he finished, Matt was sweatin' pretty bad.

Papa looked up at Ma 'n' said, "Tha's 'bout da bes' Ah kin do, Miss Penny. Trah to hol' da han' still whilst y'all wash it." He stood 'n' walked to the door.

"Thanks, Papa," said Matt.

Papa turned 'n' said, "You welcome, Missah Matt. Y'all please see dat docta'. You heah?"

Matt smiled. "I will, Papa. Wouldn't want all your good work to go to waste."

Papa nodded 'n' smiled 'n' went outside.

Ma dipped a rag in some water 'n' went to daubin' at Matt's hand real ginger-like. "Mr. Grady," she said, "Why couldn't you have waited until this hand was healed before riding that horse?"

Ma's voice was startin' to take on that scoldin' tone.

"Today was right if me an' that horse was gonna get along."

"Oh," Ma said. Seems like she didn't have no answer for that one. When she finished cleanin' his hand, she wrapped it real tight with some clean rags. Then she wrapped a bandage around his head.

Matt looked at me 'n' said, "How's ol' Dunny doin', boy?"

"Tolerable well, considerin'," I said.

He stood and kinda took in the room with a quick look. "I thank all of you for your help. I'll be re-buildin' everything that was torn down just as soon as I'm able."

Ignacio said, "Don't think of that, Senor Matt. We weel take care of everything. I would pay more than that price to see such a ride."

"I thank you again, Ignacio." Matt walked to the door. I was right behind him as he went outside.

"You find my hat, boy?"

"I forgot about it," I said.

Matt shook his head. "You gotta get your priorities right, boy."

Chapter 32

Matt rested that night 'n' left early the next morning for La Mesilla. I couldn't figure why he rode Dunny instead of Critter but he sure enough did. They looked quite the pair, what with both of 'em bein' about as beat up as a body could get, but I reckon Matt thought it was more of Dunny's necessary trainin'. Matt seemed to be favorin' his right side a bit as he climbed into the saddle. Thought I heard him grunt a bit, like maybe he had a stove-in rib. I said a prayer for him as he rode off.

The next week was a busy one. Everybody pitched in 'n' helped fix all the things busted by Dunny whilst he was havin' his fit. It seemed like it made us all closer than we was before. We all missed Matt but none of us was really worried about him. There weren't nothin' Matt couldn't fix 'n' we all knew it.

Uncle George 'n' Pedro 'n' Chester came back from Tucson with all kinds of things we needed. They had driven five head of cattle 'n' hauled a lot of vegetables from our field to help pay for things.

The Apache Gang 'n' Judd 'n' Critter kept our cattle from strayin' all over the territory, 'n' we all got better at herdin' them ornery beefs. Our big sow had seven babies 'n' me 'n' Ma watched them a lot. Mel fell kinda partial to one of 'em that had a black patch on its rump 'n' asked Ma if she could have it for a pet. Ma said she shouldn't make a pet out of any animal that we might use for food.

Tina 'n' Ebony 'n' Mel followed me 'n' Tater 'n' Pancho 'n' Billy Jo around whenever we was near the house so we stayed away most of the time, workin' the cattle or explorin'. It was gettin' a mite cold at nights 'n' the days was pretty cool too. I was sure wishin' for summer so we could go swimmin' 'n' such, but summer was a long way off 'n' I knew we couldn't keep hidin' from them girls forever.

The Peraltas had planted chiles 'n' I helped water 'em. They weren't near any irrigation 'n' they weren't near enough to dig no ditch to so the Peraltas just carried water to 'em whenever they was in need.

Seems like Christina took a likin' to me 'cause she followed me around whenever I went to waterin' them chiles. Pancho got to teasin' me about the situation, so I plumb quit waterin' the chiles.

Ol' Blue was still chasin' Judd, and he hadn't caught him yet. Critter was payin' a lot of attention to Patches 'n' showin' off a lot. He'd rear up on hind 'n' drop down 'n' kick up his heels 'n' run around a lot.

Aunt Sandra 'n' Ma talked about our "ranch" and Aunt Sandra thought maybe we should sell off the cattle 'n' plant crops. I took notice that she was callin' our place a ranch 'n' not a farm. We had just finished breakfast 'n' Ma had the dishes in a tin tub 'n' was washin' 'em. She stopped washin' 'n' looked at Aunt Sandra.

"Why, Sandra, whatever makes you think we should sell the cattle and grow more crops?" asked Ma.

Aunt Sandra put down the towel she was usin' to dry the dishes. "You know full well, Penny, that without Mr. Grady we couldn't manage to keep up with more than a few head. We all know farming. And we have the water."

"Well, we have Mr. Grady," said Ma.

"We can't count on him, Penny."

"Mr. Grady is very dependable." Looked to me like Ma had set her jaw a mite.

"The United States Army is looking for him, Penny.

Eventually they'll find him."

Ma wiped her hands dry 'n' put her hands on her hips. "So, what would you have us do, Sandra, sell the cattle and desert him? If it hadn't been for Mr. Grady, none of us would be here now."

"Oh, Penny. I don't have the answer. I really like Mr. Grady and wish his life could be better, but I don't think it will ever improve."

"Sandra! How could you say such a thing?"

Aunt Sandra looked at Ma like Ma sometimes looked at me when she was tryin' to tell me somethin' I didn't want to hear. "Penny, Mr. Grady has lost his country. I think it meant more to him than you realize. He'll never obey the laws of the United States. He'll fight with all authority. This country is growing. Soon there will not be enough open space to live away from the law or the army. Where is his future?"

Ma didn't answer for a while. She just stood real still. Then she looked at Aunt Sandra 'n' said, "I'm not selling a single steer."

Aunt Sandra kinda gave a weak smile 'n' said, "I thought you might feel that way. When Mr. Grady returns, I intend to ride with him and the others and learn what I can about raising cattle instead of corn – just in case."

Ma looked at Aunt Sandra 'n' pert near cried. I could tell by the way her eyes got real shiny. "I'll be right there with you. And thanks, Sandra. You're a wonderful person. I'm so fortunate to have you for a friend and sister-in-law."

Aunt Sandra patted Ma on the back of her hand 'n' said, "I feel the same way about you, my dear. I think you have chosen a difficult path but I'll walk it with you as long as you'll let me."

I was supposed to be doin' chores but was glad I hung around the house long enough to hear Ma 'n' Aunt Sandra talk about Matt 'n' the cattle. I was even gladder that we wasn't gonna sell no cattle ‘n’ Aunt Sandra was gonna learn about takin’ care of ‘em from Matt. Ma too, from the sound of it.

Chapter 33

It was pretty late, 'n' I'd been asleep for a spell, when I heard the commotion. It was the biggest fuss I'd heard in quite some time 'n' I couldn't rightly tell what it was at first. Could'a' been a couple of mountain lions fightin', or maybe even bears. Whatever it was scared me plumb to shiverin' 'cause it sounded so fierce.

I jumped out of bed 'n' pulled on my britches 'n' grabbed my carbine which was up on some pegs Matt had put on the wall. Ma was already up 'n' she had her shotgun in her hands. If she was as scared as me, I sure couldn't tell by lookin'. She seemed right calm, considerin' it sounded like the world was comin' to an end right outside our door.

Mel was standin' right next to Ma, on the side of her away from the door. I was hopin' Uncle George was up an' headed for our place 'cause I sure didn't wanna take on whatever was makin' all that ruckus without his help.

Ma said, "You stay right next to me, Craw."

"Yes, Ma'am," I said, an' she started to open the door.

About then I heard the chickens squawkin' somethin' awful. Then I heard a horse whinny real loud. It was Critter. I'd know him anywhere. About then there came the deepest growl I'd ever heard in my life. Sounded like maybe whatever was growlin' was at least the size of our Studebaker wagon and, let me tell you, that Studebaker was a big wagon.

I plumb forgot about me tellin' Ma I'd stay right by her side. I bolted through the door, pert near runnin' over Ma as she pushed it open.

There was better'n a half-moon 'n' I could see the

grizzly before I was halfway to the chicken coop. It was standin' on two legs 'n' swayin' from side-to-side an' snarlin' at Critter. One side of the chickencoop was all stove-in an' there was chickens runnin' everywhere. From the corner of my eye I saw a small dark shadow flash past Critter an' attack that bear at a dead run. Judd jumped up an' nipped that big ol' bear right on the tip of his nose 'n' hit the ground runnin'.

That grizzly didn't have no idea where Judd had come from an' neither did I. He spun around to attack Judd an' Critter turned 'n' let him have it with both hooves. Pert near put him on the ground but that was one tough bear. He forgot about Judd an' went after Critter. Critter held his ground for another kick an' he planted both hooves in that bear's snout but the bear got in a lick with his front paw an' I heard Critter squeal.

I cocked my carbine an' put it in my shoulder but I was far too excited for any accurate shootin'. I pulled the trigger an' pert near hit Critter. I thought the bullet had missed him an' hit the bear but I weren't real sure about it. I could hear Ma screamin' at me to get back in the house but I couldn't let that bear kill Critter an' Judd. I grabbed the carbine by the barrel an' moved closer to the bear. I reckoned I was only about twenty or thirty feet from him by then.

I didn't think about it at the time, but Ma couldn't use her shotgun 'cause me 'n' Critter 'n' Judd was in the way. A ten-gauge shotgun takes up a lot of space in front of it when it goes off. Ma was still screamin' for me to get back to the house. By now I'd got the bear's attention an' he kinda moved in my direction. I could hear Mel screamin' too. I ain't never seen anything in my life as scary as that bear. He was downright agitated an' he was about to take out his aggravation on my puny body.

I started to turn an' run for the house but, before I even got half-turned, Judd hit that bear from behind. That drew his attentions from me long enough so's I could start to thinkin' a little better. There weren't no way I was gonna do any damage to that grizzly with the butt of a carbine. He'd probably take it as an insult an' really get mad at me. I didn't have any more cartridges with me, so the only thing I could do was go back to the house an' reload, an' I wasn't sure Critter an' Judd could hold off the bear long enough for me to get it done. I could feel myself gettin' worked up to a panic. I wished I'd taken more careful aim with the shot I'd had.

That bear was takin' swipes at Critter an' Judd about as fast as I could tell it. He turned from one to the other, real quick-like. Judd was on one side an' Critter on the other, just like they was heardin' cattle, but the bear was holdin' his own. He was sure fast for as big as he was.

Right sudden I realized how much commotion was goin' on. For some reason, I hadn't paid no mind to all the noise while I was so worried about the chickens an' Critter 'n' Judd, but it came back to me all-at-once. Ma an' Mel was screamin' for me to get away from the bear. There was chicken feathers 'n' squawkin' chickens everywhere. Critter was squealin' an' kickin' an' stompin' all over the place. Judd kept jumpin' at the bear an' bitin' him whenever he could get in a shot, an' the bear was growlin' an' roarin' like nothin' I ever heard in all my born days.

About then, Ma fired one barrel into the air. I gotta admit, that ten-gauge was tolerable loud. The bear took off runnin towards the creek with Judd an' Critter hot on his heels. Uncle George an' Aunt Sandra came runnin' by me, Uncle George with his Sharps in both hands. I heard other folks comin' from somewhere. I remember thinkin' it must have been the Lincolns for they was closest to our house. It was them, sure enough an', when they passed me, I took out after 'em, havin' regained some of my senses by then. I could hear someone behind me an' I figured it must be some of the

Peraltas. Seems like everybody was runnin' after that bear. I almost got to feelin' sorry for him.

About half-a-mile north of our place we came upon Critter an' Judd. At first, I was real worried that the bear was somewhere close an' might jump out of nowhere an' get one of us but, the minute I saw Judd layin' on the ground, I plumb forgot about that bear. Judd was hurt real bad, judgin' from the way he was layin'. He was flat on his left side an' his back legs was stretched out while his front ones was curled up. Critter was standin' over him, protectin' him real proper. I fell to my knees an' tried to get a better look at Judd in the weak moonlight. Whilst I was checkin' him over, real careful, I felt blood drippin' onto my neck. I was under Critter, in between his legs, an' he was bleedin' somethin' awful.

"Ma!" I screamed as loud as I could. "Critter 'n' Judd's hurt bad!"

Next thing I knew, everybody was standin' next to Critter. I heard Chuy say that the bear was probably up in Utah by now an' that we didn't have to worry no more.

Aunt Sandra had a lantern an' she lowered it next to Judd so's I could see better. I couldn't see much blood but he was hurt sure enough. After a bit, Aunt Sandra lifted the lantern an' we all took a close look at Critter. He had cuts all over him from that bear's claws. It was the big cut on his rump that had bled on me. Chuy took off his shirt an' we wiped the cut so we could see it better an' I pert near lost my supper. It was deep an' I could see muscles 'n' bone. I had to turn my face away so I wouldn't embarrass myself in front of everybody.

Ma must have seen my sufferin' 'cause she pulled me up 'n' said, "Papa will take care of Judd. You get back to the house and wash yourself."

"What about Critter?" I said. I sure wasn't gonna argue none. I couldn't stand the sight of that gash in Critter's rump.

Chuy said, "Don' you worry about Critter. I weel take good care of heem."

I kinda nodded an' started walkin' back to the house. I wasn't sure what I was doin'. It was kinda like I was dreamin' and nothin' was real.

I hadn't gone ten yards when Tater caught up with me. "Hey, Craw. You forgot your carbine."

"You carry it," I said. I didn't feel strong enough to even carry my own carbine. Funny thing is, I didn't remember layin' it down. I guess there was a lot I didn't remember.

"You mean it?" said Tater.

"Yeah. I sure do." Tater liked to carry the carbine all the time when we was huntin'. I looked at him an' said, "Thanks for pickin' it up for me. Don't tell Matt I left my carbine layin' around an' I'll let you carry it next time we go huntin'."

"For sure?"

"For sure."

That seemed to satisfy 'im 'cause he got a smile on his face so big, I think I saw most every tooth he had in his mouth.

I washed up as best I could with a rag an' some cold water. Tater helped get the places I couldn't see or reach so good. After a bit, Ma an' Aunt Sandra came in the house an' so did Judd. He was walkin' on his own. I petted him an looked him over real good but couldn't find nothin' wrong, 'ceptin' a big knot on his head. Ma reckoned he hit his head on a rock or a tree in all the ruckus. Papa said he didn't have no broken bones an' I was sure glad to hear that. After Judd was sure *we* was all right, he went back outside an' me 'n' Tater followed him to the corral.

Chuy an' Pedro an' Chester was tendin' to Critter an' he wasn't givin' 'em no grief, which told me he knew he was hurt an' needed some help. Papa was holdin' a lantern while they did their doctorin'. Judd took up his sittin' position in front of Critter an' barked once. Critter looked at him an' gave a real soft whinny. I just knew them two was congratulatin' each other on the whippin' they'd give that bear. Each one was probably claimin' he did the most to run the bear off, but that's the way them two was. Once the work was over, they'd argue an' fight between the two of them iffen there weren't no one else to argue an' fight with.

After about an hour, Chuy said, "Thees ees wan tough horse. I theenk he be fine in a few days."

It weren't no time at all before Critter was healed. He had a scar or two but he was as good as new otherwise.

Two days before Christmas it snowed on the mountains north of our place 'n' the weather was plenty cold. There was heavy dark clouds in the whole sky.

Seemed like Ma was unhappy about somethin'. She walked to Pa's grave 'n' stood there a long time. Mel 'n' me went too 'n' just stood real quiet with her. I got to thinkin' all about Pa 'n' how he used to teach me things 'n' play mumble-de-peg with me 'n' laugh a lot. My pa was about the best man who ever was, 'n' I knew he found the next best man who ever was to come 'n' help us through our hard times 'n' grief, 'n' now we didn't even have him. I wondered how Matt was doin' 'n' if he would ever come back to us.

After a spell, Mel got to cryin' 'n' Ma asked me to take her back to the house. I was startin' to shiver from the cold 'n' was more than ready to get inside 'n' belly up to the stove.

Mel quit cryin' when we got inside 'n' I patted her on the back real gentle 'n' told her everything was gonna be all right. It seemed a long time before Ma came back but she was smilin' when she came through the door. Her eyes was all red from cryin' but she didn't want us to know she was sad.

I wished Matt was here. Ma wasn't sad when he was around.

The next day it snowed hard. I was woke up by a loud thump on the door 'n' pert near jumped outa my skin. I ran for my carbine 'n' Ma, who was already cookin' breakfast, grabbed her shotgun. I peaked out through the shutter 'n' spied Critter just as he gave a kick at the door again. Ma hadn't yet seen him 'n' the loud thump made her jump.

I said, "It's only Critter, Ma."

"Critter? What on earth is he doing?" she said.

I wasn't for certain so I said what it looked like he was doin'. "I think he's knockin' at the door."

Ma leaned her shotgun against the wall 'n' smiled. "Well, I guess we'd better see what he wants before he kicks it in."

I put my carbine on my bed 'n' opened the door before Critter could wind up 'n' give it another kick. When I got the door open, Critter looked at me 'n' whinnied real loud, like maybe he was mad at me or somethin'. It was then I noticed the snow. It was fallin' in big flakes 'n' I could tell Critter weren't havin' none of it. I thought at first he wanted me to stop the snow, which, of course, I couldn't, but Critter wouldn't know that. I said, "I can't do much about the snow, Critter."

He whinnied again, louder this time, then turned 'n' walked a few steps in the direction of the corral. When I didn't follow, he stopped 'n' looked at me 'n' whinnied again. I reckoned he wanted me to follow him so I put on my trousers 'n' boots 'n' stepped outside. Critter turned 'n' trotted to the corral with me runnin' behind him.

Patches stood at the edge of the corral 'n' nickered at us. Critter went right up to her 'n' nuzzled her real gentle. I couldn't for the life of me see anything wrong. Bess 'n' Jack stood on the other side of the corral, all huddled up. After critter got done payin' his respects to Patches, he turned 'n' whinnied at me again.

I didn't know what else to do, so I said, "What's wrong, Critter?" I felt kinda dumb, talkin' to a horse like maybe he could understand me but Critter reared on hind 'n' pawed the air. I could see he wasn't mad. He was just tryin' to tell me somethin'. I stooped between the rails 'n' got into the corral with Patches. I patted 'n' rubbed her for a minute, then she walked to the water trough 'n' stood real still.

The water was frozen. I found a big rock about twenty feet from the corral 'n' busted up the ice so Patches 'n' Bess 'n' Jack could drink, then I threw the rock out of the corral, bein' real careful to make notice of where it landed so's I could get it again if I had need. Critter was noddin' his head up 'n' down 'n' grinnin', like he was pleased about the way things was turnin' out.

The water for the milk cow was froze too so I found another rock 'n' fixed it like I had the water in the horse corral.

I went back to the house 'n' told Ma 'n' Mel about how I was learnin' to speak horse from Critter 'n' about how things was all froze up.

We put breakfast off till we took care of our animals. The chickens was the hardest hit. Three hens 'n' a bunch of chicks was already dead from the cold 'n' we set to work buildin' a fire in the middle of the chickencoop. Ma brought blankets 'n' whatever else she could find that might hold in the heat 'n' she tacked 'em up on the sides of the coop. We all brought in a little firewood 'n', once the fire was cracklin' proper, Mel stayed with the chickens while Ma 'n' me went to checkin' on the pigs. The weather didn't seem to bother them so much. They was doin' fine. I broke up the ice pretty good that was in their water 'n' went lookin' for Blue while Ma went back to the house to finish breakfast.

Ol' Blue was all curled up in a tight ball next to Judd. They was in the tack shed 'n' doin' right well. I got to worryin' about the cattle but there wasn't much I could do for them.

Aunt Sandra was helpin' Ma with breakfast when I got back to the house 'n' Uncle George had gone to the chickencoop to let Mel come back to the house. Mel came in about a minute after I got there. She smelled like smoke.

Ma said, "Craw, after you've warmed yourself, why don't you see if you can help Uncle George? We have to vent the fire or the chickens will die from the smoke."

I didn't take but a minute to warm my hands 'n' feet, then I ran to the chickencoop.

Uncle George was choppin' a hole in the roof of the coop with a small hatchet. When he finished he was sweatin' pretty heavy 'n' he bent low to get his breath. The smoke was startin' to drift to the small hole he'd made in the roof 'n', after a while, breathin' got a mite easier.

In a bit, Uncle George took a small piece of canvas 'n' some pieces of wood 'n' got up on the roof of the coop 'n' made a little umbrella over the hole so the snow couldn't fall in. By the time he was finished, he was pert near froze, so he went to the house to warm up 'n' get some coffee. After a while he came back 'n' told me I could go eat breakfast.

After breakfast, Uncle George got some chicken wire 'n' built a little fence around the fire so's none of the chickens would get burned. We still had to keep one person in the coop all the time to see to the fire.

Ma fixed up the dead chickens 'n' we had a wonderful dinner. I felt bad about the baby chicks. Mel cried a little. Uncle George said he reckoned we might have lost some of the crops but he didn't say which ones. Him 'n' Ma talked about how it hadn't snowed last year until late January. Uncle George reckoned we still had a lot to learn about this country.

Chapter 34

Christmas morning, we all got up 'n' checked the animals. Except for Aunt Sandra. She had the last watch in the chickencoop 'n' was already up. After Mel ate, she took over for Aunt Sandra while I fed the animals. It was still snowin' 'n' there was more than two feet on the ground.

About mid-mornin', the Peraltas 'n' the Lincolns was at our house 'n' the women was preparin' a big Christmas dinner while the men figured out how we could all help each other get through this cold spell.

Since our chickencoop was the biggest, everybody brought their chickens to our place. This sure made it easier to spread the watch out. Papa 'n' Ignacio 'n' Uncle George made improvements on our chickencoop an' agreed to fix up the Lincoln's 'n' Peralta's coops at the first break in the weather. By the middle of the afternoon everybody was ready to relax 'n' think about Christmas.

Our house was real crowded but it was sure a happy place. We sang songs 'n' had warm milk with honey 'n' hot coffee, 'n' little sweetcakes that Mama 'n' Missy had made.

After a spell things got a little quiet 'n' I reckon all the growed folks was thinkin' about other Christmases they'd had 'cause they sure had a faraway look in their eyes. I didn't have near as many Christmases to remember as the grownups, but the ones I did remember brought tears to my eyes. I rubbed my eyes 'n' tried to turn my back to everyone but Pancho saw me 'n' patted me on the back.

"I am sorry your father is not here, Craw," he said.

That only made me feel worse 'n' I said, "Yeah, me too."

Then them tears really started comin'. I wiped my eyes real good, till I was sure they was gone, then I turned to face Pancho. "You reckon Matt will come back soon?"

"Of this I am sure," he said.

That made me feel some better.

About this time I heard Critter whinny real loud. It wasn't the kind of whinny he'd given me the day before. This was a warnin'.

All of the men were outside in a flicker of an eye, crouchin' low or walkin' in a stoop. Next to the corral was an Indian. He was pretty bad off from the looks of him. His arm was bleedin' 'n' there was blood on his shoulder 'n' he was layin' on his back. Critter stood next to him, on the other side of the corral fence, eyeballin' him real close.

Chuy put his rifle to his shoulder.

I screamed. "No, Chuy. Don't shoot! He belongs to Cochise's tribe."

Chuy brought the rifle down but he stood real still, watchin' that Apache.

Pedro said, "Are you certain, Crawford?"

I nodded, real excited-like. "Yes. I recognize him."

Ignacio said, "Then we must care for him. Cochise has kept his word."

No matter how much Chuy 'n' Pedro hated Apaches, they wasn't about to question their father, even if they were growed men.

Mama came pushin' her way through the crowd that was gathered around that Indian. "Don't Y'all jus' stan' aroun' 'n' wash dis po' Indian die. You dere." She pointed to Chuy. "Get him inta Miss Penny's house right dis minute!"

I reckon Chuy musta thought Mama was a general in the army the way he handed me his rifle 'n' took hold of that Apache's feet. Pedro grabbed his hands 'n' they carried him to the house 'n' put him on my bed. Most of the blood was dried 'n' caked 'n' Ignacio said it looked like he might have been shot yesterday.

Ma cut his shirt off 'n' went to cleanin' the wound. She was gettin' pretty good at doctorin', what with all the practice she was gettin' on account of Matt. Mama 'n' Aunt Sandra 'n' Ignacio's wife, Consuela, was boilin' water 'n' tearin' up things to use as bandages 'n' gettin' a wad of clothes to use as a pillow so's the Apache fella would be a might more comfortable. Seemed like everybody was busy doin' somethin', 'ceptin' for me, so I went outside with Pancho 'n' Tater 'n' Billy Jo.

"Y'all think dat Injun is gonna die?" asked Tater.

"I don't know for sure," I said. "They's sure a lot of blood run out of him."

"If he dies then perhaps Cochise will come and kill us," said Pancho.

For some reason that made me mad. "Don't be talkin' that way, Pancho. We didn't shoot him."

"Cochise does not know that," he said.

'Course he was right. How was Cochise gonna know that we didn't shoot him? That got to worryin' me some. We waited outside by the fire Papa 'n' the Peraltas had made earlier. Billy Jo whittled a stick while we talked about how the Apache might have got shot.

"You think maybe the soldiers shot him?" asked Tater.

"Probably" said Pancho.

"Could'a been anybody. Dey's a bounty out for Apache scalps," said Billy Jo, still whittlin' his stick.

"Who told you that?" I asked.

"Ah heard dem soldiers talkin' 'bout it when dey was here," he said.

"Oh," I said. I couldn't think of anything else to say. I couldn't really believe someone would pay one man to scalp another.

"Women too. Chilluns even," said Billy Jo, still whittlin'.

"That ain't right," I said.

"Ain't none of it right da way ah sees it." He just kept whittlin' while he talked. Didn't seem to me like he was all that upset about it but you could never tell about Billy Jo. He didn't show his feelins a lot.

After quite a spell, Uncle George came out by the fire 'n' sat down on one of the rocks we had set around the big firepit.

"Is he gonna live?" I asked.

Uncle George nodded. "I believe he is. The bullet went clear through his shoulder. He may not be able to use that arm as well as he used to but I think he'll be fine in a month or so."

"Are we gonna tell Cochise?" I asked.

"I'd like to but I don't know how to find him. We'll just have to wait and see. Maybe the Indian will be able to tell us how to find his people when he's a little better.

The rest of Christmas day wasn't quite as happy as it was earlier but we still sang songs 'n' wished each other a merry Christmas. 'Cept for the wounded Apache, it would have been a real nice Christmas – that 'n' Matt not bein' there. I wondered if he was okay. It had been a pretty good spell since he'd left for La Mesilla.

I slept on a blanket on the floor that night. I didn't mind 'cause it was a lot closer to the stove 'n' I slept good 'n' warm.

Chapter 35

Most of the snow had melted by the end of the week 'n' the weather had turned right warm for late December. I didn't even have to wear my coat durin' the day but Ma always made me take it with me in case the weather changed. It was sure a lot easier to do chores without havin' to walk on snow 'n' ice 'n' my hands didn't get so cold while I was milkin'.

Patches was gettin' to be my pal as well as my horse. She sure was smart. Critter gave her a lot of attention too. I think he kind of liked her almost as much as I did. We never put Critter in the coral 'cause Matt never did. He just roamed around, doin' whatever he wanted. Whenever me 'n' the rest of the Apache gang went lookin' for strays, him 'n' Judd tagged along. Those two sure seemed happy when we was lookin' for them strays. Truth be known, we couldn't have done much good without 'em.

One mornin' we found a maverick in a stand of cedar. We all gave chase 'n' Tater got his rope over them long horns. Somethin' went wrong 'cause he didn't have time to dally around his saddlehorn. Next thing I knew, he was jerked plumb out of the saddle 'n' that steer was draggin' him on the ground. We didn't know what to do. We all gave chase 'n' tried to rope the steer but that only made it worse. Tater was sceamin' but I couldn't understand what he was sayin'.

Right sudden, Critter ran in front of that steer 'n' went to bumpin' into him. The steer stopped runnin' 'n' tried to gore Critter with them big horns but Critter kept just out of range. He was sure quick for a big horse. Judd jumped in 'n' started nippin' at that steer's nose. He got it a few times too. This made that steer so plumb mad that he forgot about Critter 'n' went after Judd. When he went after Judd, Critter ran back in 'n' gave him a bump. That longhorn was so confused, he didn't know if he was comin' or goin'. He stopped in his tracks 'n' looked from Critter to Judd. This gave the rope enough slack for Tater to unwrap his wrist. We all moved in 'n' got him to his feet 'n' led him away from the steer.

We took Tater home 'n' Mama took care of him. He had a real bad rope burn on his left wrist 'n' he was rubbed a little raw on his stomach 'n' knees 'n' he pert near ruined his clothes, an' he was in a tolerable amount of pain but, other than that, he was okay. I told Mama about how Critter 'n' Judd had probably saved his life 'n' Mama heated up some beans 'n' bacon 'n' gave them a proper reward, sayin' all the time she'd never seen a horse eat beans 'n' bacon. I told her Critter didn't really eat the bacon but he sure enough loved them beans. I promised her it was so but she didn't believe it till she saw the show those two put on.

While Mama 'n' me 'n' the rest of the Lincolns was enjoyin' the show put on by Judd 'n' Critter, I heard Socorra shoutin' real loud, "El Gato is here! Senor Matt is back!"

I turned around 'n' saw Socorra 'n' Pancho wavin' in the direction of two horsemen pushin' a small herd of cattle. One of the horses was Dunny. When they drew closer, I recognized the forage cap 'n' Matt. The other rider was a stranger.

They held up the cattle near the creek, south of the house. Judd ran up to greet Matt 'n' then took over watchin' the small herd as Matt 'n' the stranger rode up to greet everyone. The stranger was leadin' a pack mule loaded down 'bout as much as a full-dressed Thanksgivin' turkey, 'n' Matt was leadin' one too, loaded almost as heavy.

Matt slid offa Dunny in that smooth way that only he had of dismountin' 'n' I knew he was okay. Socorra ran up to him an' gave him an awful big hug. Matt seemed a mite embarrassed about it 'n' he looked up at Ma who was standin' off a few yards.

"It's good to see you, Mr. Grady. I trust your hand is better?" said Ma.

Matt touched the brim of his cap. "It's good to see you, Miss Penny. The hand is fine. Thank you." I saw the big scar on his palm an' was sure Ma had seen it too.

I don't know why but I wished that Matt had hugged my ma like he had Socorra, instead of bein' so formal, like he always was with Ma.

Matt turned to the stranger, who I was just beginnin' to notice. This fella was different. He looked a little bit like an Indian but not exactly. I'd never seen anyone like him before. He had dark hair, what little I could see of it under that funny-lookin' black derby he was wearin', an' his eyes was narrow, almost like slits. His skin had kind of a yellow tinge to it, like maybe he was sick or somethin'. He had on the brightest red shirt I'd ever seen 'n' a pair of green britches. His boots was real light-colored, sort of like buttermilk, an' he had a Colt Navy revolver tucked under a wide brown belt. He was real comical-lookin' 'cept for his yellowish skin. I felt bad for him for he surely musta been mighty sick to turn that color.

Matt waved a hand. "This is Chin Ling. He's a Chinaman an' he was real out of place in La Mesilla so he decided he'd like to move west. He was gonna go back to San Francisco but I suggested he might wanna look over this land an' settle nearby. We picked up a few head of cattle on the way to give him a start. He might wanna settle near here, if you folks don't mind. He's not real sure yet. Everything he owns is on that mule so he can keep movin' if you don't want him here. He isn't of a mind to stay where he's not wanted."

Aunt Sandra stepped forward. "Welcome, Chin Ling. I'm Sandra Kennsington." She shook his hand.

Chin Ling smiled real big. "So happy meet your acquaintance, Missy Sandra."

Ma was the next to welcome Chin Ling 'n', pretty soon, he was a member of our clan, for, one after the other, everyone shook his hand and bid him welcome.

I didn't say much for I had no notion of what a Chinaman was. Aunt Sandra told me later that evening all about a big country called China 'n' how the people there all have skin the color of Chin Ling's. It made me feel better to know he wasn't sick with the plague or some such thing.

Anyway, about this time, Critter came prancin' up to Matt 'n' stopped a few feet away 'n' eyeballed Dunny. Matt reached into the pack on his mule's back 'n' pulled out an apple. Critter snatched it clean as a whistle from Matt's hand 'n' walked away from the crowd so's he could enjoy it in peace. We all had a good laugh, though I caught Matt lookin' at the big scar on Critter's rump.

We got Chin Ling all situated in our schoolhouse temporary 'n' he unpacked his mule 'n' put his things inside. He sure was a smilin' fella. He seemed real happy about livin' with all of us.

Matt took most of the stuff he had on his pack mule 'n' put it on the ground next to the firepit. It was wrapped in burlap, so I couldn't tell what it was. The rest of it he took to his wickiup.

After Matt had put away his gear, Uncle George told him about the grizzly bear an' then about the wounded Apache. Matt went to visit the Apache 'n' I went along. Matt knelt next to my bed 'n' talked to the Apache a while. The fella seemed real glad to see him an' he sure looked better than he had the day before. After a spell, Matt stood 'n' walked outside. I was with him, just like a shadow.

Uncle George was just outside. He said, "How is our Apache friend?"

"His name is Chollo. He's gettin' better, thanks to everybody here, but he's real worried about the men who shot him."

"The soldiers from Tucson?" asked Uncle George.

"He says the men who shot him weren't soldiers. He says there were four of them and they were scalp hunters. They ambushed Chollo and the man with him. Chollo got away but the other man didn't."

"Scalp hunters? I've heard of these men but I didn't really believe it," said Uncle George.

"Believe it, George. They're bad men. They kill anyone with long black hair and turn it in as an Apache scalp. It might be Mexican, Papago, woman or child. They don't care."

"Good Lord!" said Uncle George.

Matt looked around the hills to the north of our place. "Chollo says it happened almost a day north of here. No tellin' which way they're headed. Pass the word to the others an' let's all keep an eye out."

Uncle George nodded.

That evening we all ate outside by the big firepit on account of the weather bein' so good. Chin Ling talked real funny English 'n' I almost laughed a few times but I knew Ma wouldn't be havin' any of that so I just held it in. He was sure fun to be around. Everything he said was funny, even if I didn't understand it. He was real interested in learnin' English in our schoolhouse 'n' I thought that was a good idea.

After supper Matt opened up the stuff he'd left layin' near the firepit. He kinda looked at all of us 'n' said, "I tried to get here before Christmas but couldn't quite get the job done. I picked up a few things for all of us in La Messilla." When he peeled the burlap away, there was a bunch of books. He looked at Aunt Sandra. "For the school, Miss Sandra. Merry Christmas."

That was the first time I ever remember seein' my Aunt Sandra speechless. She just stood there for the longest time, starin' at all them books. There musta been more than fifteen or twenty of 'em. Finally, she said, "Mr. Grady, I don't know what to say. Thank you doesn't seem quite enough."

"It's more than enough for me, Miss Sandra. I didn't know what to get for sure, so I bought every book I could find."

Aunt Sandra bent over the books 'n' started lookin' through 'em. There was books on science 'n' history 'n' everything. Aunt Sandra pert near cried as she looked at all them books with all that learnin' in 'em.

"Mr. Grady, this is a wonderful selection! I can hardly wait to read the *Travels of Magellan* to the class. And all of the others. Why, you even have two of Shakespeare's works - and Dickens ." She stopped lookin' at the books 'n' looked up at Matt. "Mr. Grady, God bless you." She stood 'n' kissed him on the cheek.

Matt seemed a little embarrassed for a second or two, then he smiled 'n' said, "I think he just did."

Everybody laughed 'n' moved in to look at the books. Pancho was real anxious to read one right away, 'n' he asked Aunt Sandra if he could take one of 'em home. She gave him one called *Tom Sawyer* 'n' you'd'a' thought he'd struck it rich. He was smilin' from ear to ear when he took it from Aunt Sandra's hand.

Matt had something for all of us. Mama got a new skillet; Tater 'n' Billy Jo got new coats; Missy got a store-bought dress. She loved it, even though it was a little big. Matt told her she'd grow into it. Chester got a new hammer an' tongs an' a bunch of horseshoe nails. Ebony an' Tina each got rag dolls. Papa got an Army Colt. It had been modified to take the .44 cartridge. Chuy an' Pedro an' Ignacio each got the same kind of pistol. Consuela got a real pretty silver crucifix. Marguerita an' Socorra each got dresses. Pancho got a store-bought shirt - a pretty green one it was too. Uncle George got a funny-lookin' pistol. Matt said it was called a Le Mat. It sure was big for a pistol. It shot one shotgun shell an' seven bullets.

I wouldn't wanna have nobody shoot me with that thing. Mel got a little tea set, made out of real porcelain. One of the cups had got cracked on the trip from Messilla, but it weren't cracked real bad. They was eight cups an' saucers. Mel went plumb crazy over it. She went to huggin' on Matt an' I thought she was never gonna quit but she finally went back to lookin' at her new tea set. Then Matt pulled out a hairbrush an' handed it to her.

Mel took it an' said, "It looks like the one Pa gave me."

"It is. I had a fella in Messilla make it brand new," said Matt.

Mel hugged him some more an' kissed his cheek a bunch, then went to brushin' her hair.

Ma got a new *serape,* like the kind we'd seen on the tables in Tucson. It was right colorful. I got the biggest bag of licorice I'd ever saw. Matt took one of the pieces when he gave me the bag an' chewed it with big grin.

Matt looked at Mel and said, "Oh, I almost forgot. I'll be back in a minute or two." He walked to the schoolhouse where he had put Chin Ling's things. A few minutes later he came walkin' back with somethin' wrapped in a small blanket. When he got by the fire, he opened one end of the blanket and I think most everyone there jumped back a couple of feet. "This is for you, Mel."

"What is it?" asked Mel. I could tell she was nervous but she trusted Matt a lot so she peeked up at the blanket to get a better look.

"It's a baby javelina," said Matt. "I've never seen one this young this time of year but me an' Chin Ling found him about two days ago. He was near dead but we gave him some water and cactus juice. Had to cut a hole in the finger of one of Chin Ling's gloves to feed him but it works. I suspect if you have any milk to spare, the little guy might have a chance."

Well, when I found out it was just a baby, my nerve

came back an' I stepped a bit closer myself. I can't rightly say it was the prettiest thing I ever saw but it was kinda cute, only because it was so small, I reckon. It had a long nose and not much hair and was only about the size of a month-old puppy.

Everybody got to lookin' at it an' I backed up a bit so's they could see better. After they all got done with their "oohin' and aahin'", I said, "What's a Javelina?"

Matt, he smiled and said, "Some folks out here call 'em wild pigs."

"Do you eat 'em?" I asked.

"Yeah, lots of folks eat 'em, but that ain't what I had in mind for this little guy. I figure we could teach him to herd cattle."

Ma said, "I'll get some milk." An' she hurried into the house.

Mel said, "Can I hold him?"

Matt handed her the blanket real careful-like an' Mel took it just as careful. She got to pettin' it an' cooin' at it, like it were a human baby. I gotta say, for no bigger than it was, it sure looked a mite ferocious-mean. I think Mel was kinda brave to pet it the way she did. She even put her cheek to it and hugged it real gentle. The little guy seemed to like it some and tried to cuddle up to her. We all laughed.

Aunt Sandra said, "I think you've made a friend."

Mel looked up at Matt. "Is he for me?"

Matt grinned real big an' said, "You think you can take care of him?"

"I promise I will."

"Then I guess he's yours if your ma says it's okay."

Ma had just stepped out of the house with the milk. "Are you sure it's not dangerous, Mr. Grady?" she said.

"No more than a dog, Miss Penny. And they're smarter than most dogs and just as loyal. We had one at San Xavier Mission. It used to play fetch and follow us kids and chase lizards and ground squirrels with the best of the dogs."

Ma looked at Mel and said, "Here, Mel. You must learn how to take care of it, beginning right now." She handed Mel the milk, which was in an old bottle that we had made up for a calf whose mama had died and it had a nipple on it that Ma had made. Mel took the bottle and most of us kids gathered around to witness the feedin'.

Ma looked at Matt an' said, "Mr. Grady, I trust you will be available help Mel teach the little Javelina to behave?"

"That I will, Miss Penny. I'll watch her real close until Mel is comfortable with him."

"Thank you, Mr. Grady."

Mel looked up from her feedin'. That little critter must have been powerful hungry 'cause he was fixin' to drink all the milk and eat the bottle it looked to me like. She said to Matt, "What's his name?"

Matt said, "I'll leave that up to you."

Mel scrooched up her face and went to thinkin' of a name for the javelina, who was about to finish eatin'. Everybody seemed real pleased he was eatin' so much. We all took it as a sign that he was gonna be okay.

After a bunch of huggin' an' well-wishin', we left Mel alone with her javelina an' Ignacio played his guitar 'n' Papa played his banjo, an' Chester his mouth organ, 'n' we all sang songs 'n' had a dandy time. It sure felt good havin' Matt back.

Chapter 36

Mel named that little javelina Squeak on account of he made some peculiar noises. Ol' Squeak, he grew like a weed as soon as he started gettin' grub regular. In a week, he was followin' Mel every place she went. It was funny to watch him try to keep up with Mel on account of he had such short legs an' moved 'em so fast.

Seems like Judd took to the little guy an' was most always nearby, kinda watchin' out for him. One day a mocking bird took after Squeak an' Judd put an end to that real quick. He put an end to the mocking bird too, with one quick jump and a snap of his jaws. I think the mocking birds left Squeak alone after that, I couldn't never figure why Judd took to the little guy like he did but we were all glad on account of Judd had a lot of savvy. That's a Mexican word that Matt used a lot. He said it meant smarts.

Squeak fit right in with everybody. Tater an' me played with him a lot, an' even Pancho played with him. He was right at home with everybody an' he was growin' like a weed.

Matt had been back for almost two weeks 'n' even though the weather had turned cold again, I was pert near as happy as I could get. Chin Ling was learnin' English real good, but he still had a ways to go 'n' everything he said was funny. He wasn't much of a hand with cattle but he sure tried hard. Whenever he got throwed by his horse, which was a mite often, all of us in the Apache Gang had to look away 'n' cover our faces on account of we didn't want to hurt his feelin's by him seein' us laughin' at him. He sure was a tough little guy though. He had to be, as many times as he hit the ground 'n' all.

One day he got throwed real hard 'n' his derby came off. It was the first time I ever saw him without that hat 'n', boy, was I surprised! He had a long pigtail. I'd never seen a man or a boy with a pigtail 'n' it was such a strange sight. I spoke without thinkin'. "Hey, Chin Ling, why you got a pigtail like a girl?" Right away, I knew I'd get a lickin' if Ma ever heard such talk but it was too late to take the words back.

Matt came ridin' up to check Chin Ling 'n' he said, "The men in China wear their hair that way, boy. It's called a queyue. You might look strange to them with your short hair."

I looked at Chin Ling 'n' said, "I'm sorry, Chin Ling. I just never saw a man with a pigtail. You won't tell my ma that I said such a thing, will you?"

Chin Ling stood 'n' picked up his derby 'n' dusted the snow off it. He looked up at me with that big grin of his 'n' said, "Chin Ling no say a word to Missy Penny. You collect. Not look so good in this country as in China." He looked at Matt, who was grinnin' almost as big as Chin Ling. "Missah Matt, you cut Chin Ling's hair?"

"I ain't a barber, Chin Ling. Besides, you may not get to the Happy Huntin' Ground without it. Maybe Craw here will help you out."

Chin Ling looked at me. "You cut Chin Ling's hair?"

I looked at Matt 'n' didn't really have no notion of what to say.

Matt kinda shook his head a little bit so's Chin Ling couldn't see it.

I looked back at Chin Ling an' said, "I reckon you oughta keep that there queyue thing on account of it's part of your religion and you shouldn't never give up your religion on account of somebody else's thinkin'."

Chin Ling smiled real big and put his derby back on his head. I took notice that he didn't tuck the queyue under the hat but left it hangin' down his back.

The next day Uncle George 'n' Pedro 'n' Chuy 'n' Chester took two of the wagons 'n' left for Tucson. Chin Ling needed some lumber to build a small house 'n' they was gonna buy some in Tucson. Chin Ling gave Uncle George four of his longhorns to trade for the lumber. Chuy 'n' Pedro would most likely herd the cattle while Chester 'n' Uncle George drove the wagons. The Peraltas had told Chin Ling they would help him build his house out of adobe but I don't reckon Chin Ling was fond of livin' in a house made of dirt.

Matt 'n' the Apache Gang 'n' Aunt Sandra went east about an hour after Uncle George 'n' them headed west for Tucson. Aunt Sandra was a fine rider 'n' she was learnin' to cut 'n' rope too. Matt always made sure she had gloves on when she went to ropin' 'n' I noticed he watched her like a hawk whenever she loosened her rope. He was always right behind her when she throwed a loop. I know he was makin' sure nothin' happened to her like it did Tater.

We had most of the cattle pretty much in the graze near the house 'n' they was mostly used to doin' things a certain way every day, 'ceptin' for a few, which we always had to chase out of the bush. This day we had found only one steer 'n' Matt thought we should go back to the ranch early, what with most all of the men bein' gone 'n' all.

Matt was ridin' Critter, 'n' Judd was runnin' our flank as we got near the house. Right sudden Matt reined Critter in. I was followin' real close behind 'n' pert near ran into him before I got Patches stopped. Matt was watchin' Judd, who'd taken a crouched position. Matt motioned for all of us to be still. He dismounted 'n' walked to Judd, an' the both of them walked to the cottonwoods by the creek. They disappeared for a little while, then Matt came walkin' back, real quick-like.

His voice was low but we could all hear him real good. "There are four men outside of Miss Penny's. Looks like they have everyone lined up by the firepit. Two of 'em are holdin' pistols on our people. I don't know what's goin' on but I know it's not good."

He took his Henry rifle from its scabbard 'n' walked up to Aunt Sandra. "Do you know how to use this?"

"If I have to," she said. I really was proud of my Aunt Sandra.

He handed her the rifle. "You may."

He looked at me. "Boy, I want you to stay with your Aunt Sandra. If she has to do any shootin' that will mean things ain't turnin' out proper. If she shoots, then you shoot. Be careful of your target. We've talked about that."

I nodded 'n' swallowed real hard an' I was startin' to shake a little bit. Matt walked up next to Patches 'n' patted my leg. "If it comes to it, boy, you'll be fine. Don't fret about it."

"Yessir," I said, just like he was my captain 'n' I was in the Confederate cavalry.

Then Matt looked at Chin Ling an' Billy Jo. They was the only other ones who had guns. "Chin Ling, I want you an' Billy Jo to get these folks as close to the house as you can get 'em without bein' seen. You two are gonna have to be pretty close to hit anything with those pistols."

Chin Ling said, "What Missa Matt do?"

"I'm gonna ride in there like I'm a stranger passin' through. I'll try to get as close as I can. Maybe I can do some good without hurtin' any of our people."

Aunt Sandra said, "I should go with you, Mr. Grady."

Matt shook his head. "No, Miss Sandra. Folks are gonna die today. I don't want you to be one of 'em. I suspect you can use that rifle." He nodded at me. "And if Craw stays calm, I know he can handle that carbine. You may end up bein' the only hope they have."

Aunt Sandra started to speak. "But, Mr. Grady..."

"Meanin' no disrespect, Ma'am, but it needs to be done

the way I've said."

Aunt Sandra didn't say nothin' more.

Matt mounted Critter 'n' lit one of his little cigars then nudged Critter with his moccasins.

Matt skirted south, so's to draw attention away from the creek, 'n' we went as fast 'n' as quiet as we could for the house, Pancho 'n' Tater bein' told by Aunt Sandra to hide near the creek and hang on to the steer we had been herdin'. We got into some pretty good hidin' places real close to the house. I was the closest. Aunt Sandra had tried to motion me back but I pretended I didn't see her. I was hidin' behind the waterin' trough that Pa had built. It weren't but twenty yards from the firepit. Aunt Sandra was off to my left 'n' behind me in some bushes, 'n' I had no idea where Chin Ling an' Billy Jo was.

I could see Tina an' Mel an' Ebony but they couldn't see me. I sure hoped they wouldn't say nothin' about Matt when he rode up. I got to worryin' about that somethin' fierce an' then I got to wonderin' where Squeak was.

I heard one of them men talkin' 'n' I heard him real plain. I'm glad I couldn't see him. I was scared enough as it was.

One man said, "Which one do you want?"

Somebody else said, "I'll take the redhead."

That first man said, "I'll take this little Mex. When I'm done with her, her scalp is mine."

Another man said, "I ain't never had a nigger. I think I'll take the young nigger."

The first man said, "Suit yourself. How 'bout you, Pete?"

This Pete fella said, "I guess I'll start with older Mexican. She looks hot-blooded to me. And, I get her scalp later."

I wasn't sure what they was talkin' about but I did understand scalpin'. I got to shakin' real bad. My stomach got real tight 'n' I thought I might vomit. But I didn't, 'cause about then I heard Matt.

"Hello the house! I could use some water. You got any to spare?"

I heard the jingle of spurs 'n' scrapin' noises as musta' been made by them fellas turnin' to see who was hailin' 'em.

One of 'em said, "What should we do, Skaggs?"

This Skaggs fella was the first one I had heard talkin'. He said, "Let him ride in. There ain't but one of him an' there's four of us. Besides, he might have somethin' worth the takin'.

"Come on in, stranger. There's plenty of water," said Skaggs. I sure didn't like this fella.

I heard Critter's hoofs hittin' the ground as Matt drew nearer 'n' I heard one of them fellas say, "He's wearin' a Confederate cap."

Skaggs said, "So he is. Let's palaver with this gent before we kill 'im."

Then I heard a few chuckles.

Saddle leather creaked as Matt reined in. One of the men said, "There's the water, help yourself."

I didn't hear Matt dismount.

"Where'd you find so many pretty women out here in the middle of nowhere?" asked Matt. I didn't hear Ma nor any of the others say anything. I reckoned they knew Matt was trying to pull a trick on them strangers and they was playin' along real good.

The one called Pete laughed. "That's the funny part of it. We just found 'em. Nothin' but an' ol' Nigger 'n' an ol' Mexican man 'n' all these women. Who was you with in the war? Iffen it was the right outfit, you just might get one of these gals."

"Fourth Texas Cavalry. Colonel Sibley," Matt said. I knowed that weren't true but I reckoned he knew what he was doin'.

"Step down, stranger. I was with Quantrill," said Skaggs.

Next thing I heard was a shot, then another. Judd growled an' one of them fellas screamed. By then, I forgot whatever it was Matt had told me 'n' I stood 'n' put my carbine to my shoulder. I heard three or four more shots as I was tryin' to find a target, but there weren't none. All of them four men was on the ground. Ma 'n' the others was scatterin' to the winds. Chollo stood in the doorway of our house with Ma's shotgun in his hands. There was still smoke rollin' out the ends of both barrels. He musta' still been pretty weak, 'cause he was leanin' against the doorframe.

Next thing I knowed, Chin Ling came fallin' off the roof. He musta lost his balance or somethin'. He was okay though, 'cause he stood up real quick 'n' went to pointin' his navy Colt at them men layin' on the ground an' jabberrin' so fast in Chinese that I couldn't tell where one word ended an' another one started.

Everything happened so fast I can't really recollect it all. Aunt Sandra came runnin' up 'n' Ma an' the others came runnin' up too. Ignacio an' Papa was tied up in a sittin' position by the fire pit an' Mama an' Consuela went to untyin' 'em real fast.

Matt said, "Ease that hammer home, boy. The shootin's done."

How he coulda taken the time to notice my carbine was cocked, I'll never know, but his words brought me back to earth 'n' my heart started beatin' again. "Yessir," I said. I took the cap off the nipple an' held the hammer back with my thumb 'n' pulled the trigger, lettin' the hammer light on the nipple real gentle. It was then I noticed that Matt still had his cigar in his mouth.

He looked around. "Is everybody okay?"

Ma said, "We all seem to be all right, Mr. Grady. How are you?"

Matt looked at Ma 'n' smiled. "I'm fine, Miss Penny.

Thanks for askin'." He looked at one of the dead men 'n' said, "I never did like Quantrill." He dismounted an' reached down 'n' patted Judd once then walked to the door of our house 'n' helped Chollo back to my bed, talkin' to him in Apache the whole time.

All of us just stood outside, lookin' at each other for a minute or two, then Ma started cryin' 'n' she hugged me 'n' Mel 'n' Aunt Sandra, 'n' Missy 'n' pretty soon, everybody was huggin' everybody else. In all the excitement, I'd plumb forgot about Pancho 'n' Tater. About the time I remembered, here they come, runnin' as fast as they could. They wasn't sure what was goin' on but they jumped right in an went to huggin', like everybody else. Squeak came around the corner of the house on them stiff little legs of his an' everybody laughed for a spell an' then went right back to huggin'

After a bit, Matt came back outside. Everybody was still huggin 'n' cryin' 'n' laughin'. Matt took a puff on his cigar 'n' smiled. As he walked to Critter, he said, "I'll drag these bodies south a mile or two 'n' let the buzzards have 'em. I'll be back in time for supper."

Right sudden Ma quit smilin'. Everybody did. Ma said, "Mr. Grady! Surely you're not serious?"

Matt looked at her like he knew he was gonna get a lecture 'n' sure enough he was right. "What else would you have me do with 'em?"

"Give them a Christian burial, Mr. Grady," said Ma.

Matt took the cigar out of his mouth. "Miss Penny, do you have any idea what these *hombres* were planin' to do to you and the others?"

Ma's face went real red. "Yes, Mr. Grady. They were very clear about their intentions."

Matt raised an eyebrow. "An' you wanna give 'em a Christian burial?"

"Mr. Grady! How could you even ask such a question?

These men are dead."

"They earned it, Miss Penny."

Ma kinda hesitated a second or two. "Then they have been paid their just rewards as men. Now we must give them a Christian burial so that their souls may be saved."

Matt pointed to one of the dead men, the one with a dark hole in the center of his forehead. There was powder burns around the hole. I noticed he had a gash on his neck 'n' figured that maybe Judd had something to do with that. "Even the one who rode with Quantrill?"

Ma nodded. "Every man deserves a Christian burial, Mr. Grady."

Matt took another puff at his cigar. I knew he was tryin' to find words. I don't know if Ma knew, but I sure did. I knew Matt real good.

He blew some smoke 'n' said, "Miss Penny, I don't reckon I'll ever understand how your mind works but if you wanna give that scum a Christian burial, you go right ahead an' do it. Just don't look for me on the end of one of the shovels." He put the cigar in his mouth 'n' walked to Critter.

Nobody said anything to him, not even Socorra. I think we all reckoned every man deserved a burial. That was sure a strange endin' to the whole thing. Matt rode Critter back in the direction of the creek. I reckoned he was goin' after that steer we had been herdin'.

Matt came back in about an hour. Ma was workin' a shovel 'n' her hair was fallin' in her face. She looked up from about knee-deep in the grave she was diggin'. "Hello, Mr. Grady."

Matt kinda got a disgusted look on his face 'n' said, "Get out of that hole, Miss Penny. I'll finish it – as long as you promise not to put that *hombre* that rode with Quantrill in it."

Ma smiled real big 'n' I knew that, for some reason, Matt offerin' to dig that grave made her about as happy as I'd seen her in a long time. Pretty soon everybody was smilin'. It was plumb peculiar that we was all smilin' whilst we was diggin' graves but we sure enough were.

Chapter 37

When Uncle George 'n' the others got back from Tucson, they was pure surprised to hear about them scalp hunters. I even told 'em how we found nine scalps on their pack horse. Ma shushed me but by then I already had it out.

They had a bunch of lumber for Chin Ling 'n' even had some money left over to give him for his cattle. Seems they brought a good price, seein' as nobody was bringin' cattle through Apache country 'n' the town was hungry for beef. Matt 'n' Uncle George 'n' Papa 'n' the Peraltas talked it over 'n' they decided to drive half of all the cattle to Tucson. Well, not Matt. Him 'n' Critter 'n' Judd would stay on the ranch until everyone else got back, then they'd head for west Texas 'n' see if they could get some more cattle.

Uncle George had registered a brand an' had two new brandin' irons.

Matt looked at the irons. "The box X? Where'd you come up with that?"

Uncle George said, "Sandra and Penny and I talked it over and decided that it would be appropriate. We have no need to attach our names on the brand for, without you, there would have been no need for a brand at all."

Matt grinned. "You know, George, that brand looks a lot like the Confederate Battle Flag. Good choice."

I don't think Uncle George had give much thought to no battle flag, on account of he seemed a mite embarrassed when Matt pointed that out to him.

I sure wanted to go to Tucson but it was so good to be with Matt, I never said a word. Billy Jo got to go 'n' so did

Pancho. Me 'n' Tater 'n' Matt 'n' Chin Ling 'n' Ignacio 'n' Papa would be the only men left behind. I reckoned me 'n' Tater was almost men.

The day everybody left with half the cattle, Matt picked out an ol' brindle bull 'n' tied a little bell around his neck. Matt said that ol' bull was a natural-born leader 'n' weren't no bunch-quitter. Matt was right. That ol' bull kinda had his own way of doin' things 'n' it was the same every day. He'd lead the rest of them steers out about a half mile or more to get at good graze an' he'd lead 'em all back home to the water before sundown. It sure made life a lot easier. 'Course there was always one or two of them critters that wandered off but we could handle them real easy.

Chin Ling got busy makin' his little house about a half mile north of us in some hills, about two hundred yards from the creek. We had a time gettin' everything up there on account of it was rough goin' for a wagon, but we got it done. Papa 'n' Ignacio 'n' Matt 'n' me 'n' Tater 'n' Socorra cleared a bunch of rocks 'n' made a sort of trail up to Chin Ling's place. Socorra was the only one of the women to come with us, 'cept for Aunt Sandra. She came up on the second day but, after that, she stayed near home 'n' helped with the chores. I sure was glad I didn't have to milk the cow. Judd an' Squeak was always nearby an' so was Mel. Squeak stuck to her like flypaper. Critter had even taken to Squeak. I found that plumb peculiar on account of I know how ornery that horse can be at times, but you could never really figure him out.

The weather was cold, but not frightful cold like it had been before Christmas 'n', if we kept movin', it was real comfortable, 'n' Matt saw to it we kept movin'. In four days, Chin Ling had a four-sided little house with a place for a stove inside. Trouble is, he didn't have a stove. Chin Ling said he'd get one though, maybe with the extra money he got from his cattle. I gotta say, it didn't look to me like the place would stand one good blow but Chin Ling didn't seem all that worried about it, so I never said nothin'.

In the middle of the dirt floor, Chin Ling made a little fire pit. Matt laughed 'n' asked him what he was gonna do about the smoke. What he did was to stay at the schoolhouse until he could get him a stove.

After Chin Ling's house was up, we stayed at our own places 'n' fixed things 'n' did chores, 'cept for Chin Ling. He stayed at his place 'n' made "improvements". Anyway, that's what Matt called 'em. He'd come in 'n' eat supper with us, 'n' him 'n' Matt would stay in the schoolhouse. I stayed there a couple of times but Matt said he thought I should stay with Ma 'n' Mel more on account of a woman always felt better to have a man around the house. It made me feel real good that Matt called me a man. 'Course, whenever he called me, he still called me "Boy." It was okay by me though 'cause that was Matt's special name for me. He didn't call anybody else that - only me.

Socorra didn't seem as happy at the ranch as she did when she had Matt all to herself up at Chin Ling's. Maybe I'm just spoutin' wind, but that's the way I saw it. Ma seemed happier to have Matt around 'n' I found out she had learned some Mexican cookin' from Consuela, 'n' Pedro's wife, Marguerita. I wasn't used to it yet 'n' found it a mite warm, but it was tolerable good-tastin so long as you had lots of water or milk at hand. Matt couldn't get enough of it. He really liked his beans 'n' chiles 'n' beef.

Sometimes Socorra would make somethin' special, just for Matt. I don't think Ma liked this on account of she'd gone to a lot of trouble to learn Mexican cookin'. No one could argue it wasn't a lot different than what we was used to eatin' in Ohio.

Chin Ling didn't take to that Mexican cookin' at all. The first time he bit into one of them green chiles, he started jabberin' in that funny language of his so fast, I ain't sure even another Chinaman could've understood him. He ran plumb to the creek 'n' didn't come back till he'd put out the fire. While he was gone, Matt finished Chin Ling's plate. After Chin Ling got back from the creek, Ma gave him some bacon 'n' beans 'n' he seemed happy about that. He kept lookin' at Matt like it was all his fault he'd burnt his mouth. Matt just looked at him 'n' grinned real big. I wouldn't 'a' been grinnin'. Looked to me Like Chin Ling wanted to hang Matt from the nearest cottonwood, which weren't all that far away.

Papa got out his banjo 'n' we went to singin'. I noticed that Matt didn't sing much when we got to a church song. Papa had a real pretty deep voice 'n' he sure sang good. He sang one song, called *Swing Low, Sweet Chariot*, that was so pretty 'n' sad at the same time that I almost cried. I think Ma 'n' Aunt Sandra did cry a mite. Squeak made funny noises sometimes while we was singin', almost like he was tryin' to sing along with us. We all got a good laugh outa that. After a spell we all turned in. It was startin' to get cold.

The next day it snowed 'n' Aunt Sandra got to worryin' about Uncle George but Matt told her that they were most likely in Tucson by then and that the weather there weren't nowhere near as cold as it was up here in the higher country. Seems like she quit worryin' as soon as Matt said it.

Matt 'n' me 'n' Tater helped Papa fix up his chicken coop real good. Matt wasn't the best hand with a hammer but he done all right. It was about the only thing I had ever seen him do that he didn't do better than anybody else. He'd hammer with his left hand, then switch to his right. Seems like he didn't know for sure which hand he was better at hammerin' with. Squeak was with us, right in the middle of the coop, watchin' all the goin's on. Them chickens didn't pay him no mind at all. It was like he was one of them. Even the rooster didn't have much to say about Squeak bein' in his coop.

Late in the afternoon Matt stopped hammerin' 'n' stood

up, lookin' all around. He went to walkin' to the schoolhouse at a right fast pace. I followed him but didn't say nothin'. He went inside the schoolhouse 'n' got his lookin' glass then climbed the little hill behind our house 'n' looked through it.

"Yankees, boy. Looks like me 'n' Critter 'n' Judd are gonna have to leave for a while. I don't wanna bring any trouble to you or yours." He looked around at the fresh snow. "It ain't gonna be easy to hide tracks in this snow, boy. Get everybody together as fast as you can."

"Yessir," I said. There I was, back in the Confederate cavalry again, takin' orders from my captain.

In ten minutes we was all standin' by the fire pit. Matt looked at all of us 'n' said, "I need some help from all of you to keep these Yankees from knowin' I've been here. If they find out, it might not go good for you. "He didn't say anything for a few seconds then he said, "I'm gonna ride out of here on Critter. I'll be takin' Judd with me. I need you to move the cattle through here 'n' do anything else you can think of to cover my tracks. I'll hit the creek an' run it for quite a spell, but between here an' there, there is need for a lot of tracks in this fresh snow. Looks to me like they'll be here in less than two hours. I'll be back when I think it's safe."

"*Adios, muchacho*," said Ignacio 'n', the next thing I knew, Matt was in our house, gettin' Chollo. He was a lot better but he still had a ways to go.

When Matt came out of the house with Chollo, Ma said, "Surely, Mr. Grady, you're not taking Chollo? He's not well enough."

Matt looked at Ma like she was a child. "Miss Penny, he's Apache. Those Yankees kill Apaches. Even if they didn't kill him, they'd put him in prison. To an Apache that's the same as dyin'."

Ignacio already had Dunny saddled for Chollo. Matt had Critter saddled real quick. Ma 'n' Aunt Sandra gave 'em some food 'n' extra blankets 'n' they was gone.

We all saddled up 'n' went after that ol' brindle bull. All of us was ridin', even Ma. We found him 'n' the others where we knew we would 'n' drove 'em home, across the creek 'n' all around the coral 'n' then we moved 'em back across the creek 'n' let 'em drift. I'd say when it was all said 'n' done, that was one confused bunch of cattle.

After we let the cattle loose, we built a big fire 'n' started cookin', kinda like we was havin' a celebration. When the soldiers got there, Ma told Lieutenant Barton all about how we got such a good price for our cattle in Tucson 'n' had decided it called for a celebration. She invited all of them soldiers to stay 'n' eat with us. There musta been close to twenty, an' Lieutenant Barton kept thankin' Ma all afternoon.

Sargent Culpepper kept lookin' at all the tracks but he never said nothin'.

Them soldiers sure paid a lot of attention to Ma 'n' Socorra once they found out they wasn't married. One soldier kept askin' Ma if he could help do anything. After about a dozen times, Ma kinda casual-like mentioned that we could always use more firewood. Next thing I knew, pert near everyone of them soldiers was cuttin' wood. We didn't have near enough axes, but them without axes used knives or little hatchets. Them soldiers cut more wood in two hours than Matt 'n' me did in a week.

Next thing I knowed, they was fixin' our chicken coop, an' then they even built a little corral next to the big one. 'Ceptin' for Matt bein' gone, I got to thinkin' it was a good idea to have these fellas stop by every once in a while to take care of chores. Now if I could only get one of 'em to do my milkin', my life would sure get better in a hurry. They did churn butter though an', I gotta say, they did a real fine job.

Just before dusk, Sargent Culpepper walked up to lieutenant Barton 'n' told him about a bunch of graves he'd found.

When Lieutenant Barton asked Ma about it, she made up quite a yarn. She told how Uncle George ‘n’ the Lincolns ‘n’ Peraltas had killed them Indians a while back. When it got to the four fresh graves, Ma had a tougher time with her yarn, seein’ as how most of our men folk were in town, but she got through it. Sargent Culpepper kinda raised an eyebrow a bit in the listenin’ but he never said nothin’.

Lieutenant Barton said, “You shot one of those scalp hunters yourself, Ma’am?”

Ma nodded. “I had no choice, Lieutenant. They were going to kill us all and take the scalps of the Peralta women as Apache bounty.”

Sargent Culppeper said, “They bein’ the scum of the earth - beggin’ yer pardon, Ma’am.”

The lieutenant put his hand on Ma’s arm. “It must have been terrifying.”

Ma smiled ‘n’ moved her arm a bit. “It was, Lieutenant, but we all did what we had to do.”

Sargent Culpepper said, “I’ll be sayin’ ye certainly did - and a fine job it was too.”

Ma smiled at him ‘n’ said, “Thank you, Sargent Culpepper.”

About this time, a bunch of them soldiers gave three cheers to Ma ‘n’ the rest of us for takin’ care of business with them scalp hunters. I got to wonderin’ what they’d do if they knew Matt ‘n’ Chollo had killed them fellers. Instead of cheerin’ they’d probably want to be killin’ Matt ‘n’ Chollo. It didn’t make much sense to me.

The soldiers camped south of us that night ‘n’ left at daybreak next day. I was wishin’ they would stay a little longer ‘n’ get a few more chores done.

Chapter 38

Matt had come back almost as fast as them soldiers was ridin' outa sight an' we carried on like they wasn't no such thing as a Yankee.

It was a day or so after the soldiers came to our place an' we was lookin' for a steer that had plumb quit the bunch an' headed south. Matt an' me 'n' Judd had been followin' his tracks for the better part of the day an' it didn't seem like we was gainin' much. All-of-a-sudden Matt reined up an' put a finger to his lips. I thought at first that he'd spotted the steer but he was actin' like it might be somethin' else.

We was in a stand of mesquite an' there was some more mesquite an' big boulders up ahead of us. Judd was standin' real still next to one of the boulders. Matt slid out of the saddle an' pulled his Henry from the scabbard. I knew that steer had caused us a bunch of grief but I thought shootin' him was goin' a mite far.

Matt put his hand out, palm down, tellin' me to dismount an' get low. I didn't wait even a second. He pointed to his Henry an' I got my carbine. I was real sure somethin' bad was about to happen an' I was just as sure it didn't have nothin' to do with no maverick steer.

Matt pointed at a boulder an' motioned that I should get behind it, then he moved towards them big rocks up ahead of us an' I lost sight of him. I just crouched behind that boulder an' didn't move a muscle till I couldn't stand it no more. I was about to get up when Matt stepped around the boulder I was hidin' behind. Liked to scared me plumb to death.

"Scalp hunters, boy. About half a day gone. There's some dead folks up there. I know you've seen dead folks but this is a mite rough. They've been scalped. I covered 'em up the best I could but I'm gonna need help buryin' 'em. Are you up to it?"

"Sure, Matt. We can't leave 'em out here without a Christian burial."

"They're not Christians, boy, but they still need buryin'."

I didn't know how he knew they wasn't Christians till we walked the horses into the little clearing; then it was pretty clear. They was Indians. There was five of 'em. Two men, two women an' a little boy. The boy weren't no more than five or six. The tops of their heads was all red with blood where their scalps had been taken. The faces of the men had been beat in with rocks or some such thing, an' then they'd been trampled by horses. The women, well, I couldn't get much of a look at them 'cause Matt had covered 'em right proper with clothes 'n' such that was layin' around, but I could tell they was naked under all them rags Matt had piled on 'em.

My stomach got to turnin' over an' I had to walk away for a minute. When I came back, Matt was lookin' at the face of one of the women. Tears was runnin' down his cheeks. I didn't know what to think. I had never seen Matt cry. I was scared plumb speechless. All-of-a-sudden Matt stood up an' looked at the sky. He clenched his fists an' screamed a kinda scream I hadn't never heard before an' I almost wet my britches. The sound musta carried a hundred miles. I just stood real still, not knowin' what was gonna happen next an' hopin' I wouldn't find out the hard way.

He looked at the sky for a long time, then he turned to me an' said, "You better go home, boy. Can you find your way?"

I know my voice was shakin' as bad as the rest of me but I said, "We gotta bury 'em, Matt. We can't leave 'em like this."

Matt looked at me a spell an' it was almost like I could see life comin' back into his eyes. "Yeah. You're right, boy. We gotta bury 'em." He walked to a pile of stuff layin' by an old campfire an' picked up a small ax. It had blood on it. "Find yourself somethin' to dig with an' let's get it done."

Neither one of us said a word the whole time we was diggin' them graves. Judd musta knowed what we was doin' for he dug next to Matt. It was more 'n two hours before we was finished. We put the bodies in the graves together, 'ceptin' for that one woman. Matt tended to her himself. He wouldn't let me near her. I stood back a bit while he put her down in that hole about as gentle as if she was a delicate flower. When he had her covered, he knelt next to her grave an' rocked back an' forth for a few minutes. He was sayin' somthin' in Apache, I think, but I had no notion what it was.

Right sudden he stood up an' looked at the sun sinkin' low in the west. "It's late, boy. I reckon you're gonna have to stay with me tonight."

I hadn't planned on doin' anything but that in the first place so I was glad when he said I could. "What are we gonna do now, Matt?"

"I can't let you go home alone with the scalp hunters out here, boy, so I reckon we're gonna catch us some scalp hunters tomorrow." He started walkin' around the camp, lookin' at the ground an' the mesquite an' the big boulders.

After a bit he stopped an' took a cigar out of his pocket. After it was lit, I said, "How many you figure they was?"

"Six," he said.

Not five or six, or six or seven, but "six".

"You sure?" I said.

"Six. At least one is sittin' a California saddle. His horse is about fifteen hands and the rider is a big man for a Mexican. Two of the others are on Morgan horses. Probably stole 'em from the Yankee cavalry. One is ridin' a small horse, probably from hill country somewhere, judgin' by the way the horse walks. One is ridin' a chestnut with a silver saddle. The last one is on a palomino with a bar shoe on the right hind. They're leading two burros."

Now there ain't no way in the world he could have knowed all of that but I was sure he did. I guess I musta looked a mite befuddled 'cause Matt said, "It's all here, boy. Come here. I'll show you."

I followed him to one of the boulders. He pointed at it an' said, "They surprised the camp but the Apaches put up a short fight before they went down." He pointed to the side of a boulder. "See this?"

I leaned into the boulder but all I saw was a mark on it about waist high.

"If you look real close, you'll see a small splinter of wood. The kind of wood that comes from the stirrup of a California saddle. There are still a few of 'em out here, mainly used by Mexicans." He pointed to the ground. "One of the Apaches must 've got enough of a grip on the bridle to bring the horse down. This is where his shoulder hit and this is where his head hit. See the imprint of the stirrup? Long from top to bottom. Big man. Tall. When the horse gets up, he moves over here." Matt pointed. "His rider gets off. The horse takes a few steps from side to side. Much shallower track without the weight of the man. See this mark in the dirt? It was made by a Mexican spur with a big rowel."

There was a pool of dryin' blood next to the marks of the horse's head. That musta been from the Apache.

Matt pointed to the pool of dried blood. "See the hair next to the blood?"

I nodded.

"It's not Apache. The poor guy musta got a handful of mane when he took the horse down. It's white beneath all the blood, so the horse is a grey or paint. Most likely a grey, as big as he is."

I almost forgot about the terrible things I'd just seen on account of Matt was readin' so much out of the signs left behind by them scalp hunters, an' I was findin' it downright interestin'.

He moved closer to where we buried the Indians an' pointed at a sharp edge of a boulder. "Horse hair. Chestnut, from the right flank, close to the saddle. A small silver concho is layin' on the ground."

My mouth musta surely been wide open but I can't swear to it on account of I couldn't see myself.

Matt stepped a few feet towards the south an' pointed at the ground. "Bar shoe on the right hind. Probably got a split hoof." He followed the tracks about fifteen yards an' pointed to a mesquite tree. There was some gold-colored hair in the branches. "The bar shoe is a palomino."

He walked back past the graves an' pointed to a bunch of tracks. "This is a smaller horse. You can't be for sure just by lookin' at the tracks where he was standin', but if you look here," He pointed to another spot. "You can see the horse's stride pretty clear. Probably about thirteen hands or less. See how his stride is shorter an' how he walks with more pressure on the outside of the hoof? Kinda like he's always tryin' to be sure he's keepin' a good balance."

I wasn't none too sure of all of that but I reckoned it could be true. I couldn't see no way he could tell the other two horses was Morgans. Matt musta read my mind, 'cause the next thing he did was walk down the trail a ways an' point to some more tracks.

He said, "See the length of the stride? It's long. Longer than most. Take a look at the rear hoof prints. See how the front of the hoof makes a real deep mark?"

I nodded. I didn't wanna say anything on account of I

didn't want Matt to lose track of what he was sayin'. It was like I didn't wanna break the magic spell.

"These horses aren't runnin' here. They're just walkin'. A Morgan walks that way. The last Morgan I saw was ridden by a Yankee cavalryman. We had 'em too. When we could get 'em. Best horse in a fight you can get."

Matt walked a few more feet down the trail an' pointed to a big Palo Verde tree. "If you look around over there, you'll see burro tracks. Two sets."

I ran to the Palo Verde an' looked an', sure enough, there was two sets of smaller hoof prints. I was plumb amazed. I figured Matt was about the smartest man I ever knew. Almost as smart as my pa.

It was gettin' dark so we moved up hill a ways from the graves an' set up a cold camp. Matt wouldn't allow no fire on account of it could be seen from quite a distance. Judd disappeared into the rocks 'n' brush an' Critter kinda stood in a clump of mesquite. He was hard to see standin' there an' I wondered if that was why he'd picked that spot. I reckoned he was savvy enough to know how to hide like that. Patches was tethered to a mesquite only about ten yards from where I was fixin' to go to sleep.

I didn't think I'd ever sleep again after seein' them dead Indians but I musta fell asleep as soon as my head hit my saddle. I woke up about half-an-hour before sunup an' saw that Matt wasn't next to me. His soogans was there but he wasn't. I got up, real quiet-like, an' walked down to them graves. Matt was there, kneelin' next to the one that he put that one woman in. In the dark grey of the early mornin' it was hard to see real plain, but I think Matt was cryin' again. Not 'cause I could see tears or nothin' like that but because he was sittin' so still, like the way Ma sometimes did next to Pa's grave. I knew Ma was cryin' when she did that. I didn't know what to say or do so I turned around to go back to our camp.

Matt said, "It's okay, boy. You can come down here if you like."

His voice was soft but, in the quiet of the dawn, it seemed loud.

I walked up to the grave an' knelt next to him. He still didn't say nothin'. After a while, I said, "Did you know her, Matt?"

The sky was turnin' grey an' I saw him nod.

"She was Taza's sister. We used to play together when we were kids. She used to follow me around so much, Taza started teasin' me about it. I couldn't stand the teasin' so I avoided her after that." He sat there for a spell, lookin' down at the grave. After a bit, he looked at me an' said, "Boy, I'm goin' after six men. I'm afraid to send you back home in case they circled north. That decision, I'm leavin' up to you. You wanna ride back home or take up the trail?"

That wasn't even a choice insofar as I was concerned. "I wanna stay with you, Matt. I wanna get them scalp hunters too."

"Okay, boy. I want you to ride behind me and a little to the right. Keep your eyes open and your hands on your carbine."

"Yessir!" I said.

Matt stood up an' looked at the grave then he started off for our camp. "Let's have a biscuit and some coffee. It's light enough now."

We tracked them scalp hunters for the better part of the day an' we caught up with 'em, sure enough. Trouble is, Cochise had caught up with 'em first. We was ridin' into the mouth of a draw when Matt drew rein an' sat real still. Looked to me like he was sniffin' the air. Pretty soon he pulled his Henry from it's scabbard an' fired three shots in the air. In less than a minute ten Apaches came ridin' from the draw with Taza in the lead. They pulled up about ten yards from us an' was I ever scared. I wasn't sure what they was gonna do.

Matt nodded at Taza an' said somethin' in Apache. Taza said somethin' back an' Matt said some more. This time he musta told the story about the Indians we buried 'cause Taza looked up at the sky an' let out a yell like Matt had done the day before. He turned his horse an' rode back up the draw as fast as he could. The rest of the Apaches followed an' we followed them.

Up near the head of the draw, them six scalp hunters was all staked to trees, upside down. There was still coals glowin' in fires next to their heads. I could smell the burnin' flesh an' reckoned that's what Matt was sniffin' for earlier. My stomach started turnin' flip flops an' I reined up a ways short of the rest an' kinda backed Patches up a few feet.

One of them scalp hunters was still alive. He was screamin' but his screams seemed a mite weak to me. Taza ran up to the glowin' coals of the fire next to his head an' kicked 'em away, like maybe he was gonna let the man live. Turns out, he wanted him to suffer longer, but the man was too far gone. Taza started skinnin' his belly an the man up an' died.

It was plumb strange how it got deathly quiet as soon as the man died. Nobody moved for a spell. Cochise was there with about thirty more Apaches an', after a bit, he walked up to Taza. They talked Apache for a few minutes, then Cochise walked up to Matt, who was still mounted. They talked Apache for quite a bit then Cochise turned to me an' said in English, "You help find these Mexicans?"

"Yes, Sir," I said kinda quiet-like.

He looked at me for a spell an' I swear I saw his face soften up a bit, kinda like Ma's after she's scolded me too much for somethin'. "You should go home now, Crawford. This is a sad day. Give greetings to your family."

Matt nodded at Taza an' Cochise an' turned Critter

around. As I turned Patches, I saw six horses ‘n’ two burros tied together near a big tree. There was a big grey, a chestnut, a small pinto, two big blacks and a palomino. Matt hadn’t missed a one.

Judd took off on our right flank, an’ we rode outa that draw an’ headed for home.

Chapter 39

It was pert near two weeks before Uncle George ‘n’ the others got back from Tucson. Matt ‘n’ Chin Ling ‘n’ Chuy left for Texas the next day.

Chollo was doin’ real good ‘n’ he was learnin’ English in the schoolhouse, just like the rest of us. One day a week, Aunt Sandra called it language day, we all tried to learn Mexican ‘n’ Chinese ‘n’ Apache. I got to where I could understand some Mexican but I never really got very far with Apache ‘n’ didn’t do much better with Chinese, but it was fun to say the different words ‘n’ point out things. I did learn a few words for everyday things like horse ‘n’ cow ‘n’ house ‘n’ man ‘n’ such. Things like that I could say in four languages. It made me feel kinda smart.

Chollo helped as much as he could with chores ‘n’ got stronger every day. I got to likin’ him pretty good. He scared me a little at first but once I got to knowin’ him, he didn’t scare me no more than Tater.

We got a good price for the cattle ‘n’ Uncle George had brought back a bunch of supplies ‘n’ some blacksmith tools. He even had a small forge. Turns out, Papa an’ Chester both knew the blacksmith trade. They set about makin’ plans to build a small blacksmith building near Papa’s place.

When I got to thinkin’ about it, I reckoned I was about the luckiest kid in the world. I lived in a place where there was Mexicans, ‘n’ Negroes ‘n’ Chinese ‘n’ Confederates ‘n’ Apaches ‘n’ white folks ‘n’ none of us knew the difference. We all helped each other ‘n’ watched out for one another. It turns out that none of the families had the same religions either but we didn’t let that bother us none. The Peraltas was Catholic.

The Lincolns was Baptist. I weren't real sure what Chin Ling was, 'n' Chollo believed in spirits in the mountains 'n' such. I wasn't real clear on Matt's views, 'ceptin' maybe he believed more like Chollo than anything else. Uncle George 'n' the rest of us was Presbyterians.

With all the differences we had amongst us, I got to wonderin' why it was so hard for the rest of the world to get along. We was doin' fine; why couldn't they? Aunt Sandra said most folks that didn't get along had problems because of religions or greed. She tried to explain that some folks thought everybody should be like they were 'n' believe like they believed. That sounded kinda borin' to me. I couldn't imagine me 'n' Tater 'n' Pancho bein' the same. Things was different out west, 'n' I liked it the way they was here, 'ceptin' for the bad people, 'n' they sure seemed to be plenty enough of them. Aunt Sandra said someday there would be law 'n' order in this country 'n' things would get better. I wondered if that meant we were all gonna have to be the same. I'd rather have the bad men if that were so.

Me 'n' Tater 'n' Pancho 'n' Billy Jo made a sled out of some little tree trunks with some branches laid across between 'em. Papa smoothed out the bottoms 'n' rounded the fronts of them trunks for us so's we could get up some pretty good speed. We'd drag our sled up to the top of the hill behind our house 'n' all jump on board 'n' have a grand time slidin' down the hill. It was a chore draggin' it back up the hill until we hooked Jack to it with a rope 'n' he did the draggin' for us. Jack seemed to have as much fun as we did. He sure was a good mule. Blue chased us down the hill a bunch of times, barkin' 'n' howlin' till he got plumg tuckered out. Squeak did his best to follow us down the hill but he got lost in the deep snow, so Mel held him an' rode down with us.

In late February it commenced to snowin' real hard. Seemed like it was never gonna stop. I didn't remember any snow like that the year before. I guess maybe the weather out here ain't always the same. Matt 'n' Chuy 'n' Chin Ling came ridin' in, pushin' more than two hundred head of cattle in the middle of that storm. Everybody turned out at our place to greet 'em 'n' we had a real nice supper. Chuy told stories about how Judd 'n' Critter had practically kept the herd movin' in the right direction with hardly any help from him or Matt or Chin Ling.

Matt thought we should take most of the cattle to Tucson 'n' sell them while the price was still high. Uncle George 'n' the others agreed. I don't know much about how the money was to be split up but everybody seemed happy with the arrangements.

Chin Ling had a small pot-bellied stove on the back of his mule, an' a bunch of us helped him put it in his little house. Before long he had a fire goin' 'n' was jabberin', real happy-like, in Chinese. I will say, it sure warmed up that little place in a hurry. It got so hot we had to open the door to cool things off a mite.

Chuy told how they had met up with some of Cochise's tribe south of Fort Bowie 'n' had given 'em ten head of cattle an' some tobacco. Seems like the Chiricahuas was havin' a rough winter 'n' the army had poisoned some of the water holes 'n' some of Cochise's people were sick. It didn't seem right to me. Chuy said Matt was ready to attack Fort Bowie but him 'n' Chin Ling had talked him out of it, sayin' they should get the cattle home first, then maybe they could attack Fort Bowie.

Matt looked over Papa's little blacksmith shop 'n' asked him to shoe Dunny. They agreed on a price 'n' Papa went to work. Matt had Critter shoed in El Paso Del Norte, so he was in good shape.

I showed Matt our sled 'n' he rode down the hill a few times with us 'n' then he made "improvements" by putting a little rudder on it so's we could steer it. Papa had the rudder made in about an hour. Next thing, we was steerin' that sled like a little boat 'n' havin' even a better time than we had before.

Matt had supper with us that evenin'. I could tell Ma was glad to have him. What with the snow, every family ate at their own place, 'cept Chin Ling 'n Uncle George 'n' Aunt Sandra 'n' Chollo. They ate with us that night. Chin Ling helped fix the food 'n' he made some kinda rice with beef in it. Matt wasn't crazy about it but I thought it tasted good. I could tell Matt would'a' rather had some chile 'n' beans. He didn't let on but I think Ma knew too.

The wind died down with dusk 'n' the snow was fallin' in big, soft flakes. The fireplace kept us all warm 'n' Ma looked real pretty in the soft glow of the light from it. I got to feelin' lonely for Pa even though Matt was there. I remembered lots of times when Ma 'n' Pa sat by the fireplace 'n' just held hands.

Then I got to thinkin' how it would be to have Matt for a pa. I know he liked Ma. 'N' Ma liked him. I was sure of it. I liked Matt more than any man I ever knew, 'ceptin' for my pa, an' I got to wishin' he would stay forever 'n' be with us always, but I had trouble drawin' that picture. Mel liked Matt too. I heard her ask Ma once if Matt was gonna marry her 'n' be our new pa. Ma looked at her 'n' said, "I don't think Mr. Grady will ever marry anybody, Honey."

"Why?" asked Mel.

Ma had put her arm around Mel 'n' said, "Mr. Grady is a fine man, Mel, but he's also a troubled man."

"What does that mean, Ma?" I had asked.

"He has no country and that bothers him more than we know."

"Oh," I said. I was a mite confused but I didn't want to let on.

"Why does he need a country when he has us?" said

Mel.

Ma smiled 'n' kissed Mel on the forehead. "That's a real good question, Hon. Maybe I'll ask him someday," she said.

I got dragged out of my private thoughts when Uncle George cleared his throat 'n' said, "Mr. Grady, I know it's none of my business, but I feel compelled to speak on a matter of importance."

Matt smiled. "Speak away, George."

"Well, we were wondering, that is, *I* was wondering, what your plans are for the future. None of us would be here now if not for you, and we all know it. You have protected us and helped us prosper. You seem to want little for yourself and show no clear commitment to remaining here with us. This concerns me."

Matt grinned. "I got no plans to leave you in a tight, George."

"Mr. Grady, won't you please consider ending your war with the United States?" asked Uncle George. It almost sounded like he was beggin'.

Matt quit grinnin' 'n' got kind of a sad look on his face. "I wish I could, George. But I can't."

Aunt Sandra said, "Mr. Grady, you are a kind man and we all love you for what you have done for us and who you are. None of us want to see you live in pain like you have been. You have a home here, Mr. Grady. Please reconsider."

Matt looked at the wall behind Aunt Sandra but he wasn't seein' it. He was lookin' plumb through it to a place only he could see. "While I was in El Paso Del Norte, I heard some talk that a Confederate unit was bein' formed in Mexico. I been givin' some thought to ..."

"No!" Ma said. She'd been sittin' but now she was standin'. "No, Mr. Grady. You cannot be thinking such a thing! The Southern Confederacy is dead! You have people here who care for you and need you. If those people in Mexico try to continue the war, they will all perish. If you join them, you will see the same end. It would be a terrible waste of a life as good as yours."

I gotta say, I was plumb speechless. Ma had really give Matt what for. I'd never heard her speak like that to nobody.

For a second nobody said a word. Chin Ling kinda sat with his mouth half open. Aunt Sandra 'n' Uncle George didn't look much different. Ma had her hands on her hips 'n' was lookin' real hard at Matt, like maybe she was gonna knock some sense into him. I wasn't too sure about that idea. I got to feelin' real uncomfortable but didn't dare say nothin'. I'd never seen my ma act this way.

I think Matt musta knowed that somethin' powerful was ailin' Ma 'cause he didn't say a word. He just looked right into Ma's eyes. Ma met his stare, eyeball for eyeball. Looked to me nobody was ever gonna say another word. The only sound in the room was the cracklin' of the fire in the fireplace. Nobody was even breathin'.

Finally Ma turned away 'n' walked to the door. She picked up her coat on the rack 'n' went outside into the softly fallin' snow. I started to follow her but Uncle George said, "Stay put, Craw. This is something your mother must work through."

I looked up at Matt. "Matt, Ma loves you. We all want you to stay. Please, Matt, don't go join them Confederates." There's no doubt, *I* was beggin'. I felt Aunt Sandra pattin' me real gentle on the back.

Matt looked at me 'n' I swear his eyes was wet. He said, "That's the problem, boy. I love your Ma 'n' you 'n' Mel 'n' all the rest of the folks here. The big problem is, I love your Ma more than I have a right to."

I couldn't stand it no more. I jumped up 'n' threw my arms around him 'n' held on real tight. Next thing I knew, Mel was huggin' him too.

Uncle George said, "Good Lord, man, who has more of a right to love her than you, Mr. Grady?"

I could feel Matt's hand on my back, huggin' me to him. "Your brother, George."

Aunt Sandra said, "Mr. Grady, please don't think that way. Paul has left us and can do nothing to love and comfort Penny in this life."

"He'll always be with Miss Penny," said Matt. "That's just how things are, Miss Sandra."

"Poppycock!" said Uncle George. "Paul was my brother, and a good man he was too, but he would want Penny to carry on with her life."

"I'm sure he would, George. I can tell he was a fine man and I don't aim to try to fill his boots. I don't think they'd fit."

Aunt Sandra was standin' behind me. Her hand was on my back 'n' I could feel it push against me when she said, "Mr. Grady, in the short time I've known you, I've known nothing but a man of honor and integrity. You are throwing lives away, Mr. Grady. Please. Think it over carefully."

I heard Matt say, "Yes, Ma'am," real soft-like. Then he knelt down in front of me 'n' Mel. "I need you two to know somethin' real plain."

Mel 'n' me both stopped blubberin' 'n' I wiped my eyes with the back of my hand.

He hugged us both 'n' said, "You two are as important to me as almost anything in my life. I hope someday you'll understand why I do whatever it is I end up doin'. I'm gonna go 'n' do some thinkin' for a while. Remember that I love you both. That's a hard word for me to say, but it's true."

He stood 'n' walked out the door.

Chin Ling, who hadn't said a word whilst all of this was goin' on, said, "Wha' hoppen?"

Chollo, who probably understood a little more of what went on, just said, "*Malo.*"

I knew that was the Mexican word for "bad." Chollo didn't say much but, when he did, he said a lot without a bunch of words.

Ma came in out of the snow about ten minutes later. I knew she'd been cryin' 'n' I knew she'd been to Pa's grave.

Chapter 40

Chollo stayed with Chin Ling that night 'n' took it up permanent. Matt 'n' Critter 'n' Judd were gone the next mornin' but most of Matt's gear was still in his wickiup so I knew he'd be back. Papa shoed Dunny 'n' put him in the corral with the rest of the horses. Uncle George 'n' everybody else waited for Matt to come back so they could drive the cattle to Tucson. The snow was gone in a few days 'n' the weather got real warm. I was sure glad to see it. I kept lookin' around for Matt 'cause I knew he was gonna show up at any minute. Ma cried a lot. Aunt Sandra was with her a lot. Seems like she was watchin' over her or somethin'.

About a week went by an', late one afternoon, Judd came trottin' up to our porch. Ma 'n' Aunt Sandra was hangin' clothes out back of the house 'n' I called to 'em real quick. "Ma! Aunt Sandra! Judd's here!"

They came runnin' around the side of the house 'n' we all waited for Matt to come ridin' in on Critter while Mel petted 'n' hugged Judd. After a few minutes, I looked at Judd 'n' said, "Where's Matt?'

Judd picked up his ears 'n' sat up real straight.

"Where's Matt?" I said again.

Judd stood 'n' trotted about ten yards in the direction of the creek 'n' stopped 'n' turned his head to see if we was followin'. He waited real patient.

Ma said, "Oh. He may be hurt. Quick. Saddle some horses. Craw get your carbine."

In five minutes, me 'n' Mel 'n' Aunt Sandra 'n' Ma 'n'

Uncle George was saddled 'n' followin' Judd, who seemed not to be in any particular hurry. We splashed across the creek 'n' headed north, toward that big ol' mesa. When we got near the cave which had brought me 'n' the rest of the Apache Gang a passel of trouble, Judd slowed to a walk.

"Where's Matt?" I asked him. I was gettin' a mite anxious. Judd was actin' real weird - like not a thing in the world was wrong. Judd stopped walkin' long enough to look at me then turned and started walkin' again, even slower than before. He could be a little aggravatin' at times.

"Surrender or die!"

Them words was so close 'n' so loud my heart plumb quit beatin' for a second.

"Mr. Grady?" Ma said.

"Great." I recognized Matt's voice this time. He stood from behind a big boulder about twenty yards above us 'n' to the right. He was holdin' his Henry rifle. He started down the hill 'n' looked a little odd as he almost stumbled a time or two. When he got to where we was, he tipped his hat.

"Howdy, folks. You out for a little ride?" said Matt.

Somethin' about him didn't seem quite regular to me but I couldn't put my finger on it.

Ma looked at me 'n' Mel, then at Matt. "Mr. Grady, have you been drinking?"

Matt grinned. "That I have, Miss Penny. It's just another one of my bad habits when I have any serious thinkin' to do."

Matt was standin' between my horse 'n' Ma's 'n' I could smell it now. I'd smelt it before on a bunch of soldiers in Tucson. I didn't much care for the smell.

I said, "Judd came home 'n' we thought maybe somethin' bad had happened to you."

Matt squinted one eye at Judd. "You really oughta mind your own business," he said. Judd tucked his tail between his legs 'n' pert near crawled into some bushes.

I could see that Aunt Sandra was havin' a tough time holdin' in a laugh.

"Mr. Grady. What will the children think?" said Ma.

Matt answered. "I dunno. Why don't we ask 'em?"

Aunt Sandra said, "You're a very resourceful man, Mr. Grady. Where did you find spirits way out here?"

Matt smiled at Aunt Sandra. "Thank you for the compliment, Miss Sandra. But I'm really not all that resourceful. I picked up some whiskey 'n' tequila in La Mesilla last trip. I was gonna save it for some kind of celebration but other matters came up."

Sounded to me like Matt's words wasn't quite as clear as usual.

Uncle George said, "How do you feel, Mr. Grady?"

"Like a street light in New Orleans, George. Pretty well lit. How 'bout yourself? Everything okay at home?"

"Fine, Mr. Grady. Thank you for asking."

Matt said, "Slide outa them saddles 'n' let the horses rest. It's good to see you."

We all dismounted 'n' tied the horses to bushes 'n' trees. Everything seemed kinda strange to me. I can't really explain it.

Matt had walked over to the mouth of the cave, where the overhang gave some shade, 'n' sat down. We all crowded in 'n' sat. Matt pulled some jerky from one of his saddlebags 'n' offered us all a chew. I was the only one who took a bite.

All this time, Ma was watchin' Matt real close. I saw five or six empty bottles toward the back of the cave entrance. Ma saw 'em too.

"How much have you had to drink today, Mr. Grady?" She said.

Matt kinda leaned over in the direction of them bottles 'n' squinted real hard. He looked at me 'n' said, "How many bottles are there, boy?"

I took a careful count 'n' said, "Six."

Matt looked at Ma 'n' said, "Three."

"Today?" asked Ma. 'N' I could tell by the sound of her voice that three was not a good thing.

"Yes'm. Three yesterday 'n' three today. I've got three left for tomorrow."

"Mr. Grady! A man cannot drink that much hard liquor in one day," said Ma.

Matt arched an eyebrow. "Oh?"

I thought I heard Uncle George chuckle but, when I turned to look, his face was as serious as a preacher's at a funeral.

Seemed like Ma was gettin' more aggravated by the second, what with Uncle George 'n' Aunt Sandra not seemin' to take matters as serious as her, 'n' me 'n' Mel not havin' any idea of what was goin' on.

Ma said, "Mr. Grady, you are not setting a very good example for Craw and Mel."

Matt took off his cap 'n' looked at Ma. "Miss Penny, I wasn't intendin' to set an example of any kind for anybody. That's why I came out here. This is a safe, quiet place. There's no Yankees, an' no kids to set a bad example for, an' no...." He kinda hesitated. "An' no beautiful redheads, which is the reason for the bad example. Now, if you'll excuse me, I have to get some sleep."

Just like that, he laid back, put his forage cap over his eyes, 'n' went to sleep.

Uncle George looked at him a minute then said. "Amazing." He got up 'n' walked over to the empty bottles. One-by-one, he picked 'em up 'n' sniffed at 'em. When he was all done, he said. "I believe him. He drank six of those bottles in two days."

Aunt Sandra started to lookin' a mite worried. "Penny, maybe you had better try to wake him."

Ma patted Matt on the face but he didn't pay it no mind. All it did was cause him to snore a little bit. Finally Ma slapped him a good one 'n' I figured for sure the world was gonna come to an end, but Matt just kept snorin'.

"Perhaps we had better get him to the house," said Uncle George.

Well, we did, but it weren't no easy matter. It took all of us to get him on Critter's back, 'n' Judd kept runnin' around like a nervous chicken in a fox den, almost gettin' in the way from time to time. Judd settled down when he saw Matt was in the saddle. Once we had him there, we couldn't figure how to keep him there. We thought of tyin' his moccasins to the stirrups but reckoned that might not work. Finally, Ma said she would climb on behind him 'n' hold him up.

We all knew that would be suicide – that's what they call it when you deliberately kill yourself – but Ma insisted. Nobody had ever rode Critter but Matt, an' we'd all seen him buck. I got real scared for Ma but, when she climbed up behind Matt, Critter turned his head 'n' looked at her 'n', I swear, that horse showed his teeth in a big grin. Ma smiled at him 'n' reached around Matt 'n' patted him real good 'n' we all headed for home.

Chapter 41

It was about noon the next day when Matt woke up. Uncle George said he would probably sleep for a week but he didn't. When he woke up, seemed like nothin' had ever happened. Matt was his old self. He crawled out of my bed 'n' put on his britches 'n' one of Pa's shirts Ma had left hangin' in the room.

Me 'n' Mel was churnin' butter 'n' Ma was mendin' a pair of my britches when he walked into the room. He looked at Ma kinda shy 'n' said, "Good mornin', Miss Penny."

Ma kinda half smiled 'n' said, "Good afternoon, Mr. Grady."

"Oh," he said, then looked at me 'n' Mel. "Howdy, you two."

Mel jumped up 'n' hugged him 'n' so did I. He bent down 'n' hugged Mel 'n' messed up my hair 'n' then stood up.

"Say, Miss Penny, uh, well, that is, how did I get here?" said Matt.

Now Ma was smilin' real pretty. "Why, Mr. Grady, don't you recall the events of yesterday?"

Matt looked at me, then at the floor, then back to Ma. "Not quite all of 'em apparently. To tell you the truth, the last thing I recall was hearin' riders up by the cave. I figured they was Yankees so I laid an ambush. They must not 'a' been Yankees. Either that or they didn't put up much of a fight. I don't even remember what happened. 'Course, I had tipped a little of the spirits earlier 'n' wasn't in top fightin' condition."

Ma put down the britches she was mendin' 'n' stood real

close to Matt. "You mean you don't recall the words you said to me?"

Matt started to lookin' real worried. "Words I said to you?" He swallowed hard.

"Perhaps you were in a state of incapacitation. Don't worry, Mr. Grady. I'll not hold you to what you said."

"Won't hold me to what I said? What do you mean by that, Miss Penny?"

"Well, it isn't often a woman hears those kinds of words from a man such as yourself, Mr. Grady."

"Those kinds of words?" Matt kind of had a trapped look about him. "What kind of words are we talkin' about, Miss Penny?"

I couldn't stand it no more. I said, "You said Ma was a beautiful redhead."

"That's all?" asked Matt.

"That's all. Then you went to sleep," I said.

Ma looked at me, kind of irritated. I knew she was funnin' with Matt on account of he couldn't remember, 'n' I messed it up, but Matt was lookin' real upset 'n' I couldn't stand it no longer.

Matt cleared his throat. "Well, that was surely rude of me. I apologize to all of you. Then he looked at Ma 'n' said, "If all I said was that you're a beautiful redhead, I did you an injustice, Miss Penny. You are the most beautiful woman I've ever known; in every way beauty describes a person."

Now it was Ma's turn to be uncomfortable. "Well, thank you, Mr. Grady."

Matt said, "Don't thank me. Thank your Christian God. I'm just speakin' a fact. Where's George?"

Just like that, the subject was ended.

Ma didn't say anything right away so I said, "Him 'n' Chuy 'n' Pedro 'n' Chester 'n' Billy Jo 'n' Socorra took a wagon 'n' a bunch of the cattle 'n' started for Tucson at daybreak."

"Chin Ling?" asked Matt.

"Him 'n' Chollo are up at his place. Chollo's gonna help him make 'improvements.'" I was gettin' real proud of that word.

Matt smiled. "I see."

Ma got her voice back. "Would you like some coffee, Mr. Grady?"

"I surely would appreciate it, Miss Penny."

"And something to eat?" she asked.

"Please."

"What would you like?"

"I'm sure whatever you serve will be perfect."

And I gotta say it was. At least from how Matt looked at things. He had eggs 'n' beans with somethin' Pancho called *machaca*. It was shredded beef with chili 'n' stuff in it. Matt liked it a lot. Consuela Peralta had give Ma some tortillas that mornin' 'n' Matt had one of those too. He even had some milk. When he finished, he helped Ma clean up the dishes 'n' then he saddled Critter 'n' headed for the Lincoln's place. Said he was gonna talk with Papa about somethin'. In a minute or two he was back at our place. Mel 'n' me quit churnin' the butter 'n' walked outside with Ma.

"Did you forget something, Mr. Grady?" asked Ma.

"How did you get me here?" he said.

"On Critter," said Ma.

"How did you keep me in the saddle, or did you just drape me over his back like a sack of flour?"

I said, "Ma rode behind you on Critter 'n' held you up."

"She did, huh?"

"She sure did. I thought Critter was gonna get mad 'n' buck but he didn't do nothin'. He just let Ma get up behind you like maybe it weren't nothin' unusual."

Matt patted Critter on his neck 'n' turned him back towards Papa's place. "Thanks. I was just wonderin'."

Ma watched him go. “I wonder what that was all about?” she said.

Chapter 42

We didn't see much of Matt around the house after that. Oh, we all knew he was close by, workin' on somethin' or another, but he didn't spend no time with us. Seems like he was stayin' away deliberate. He took his meals at the Peraltas, 'ceptin' on those days when we all ate together.

Squeak was gettin' bigger an' takin' charge of things from time-to-time. By that, I mean he mostly buffaloed Ol' Blue. I reckon Blue just never got used to the way Squeak looked. Them big teeth in the bottom of his mouth was gettin' dangerous lookin' even though Squeak weren't no bigger than a small dog yet. I reckoned by the time he was full growed, he was gonna be a might hard to boss around. I think maybe Blue knew that too. Squeak never let on that he was mean, even though he looked it. He followed Mel everywhere she went and his little tail would swish back and forth like maybe he was the happiest javelina in the world. I gotta say, he was the cuddliest little guy I ever knew. He loved to be petted an' rubbed.

It was ten days before Uncle George 'n' the others got back from Tucson 'n' they was all excited about how much money they'd made sellin' them cattle. Seemed like they could'a' sold a thousand head is what Uncle George said.

The wagons was full of all kinds of good things but the most important to me was the licorice. Uncle George gave me a whole handful of it. That sure tasted good. I saved some for Matt 'cause I knew he liked it. Gave some of it to the Apache Gang too, 'n' still had plenty left. Uncle George said I was workin' real hard 'n' had earned it proper.

Later, Matt sat with his back up against a cottonwood an' his fishin' pole hangin' out over the creek. His forage cap was pulled low over his eyes an' I couldn't tell for sure if he was sleepin' or not. Chollo was upstream a bit, sittin' real still an' just lookin' at me an' Matt an' the rest of the Apache Gang. I don't reckon he had any idea of what we was doin'. I don't think he'd ever seen anybody fishin' before. He looked like maybe he was waitin' for somethin' to happen. If the truth be known, so was I. When I went fishin', if I didn't get a bite pretty quick, I'd pull the line out an' throw another cast. Not Matt. He threw the line in the water an' leaned up against that tree an' looked like he didn't care if he ever moved again till he got a bite. He sure was patient.

I was just a couple of feet on Matt's right an' I'd probably cast my line about fifty times while he'd been leanin' into that tree. I weren't havin' no better luck than Matt but I was sure workin' at it a lot harder. I found that right peculiar 'cause I was usually able to get a couple of fish in pretty short order. I figured maybe Matt was jinxin' me an' decided to move downstream about twenty yards.

When I got up to move, Chollo was up like a cat on his way to a birdbath. He followed me a ways an', when I stopped an' threw in my line, he took up a position about in the middle of me 'n' Matt an' sat down an' looked straight ahead. I figured he was watchin' me 'n' Matt both out of the corners of his eyes by lookin' at the creek.

I looked behind us for the horses an' Chollo's sorrel was still tied next to Patches. I couldn't see Critter but I knew he was back there somewhere, most likely seein' what kind of trouble he could stir up. Judd was layin' down on Matt's left side, like he didn't have a care in the world, an' Matt hadn't moved a muscle since I'd moved downstream.

I sure couldn't figure him. He seemed to always be busy doin' somethin' an' this was the first time I'd ever seen him sit still for more 'n a few minutes. It didn't seem right somehow an' I wondered if maybe he wasn't sick.

Pancho musta got bored or somethin', 'cause he tossed a little pebble into the creek.

Without liftin' his cap, Matt said, "That ain't gonna catch you any fish, Pancho."

Pancho, he kind of jerked his head in Matt's direction an' held on to his fishin' pole real quiet-like. I could see Matt smile under his cap.

Tater 'n' Billie Jo just looked at each other an' didn't move a lick.

'Bout this time, here came Mel 'n' Ebony 'n' Tina 'n' Squeak. They sure didn't make no bones about their comin'. They was makin' more racket than a team of runaway horses. Mel 'n' Ebony was singin' some song about spring flowers in the winter or somethin' like that, an' Tina was bein' her usual self an' leadin' the way. I suspected Matt was gonna give 'em what-for on account of they was messin' up our fishin', but he just lifted the bill of his forage cap an' smiled, then put it back down over his eyes.

The girls stopped in about the middle of all of us an' finished their song. When they was done, Matt sat up an' clapped his hands.

"Well done, ladies," he said.

I sure couldn't figure him.

Tina said, "Would you like to hear another one?"

Matt sat up real straight and said, "I surely would, but before you gals entertain us with another melody, I figure us men should return your kindness an' sing a song for you."

Tater said, "Does we have ta do dat, Missah Matt? Dem girls allus make fun a' ouhah singin'."

Matt looked at Tater, then to the girls. "Is this true, Ladies? Do you scoff at these young men when they burst into song?"

Mel giggled.

Tina said, "Is that what they call it: singing?"

Matt clucked. "Now, now. Be careful what you say. One of these days you may need the able-bodied assistance of one of these fine specimens of young manhood."

Mel giggled again. "Oh, Matt, you're so funny."

Matt tousled her hair. If anybody else had done that, she'd have pitched a hissy-fit, but she seemed to like it when Matt did it.

Ebony said, "Missuh Matt, what means dat word?"

Matt looked at her an' said, "Which word, Ebony?"

"Scotch."

Matt grinned real big. "The word is 'scoff', with two fs. It sort of means to make fun of someone or to belittle 'em a might."

"Oh," she said.

Ebony was real serious about learnin' proper English. She understood most everything that was said but she could be a might tough to understand when she started talkin' Georgia talk. I figured that was one of the reasons them Confederates had lost the war on account of they couldn't all talk proper.

Matt looked at me 'n' Tater 'n' Pancho 'n' Billie Jo. How 'bout it, gents? You feel. like singin' a song for these lovely ladies?"

Pancho said, "I much prefer to fish."

"Me too," I said. I sure didn't wanna sing no song in front of them girls.

"But we don't have enough poles for the girls." He looked at Mel 'n' Tina 'n' Ebony. "You girls wanna try your hand at fishin'?"

Mel jumped up an' down an' said, "Can we?"

Matt looked at me an' I held up my pole. I'd rather let Mel use it than sing in front of Tina. Mel ran over an' grabbed it before I had a chance to change my mind. Next thing I knew, Tater an' Poncho gave up their poles. Guess they felt the same way about singin' in front of them girls as I did.

Me 'n' Tater 'n' Poncho hadn't even moved away from the bank of the creek when Mel caught a fish. She hadn't even landed hers when Ebony caught one an' was pullin' it in. About the time Mel had hers up on dry land an' was squeelin' for someone to take the hook out, Tina got a bite. It was the darndest thing I ever saw. Us menfolk had been at it for quite a spell an' hadn't caught nothin' but a sunburn, an' here these girls came up to the creek, singin' an' carryin' on an' makin' all sorts of noises, an' every one of 'em caught a fish in less than one minute.

Matt pointed to the cuttin' board Ma had give us for cleanin' the fish 'n' said, "I guess you boys had better start to cleanin'. Looks to me like we may have a time keepin' up with the ladies if we don't get a quick start."

We all moaned an' complained a mite but it didn't do no good. Matt picked up one of them fish 'n' sliced it open an' went to work cleanin' it. I took out my knife 'n' so did the others, 'ceptin' Chollo. He just stood off to the side an' watched us all while we went to the dirty work.

I gotta say, Matt was right, sure enough. Them girls caught fifteen fish before you could blink an eye. We was still cleanin' fish when the girls laid our poles down an' skipped back towards the house, Squeak bein' the last one outa sight, his little tail swishin' back and forth.. Tina gave me one of her smarty-pants smiles as she bounced by me. There wasn't much I could do about it 'cept swallow my pride.

Billie Jo looked at me an' said, "Don't dat beat all you evah saw? Dem girls is here five minutes an' dey ketch pert-near ev'ry fish in da stream an' dey ups an' leaves us to do dah dirty work."

I reckoned Billie Jo was lookin' to me to do somethin',

so I said to Matt, "Yeah, Matt, how's come the girls get to have all the fun an' we gotta do all the work?"

Matt finished cleanin' the fish he was workin' on an' looked at me with a big grin. "'Cause they caught all the fish. You wouldn't expect them to do everything, would you?"

He had me there. I didn't know how to answer that one without soundin' plumb stupid. Pa had always shared the work with Ma. As a matter-of-fact, all of us shared chores. "No," I said, real quiet-like. Billie Jo kinda scowled at me for a second but he knew Matt was right, so he went back to cleanin' his fish pretty quick.

Chapter 43

I was pretty excited about goin' to La Messilla. Chin Ling 'n' Billy Jo was drivin' the wagon but me 'n' Matt 'n' Chuy was ridin' horseback. I was leadin' Jack but he weren't no particular trouble. He was a real good mule. Judd was out in front an' off to the right a bit, kinda scoutin', an' I could tell he was havin' a great adventure.

We made good time the first day an' even better on the second but Matt left us early in the mornin' of the second day an' said for us to take the Butterfield road so's to make the most of our time. He said he'd loop around a bit an' meet us where the road crossed San Simon wash on the other side of Fort Bowie. He figured there weren't no sense in him takin' the chance of meetin' up with the Yankees.

On the evenin' of the third day we met at the wash and headed for the little range of mountains south of Silver City. Once we hit the down-side of the mountains the goin' was real easy. After a long gradual uphill spell we hit some real flat land an' it stayed that way for most of the way into Messilla.

Late afternoon of the seventh day we topped a rise an I was lookin' into a valley that seemed right pretty to me. There was a big river runnin' through the valley an' east of the river about two or three miles was Messilla. About fifteen or twenty miles east of the town was some mountains that looked like organ pipes on top. I had never seen anyplace like it. It was almost like lookin' into a storybook.

"Let's let the horses blow," said Matt. An' we all dismounted an' loosened our cinches. Matt lit a cigar an' Chuy took some tobacco out of his pouch an' rolled himself a smoke.

Chin Ling lit a funny-lookin' pipe an' they all sat together an' looked at the valley. Me 'n' Billy Jo looked at the river for a spell.

"How far you figure it is to the River?" I asked Matt.

"About an hour," he said, talkin' around the smoke.

"Dat don' look like it be no hour, Missuh Matt. Looks like we be dere in 'bout ten o' fi'teen minutes," said Billy Jo.

"Things out here are always farther away than they look, Billy Jo," said Matt.

"Yeah. I s'ppose y'all raht. Dis here hill we jus' clum' di'n't look like so much at da' beginnin' but by da time we gots here I was plumb tuckered."

Chuy said, "Thees place is very beautiful. Is that the right word, *Senor* Matt?"

Matt smiled. "That's the right word all right."

Chin Ling kinda bobbed his head up an' down. "Velly pletty up here. Not so pletty down there."

"What is wrong with it?" asked Chuy.

"Too many white men. No Chinee."

Matt laughed. He looked around at all of us then said, "I'd say you got a pretty good mix of all kind of folks in our little party."

Chin Ling pulled his lips back in a grin. "Too bad Mesilla not like our party. Too many Mexicans and white men make fun of Chin Ling."

"You stay with me, Chin Ling," said Chuy. "I will not let them make fun of you."

Matt said, "I hope there's no trouble - but Chuy's right, Chin Ling - nobody'll be makin' fun of you."

"Missa Matt no can make fight. Big trouble with soldiers. They not know Missa Matt never give up."

Matt kinda shrugged. "We'll do whatever it is we have to do."

Chuy looked at Matt real hard for a spell then said,

"*Senor* Matt, this war, it is over?"

Matt took a deep puff on his cigar. "I reckon it is - for most folks. I don't think I'm ever gonna get there, amigo."

"Why is this?" asked Chuy.

"The way I look at it is real simple. The folks in the south, and out here in Arizona, voluntarily left the Union that they had voluntarily helped form. It was their right to do that. The central government in Washington City said they couldn't do it and, because they had the firepower, they imposed their will on the peoples of the Confederacy. To my way of thinkin', that's wrong."

I ain't sure Chuy had a notion of what Matt was talkin' about but he nodded an' went back to smokin'. I had no idea what Matt meant but I knew it was powerful in his chest. It worried me more than a little.

Billy Jo said, "Dat ribber got a name?"

Matt grinned real big an' said, "That, my friend, is the Rio Grande."

"We cross dat ribber on da way out wes' but ah nevva knowed da name a' it."

"Now you do," said Matt.

After that, nobody said much of anything for quite a spell. We musta sat there for half an hour just watchin' the Rio Grande an' Mesilla. From up in the hills where we were it sure looked peaceful. Finally Matt said, "Let's get it done. We'll camp on the west side of the river tonight and ride in after daybreak."

It wasn't much passed first light when we crossed the Rio Grande an' rode into La Messilla the next morning. It was bigger than Tucson an' I reckoned Matt figured there was less chance of him bein' noticed by any Yankees. He still wore his forage cap but I seen some others wearing parts of old uniforms too, so I reckoned things was different than in Tucson.

We tied up near the livery an' Matt saw to it our horses was cared for an' given some real oats for their long trip. He asked the man at the livery to grease up the wagon an' check it over real good. When he was done doin' all of this, we went to a real café, where Matt knew the owner from the war days.

We all found seats an' ordered up our food. I ordered me some eggs an' pancakes an' ham. While we was waitin' for our food, Matt talked with the owner of the place, whose name was Mr. Gonzales. Seems like they both knew Captain Hunter, an' Matt asked after him, but Mr. Gonzales said he hadn't seen him since he'd passed through on his way to San Antonio with the Arizona Rangers. He said that Captain Hunter had never come back to his place near Deming as far as he knew. They both wondered about what might have become of him for a spell, then they went to talkin' about the weather an' a bunch of other stuff.

Mr. Gonzales said the stage was back in operation from El Paso to Tucson but not many of them was gettin' through on account of Cochise had stopped most of 'em an' killed all the people an' stole the horses an' other valuables. Matt said he was sorry to hear such a thing. Then Mr. Gonzales said a man named Tom Jeffords had got a stage contract an' swore his coaches would get through to Tucson but he hadn't had anymore luck than the others. Matt sighed an' said that was a pity.

When our food came, I dug into mine right quick. I was most starvin'.

After eatin' we walked down the main street and looked at all the things that was for sale. They sure had a lot more stores than Tucson. There was a mercantile with lots of hardware an' Matt went inside an' talked to the man behind the wooden counter while the rest of us just looked at all the stuff. It had lots more than Mr. Warner's store in Tucson.

After a bit, Matt an' the man went to the back of the

store. In a few minutes they was back an' Matt had a funny-lookin' metal piece in his hand an' some kind of washer. He paid the man some money an' walked outside. We all followed him an' asked what in tarnation was that thing he'd bought.

He held it up a bit so's we could all see it an' said, "I think this is the piece that your Uncle George has been waitin' for so he could get that pump to workin'. If it fits, you won't be carryin' water from the creek. You just grab the handle an' pump."

I couldn't think of any more welcome news than that. Uncle George had written a bunch of letters to St. Louis, askin' about that part an', each time, the company said they had shipped it. Uncle George figured that Cochise must have about a dozen of them things by now.

We walked down to the livery where Matt put the parts in his saddle bag. We all checked our horses to see they was bein' proper cared for then we went back out on Main street. The town was really awake by then an' there was lots of folks walkin' up an' down the streets. I took special note that there was a lot more womenfolk in La Mesilla than there was in Tucson. Mostly folks was Mexican but there was lots of whites too. I didn't see no Chinese though and I took notice that a lot of folks looked at Chin Ling real peculiar.

Chuy said him an' Chin Ling was gonna explore the north side of town an' they left, headed in that direction. Me 'n' Matt 'n' Billy Jo went into a saddlery an' looked at all the tack. Uncle George was in need of harness an' such an' Matt pulled out the list Uncle George had give him an' ordered up everything on it.

We was loaded up pretty good when we walked out of the saddlery an' we was strugglin' for the livery to put the tack in the wagon when I noticed a commotion on the street in front of us. A big crowd was gathered right in the middle of the street, watchin the goin's on. When we got closer I could see that Chuy an' Chin Ling was smack-smooth in the middle of it.

Two white men an' a Mexican was beatin' up on Chin Ling an' Chuy. It didn't seem fair to me. I reckon Matt felt the same way 'cause he set his load on the dirt street an' said, "Watch our gear." Then he pushed his way through the crowd an' dove right in to that fight.

Two of the men was beatin' up on Chuy, an' Matt went after them first. He grabbed one an' spun him around an' laid him out right proper with one punch. The other man beatin' up on Chuy stopped hittin' Chuy an' turned on Matt. Chuy fell to the dirt.

As Matt stepped closer to the big gent that had been beatin' up on Chuy, the fella reached down to his belt an' pulled out a knife. The crowd backed up a mite an' got real quiet. The Mexican beatin' up on Chin Ling pushed him down an' turned to see why the crowd had got so quiet. When he saw his friend holdin' up a knife, he kinda grinned an' pulled out his own knife.

"You keep real bad company, senor," he said. I noticed he was missin' one of his front teeth.

Matt said, "I'm not gonna take you both on at the same time."

The white man said, "It don't look like you got much say in the matter, Mr. Butt-in." An' then he took a step in Matt's direction. They was only about ten feet apart an' things happened real fast. Matt reached up behind his neck an' pulled out that dagger knife that he carried on a thong an' threw it at the white man. The man's eyes got real big when he looked down at that dagger stickin' in his chest. He grabbed at it an' held onto the handle but he never pulled it out. He was still holdin' onto it when he fell back.

Before the white man had hit the ground, Matt had got out his Bowie knife an' was facin' the Mexican. The smile was gone from the Mexican's face. Matt slashed at him with his

Bowie knife an' the man dropped his knife on account of part of his right hand was gone. The knife an' one of his fingers fell to the street. The man turned an' ran, screamin' real loud. Nobody in the crowd said nothin' for a few seconds. Matt was eyeballin' all of 'em, waitin' to see if anyone else wanted to try his luck, I reckon. They weren't no takers though. Chin Ling got up an' staggered into a hitchin' post then took a look at the two white men layin' on the ground, one of 'em with a knife in his chest, buried to the hilt.

"Wha hoppen?" he said.

Chuy got to his feet an' stood next to Matt, his feet spread an' ready to fight. They still wasn't no takers.

Matt sheathed his Bowie knife an' walked over to the man with the knife in his chest. He bent down an' got real close to the man. After a bit he stood up an' said, "Get a doctor. This man's still breathin'."

A man stepped out of the crowd an' said to Matt, "Hello, sir. I see you're feelin' well." Then he knelt next to the man."

Matt said, "Howdy, Doc. He's all yours. When you're done with him, I want my dagger back. I'll be by later to pick it up. Your office still in the same place?"

The doctor looked up an' said, "Yes." Then he turned to the crowd an' said, "I need some help here to get this man to my office." A bunch of men stepped forward. Seemed like nobody was holdin' a grudge against Matt. I don't reckon they should have. It was a fair fight, an' Matt didn't start it.

While they were carryin' the injured man off, Matt knelt next to the other man, who was still not movin'. After a bit he said, "You can get up now, mister. The fightin's over."

The man opened his eyes an' looked at Matt an' said, "We was just funnin'. We didn't mean nothin' by it."

Matt picked him up by the front of his shirt an' stood him up real straight, then he hit him right in the nose with a tight fist. The fella fell backwards an' landed in the dirt. As he walked back to me ‘n’ Billy Jo, rubbing his knuckles, he said to the man, “I’m just funnin’ too.”

The man just laid there. I don’t think he wanted to get up an’ get hit again. The crowd busted up an’ no one helped the man Matt had just hit. They plumb ignored him.

Matt looked at Chin Ling an’ Chuy an’ said, “You two okay?”

“Chin Ling okay but velly solly about fight.”

Chuy said, “My jaw and my pride are hurt, but both weel heal.”

Matt grinned an’ said, “That’s all that counts.”

We picked up our tack an’ carried it to the livery. Matt never even asked Chin Ling or Chuy what started the fight, an’ they never said. Me ‘n’ Billy Jo was plumb quiet on account of we was afraid to say anything at all. We had no notion of what to expect next an’ we kept a close eye on everybody around us but nobody paid us any mind. Back in Cincinnati there would’a’ been about five or six constables arrestin’ everybody. Things sure was different out west.

We spent the better part of the day gettin’ supplies an’ then we went an’ got our horses an’ wagon. Matt stopped for a minute at the doctor’s place an’ got his dagger an’ when he came back outside an’ mounted Critter, he said, “I guess that gent’s gonna pull through.”

That’s all he said an’ nobody said nothin’ else until we forded the river. We was climbin’ the hill west of town when Chuy said, “Thank you, Senor Matt, for helping us back there.”

Matt didn’t even look at him. “You’d ‘a’ done the same for me,” he said, an’ that was the end of the conversation.

Chapter 44

Since we'd got back from La Mesilla we'd had water right outside our door. That part Matt got for the pump worked real good an' it was like a miracle to have water without carryin' it from the creek. It sure cut down on the chores. Uncle George was talkin' about gettin' a bunch of pipe an' runnin' a line to the Lincolns as soon as we could. From there, the Peraltas would get water next.

Me 'n' Matt was ridin' south from our place, not bein' in any particular hurry. I was sure excited about seein' Cochise's mountains. Matt said they was real special an' there was no place else on earth that was quite like 'em. I had an itchy feelin' to move a little faster but Matt wouldn't have none of it. He said we'd get there when we was supposed to. Besides, we had five head of cattle we was takin' to Cochise an' his people.

When we hit the big flat about twenty miles south of our place we bedded down in a little wash. Matt said it was okay on account of there weren't no rain in sight, not even up in the mountains. From the flatland I could see Cochise's mountains. At this distance, except for bein' real high, they didn't seem all that much different than the other mountains I'd seen out west, but I knew Matt wouldn't lie to me an' that these mountains was special.

The next afternoon we rode into them mountains, an' I hadn't never seen nothin' like 'em. They had funny-shaped rocks that went straight up to the sky in tall columns everywhere. Some of 'em looked like they was balanced real delicate on top of others. There was windin' passages through the rocks an' steep cliffs an' streams too. In places there was lots of trees an', in other places, there was big rocks, some of 'em with little caves in 'em. There was a million places to hide an' ambush folks from. No wonder to me that the cavalry weren't too keen on chasin' Cochise an' his people into them mountains. The cattle was followin', single file behind us an' Judd was behind them.

About two hours into the mountains we was on a particular narrow trail with rocks on both sides an' Matt reined up next to a big ol' boulder that overhung the trail an' had a big cave openin'. He got off Critter an' loosened the cinch. I did the same with Patches. Judd sat down in the shade of the big boulder an' pert-near smiled. He was havin' a grand time. The cattle milled around an' munched tall grass.

There was a small pool of water in one of the big boulders just up the trail a few yards an' Critter an' Patches walked to it an' took a drink. The cattle mosied to the water when they was done. There was a gentle breeze blowin' an' it felt real good. It sure was cooler in them mountains than it was on the desert, or even at our place.

I took a sip of water from my canteen an' said, "How much longer before we get to Cochise?"

Matt lit a little cigar an' said, "We're there."

I looked around real quick but didn't see nothin', so I said, "You sure?"

Matt said, "You might as well have one of your biscuits an' settle in a spell. This is most likely where we'll meet."

I started to walk up to Patches an' get a biscuit from my saddle bags when I spied an Indian sittin' on a big rock, not twenty feet away. It like to scared me plumb senseless but I saw quick enough it was Taza. None of the other Apaches looked like him.

He grinned real big, "You like horse?"

I knew he was talkin' about Patches. "Yes, Sir. I sure do. She's a right fine horse."

Taza slid down from the boulder an' walked up to me. I never really got real comfortable with that first few seconds of meetin' an Apache. None of Cochise's people ever did me no harm but I knowed they was fightin' a loosin' battle with all them soldiers, an' they weren't none too fond of the average white man neither, so I guess I always expected the worst. I'm kind of ashamed for thinkin' that way but I couldn't help it. Them Apaches was fierce-lookin' folks, an' they was reg'lar mad at whites, an' if one of 'em wanted to, I reckoned they could have killed me in a second. An' I knew it.

Matt stood an' walked to meet Taza. They hugged real quick an' Matt gave Taza a little cigar. Judd walked up next to 'em an' wagged his tail once an' sat. Taza rubbed his head, then him an' Matt sat an' smoked together, neither one of 'em sayin' a word. They just sat an' stared down the trail. I knew them two was close on account of it felt like they was communicatin' just by sittin' there an' smokin' them cigars together. Just about the time I couldn't stand the quiet no longer, they finished their smokes. Taza crumbled the stub of his cigar and put the loose tobacco in a leather pouch he carried around his waist. Matt gave him his cigar stub and Taza crumbled it just like he done his own.

Taza said, "You know a white man name Tom Jeffords?"

"I've heard of him but I don't know him personally,' said Matt.

"He is brave, I think, but very foolish," said Taza.

Matt smiled. "What did he do? Attack you single-handed?"

Taza laughed that real short, deep laugh of his. "He is not that foolish."

It sounded almost like Taza had gravel in his throat

when he talked.

"Why do you say he is foolish?" asked Matt.

"He came into our country, alone, looking for Cochise."

"Did he find him?" asked Matt.

"No, but we found him."

"Do you now ride his horse?" asked Matt.

"No. I wanted to kill him but our father said we would listen to his words."

Matt didn't say nothin' an' Taza went on. "He said he had a contract, like my father had many years ago at Fort Bowie, but his contract was not for wood. He said his contract was for passengers in a coach. He asked my father to let his coach pass. He promised he would carry no guns or soldiers to the Presidio if we would do this, and he would not stop on our land."

"He rode into your country to say this thing to Cochise?" said Matt. I could tell he was a mite surprised.

Taza nodded.

Matt said, "What will Cochise do with this white man?"

"He let him go and told him he would think on it."

Matt raised an eyebrow. "That don't sound like Cochise. Why did he do that?"

Taza looked at me an' smiled. I swear, when he smiled, he reminded me of Billy Barnes. Not that he looked like 'im or anything, but it was a real friendly smile, just like Billy's.

Taza looked back at Matt an' said, "He is brave. My father likes brave men. And he has hair like Crawford mother."

For a second Matt didn't say anything. I reckoned he was tryin' to figure out what Taza meant. Then, all-of-a-sudden, his eyes lit up. "You mean he has red hair?"

Taza nodded. "Not like yours but like Crawford mother. Our father would speak to you of him."

Matt stood. "I don't know what I can tell him but I'll speak to him about this man."

Taza stood an' we walked down the trail. Critter fell in behind us an' Patches followed him. I had no notion where Judd was but I'd have bet he was on our flank somewhere, takin' care of the scoutin' business.

We hadn't gone two hundred yards when Taza took a small trail to the right an' we went down a steep hill. At the bottom of the hill was a stream an' a bunch of trees an' about fifty Apaches. Cochise was one of 'em. Na'itche was there an' I was glad to see him on account of he was closer to my age than anybody else. I hugged him just like I'd seen Matt do with Taza an' I think it kinda took him by surprise but I could tell, after he thought it over, he was glad I'd done it. He was right friendly after that.

After Matt an' me did our greetings, Matt went to Critter's saddlebags an' took out all the tobacco he'd brought. He gave it to Cochise, who passed it around. About then, here came the cattle. I guess Judd had a little trouble gettin' 'em to come down that steep slope but he got the job done. All five of 'em was there.

Cochise walked up to Judd, who wagged his tail once an' sat. Cochise squatted an' looked at Judd a long time, then he smoothed the hair on Judd's head back. He didn't say nothin', just smoothed the hair back. After a bit, he stood an' looked at Matt. "He is a fine warrior. And he herds cattle good."

Judd musta knowed Cochise was talkin' about him 'cause he stood an' wagged his tail once an' sat back down. Everybody who saw it laughed.

Cochise looked at the cattle an' his eyes went far away, like he was thinkin' real deep. He turned to Matt. "You are a fine son and a friend. My people can use the food."

My heart felt real heavy to hear him say that. It was his country an' yet his people was hungry on account of they couldn't stop nowhere an' rest. The cavalry was always tryin' to kill 'em. It just weren't right.

"When we can spare more, I'll find a way to get them to you."

Cochise looked at Matt real close. "You have always been true to your brother and his people. I would like to know about a white man name Tom Jeffords."

"I don't know the man like I know you. I have never met him. I've heard of him."

"What have you heard?"

"Not much. Except that I heard no man calls him a liar. From what I heard, he is true to his word but I do not know that for sure."

"He has hair like Crawford mother," said Cochise.

Matt grinned. "So I've heard."

"I like this white man," said Cochise.

"I figured that or he'd be dead now," said Matt.

Cochise seemed to think real hard for a spell, then he said, "I will let his coach pass through our land. If he keeps his word not to carry guns or soldiers, or to stop on our land, his coach will be safe."

I was real pleased that Cochise was gonna let this Tom Jeffords fella's stagecoach pass through his land. I don't know why but, maybe I saw it as a first step in the direction of endin' all the killin'.

After the short meetin' was over, Cochise's people drove the cattle off to wherever the rest of his people was stayin'. Matt an' Taza an' Cochise visited after the others was gone. I heard Matt tell Cochise about Chollo but I didn't hear what Cochise said back to Matt on account of me 'n' Na'itche was explorin' the rocks. We had a swell time lookin' for hidden treasure an' secret hidin' places. After a couple of hours, me an' Matt headed for home. I think I'd always remember that day an' how peaceful it was an' how close I felt to them Chiricahua Apaches. An' how wrong I thought everything was.

Chapter 45

About a week after our trip to Cochise's mountains, Matt came up to the house about midday 'n' said he was goin' to La Mesilla again. He took Jack with him 'n' we all wondered why, since he had other horses he could have used for packin', an we all used Jack for field work, but nobody said nothin'. Chollo went with him 'n' Critter 'n' Judd 'n' Jack. He didn't say nothin' about takin' Chuy 'n' gettin' some more cattle. Uncle George said somethin' about that at supper that evenin'.

"Penny, don't you find it odd that Mr. Grady left with Chollo? He knows he could have taken Chuy with him and they could have acquired some more cattle. Tucson is a goldmine for anyone with cattle to sell."

"Yes, I find it odd. But, then again, most of his ways are quite peculiar to me. I think I'll never understand him," said Ma.

Aunt Sandra said to Uncle George, "We saw very little of him while you were gone, Dear."

Uncle George kinda grunted. "I have a strange feeling that whatever he's up to this time is not in keeping with his permanence around here."

I had no notion of what Uncle George meant. Sometimes him 'n' Aunt Sandra 'n' Ma would talk such that I couldn't quite understand the meanin' of all the words, even though they was speakin' proper English.

"Why do you say that, George?" asked Ma.

"He took all of his animals with him, except for Dunny."

I said, "But he left all of his stuff."

Seemed like Ma's face loosened a bit. "Are you certain?" she said.

I nodded real plain. "Positive. He didn't take nothin' but his soogans. Most everything else is in his wickiup." I had done a little snoopin' on my own after Matt left. They wasn't the only ones thought it was peculiar that Matt had took Jack with him.

Pert near three weeks after he left, Matt came ridin' up to the house without Chollo. He was leadin' Jack but there weren't no heavy load on 'im. It was just before sunset when he rode up 'n' most everyone was standin' around the campfire. We was just finishin' supper 'n' Papa had broke out his banjo 'n' was just tunnin' up. Everybody stopped what they was doin', includin' Papa, 'n' we all stepped next to Critter 'n' greeted Matt proper. He eased offa Critter 'n' greeted everybody back. He had presents for everybody, 'n' when he got done passin' 'em out, they wasn't much left in Jack's pack. Seemed real peculiar that he'd gone all the way to La Mesilla with Chollo just to get presents. 'N' I got to wonderin' where Chollo was.

While everybody was lookin' at all the presents, Matt asked Mrs. Peralta, for that's what we had taken to callin' Consuela, Ignacio's wife, if she had any tortillas 'n' beans. She beamed a big smile 'n' said, "*Si, si, Senor Matt.*" 'N' she handed him a plate.

"Where's Chollo?" I asked.

"He's out there in the hills somewhere." Matt kinda waved his fork in the direction of the east.

"Ain't he comin' back to stay with us?" I asked.

"Maybe." I could tell by the way he said it, he didn't wanna talk no more about Chollo.

Matt filled his plate 'n' started eatin' like he hadn't been gone but a few hours instead of three weeks. Squeak walked right up to him and stood real still until Matt rubbed his ears, then he walked back to Mel. Around a mouthful of beans, Matt said, "Well, Papa, don't let me hold up the preceedin's. Play somethin' pretty."

Papa started playin' 'n', pretty soon, everybody started dancin' - well, everybody 'ceptin' Matt. He was still eatin'. He ate like he wasn't ever gonna get fed no more. I never seen a hungrier man. I saw Ma watchin' him too.

When Papa played certain songs, we all stopped dancin' 'n' sang. I ain't rightly sure how we picked which songs to sing 'n' which songs to dance, but it seems like we all knew.

After a bit, Matt washed his plate in a tub away from the fire 'n' rinsed it in another tub, then stacked it with the others by our front door. He excused himself 'n' said he was tired. He didn't go to his wickiup though. He mounted Critter 'n' rode east, across the creek 'n' out of sight.

Later that night, after Mel 'n' me was in bed, I heard Uncle George 'n' Aunt Sandra 'n' Ma talkin'.

Ma said, "He's different, Sandra. Something is different. He hardly spoke to anyone. He just ate and left."

Uncle George said, "I'm sure he's exhausted, Penny. It's a long trail to La Mesilla,"

"I think Penny's right, George," said Aunt Sandra. "Mr. Grady has never acted in this manner, and I'm sure he's been exhausted on other occasions."

"The man has a lot on his mind," said Uncle George.

Ma said, "He always has, George. And he's never acted this distant."

I heard Uncle George yawn. "Well, let's sleep on it. Maybe tomorrow he'll be back to normal."

Chapter 46

Uncle George was right. Seems like Matt was his old self the next mornin'. He helped me do my chores, 'n' I gave him a piece of licorice. He musta thanked me a hundred times. After mornin' chores we saddled up 'n' rode around the hills north of the house in search of a couple of missin' steers. We found 'em 'n' had 'em pushed into the rest of the herd by early afternoon.

The next day Ma 'n' Mel 'n' me 'n' Uncle George 'n' Aunt Sandra saddled up 'n' we all went on a ride. Matt was with us 'n' he showed us lots of things about the desert. It was a real special day. We wasn't really workin', more like we was just enjoyin' each other's company.

About mid-mornin' Matt stopped, 'n' Critter stood real still. Matt took out his lookin' glass 'n' pointed it west. I could see a small cloud of dust but nothin' else. Matt looked through that glass for a while then said, "You folks might want to ride on back to the house. There's about twenty Yankees ridin' this way.

Ma's face got kinda pale. "What will you do, Mr. Grady?"

"What I have to do, Miss Penny. Don't worry yourself. Get on home an' act like nothin' in the world is out of order." He turned Critter 'n' rode off without another word.

It took Lieutenant Barton 'n' Sargent Culpper 'n' their men about two hours to get to our place, an' when they did, I was in for the surprise of my life.

Lieutenant Barton sat his horse in front of our place 'n' said good mornin' to Ma 'n' the rest of us. Ma asked him to dismount 'n' have a cup of coffee. That's when I got my surprise.

"No, thank you, Mrs. Kensington. We haven't the time. We have received word from a friendly Indian that a Rebel is in this area, in those hills northeast of here. He pointed to the big mesa northeast of our place.

I thought Ma was gonna swoon. She put her hands to her face 'n' started shakin'.

Lieutenant Barton said, "I wouldn't be too concerned, Mrs. Kensington. He most likely would not come near a place with this many people. We'll have him by tomorrow, one way or the other."

I didn't like the way he said that.

Ma finally found her voice. "Are you certain of your information, Lieutenant?"

"Very certain. Seems one of the friendly Apaches told the commander at Fort Bowie. He sent word to Camp Lowell that he couldn't spare the men to search for a die-hard Reb with Cochise still running rampant. My unit was assigned the task of ending this rebel's war."

Lieutenant Barton paused for a second or two then said, "This friendly Apache even drew a crude map to a box canyon where this rebel is supposed to be camping. And he rides a blue roan with four white stockings."

I thought for sure Ma's legs were gonna fold up 'n' I thought I knew why Chollo didn't come back with Matt. I couldn't believe Chollo would turn Matt in to the Yankees but it surely must be so.

"Don't you worry. You'll be safe with my company here."

Aunt Sandra said, "We surely thank you, Lieutenant" Then she turned to Ma. "Come, Penny. Let's go in the house and sit down."

I ran for the coral 'n' saddled Patches while everybody was talkin'. Nobody noticed anything until I lit out for the creek, then I heard Ma shoutin', "Crawford! Come back!"

But there just weren't no way I was goin' back. I had to warn Matt them Yankees knew where he was. Patches was fairly fast 'n' she was real sure-footed 'n' I was a lot lighter than them soldiers with all their gear. I reckoned I could reach Matt in plenty of time to warn him.

I was plumb out of breath, 'n' so was Patches, when we reached that box canyon. Matt was there all right. He was sittin' at a small foldin' table, in front of a tent, about twenty yards from the end of the canyon. He'd be trapped for sure if them soldiers rode up on him. The walls of the canyon was real steep 'n' only had a little scrub brush on 'em. There weren't no cover to speak of.

I reined Patches to a walk 'n' took real particular stock of Matt's camp. I had no idea he had a tent. I wondered why he didn't bring it to our place. It would'a' been a lot better than his wickiup, to my way of thinkin'. Next to the tent, there was a flag on a wooden pole. I had never seen a flag like that before 'n' I reckoned it was the flag them Confederates used. It was mostly red with a blue X in the middle that ran to the corners. Spaced even-like in the blue X was thirteen white stars. I gotta say, it was a pretty flag, but seein' it made me real afraid for Matt. I don't know why, but it sure 'nough did.

Matt looked up from a paper he had on his little foldin' table 'n' stood up from his foldin' stool. "What are you doin' here, boy?"

I could see that Matt had on his fancy uniform, the one he'd never worn before. He sure looked handsome in it. I wished Ma could see him.

I jumped out of the saddle 'n' pert near broke a leg, but I caught my balance in time. "Soldiers, Matt! They know where you are! They say a friendly Apache told 'em."

Matt smiled. "That so? I reckon you just can't trust anybody nowadays."

"Matt, you gotta leave! Them soldiers'll be here any

minute!" I could hardly say the words. I was so out of breath.

He took a step or two in my direction 'n' knelt in front of me. "Boy, I want you to leave this place."

"But, Matt..."

"No buts, boy. There is a serious matter about to occur here. You could get hurt. I don't want that to happen. Now get on home."

"But, Matt, there's too many of 'em. Please don't fight all them soldiers." I couldn't help it. Tears was runnin' down my face, like maybe I had a river behind each eye. I could hardly see.

Matt put his arm around me 'n' hugged me real tight. "Boy, I have to do what I have to do. Some day maybe you'll understand."

I had my face up against his neck 'n' I said, "But, Matt, I don't wanna understand someday. I want you to be safe. There's too many soldiers, Matt. Please don't stay." I was sobbin' so hard I don't reckon he understood much of what I said.

"You gotta go, boy. Now." He stood up 'n' walked back to his little foldin' stool 'n' sat. He looked at me 'n' said, "Go on, boy. Get home to your family. They need you."

"But they need you too, Matt. Please."

"Go, boy. That's an order."

"Yessir," I said. Matt knew I'd never disobey an order. Patches was still blowin' pretty hard but I mounted 'n' took one more look at Matt, hopin' he'd change his mind, but he didn't. He just sat there real straight 'n' looked at me. I turned Patches 'n' rode away real slow.

I hadn't gone two hundred yards when I met the soldiers. But they wasn't alone. Seems like everybody from Cherry Creek was with 'em.

Chapter 47

Them soldiers was so nervous, they pert near shot me but I heard Lieutenant Barton say, "Hold your fire!"

I stopped Patches 'n' didn't move, like maybe them soldiers couldn't get around me if I stayed put.

Ma said, "Crawford! Come here!"

I said, "Don't let 'em do it, Ma." I was cryin' again.

Lieutenant Barton looked at me, then at Ma. "Does your son know this man, Mrs. Kensington?'

Ma nodded. "We all know him, Lieutenant Barton. He helped keep us alive. He taught us about the desert and these mountains, and how to take care of our cattle. He's a good man, Sir."

Lieutenant Barton looked at my ma most strange. "I see." Then he looked at me. "Is he alone, son?"

I saw this as my chance to save Matt. "No, Sir. He has a hundred Confederates with him."

Sargent Culpepper looked at me 'n' smiled. "That's a mighty big number of Confederates, me boy. Are you sure it was a hundred?"

"Maybe two hundred," I said.

"Oh, two hundred is it now?" he said. Then he looked at me real gentle-like. "He's all alone, isn't he, me boy?"

For some reason I couldn't lie to Sargent Culpepper. He was my favorite of all the soldiers.

I hung my head. "Yessir. He's just sittin' in front of a tent, waitin' for you."

Lieutenant Barton said, "Sitting in front of a tent?"

"Yessir," I said.

"You warned him we were coming after him and he remained sitting in front of a tent - alone?" asked Lieutenant Barton.

By now I was cryin' fer real. I was afraid to death this was the end for Matt. "Yessir." I looked at Ma. "Ma, it's like he's just waitin' to die. Don't let 'em do it, Ma. Matt never did nothin' to nobody."

Ma looked at Lieutenant Barton. "Surely, Lieutenant Barton, you aren't going to ride into a box canyon with twenty soldiers against one man without affording Captain Grady an opportunity to surrender peacefully?"

I had never heard Ma call Matt "Captain Grady", 'n' it so surprised me, I plumb quit cryin'.

"Are you certain this man was a captain?" said Lieutenant Barton.

"I'm positive he's a captain, Sir," said Ma.

"*Was* a captain, Mrs. Kensington. There is no longer a Confederacy."

Sargent Culpepper said, "Beggin' your pardon, Sir, but if the man hasn't yet surrendered, he's still a captain."

I pert near let out a cheer for Sargent Culpepper.

Seems like Lieutenant Barton cleared his throat 'n' looked kinda stern at Sargent Culpepper 'n' then Ma, 'n' then he said, "Under the circumstances, Mrs. Kensington, we will confront this rebel officer with a show of force and offer him the opportunity to surrender peacefully."

"Thank you, Sir," said Ma. I heard Chester 'n' some of the others mumblin' from somewhere behind them soldiers but I couldn't tell what they was sayin'.

Lieutenant Barton turned in the saddle 'n' said to his men, "Bare arms, men. But there will be no shooting until the order is given by Sargent Culpepper or myself. I don't know what this rebel's intentions are and I want every man ready to fire upon command." He looked at Ma 'n' said, "Mrs.

Kensington, you and your party are to remain behind and to one side of my troop. I don't want any civilian casualties in the event your rebel captain starts shooting."

Ma nodded. "Thank you, Lieutenant Barton. I appreciate your consideration."

Lieutenant Barton put his hand to his hat 'n' said, "My pleasure, Mrs. Kensington. Now if you'll excuse me, I have a die-hard rebel to capture." He looked over his shoulder 'n' said to his men, "When we approach the tent, form a semi-circle so we have the rebel hemmed in. Stand ready with your arms." He waved his hand in a forward motion 'n' started ridin' for the canyon. Sargent Culpepper was right behind him, 'n' the rest of them soldiers followed. All the rest of us followed them soldiers.

I don't know what I expected when we rode into view of the tent, but I expected somethin'. I didn't figure Matt to still be sittin' in front of that tent with that nice clean uniform on 'n' smokin' a little cigar. But he sure enough was. I gotta say, He looked right splendid.

Lieutenant Barton's voice scared me - for he spoke so sudden - when a second before the only sounds in the canyon was the muffled noise of the horses' hooves in the soft dirt. "Good afternoon, Sir. I am here to discuss surrender."

Matt stood real slow 'n' waved a hand at his little table. "That's a fine idea, Lieutenant. Please dismount and approach my table."

I hadn't even noticed it before but there was another foldin' stool at the table. Seems like Matt had planned this whole thing out pretty proper. I felt pretty happy inside. It looked like maybe Matt was gonna fergit the war 'n' all them Confederates 'n' stay with us for good.

Lieutenant Barton looked at his soldiers, who had formed sort of a half-circle in front of the tent. Some of them soldiers was lookin' at Matt's flag 'n' some others was lookin' at his fine uniform. I saw Critter standin' about ten feet behind Matt an' noticed for the first time that he had on a fine saddle blanket. It was grey with gold trim an' had the letters "CSA" in gold written on the bottom rear. Seems like even Critter was in uniform for the surrender. He looked almost as splendid as Matt. I figured Matt musta had that blanket made up special for Critter when he was in La Mesilla. I could tell when Lieutenant Barton noticed it too. He kinda stiffened up a mite. He said, "Stand easy, men. Sargent Culpepper, accompany me." He dismounted 'n' walked up to Matt with Sargent Culpepper only a step behind.

He was only about three or four feet away from Matt when he stopped. He stood real straight 'n' saluted. Matt stood real straight 'n' saluted him back. Sargent Culpepper saluted 'n' Matt gave him a right snappy salute back. Then Matt 'n' Lieutenant Barton sat in them little foldin' stools at the little table while Sargent Culpepper stood, kinda stiff-like, next to Lieutenant Barton.

I couldn't hear what they was sayin' so I dismounted 'n' walked up next to one of them soldier's horses that was real close to the front of the tent. The soldier looked down at me 'n' smiled but he didn't say nothin'.

I heard Lieutenant Barton say, "Captain, I am willing to offer you the same terms General Grant offered General Lee at The Appomattox Courthouse. You may keep your sidearms and your horse."

Matt kinda squinted at the lieutenant. "That's all fine an' well, Lieutenant, but I think there's a grave misunderstandin' here. My terms of surrender for you and your men are even more generous. I intend that you may keep your rifles an' carbines as well as your sidearms since you are in Apache Country. Turnin' a man out in this country without a rifle is a bit on the cruel side. Don't you agree, Sir?"

Lieutenant Barton looked at Matt like maybe he was

crazy. "You think I'm here to discuss terms of *my* surrender?"

"Certainly, Sir. Why else would you ride into my camp?" said Matt, like he was plumb serious.

I didn't have no idea what Matt was thinkin' but I do know that, about that time, I was thinkin' maybe Matt had lost his mind.

"To accept *your* surrender, Sir," said Lieutenant Barton.

"Whatever in the world put you of a mind that I would surrender to you, sir?" said Matt.

I could feel my body startin' to shake a little.

Lieutenant Barton smiled 'n' kinda waved his hand at all them soldiers.

Matt leaned a bit forward 'n' said, "Lieutenant, you've made a grievous error in judgement."

"How so, Captain? I obviously have the superior force."

"Well, it might appear that way at first glance but let me ask you a question, Sir. Have you ever heard of the guns of Val Verde?" said Matt.

I had no notion of what them guns of Val Verde was but Lieutenant Barton sure did, 'cause he wasn't lookin' so much like the cat that ate the canary no more.

"You Yankees never found 'em, but I did. And your men are lined up perfect for a slaughter, Lieutenant. I loaded 'em with grapeshot, Sir, and if so much as one of your men attempts to move, there'll be a lot of dead horses 'n' Yankees in this little canyon in short order."

Them soldiers started lookin' all around that canyon with their eyes, but not a one of them moved much of anything else.

Lieutenant Barton said, "You're bluffing, Captain."

"You seem to be a decent sort - for a Yankee - , Lieutenant, so I'll spare you the suspense." He pulled on a rope that lead to the cliff wall behind him. A bunch of bushes on the side of the hill, about twenty feet above the ground 'n' about forty feet to the rear of the tent, fell to the canyon floor. Behind where them bushes had been was two cannons, leastways, that's what I call 'em. They was pointed right over Matt's head at the area in front of the tent.

A few of the soldiers' horses kinda shied a bit when them bushes fell, but them soldiers was holdin' 'em real tight with the reins. They settled down quick.

The Lieutenant looked at them cannons with his mouth open. For a long time, he didn't say nothin'. Then he looked at Matt like, if looks could kill, Matt woulda' been dead a hundred times.

Matt held up his hand again. This time there was a different rope in it. He smiled at Lieutenant Barton. "Lanyard."

Lieutenant Barton said, "Sir, those guns may get most of my men but some will survive."

Matt said, "Are you really ready to lose fifteen or twenty men for one, Sir? And I'm not worried about the survivors. By the time they're able to return accurate fire, I'll have killed every last one."

"You forget about myself and Sargent Culpepper," said Lieutenant Barton.

"Not at all, Lieutenant. While I'm pullin' the lanyard, I'm shootin' Sargent Culpepper with the other hand." Matt looked at Sargent Culpepper kinda sheepish. "No offense, Sargent Culpepper, but I reckon you to be a pretty good trooper an' I have to get you first."

Sargent Culpepper stood a little stiffer 'n' said, "No offense taken, Sir. I understand."

Matt smiled 'n' said, "I kinda figured you might."

Lieutenant Barton said, "I'll have no more of this. You, Sir, will surrender to me or my men will open fire. You have one minute to make your decision." He looked at Sargent Culpepper 'n' said, "Have the men take aim and fire on your command, Sargent Culpepper."

"Yessir."

Matt just looked at Lieutenant Barton 'n' said, "If you're a God-fearin' man, Lieutenant, make your peace with 'im within the next minute."

I'd never been so tense in all my born days. I was plumb tuckered out just concentratin' so hard on every word that was said 'n' every move that was made. I couldn't move.

From all around me, I heard Ma's scream. It seemed to come from everywhere at once. "No!" Next thing I knew, she had run through that semi-circle of horses 'n' was standin' next to the table. "No! There will be no bloodshed here today."

Lieutenant Barton said, "Mrs. Kensington, this is no place for a woman. Please retire so you won't be injured."

Matt looked at Ma with his mouth half open. "Miss Penny. What are you doin' here? Please, listen to the lieutenant. It's the only right thing he's said so far today."

I thought Sargent Culpepper smiled a little when Matt said that but I can't be sure.

Ma looked at Matt like Mel had looked at her when she was wantin' to keep that little javelina for a pet. "I beg of you, Captain Grady. Don't go through with this madness. What have you to gain by killing these men? I know them all. I don't want to see them killed - not by you nor anyone else. And, Captain Grady, even more than that, I don't want to see you killed. Nor do any of us." Ma was plainly cryin' now. "Please, Matt. Don't do this."

Ma had never called Matt by his given name 'n' it sure took me by surprise. Matt too. That was real plain in his face.

"Miss Penny - please - leave this place," he said in a real soft voice.

Ma looked him right square in the eyes. Tears was streamin' down her face. "I can't, Matt. I just can't."

Next thing I knowed, Chester 'n' Uncle George 'n' Aunt Sandra was standin' next to the table. Then it seemed like everybody was there. We was all standin' around the table. Everybody was mumblin' somethin' or the other 'n' I couldn't make no sense of any of it but, when Matt spoke, everybody shushed up real sudden.

He was lookin' right at Lieutenant Barton. "Lieutenant, I have a new proposal."

Lieutenant Barton seemed about ready for anything that might change the way things was lookin'. "What is it, Captain?"

"I propose that, for this day, we declare a truce. I will remove myself from the field of battle and leave the guns of Val Verde for your taking at sunrise. I will not surrender to you, nor you to me, unless we meet again someday on the field of battle to decide this matter once and for all."

Lieutenant Barton looked at Sargent Culpepper. Sargent Culpepper said, "As you know, Sir, this kind of thing is done o'er and o'er again by armies in the field. I see no harm in it."

Lieutenant Barton stood 'n' turned to his men. "Stand easy in the saddle, men. The Confederate Captain and I have agreed to a truce for one day." I took note that Matt weren't a die-hard secesh or rebel all-of-a-sudden. He was a Confederate captain.

I could feel the men beginnin' to breathe again.

Ma was still cryin' but it was a quiet kind of cry, like maybe she was glad but not sure she was glad. Matt looked at her, then at Lieutenant Barton. "I'll be moving my headquarters for the evening, Lieutenant. I trust our truce applies to the ranches at Cherry Creek?"

Lieutenant Barton said, "As you wish, Sir. My men will also set up camp nearby."

They saluted each other 'n' Lieutenant Barton walked back to his horse 'n' , mounted. He looked at Sargent Culpepper 'n' said, "Sargent Culpepper, stay with the Captain and assist him with his needs."

"Yessir," said Sargent Culpepper.

Lieutenant Barton and the soldiers rode back towards our place.

Matt looked at Sargent Culpepper 'n' said, "I don't need a nanny, Sargent. You can accompany your troop if you like."

Sargent Culpepper smiled real big. "I'm sure you've no need of a nanny, Sir, but I'd consider it a privilege if I could be a mite of help in some small way. And besides, I'd rather not be around the good lieutenant for a bit. He'll be needin' some time to lick his wounds. You gave him good lickin' today, Sir. He'll not be in such a good mood for a while."

Matt smiled. "Too bad you're wearin' that blue uniform, Sargent. I got a feelin' we'd 'a' made a good team."

"Aye, that we would, Sir. That war was a terrible thing."

"Ain't they all, Sargent?" said Matt.

"Aye. That they are, Sir. That they are."

Everybody was crowdin' around Matt 'n' smilin' 'n' pattin' him on the back. We was all glad that nobody was killed.

Shortly, he looked at Ma 'n' said, "Miss Penny, I really wish you hadn't put yourself in the line of fire. That was a foolish thing to do. Brave, but very foolish. I'm truly honored by your concern but must ask you never to do such a thing again."

Ma said, "Mr. Grady, there are some of us here who don't want to see you killed in a lost cause." Ma was back to callin' him Mr. Grady again.

Matt smiled. "I take it, you're one of them?"

Ma turned redder'n a strawberry roan. When she got herself together again, she said, "Mr. Grady, good cattlemen are hard to find. We need your help."

Chuy laughed real loud 'n' pretty soon everybody was laughin', even Sargent Culpepper.

Chapter 48

We all went back to the house, 'ceptin' Matt 'n' Sargent Culpepper. They stayed behind to take care of some kind of war business I think. Pretty soon they came ridin' up to our big fire pit 'n' dismounted. All the women was busy fixin' supper for everybody 'n' them soldiers from Tucson was helpin' where they could. It seemed real peculiar to me that them fellas was gonna kill Matt a little while ago 'n' now they acted like everything was okay. I guess, if that's what a truce is, a truce is a good thing.

Ma still looked worried. I guess most of us was - even the soldiers from Tucson - for none of us knew what would happen in the morning. It was a real strange kinda evening. Everybody ate together: Confederates 'n' Yankees 'n' Mexicans 'n' Chinese 'n' Negroes 'n' us folks from Ohio. The only one missin' was Chollo 'n' I just figured he went back to Cochise. I missed him though, 'n' so did Chin Ling. When I thought of the comin' mornin', I got to worryin' about Matt.

Matt, he didn't seem worried about much of nothin'. As a matter-of-fact, he ate his chile 'n' beans with Sargent Culpepper 'n' Chin Ling mostly - me too, of course. Ma kinda stayed busy servin' food 'n' stuff like that, along with the rest of the women, but she looked at Matt a lot. I caught her doin' it a bunch of times. Matt didn't seem to pay her no mind 'n' I couldn't figure it out.

Aunt Sandra 'n' Uncle George watched Matt a lot too 'n' I got to thinkin' that maybe they all had some kinda plan to help Matt 'n' it was only for grown-ups. After a while though, I gave up on that idea, 'cause I was watchin' Matt a lot too, 'n' I sure didn't have no plan.

After supper, Papa took out his banjo an' Chester took out his mouth organ an' they played some songs. Them soldiers from Tucson asked him to play lots of songs I never heard of an' they played lots of them, but there was some they didn't know. Them soldiers sang along with Papa's playin' an' most everybody else who knew the song joined in. After Papa played *"When Johnny Comes Marchin' Home Again"*, things got real quiet. After about a minute, Matt said, "Papa, would you mind playin' *"God Save the South"*?"

Papa looked at Matt real sad 'n' said, "I'd be proud to play that song for you, Missah Matt."

I gotta say, Papa played that song about as pretty as I reckon it was ever played. He played it slow an' loud, each note bein' real clear an', by the time he finished, I don't reckon there was a dry eye amongst us, even them soldiers from Tucson. I couldn't figure out why they was affected so by that song, but they sure enough was.

After that, everybody went to their own house or camp, 'ceptin' Matt. Uncle George asked him to come to our house for a spell. When Matt got inside the house he sat in the chair Pa used to use. He looked real natural in it 'n' I sure didn't bear him no grudge for sittin' in it. I liked him there 'n' wished he might stay forever.

Uncle George 'n' Matt lit cigars 'n' then Uncle George said, "Mr. Grady, I see no way out of this but for you to surrender and accept parole. Are you willing to do this?"

Matt took a long pull on his little cigar 'n' looked Uncle George square in the eyes. "No, George, I'm not."

Ma was puttin' dishes in the cupboard when he said this 'n' she dropped one. It made a real loud noise when it broke on the floor 'n' before I even knew what happened, Matt had whirled around 'n' had that short-barreled Remington in his left hand 'n' pointed at Ma. When he figured out what had happened, I knew he was embarrassed 'cause he put that pistol back in the holster almost as fast as he took it out.

"Sorry, Miss Penny. I don't really trust them Yankees. It's a habit," he said.

Ma just stood there for a long time, lookin' at Matt, 'n' not payin' any attention to that broken dish on the floor. Aunt Sandra, who'd been helpin' Ma, didn't make any move to pick up the pieces either. She stood next to Ma, kinda watchin' her 'n' Matt both. After a while, Ma said, "You're going to fight the soldiers from Tucson, aren't you, Mr. Grady?"

Matt took a long pull on his little cigar 'n' said, "No, Miss Penny, I'm tired of fightin' Yankees. I'm leavin' tonight."

Uncle George said, "Surely, man, you can't mean that. Not after all you've done here."

"Oh, I mean it all right, George. I've been talkin' to Chin Ling an' he told me how to find his family in China. I've never been to China, so I guess it's time I gave it a look."

It was about here I couldn't be quiet no more. "No, Matt! You can't leave us. You can't!"

Matt said, "Come 'ere, boy. I wanna talk to you a minute. I don't have a lot of time, so let's get it done."

I walked over to him 'n' stood by his side.

"I'm takin' Dunny with me to California. That's where I'll sail for China. I'm leavin' Critter 'n' Judd here to help you take care of the cattle if you think your Ma will let you have 'em."

"No, Matt. Please." There I was cryin' again.

Matt put his arms around me. "I have to, boy. It's the only thing I can do. I'd like to know that those two have a good home – where folks understand their peculiar ways. Can you help me out with this?"

"No, Matt. Don't leave." I couldn't say nothin' else, I was sobbin' so hard.

Uncle George said, "Don't worry about those two, Mr. Grady. They'll be well cared for until you return."

"Thank you, George. And for you, I'd like you to have my Whitworth. I hope you never have to use it against a man but, if you do, it'll even outreach that Sharps of yours. It's served me well."

"Thank you, Mr. Grady. I'll use it wisely," said Uncle George.

Matt looked at Mel. I hadn't noticed before, but Mel was cryin' too, 'cept she was hangin' onto Ma's dress 'n' huggin' her real tight. Squeak was at her feet, lookin' for all the world like he knew something bad was happening. "Mel, I'd like you to have my lookin' glass. I don't have much in the way of things for a young lady but I think you'll like it fine. It was made in Richmond, Virginia."

Mel just kept cryin' 'n' huggin Ma.

"Miss Sandra, I'd like you to have my Colt. I won't have much use for so many weapons, so the Colt is yours. It's a lot easier to carry horseback than a rifle if you have need."

Aunt Sandra didn't say a word. She just nodded real slow.

He looked at me an' said, "Boy, all I have left of value is the battle flag. Keep it as a souvenir and remember our days on the trail together. Take care of your Ma."

He faced Ma. "Miss Penny, I have nothin' worthy of givin' you that would convey your importance in my life, but I offer you my uniform 'n' saber if you'll accept it. You're the only Yankee in this world who ever earned it."

Ma fell plumb apart. "Oh, Matt, Please." She took a step toward Matt 'n' he stood still. Ma put her arms around him 'n' just held him real tight. Matt put one arm around Ma 'n' the other around Mel's shoulders, for she was still hangin' onto Ma. I ran up 'n' put my arms around everybody 'n' we all stood there for a long time. Nobody said a word. Nobody hardly moved.

After a while Matt pulled away real gentle 'n' said, "I

wish things were different, Miss Penny. I really do." He picked up his hat from the table 'n' walked outside.

Ma put her hand to her mouth 'n' just cried, kinda quiet. I didn't know what to do, so I just stood there. Mel was still huggin' Ma. Uncle George 'n' Aunt Sandra was lookin' at each other with sad looks.

At daybreak Matt was gone. The Whitworth 'n' the Colt 'n' lookin' glass was next to our front door. Folded real neat next to 'em was that fine uniform 'n' saber. The flag was folded, real neat-like, on top of the uniform. Judd 'n' Squeak was standin' next to the uniform an' Critter was next to the porch. I was so lonely for Matt, I wanted to die. I couldn't believe he wouldn't come strollin' up from the creek at any second.

About an hour after we found Matt's stuff, Sargent Culpepper rode by the house 'n' stopped long enough to say goodbye. Seems like Lieutenant Barton weren't in no mood to pay a call. When the soldiers went to the box canyon to get them Guns of Val Verde, they discovered that them guns was made out of wood. Matt had left the lieutenant a note explainin' that he knew a good wood carver in La Mesilla should he ever have need of one. Even though we was all sad at Matt bein' gone, we all had a good laugh, even Sargent Culpepper. Matt had bluffed them soldiers with wooden cannons. Ma even smiled a little when she thought of it later.

Things weren't the same after Matt left. Critter 'n' Judd missed him about as much as the rest of us, I reckon. Judd didn't eat for a few days but he got to feelin' better when the Apache Gang went lookin' for strays an', this time, we had a real Apache with us for Chollo had come back the same day the soldiers had left. It turned out he was the friendly Indian that told the soldiers about Matt. Matt had put him up to it. I rode Critter 'n' remembered real good that Matt had told me to hold the reins in my right hand when mountin' him first thing in the mornin'. Most days he didn't give me much trouble.

In the early fall we got a letter from Matt - three letters really. One was addressed to everybody at Cherry Creek ,'n' one was for Ma. The other was for me. In my letter, Matt said how he missed me 'n' how he was sure I was doin' good 'n' helpin' Ma as much as I could 'n' how I was a good hand with cattle. He asked after Critter 'n' Judd 'n' Jack 'n' the Apache Gang an' Mel an' everybody.

In the letter to everyone, Matt told of his adventures on the Pacific Ocean 'n' how he learned all about sailin' on a clipper ship. He spoke of Chin Ling's family 'n' said he was sendin' Chin Ling's sweetheart to him as soon as he could figure out a way to get her safely to Cherry Creek. He said Chin Ling's sister was teachin' him good Chinese. Said she was real pretty too but not as pretty as Ma. Accordin' to Matt, the Chinese didn't eat proper, an' they sure didn't know much about cattle. He hadn't seen a pinto bean or a tortilla in all these months either. He had somehow managed to take Dunny to China with him 'n' he said Dunny didn't much care for the place.

When Ma finished readin' her letter from Matt, she put it down 'n' just sat at the table 'n' stared at the wall for the longest time. After a spell a tear fell from one of her eyes. She stood up 'n' walked outside. I watched her walk in the direction of Pa's grave. Matt's letter was still sittin' on the table. I walked over 'n' looked down at it. I couldn't help myself. I just had to read it.

Dear Miss Penny,

You are a most extraordinary woman and I admire your grit. Had I been a better man, I'd have stayed on in the hopes that someday I could forget the Union Army and the war, and have the nerve to ask you to marry me. Mel and Crawford are the finest youngsters I've ever known and I felt very close to both of them. I find it difficult to put into words, but I felt as though they were my own children. I never had that kind of feeling before and have no right to it now. I know I could never take the place of their Pa, and your husband, and chose to leave for all those and other reasons, but I have need for you to know that I truly know the meaning of love. You and the children have given me this experience and I am forever in your debt. My final honor was in the leaving, as I knew I could never surrender, nor could I allow you and the children to live a life of fear rooted in your own country's victory over mine.

Matt

It sure wasn't a very long letter but it said an awful lot. I felt the tears rollin' down my cheeks, 'n' I walked out the door 'n' to Pa's grave. Ma was there, just like I figured she would be. I didn't say a word. I just walked up 'n' put my arms around her. We stood there, next to Pa's grave 'n' hugged each other 'n' said nothin', for there was nothin' needed sayin'.

The End

www.ingramcontent.com/pod-product-compliance
Lightning Source LLC
Chambersburg PA
CBHW031429240626
47154CB00001B/268
9780692449639